GIRL BRAIDING HER HAIR

MARTA MOLNAR

ISBN: 978-1-940627-65-6

"You have to be hard on yourself. You have to be honest. You have to look yourself in the face."
Suzanne Valadon

———

As always, this book is dedicated to Linda, Toni, Sarah, and Diane. Your help and support are appreciated beyond words. And many thanks for first feedback to Denise McDonald, Kaela Mays, and Sue Chatterjee.

CHAPTER ONE

Ellie

Friday, March 3rd

I WANT SOMEONE TO TELL ME THAT IT'S GOING TO WORK OUT. That I won't lose my mind, or myself. That I won't fall apart.

That I won't murder Joshua Jennings in a fit of fury.

Bam. Bam. Bam.

He's ripping out my kitchen cabinets—his kitchen cabinets now—across the street. He lives in my house. Mrs. Martinez's above-the-garage apartment is where I live.

A rusty dumpster lies in wait at the end of my old driveway, a rectangular abyss of a grave. It's swallowing my life one beastly bite at a time: the old tub that came with the house, the pedestal sinks I found at the Philadelphia Architectural Salvage Yard, and the Formica countertop where I'd prepared every meal. Bit by bit, years of my life march into the dumpster's dark mouth and disappear, everything I bought and made.

My entire life will be gone by the time Joshua Jennings is finished.

Joshua Jennings is a flipper.

I hate him.

I want to buy my house back, but to do that, I'll have to ask for a raise, and to do that, I'll have to go to work, except I've been staring daggers at the flipper for the past twenty minutes.

Stop.

Okay.

Keys.

I ransack the piles of mail and makeup on the counter for my key ring. I used to be more organized. I used to have the space for it.

The hardcover copy of *The Stages of Grief*—my sister's well-meaning gift—slips to the white linoleum floor. Relentless nonsense, really. There's only one stage of grief—the one where you feel you're going to die from heartbreak. I toss the book in the garbage, unaware that I'm about to experience another major life change.

"Ellie?" Mrs. Martinez—my landlady, sixty-nine years young—peeps in the door. She has pink hair, a grandmotherly smile, and an unshakable belief that I need my chakras realigned. "I brought you Mexican hotcakes."

Mexican hotcakes are like American hotcakes, except with cinnamon and vanilla in the mix. Obviously, I let her in.

"Just made them." She sets down her work-of-art pottery plate.

She goes to pottery class. And knitting circle. And book club. And energy-healing workshops. And on Viking River Cruises. She's not the recliner-and-Wheel of Fortune type of retiree.

She whisks the napkin off her Leaning Tower of Pancakes. "Do you have time to eat?"

Definitely not.

"Thank you so much." I sit.

Mrs. Martinez conjures a small jar from her pocket. "Cajeta."

I drizzle on the thick, sweet sauce, kind of like caramel, made from goat milk. "You spoil me."

"I thought you might not have maple syrup."

I don't usually do breakfast. I'm more of a coffee-and-hop-on-the-road type. The morning commute to Center City Philadelphia is insane. Also, I've been drowning my feelings in food way too much lately, and it's beginning to show. I need to pay more attention to what I eat. And I will, starting tomorrow.

The first bite is... "Mmmm."

Mrs. Martinez watches me with the deep satisfaction of someone who just rescued a kitten from the middle of the road.

But then...

Bam. Bam. Bam.

It's difficult to eat through gritted teeth.

Bam. Bam. Bam.

My left eye twitches.

"Have you tried meditating?" Mrs. Martinez is not without sympathy.

"Hard to find Zen in a construction zone."

"Will you come to book club tonight?"

I swallow pancake, but all I taste is guilt. "I didn't have time to read the book." I can't even remember what title we're supposed to be discussing. "About sunflowers, wasn't it?"

"A story about Vincent van Gogh's sister-in-law. Brenda said she'd invite her son along. He's an editor. I bet he'll have all kinds of interesting things to say."

Mrs. Martinez used to be a romance writer. She's an incurable romantic. She means well, but I'm not interested in matchmaking. "I'm swamped with projects. I'll be working late."

Scratch. Scratch. Scratch.

My landlady doesn't react. She has problems with her hearing.

Scratch. Scratch. Scratch.

A mouse lives in the back wall of my apartment. I'm not going to complain. Mrs. Martinez wouldn't know what to do, and I don't want to be trouble. I don't know how to handle the squatter either. I don't really mind him. Another living being nearby makes me feel less alone, and I've grown used to the barely-there scratching.

4

Bam. Bam. Bam.

Now *that* gets on my last nerve.

Mrs. Martinez slips the small jar of cajeta back into her pocket. "He's almost done."

"Are you sure? There must be a doorknob somewhere he hasn't replaced—" I swallow the rest of my words. No need to drip sarcasm.

"I talked to him when I took Karma out for her walk this morning. He'll be putting the house on the market."

The last bite of my breakfast sticks in my throat. *Cough.* "He is?"

"He has a short-term loan on another property that he has to pay back."

The floor disappears from under me. My chair and the table are hanging in midair over a bottomless abyss—a malevolent magician's trick. I've been so focused on resenting the flipper for destroying my house, I didn't think about what would happen when he was finished.

"I knew he'd sell at some point." Obviously. "Chris and I only had the house for four years. People probably think it's nothing, it wasn't that long, but it was…"

"That house was your home for most of your marriage. You were happy there. It was everything."

"I don't know how to be without him." Chris was my only serious relationship ever. We met at the start of college. He had a girlfriend in high school, but he's only ever been in love with me. I was a late bloomer. He was my first everything, my one and only. "I will learn, right?" I smile to counteract how desperate I sound. "You're always happy."

"Oh, honey." The love her voice carries wraps around me like a hug. "Divorce is different. I didn't lose my husband. Going my own way was my choice. But, yes, I can promise you that you'll be happy again."

"Do you ever miss him?"

"No. He only liked the dependent me. He liked it when I was trying to get published. He liked being the one with the money. First, he never thought I'd sell a book. Then, when I did, my initial advances were low. He liked saying I played at being a writer. *She's trying to write those bodice rippers*, he'd tell people, and snicker. Then I got my first big advance. The year I outearned him, he started cheating on me. While I was on a book-signing tour."

"I'm sorry."

"Don't be. When people marry young, sometimes, they're not done growing yet. Then they end up growing in different directions. It's nobody's fault. The man I married was just the first draft of himself. And so was I. We realized we couldn't live with the final versions of each other. Goodness, I was barely sketched. We needed to be tested by life for our true characters to be revealed. We accepted that we weren't a match. Regardless, I've had a happy life."

"What's your secret?"

"Have purpose. Build the life you deserve. Don't settle for less."

She didn't. She is creative and active. She has her garden, and her friends and her trips. Mrs. Martinez is the wisewoman of the neighborhood. She is loved and respected.

"I suppose, letting go is the first step." I just can't do it. "How do I let go?"

"You don't." The two short words are full of sympathy. "You grow the necessary muscles to carry the weight of your grief. The stronger you get, the lighter it feels."

Light seems impossible at this minute. "Do you know when the house will go up for sale?"

"Another week? Two at the most. I want to talk to Joshua before he moves on. I need his advice on my back porch. The pines are too tall and keep the porch in the shade. The rain wets the wood, but the sun never reaches it to dry it. I always sit out in the front, so I keep forgetting…"

The words flutter past me.

Two weeks.

This is how change happens—in a blink. You know it's coming, you know it's coming, then you blink, and you are in a new world, the door behind you sealed, no return.

In a blink, a new family will move into my house. They might stay for decades. Who knows when the property will be relisted?

My home, the life I used to have, the memories of my happiness, will be lost to me.

• • •

"FRANK HAS HEMORRHOIDS," MY SISTER SAYS OVER THE PHONE as I cut across the office parking lot in Manayunk, a western suburb of Philly. I didn't call her from the car, because she would have hung up on me. She doesn't approve of cell phone use while driving. She doesn't believe me when I tell her that Bluetooth makes it safe.

Her revelation about Frank's condition explains one thing and justifies another.

Explains why Frank has been so fidgety lately.

Justifies why I don't move in with Abby. There are aspects of her and her boyfriend's lives I don't want to be involved in.

I turn up my coat collar against the late-winter wind. "Isn't he too young for hemorrhoids?"

"He's only two years younger than me." Abby's teacher tone warns that she doesn't appreciate the dig.

I don't appreciate Frank who—at age thirty-seven, just eight years older than I am—likes to pretend that he's my father, just because he's living with my older sister and we don't have parents.

"He'll have to have a procedure," Abby goes on. "I'll tell you about it on Sunday when you come over."

"You do realize that's a threat and not a treat?"

"Ever thought about putting together a comedy act? You're so funny."

"It's nice to be appreciated. On another note, I want to bring Bubbles home."

"She's an escape artist." Teacher tone is back.

"You'll just lose her again. She's too old to be moved back and forth."

Chris adopted the lizard in high school from a rescue. She's past middle life, according to the vet who wouldn't commit to a specific age. Bubbles is a live link to Chris, more than his books that I kept, or his favorite sweater, or his college basketball jersey that I sleep in.

"She only got out because I had the window open a crack." The weather faked me out with two days in the mid-sixties. I grabbed the opportunity of the unseasonably warm weekend and painted my apartment. "I'm not used to not having screens on all the windows."

I covered the terrarium, but Bubbles snuck out anyway, then kind of *froze* out of reach outside, high up the wall, under the eaves.

The flipper saved her with his extra-tall flipper ladder.

I don't owe him undying gratitude. It was his fault that Bubbles was out there in the first place. If Joshua hadn't bought my home, I wouldn't have moved across the street, and I wouldn't have had to paint the apartment and crack the window, etc. etc.

Since I wasn't done with painting yet, Bubbles went to live with Abby. "Our arrangement was supposed to be temporary."

"Wait until the renovations across the street are over. Once the noise is finished, Bubbles will be less frazzled. She loves having the run of the whole house here. She's sprawled out in the sunroom. You don't have any south-facing windows. And don't say that artificial light is the same. We'll talk about it on Sunday."

I walk into the redbrick building that used to be an old gristmill, and crossing the threshold reminds me of all the work on my plate. "Would you mind if we skipped Sunday lunch? I'm swamped. I want to finish my current project over the weekend."

My grand plan for a promotion is to offer my boss extra help, and *then* ask for a raise.

"You work too much."

"So do you, and you're a teacher. You do half of it for free."

"David is coming up from Virginia Beach tonight. He'll be staying the weekend with us. If you can't come over, we'll come to you."

"No matchmaking, please. Never going to happen. David is in love with Lilly."

"Lilly would *never*." Abby's shock is genuine. Lilly is married. "All Frank and I want is to see the both of you settled. I want you to be happy."

She doesn't understand that part of me is missing, and it's the part where *happy* lived.

"How about lunch Monday? Somewhere near your school?" At least, it'd just be the two of us, alone.

"Can't. Doing something else with Frank."

"What?"

"Tomorrow is better for us. We'll bring you breakfast."

It's not like my sister to be secretive, but I don't

call her on it because I've been carrying my own dark secret. What she's hiding can't possibly be worse than what I've been concealing from her for the past two decades.

I walk down the hallway's orange carpet and reiterate that I'll be working all weekend, and no matter how great a guy Frank's brother is, I don't want to date him.

When we hang up, I haven't a single doubt in my mind that they'll be coming, and they'll be bringing David.

I might not know much, but I know this:

1. I will reclaim Bubbles.
2. I will buy my house back.
3. I will never forget Chris.

I wear my resolutions as a shield as I walk into the office that's designed to be a contrast to the historic outside of the gristmill—ultramodern, all glass and steel.

Grace and Jack wave at me. They mouth *good morning* but can't say much more; their phones hold them captive.

I plop onto one of the red balls we're all pretending are chairs, but before I can open my laptop, my boss pops out of the mailroom.

"Eleanor."

Tim is the only person, other than strangers, who calls me that. To everyone else, I'm Ellie. My mother named me after Eleanor Roosevelt, who visited her school when she was in the first grade—one of her earliest and fondest memories. When Mom was still alive, she used to bring it up at least once at every dinner party.

"You're in," Tim says with an unspoken *finally* hanging in the air, as if I'm late, which I'm not. I'm five minutes early.

He's tall and skinny, with eyes that are always alert and eyebrows that are always halfway to alarmed. When he rolls onto the balls of his feet, as is his habit, he looks like a meerkat on guard duty.

"I was about to look for you." My smile is pure fiction. "I'll have time next week to help out on extra projects if you need me. And if you have a minute today, could we talk about my evaluation? You said last year that this year we'd talk about a raise. I'm ready." Could be smoother, but I make my point.

"Let me think about it."

"Since recommendations are made this month, could I send you a recap of the projects I worked on over the past year? In case justification is needed? Harris & Co., Milford's, Thurgood, Wallan & Wirt." His expression tips from annoyed to aggravated, so I course correct. "Anyway, what can I help you with?"

"I want you to take over the Gibbler project. They're ready for branding."

"I'll finish the MacKinnon brand equity report today, then start on Gibbler on Monday."

"I need you on Gibbler now. MacKinnon can wait."

The MacKinnon project is mine, and the Gibbler

project is his. We're both branding specialists, he just has higher ranking. I'm not even supposed to head single projects yet, let alone multiple. I'm not a project manager. Year after year, no matter how well or how much I do, Tim keeps me an associate.

He picks up the pad of Sticky Notes from my desk and scribbles on the top page, then sticks it onto my shoulder, rubbing with his thumb a few seconds longer than necessary. "The client wants a specific image on their new skincare product line for babies."

Toilet desenfants dance le jardin, according to Tim's bastardized French.

"Toilette des enfants dans le jardin." The payoff of four years of high school French, right there. *"Children Dressing in the Garden."*

"The Philadelphia Museum of Art has the original. Call them."

Then he retreats behind his glass door and glass walls. He tells us that he's like a shepherd who needs to keep an eye on his sheep. He is not. He's a meerkat, always on the lookout for a juicy grub—anything that would push him higher on the career ladder's rungs.

I'm no sheep either.

I'm a resourceful, self-sufficient woman who knows how to get her job done. I don't call the Philadelphia Museum of Art. I don't want an appointment for next week. If my boss wants results today, I'll give him results today. I'll drive over and see if anybody has a minute to talk to me.

13

Have purpose. Build the life you deserve. Don't settle for less, Mrs. Martinez said.

And I'm going to do just that.

"What did Tim want?" Grace comes by as I close my laptop. She holds out her bag of truffle chips to share.

"The usual."

"For you to do his job?"

I shove a chip into my mouth so I don't say anything I'll regret.

"We could go out for drinks tonight." Grace takes a chip for herself. "We haven't had a girls' night for a while."

"I'm drowning in work right now. But soon," I promise.

"Before I grow wrinkles?"

"Sure, Aphrodite." Both her parents are Greek. She has sun-kissed skin and dark, lustrous hair most people can only get from phone filters. She's so unfairly, effortlessly beautiful, if we weren't friends, I could be seriously bitter. "Hey, wasn't your name change supposed to be official today?"

She squeals. Catches herself. Glances around. Tones it down. "I'm officially Grace Papadopoulos." She only bounces a little. "My Greek ancestors can finally rest in peace."

She's been Grace Papas for as long as I've known her, her great-grandfather's name shortened at Ellis Island. Recovering her original family name has been part of a recent self-discovery journey.

14

"We're going out to celebrate this. Just not tonight?"

"Mykonos Grill when I come back from LA?"

"Definitely. When are you coming back?"

"Three weeks. I'm tucking my vacation onto the tail end of the business trip. I'm sick of winter. I want to spend time in the sun with old friends from UCLA."

"Can't let your surfing skills go rusty."

"Or my dating skills," she adds with an air of mystery.

Before I can ask whether she's reconnected with an old boyfriend online recently, her phone rings, and she leaves me.

I cancel a phone meeting with one of my own clients, which is always a risk. I don't want anyone to complain. But the gamble pays off. When I show up at the art museum, one of the curators, Wanda Abara, has twenty minutes to spare, and she's willing to see me.

I like her on sight. She's swathed in all-natural colors and fabrics—knitted top, long wool skirt. She has a warm, welcoming manner, and a quiet authority I appreciate.

"Let me show you to the vaults under the building. We'll visit the treasures nobody ever sees."

"Yes, please. Libraries and museums are my catnip."

Upstairs, the museum is a well-ordered, sophisticated, classical museum. Downstairs, I'm sneaking into the belly of a magic kingdom to see the troll king's secret hoard. The treasure trove that Wanda reveals reminds me of the fantasy novels Chris was always reading.

"It's like you have the secret password to Aladdin's cave." I barely know where to look and end up staring too long at everything, stopping at every display case. "Sorry."

"I've been here for almost twenty years, and the view hasn't yet failed to thrill me. I feel like I work at the giant warehouse in that Indiana Jones movie where the Ark of the Covenant is pushed past endless rows of artifacts as the credits roll."

"Excuse my open envy."

The storage rooms we walk through are temperature and humidity controlled. Statues are wrapped in padding that offer tantalizing glimpses. A corner of a painting peeks from here and there. Ancient Persian rugs are stacked to the ceiling. Medieval armor, bronze-age weapons—you name it, they have it.

Wanda stops at a white drawer cabinet. She consults her notes, then pulls out the appropriate drawer with white gloved hands. "I love these." She places three plastic-sleeve-protected pieces of paper side by side on the top of the cabinet. "Are they what you're looking for?"

I read the tags, from smallest to largest. "Portrait of the Artist's Son, *Catherine prépare le tub et Louise nue se coiffe*, *Toilette des enfants dans le jardin*. These are good. The subject and style remind me of Mary Cassatt."

"The artist, Suzanne Valadon, worked in Paris at

about the same time as Cassatt. They were both part of the circle of Impressionists. I wrote a paper about them a million years ago, in college."

I sink into a daydream, drinking coffee in Paris with Degas and Renoir. "Suzanne must have had quite a life."

"She was actually born Marie-Clémentine." Wanda steps aside to allow me room for closer inspection. "She changed her name to Suzanne, later. And you're right, she had a life wild enough to be a movie."

"Did she create paintings based on these sketches? Do you have any upstairs?"

"We don't have any of her paintings."

"I suppose she wasn't as famous as Monet or Van Gogh."

"As famous and more."

"What happened?"

"What usually happens. History has a tendency to forget women."

I scrape my brain for any memory of ever having heard the name. *Valadon. Valadon. Valadon.* The closest I come is… "My last name is Waldon. My husband's name. I wonder if it's a variation of Valadon."

"A lot of names were changed at Ellis Island, back in the day."

"A friend of mine just changed her last name back to the original. It's a lot of work," I tell Wanda, then refocus at the work at hand. "May I take a photo of this one?" I bend to the largest piece that depicts mother and grandmother lovingly tending to a young boy and a girl. *Toilette des enfants dans le jardin.* "This is the image our client wants."

"Without flash, please." Wanda consults her records again. "As long as you know that they all come with copyright restrictions."

"My boss will be sad to hear that." I'm disappointed too, not only that nobody else would see these touching sketches from a female artist unjustly forgotten, but that nobody would see any of the artwork we walk by again on our way out. The amount of shelving and cabinetry is staggering. "There must be as much down here as you have on display."

Wanda tugs her gloves off with a hint of regret. "Most museums only show about two to four percent of their inventory."

"That's a shame."

As I hurry down the museum's famous front steps, that thought refuses to leave me. Most of the best artworks in the world are owned by museums, either donated or purchased at great cost. And they keep over ninety-five percent away from the public, in cold storage. *Crazy.*

Not even crazy, it's a tragedy, but I have more urgent worries. I'm going back to Tim having failed the task he assigned me.

I inform him as soon as he returns to the office from lunch with his sidepiece. Tim and Frederica do lunch on Mondays and Fridays. I've hoped for years that his wife would pop in unexpectedly, but she never has. Tim tends to get away with everything.

He doesn't pass on the luck. He lets us get away with nothing.

"Did you explain how important this is for us?" he snaps.

"Copyright restrictions." I silently kiss my promotion goodbye. "It's out of their hands." But since I'm not the type to present a problem without a solution, I continue with "Sometimes, artists make multiple sketches for the same work. Just because the Philadelphia Museum of Art doesn't have one we can use doesn't mean nobody else does."

His Adam's apple bobs as he swallows the rebuke he had on the tip of his tongue. "Ask around. And don't forget to pad your hours. I want you to bill twenty percent more this week. The more hours the office bills, the better I look." He checks his cell phone. "Simon is calling in a minute to talk about me going to the next level."

That explains why he's been even more brash this morning than usual.

"Pull me along?" I joke, but not really.

"I thought about it while you were out. I'm sorry, Eleanor. You're not ready. Several of your projects were late recently."

Because I've been doing your work!

"You need more experience. You're only twenty-nine. You have plenty of time to score career wins."

As his office door closes behind him, I don't throw anything at it. I just go back to work. Really, I'm a dream employee. Hopefully, someday, somebody will notice.

I yank out my Irish grandmother's shamrock hairpins I'm wearing for good luck, shake my hair loose, and search the websites of several museums for Valadon.

With the images, come bits and pieces of Valadon's life. Must have been a dream to live in Paris in the age of the Impressionists. *Or not.* My naïve illusions are dispelled as soon as I read her notes about her childhood.

She grew up in a very different Paris than the one I know from romantic movies. Her colorful account draws me into another world, until I nearly forget the one I am in.

When my phone rings and the name *Simon Sanders* pops up on the screen, it jolts me with adrenaline. The big boss usually communicates his wishes through Tim. That Simon is calling *me* might mean that he's aware of my hard work. This call could be my ticket to the next level, to a bigger paycheck, to buying my house back.

My heartbeats are hammer falls. *Bam. Bam. Bam.*

"Tim is up for a promotion." Simon picks another direction, oblivious to my hopes and dreams. "We use the three-hundred-sixty-degree feedback method, where both people below him and above him make supportive statements. He put your name on the list."

"Okay?"

"The feedback from our clients is nothing but praise. Everybody loves him. Harris & Co, Milford's,

Thurgood, Wallan & Wirt are all raving." Simon rattles off *my* client list.

No wonder upper management never thought I was ready for a promotion. I've been doing the work, and Tim's been taking credit. I'm not even completely surprised, it's so on brand for him. "I see."

"Can I send over the form? It's nothing complicated. You just write up what you think about Tim."

"I don't need the form," I tell the regional director through my teeth, as I bob on a sea of fury. How did I not see this coming? In hindsight, the betrayal is utterly unsurprising. It's Tim. He knew the year I've had, and he didn't give a... "Here's what I think about my boss. He's so dirty, I wouldn't wipe my ass with his tongue."

And that's how I lose my job.

CHAPTER TWO

Suzanne

1876/Age 11

All the world hates a bastard.

Whenever we have to write Bible verses on our slate at school, the priest always gives me the same one: *A bastard shall not enter into the Lord's flock.*

To be a bastard is to be chained. To climb is to be free. To climb is to fly. To climb is to be safe. When I'm on them rooftops, I can see the city, but ain't nobody can see me.

Except them blasted nuns at St. Vincent de Paul. Nuns see everything.

"Marie-Clémentine Valadon!" Sister Marguerite hollers up, her black habit whipping in the wind. She might yet sail away. *If only.* "You come down this second."

I flatten myself to the convent roof, still and silent as the dead, but for my growling stomach. The thin cabbage soup for lunch was little more than water.

"Marie-Clémentine Valadon!"

I don't so much as twitch. Maybe she hasn't really seen me this time. She might well be guessing.

Except, she's looking right at me.

I push to my feet, with the pretty little stick I picked out of the rain gutter. "I ain't scared! I'm staying up here."

And since I'm standing, I might as well stand tall. I pose like the statue of Jeanne d'Arc they say will stand atop the Basilique du Sacré Cœur, holding my stick like a sword.

My boring classmates pelt me with jeers from below. I look at them right down my nose. I bet Jeanne d'Arc didn't even have to go to school. Persecuted is what I am. I stick out my chin. I'm more than a bastard. I'm more than a washerwoman's daughter. Someday, I'm gonna be *somebody*.

"Marie-Clémentine."

"You ain't gonna catch me!" I dart along the edge, roof tiles clanking under my feet. "I'm a monkey!"

The black-and-white nuns below and the girls in their drab dresses don't interest me. The brilliant blue sky above and the red tile rooftops, the fields in the distance that are about to come alive with green, those are my territory. Color and life are what I crave.

I could stay on that rooftop forever and watch

Paris. Sadly, while the nuns can't bring me down, Monsieur Winter does, eventually.

I slink into the classroom, to the back row, with frozen hands and feet. The stone wall radiates cold, ain't much of an improvement, but at least I'm safe from the wind.

The back is where the worst students sit, farthest from the stove in the front. The girls in the first row—the ones the nuns like, the ones who stupidly hang on Sister Marguerite's every word—don't even have coats on.

I envy them the heat, but the back has an important advantage. The sisters can't see what I doodle on my slate. I draw a little dog scratching his ear, exactly the little dog I want, even if there ain't an abundance of puppies in Paris. We ate the dogs and cats and rats during the Prussian siege.

Maman says I shouldn't remember—I was only six. But I remember that for months, all anyone ever said was *Do you have anything to eat?*

"Lemme see." Clelia—my best friend, also a bastard—peers at the puppy. She's worse off than I am, on account that she's Italian, an immigrant. She lives in an even poorer tenement and is even scrawnier than I am. Her thin lips round in a silent *ooh* at my drawing, but then she drops her chin and whispers, "Duck!"

Duck's our nickname for the sisters, because they waddle like mallards.

I wipe the slate with my sleeve and scribble a short sentence about the Third Republic, the topic of

Sister Marguerite's quacking. Then I slide down in my chair. Unless I misbehave, the nuns rarely notice me. I'm the smallest in class. I'm planning on growing *a lot* once we have enough food to eat.

"Terrible penmanship." Sister Marguerite bends to my slate. "There is no point in you being here if you refuse to learn. You are not even trying." She raps her knuckles on my head, then moves on. "You all must practice at home tonight. Tomorrow, you'll be writing on paper, with ink."

The girls groan. Ink and paper are expensive. If we make a mistake, Sister Marguerite will crack her switch. Yet I can barely sit still, I'm so excited. *Thank you, Sister Marguerite.*

"And now," the sister waddles back up front, "we'll memorize another fable from La Fontaine. *The Frog That Wished to Be as Big as the Ox.*"

She recites the poem a verse at a time and makes us repeat.

"The tenant of a bog,
An envious little frog,
Not bigger than an egg,
A stately bullock spies,
And, smitten with his size,
Attempts to be as big."

The little frog puffs himself up, bigger and bigger, until—no surprise—he explodes and dies gruesomely.

The sister's eyes snap to the back row. "What have you learned?"

We slink down in our seats.

Louise in the front—always a show-off—jumps to her feet and shouts the response. "We shouldn't try to reach above our station."

I hate her and the stupid tale. I like *The Raven and the Fox* much better, where the raven sits on a branch above the fox with a wheel of cheese in his beak. *What beautiful midnight feathers. What sleek wings,* the fox flatters him. *I can scarcely imagine the heavenly voice of such a magnificent creature.*

Of course, to prove that he does have a heavenly voice, the raven croaks and drops the cheese to the waiting fox below.

If you want cheese, you have to be sly. That's what I've learned from that. You want something, you do what it takes. Oh, how I want cheese…

"You'll practice your homemaking skills for the rest of the day." The sister moves on without allowing us another break. "Housework is the only knowledge a Christian woman needs."

Halfway through the afternoon, I run away. All the darning, stitching, and embroidery is mind-numbing. Learning is the worst part of school. The best part is that we get fed. That's why I keep coming back.

Montmartre covers a flat-topped hill overlooking the rest of Paris. It used to be little more than a village, dotted by gardens and edged by fields, until Paris gobbled it up and named it the eighteenth arrondissement in 1860—at least, that's what the nuns say. People come for the dance halls, drinking establishments, and artist cafés. The nuns have their work cut, praying for that crowd to suddenly turn into saints.

I run around a nanny and her charges. The children of the rich don't go to school at St. Vincent's. They have tutors coming to them. They don't have to work either, in the evenings with their mothers. The two boys and the girl I pass all have toys in their hands. The girl carries a doll, with real hair, the smaller boy shakes a toy soldier, and the older boy is riding a stick with a carved horse head. I make a face, mocking them as I pass them.

I slow at the nearby Moulin de la Galette, one of the last windmills Montmartre has left, now turned into a dance hall. Once they were famed for their brown bread, but even if they still served some, sadly, I ain't have a single centime in my pocket.

I do what I always do, watch the men who've come to paint the mill. And keep an eye out for the nuns. Sometimes they chase after me.

I know most of the painters in Montmartre. I step up behind my favorite, Pierre-Auguste Renoir. He is old enough to be my father and looks like all the others: short hair, beard and mustache, bags under his eyes.

His brush dances across the canvas. As people and buildings appear from thin air, I forget that I'm hungry. If he can make something from nothing, maybe so can I. This is an important possibility for someone who has nothing.

It's as if hope is one of the colors in his painting.

He dabs his brush into crimson without glancing at his palette.

"How do you do that?"

"I always squeeze the same color on the same spot. I know the order by heart."

Now that's smarts. I bet he didn't learn that from no nun.

"Do I hear the sweet song of Limoges in your voice?" he asks without looking at me. "I'm from Limoges myself."

"Bessines." A small village outside Limoges, to the southwest of Paris.

"Neighbors, then. What's your name?

"Marie-Clémentine…Villon."

"Any relation to François Villon, France's greatest poet?"

"He is my father."

His eyes cut to me, startled. "You are well famous then, Mademoiselle." He lifts the blank canvas leaning against the foot of his easel. "Will you sign the back?"

I do, with the brush in his hand.

Then he returns to his work, and we speak no more. I wouldn't want to disturb him. I know he must capture the scene before the light changes.

When he shifts closer to the canvas for more delicate brushwork and blocks my view, I back away to move on, and manage to trip over a drunk.

"Watch where yer goin'!" He kicks at me as I scramble away, then he mumbles, straightening his faded military uniform. "Sewer rat."

"I ain't no rat." I stamp my feet from a safe distance.

He huffs. "Aye, yer the queen's own cousin."

I huff right back at him. "The queen got her head chopped off." Sister Marguerite told us the story in detail. "I'm gonna be an artist."

The stupid drunk laughs. "Born in the sewer, die in the sewer." He knows I'm a tenement girl from my threadbare clothes. "That's us, little pigeon. Our kind don't choose where we go in life. People at the bottom of the hill stay at the bottom of the hill. The rich use us up, then throw us away. Nobody will remember our names."

"You can die in the sewer if you want, but I ain't." I chuck a pebble at him and run. I won't always live in a tenement. Someday, I'm gonna have enough money to rent an apartment, with a whole separate room for me, and one for Maman. Someday, I'm gonna be *somebody*.

I look for nuns. Not one in sight. Promising.

I run until I see another artist, Édouard Manet. He's painting people through a café's front window. I stop to watch them eat. My stomach gnaws, and it moans and it creaks.

Someday, I'm gonna have enough money to go inside a café.

When the wind chills me through, I dart over to the stables and warm up among the horses.

"You again?" The stable master catches me before my teeth can stop chattering. "Git!"

I'm not scared of him. He's got a bum leg, shot in

the war. I'm faster than he is. "I'll walk a horse for a franc."

"How old are you?"

"Eleven."

"Ha!" he says, even though I ain't lying. "You're the size of a flea."

I jerk my head toward the six horses he has in the stalls. "For two francs, I'll walk them all."

He won't get nobody for that kind of money and he knows it. He spits on the ground. "What's yer name?"

"Marie-Clémentine Valadon." I doubt he even knows Villon.

"If you get trampled, don't come to me cryin'. And if you lose one, I'll find you and tie you in front of the carriage in her place."

My heart rattles around in my chest like a wind-mill's sails. I didn't expect him to accept my offer, least not without further bargaining. "Oui, Monsieur."

I scramble to untie the nearest mare. I only come up to her shoulder, but I can reach her rope and that's all that matters.

"Careful." The man sucks his teeth.

"I ain't scared." I ate horse during the siege. I used to be scared of rats, but Maman says you don't have to be scared of nothing you can eat.

I walk the horses until twilight, warming up at the stables in between turns. All those boring nuns don't even know what a great day I'm having.

When the last horse is tied back in her stall, I

hurry to the convent—drunk with the thought of my secret riches nestled deep in my pocket.

"You missed a lesson on modesty," Clelia tells me as we walk home together.

"Did the sister say any more about Villon?" Tales of the famous poet, Paris's favorite son, are the only ones I want to hear.

"Why do you like him so much?"

"He was born poor and without a father, like us. And he didn't let nobody hurt him. When he was attacked on the street, he killed the man who attacked him." I hold out my arm as if holding a dagger, and I thrust forward savagely.

"They locked him up."

"He was pardoned later."

"Shouldn't have been, the sister said. He became a thief."

"He stole five hundred golden crowns from a chapel." Oh, the adventure of it all—not to mention the money. I'll never grow tired of thinking about how the nuns must have run around in utter despair, wailing about him. "Too bad he was banished from Paris." *I hope he kept the five hundred.*

"I thought he was condemned to be hanged."

"He escaped again. He didn't sit around all his life listening to nuns and the like."

"St. Vincent's ain't that bad. Are you skipping again tomorrow?"

"Why would I? We'll be getting paper and ink. After school, we can run to the fountain and wash the ink off the pages. Then we'll have the paper for drawing."

If I had paper, I wouldn't have to erase what I draw. I could keep it all. I fair tremble with want.

Clelia kicks a pebble down the cobblestones, uninterested in my grand scheme. She sniffs. "Why do you smell like horses?"

Why do you smell like this, why do you smell like that? girls at the school ask me all the damned time. Maman gets tired of carrying and heating water by the time she's done with all her customers' laundry.

I turn my back on my friend. "Washing is for pigs."

Manet is still at his easel.

He dilutes his paint with a drop of spirits, holds the brush by the end, steps back—

Clelia grabs my arm. "Come on. We'll miss Mademoiselle La La."

We scramble on, to the Cirque Fernando on the corner of boulevard de Rochechouart and the rue des Martyrs, then sneak around the back. We shove in among the street kids and peek through the cracks.

"Ooh." The audience inside is as impressed as we are. "Aah."

Mademoiselle La La flies through the air. Truly flies. Truly free. My heart flutters every time I watch her on the trapeze. Her costume is a sea of sequins, catching the light. She looks as if she's been dipped in jewels. Her black hair is pinned up in a tight crown.

"She is a queen." I follow her every move, while keeping an eye out to guard my back.

I've run with some of the ragtag crew around us, but they're not my friends. I have a place to go home to, to sleep. They're feral. The boy called *Petit Raton*, Little Rat, is eyeing the worn-out shoes on my feet. If he knew I have coins in my pockets… I watch the show, but I'm prepared for a scuffle. I keep my hands free and elbows ready.

Mademoiselle La La bends backward over the trapeze as she swings. Below her, another circus acrobat gallops around the ring on a horse, standing in the saddle. It's the most glorious spectacle.

"How does she do that?" Clelia whispers, and we stare, mesmerized, while the audience cheers.

We stay until the end of the last act. We're so cold, we can barely move our legs. The boulevard is dark and filling with night revelers.

"I wish we didn't have to go home." I wish we could watch people dance. Someday, I'm going to be among them. I ain't always gonna be stuck in our dank room with Maman, or trapped at the convent.

"See you tomorrow." Clelia turns down the side street. She has to go home to help her mother with her embroidery.

I hurry along, weaving among the yellow cabs drawn by white horses, to help Maman with the ironing. She would be long back from her rounds by now. In the evening, she does laundry pickups. In the morning, she makes her deliveries.

I run, ducking carriages and men.

I'm late, late, late, and I know it.

I stumble into our tenement yard, out of breath.

One of our neighbors is standing in the middle of the courtyard, yelling at Maman. "You stay away from my husband!"

Maman's fists are at the waist of her brown dress that's a sight better than the other woman's moth-eaten wool skirt and jacket. Our clothes might be simple and worn, but they're always in good repair, and they ain't faded either. When Maman colors fabric for one of her customers, she dips what we have in the leftover dye. And if she has a scrap of ribbon left from a job, she sews it on my sleeve or my collar.

She shakes her head at her accuser. "You know me better."

I lurch forward to defend her, but before I can say a word, the stupid woman—cursed with a lazy eye and chin hairs that would make a goat proud—points right at me. "Do I?"

I bare my teeth. *I'm going to bite her hand.*

She must feel my teeth coming because she whirls and stalks away.

"Why did she say that, Maman?"

"You don't listen to her." Maman leads me home, away from the curious eyes in the windows. "I have naught to do with her or her gimp of a man." She unclenches her fingers and massages her temples. "It's the same every time. Someone's husband is late coming home, and I get the blame. I must be a light-skirt, since I already have a bastard."

I hate that word more than I hate being cold, more than I hate being hungry. "She's a stupid peasant."

Of course, we're all stupid peasants, come up from the country.

I don't care. Tomorrow, I'm going to have paper and ink. I'll be as good as an artist.

Inside our room, Maman sits on a turned-over bucket by the hearth. Chairs are still scarce in the tenements, as we burned most of our furniture for heat during the siege. "Where were you?"

"At school."

She huffs at the lie. "Useless child. Why can't you be more like your sister?"

My half sister Marie-Alix married her Georges and moved to Nantes years ago, and I'm glad. Not to see her settled, but to have her out of my hair. She's twelve years older and *not* a bastard. She had her father's name all her life, and how she lorded it over me. A blacksmith! *La-di-da.* As if he didn't die in a penal colony halfway around the world, convicted of forgery.

Maman picks up a shirt that's missing a button and nods toward the stove. "Turnip stew."

I smelled it from the door. I gobble down a few spoonfuls at the unsteady old table, mindful to leave most for her breakfast. It's all she'll have, while I'll have milk and bread from the nuns.

I draw another puppy on my slate to distract myself from being hungry still. His ears go up just so, then bend down with a sweet curve. The trick is in the shading. I don't erase him either. Depending on how long we'll practice on paper at school, I might be able to keep him for a whole week.

Maman eyes the empty green bottles on the windowsill, then snaps at me. "Stop your playin'and get to your ironin'."

In the steam of the iron, I daydream about paper and ink. What if we receive a notepad? I'll draw a puppy on the front and keep him forever. I'll draw kittens too. And I'll draw myself in a circus costume.

I iron shirt after boring shirt, petticoat after insufferable petticoat, bedsheet after drab bedsheet, and I dream of gleaming sequins.

"Sprinkle on some water," Maman orders from her bucket by the dying fire. "Make them shirts smooth like them gentlemen like."

"Aye."

By the time I finish, my arms are cramped and my back is stiff.

"Time for bed, then." Maman finishes the last torn skirt at the same time, and straightens degree by degree. Her back is always bent to her work. Her brown hair is shot through with silver at the temples, the corners of her eyes are crosshatched with lines from squinting, working by candlelight. Her hands are rough from the lye soap and the laundry. She's an old woman, at forty-nine.

That won't be me.

"We'll be practicing our writing on paper at school tomorrow." Images of all I'll draw skip around in my head the way the front-row girls hop from cobblestone to cobblestone in the convent's yard, playing one of their games that they never let us back-row girls join.

"No more school for you." Maman picks through the bottles on the windowsill and finds one that has a swallow of wine on the bottom. "Them sisters sent word. They said don't bother comin' back."

I snap up my head. *Nonono.* "Where will I eat breakfast?"

"Got you an egg in the cupboard. And I already talked to the milliner. You'll see her in the mornin'." She is well pleased with herself. "You'd better not get up to your usual tricks either. You do good work or I'll wring your neck, you hear?"

An egg is a fine meal, but the ink and paper... It's as if Maman swallowed all the air in the room with that last gulp of her wine. *The little dog, and the kittens...*

I dive into my bunk and pull the blanket over my head. I don't want nobody to see my tears. "Don't care. I can't stand the stupid nuns. I never want to go back!"

Doesn't matter. Doesn't matter. Doesn't matter.

I wish I were someone else, somewhere else. I wish I were at the circus. Nothing hurts at the circus, I suspect, not in such a dreamland.

When I can no longer breathe under the blanket, I stick my head out and turn my back to Maman.

I have a small piece of charcoal in my pocket I found on the street last week, fallen off a cart. I sketch a woman's figure on the wall. Maman will beat me for it, but not until the morning. Right now, I'm a magician, making something from nothing. I draw

Mademoiselle La La as she flies through the air. And I'm her, in a sparkling costume instead of my rags, free. I draw so I don't think of the milliner, so I don't notice that I'm still hungry.

When I grow up, my family will live in a fine house. My children will never go hungry to bed. And they won't have to work too hard, I swear.

I draw so I won't cry over the prospect of spending my days on my knees again, scrubbing floors and getting kicked day after day for not being fast enough. At every job I ever had I was beaten. The shopkeepers beat children worse than the nuns. And none of them ever fed me neither.

"Stop your rustlin'." Maman throws her shoe at me, and it bounces off the wall. "Go to sleep. You'll need your strength tomorrow. You'll 'ave to work hard for Madame Mabbit."

No, I won't.

I add one last feather to Mademoiselle La La's headdress, then hide the piece of charcoal in my pocket next to my two coins. *'Cause I'm running away in the morning.*

CHAPTER THREE

Ellie

Friday, March 3rd

I HAVE NO JOB. I HAVE NO SOURCE OF INCOME. MY
REFERENCES ARE SHOT.

I turn the car down my street, and the headlights
hit the house that used to be mine, but now Joshua
Jennings is ripping apart. A shadow moves past the
window, carrying a hammer.

"He looks like a serial killer," I tell the latest pop
idol on the radio. My phone is low on battery, so I
can't play music from there. "He fits the part."

I pull up to Mrs. Martinez's garage and shut off
the car. If I darted across the street for a sneak peek, I
doubt the flipper would see me. He's too hell-bent on
dismantling the home where I was going to raise our

children with Chris, where our grandchildren were going to visit.

The flipper is erasing every last trace of us. I tamp down the masochistic need to see it.

I ignore Joshua Jennings and plod up the outside stairs to my apartment. I ignore him at the front door. I ignore him inside the entry. I ignore him as I walk across the dark kitchen. I lose my resolution at the counter.

Bam. Bam. Bam.

Across the street, the flipper passes by the windows again—the shadow of death.

"He stole my past, and now, by selling the house before I'm ready, he's trying to steal my future," I tell House Mouse as I close the blinds. "I'm not going to let him steal this present moment."

The fridge offers leftover Chinese and a bottle of rosé. To keep from thinking about the house, I look up Valadon again.

Scratch. Scratch. Scratch.

"She lived in interesting times. Hard times for children. I've never heard of the Prussian siege of Paris before." I bet House Mouse hasn't either. "It's weird to think of all the incredible hardships people have gone through in the past. I guess the lesson is that we'll survive." I drink a glass of wine.

At seven, the sounds of construction across the road stop. I do the dishes and peek out the window. The security light on Mrs. Martinez's gable illuminates the dumpster at the end of my old driveway, heaped with broken tiles.

"The idiot ripped out my kitchen backsplash." After the dishes are done, I rub lotion on my winter-cracked hands. Then I might or might not use the next two hours to complain to House Mouse about the man.

At nine, I tap the empty bottle against my forehead. In went wine, and out comes an idea. "I could take unbroken pieces of travertine and clean them."

I could use them as coasters, souvenirs of my former life. *Brilliant.*

At ten past nine, I make a fool of myself.

The easy part is climbing into the container. Once inside, however, my feet sink into the rubble, and it traps me like quicksand.

Ooh, a whole tile.

I pick up my find, then I pick up another and another. *I'd better free my feet.* Except, they are cemented into the bucketloads of small chunks of mortar that used to hold the tiles to the wall. I heave. I fall back.

I shiver. I forgot my coat. Is it cold enough for hypothermia? Because I'm pretty sure hypothermia kills people. That would be an inglorious end.

"I don't want to die in a dumpster," I tell the unsympathetic stars above my head.

Too damn bad, they blink back.

I close my eyes.

"Are you all right?"

Aw, dammit.

The flipper is balancing on the edge of the dumpster, backlit like a comic book character. Scuffed work boots, ripped jeans, green T-shirt, red-and-black flannel. All he's missing is a hard hat. Maybe he doesn't want to ruin his hair. Anyway, hard hat or no, he's the epitome of cliché construction man. He's a few years past thirty, full of himself. He thinks he has life all figured out, building his real-estate empire.

I might dislike him a little extra for that, for having his life together. He has a plan, and he's working his plan, and his plan is actually working for him.

I can't say the same for myself.

Also, I envy his incredible balance. I lack balance on a good day, and I couldn't even spell it at the moment. "I'm fine."

"I heard noise out here. I thought I might have a raccoon. Should I leave?"

"Do whatever you want."

He sits on the four-inch-wide metal edge with an easy grace. "Mind if I ask what you're doing?"

"Rescuing the remnants of my life." I clutch the tiles tighter. He's going to have to pry them from my cold, dead hands.

"If you asked, I would have brought some over."

"You don't ask your enemy a favor."

"Are we enemies?"

"You bought my house."

"You sold it. That's how houses change hands. It's a time-honored tradition."

"Don't mock me." I hiccup.

He tilts his head. "Have you been drinking?"

"What's it to you?"

"Legal liability? I'm not sure what the law says about you getting stuck in my dumpster."

"I'm not hurt."

"That's a relief."

The night is silent around us. Early March. No bugs, no birds. Then a car turns down the street.

Joshua thumps into the dumpster and sits down next to me. He smells like wood shavings and the polyurethane used to finish hardwood. "They might wonder why I'm sitting up there and stop to ask."

Good thinking.

"So," he says. "You had a rough day."

"I quit my job." When I said what I said to Simon, I knew I was going to be fired, so that counts as quitting.

"Why?"

"I can no longer work for a dishonest idiot."

"Valid reason."

"I told the director that my boss was so dirty, I wouldn't wipe my ass with his tongue."

A huff of air shoots out of Joshua's nose. "Harsh."

"Sometimes, the truth has to be said." I sit up and pretend I want to be sitting there, not stuck whatsoever.

He stands up and reaches out a hand. "Here. Let me pull you out. You'll be doing me a favor."

"I'm not going to sue."

"So you say now, but you've already established that you're my enemy. You must allow me a certain amount of skepticism."

"I'm not your enemy. You're my enemy."

He drops his hand. "And the difference is?"

"I didn't take anything from you. You took my house from me."

"I didn't know you were reluctant to sell. I didn't know anything about you. My real estate agent talked to your real estate agent."

"My husband and I could afford the mortgage together, but I can't afford it on my own."

"I'm sorry. Mrs. Martinez said... I've heard about Chris."

His name is a blessing and a death wound. It brings back memories of the only real happiness I've known, and then it stabs me with them. "I don't want to talk about him with you."

"No. Of course."

"He was an anthropology professor at West Chester University. He was an anthropology major there when we met in college. He wore these bulky hand-knit sweaters his aunt would send him for every Christmas and birthday. He had square, black glasses. He was ridiculously smart, and endlessly kind. Major hot nerd vibes." My eyes fill with tears. "All the girls wanted to go out with him, but he picked me."

Joshua has that look that men get when they know they should be doing something for a woman in distress, but they have no idea what it is—pure bewilderment. "Should we get out of here?"

"I'll go when I'm ready."

I shouldn't have drunk the wine. I'm not going to

embarrass myself further by falling on my face. He can wait ten minutes, until I'm steadier.

"I like Suzanne Valadon," I tell him.

He considers this. For a long time. His constipated expression does not ease. He considers his words very, very carefully before he says, "It's okay to be bisexual. Or anything. Every color of the rainbow is valid."

I choke on a laugh. I *will* choke before I let it out. He's *not* funny.

"Suzanne Valadon was an artist. She painted with the Impressionists and Modernists in Paris in the late nineteenth and early twentieth century." I want to read more about her. I find everything I've learned about her so far fascinating.

"Never heard of her."

My point exactly. "Most nobody has. Once those artists died, history only remembered the men. Renoir, Degas, Matisse, Monet, and Van Gogh are upstairs. Valadon is in the basement."

"Is that a metaphor?"

I'm losing sensation in my legs below the knees. "She was a bastard. I can relate. I didn't have parents."

"Just the egg, then?" Joshua deadpans.

That time I almost laugh. "My parents died in a car accident when I was ten."

He flinches. "I'm sorry."

"Me too. My sister raised me."

"How old was she?"

"Twenty."

"Pretty young. What about your grandparents?"

"My father's parents weren't that healthy and wouldn't have had the money to feed one more mouth. They didn't have the energy for a preteen. And I didn't want to move to Kentucky anyway. And then my grandfather died in a hunting accident, a year after my parents. My grandmother died of a stroke sixteen months later."

"I'm sorry. That's a lot of hits to take."

"My mom's dad left the family when she was in kindergarten, and they never heard from him again. Her mom had a heart attack when I was five. It happened at our house, but I don't remember."

"How did your parents meet?"

Same way Chris and I did. "In college. Why are you asking me all this?"

"Establishing rapport so you feel comfortable enough with me to let me pull you out. It's getting cold."

I gather up the tiles I dropped. "I can do this. I'm going." Then, to distract him from my ungainly efforts, I say, "I have no idea what I'm going to do about work."

"What would you do if you knew you couldn't fail?" He's so damn earnest. You can tell he actually thinks he's helping. "That's what my father always asks."

It's unfair. A, that he has a father. B, that he's tossing out questions like *What would you do if anything were possible?* I would bring Chris back. "I want to go home."

"Please, let me help."

When he pulls me out of the rubble, my tiles fall again. I accept that I'm not going to be able to climb out of the dumpster with my arms full, and I leave my treasures behind.

I've made a complete fool of myself, and I'm still going home empty-handed.

"I could bring over a dozen tomorrow," the flipper offers. "Would that be all right?"

My response is one I'll soon come to regret: "Yes."

Saturday, March 4th

"ARE YOU HUNGOVER?" My sister peers at me from way too close, as if searching for tiny puddles of wine in my pores.

Abby is a single inch taller, with the same long brown hair, same hazel eyes, but we no longer look alike. It's *put-together* vs. *falling apart*.

"I had a few glasses of rosé last night." I'm twenty-nine. I'm sick of being supervised. "All right?"

She stops inside the door to examine me, and I feel like a teenager undergoing parental inspection. Except that I didn't have parents when I was a teenager.

"Why are you wearing those gray sweatpants?" She moves on before I can respond. "Do you want the number for my hairdresser?"

"No."

"David is here," she whispers. "He's coming up with Frank. We brought over the waffle iron. I'm making breakfast." Abby's vocabulary is missing the word *boundaries*. She thinks nothing of popping in whenever, and bringing guests along for the visit.

"I'm going to barf. Hi, Frank."

My sister's boyfriend is carrying the waffle iron box, huffing as if he's hefting an anvil. He lumbers forward in his brown corduroy pants and a blue sweater vest. I've never seen a thirty-something who looks more like a grandfather. He's the only man I know who'd wear a tie for a family breakfast. He looks as if he just popped in, on a break from his work at the bank.

He can't speak, so he grunts a greeting at me. Then he steps away because his phone pings.

"Hi, David."

Frank's brother—who is appropriately dressed in jeans and a Philadelphia Eagles hoody—lifts a brown paper bag. "Blueberry syrup and fresh blueberries." He is the most beautiful man I know. His father (shared parent with Frank) is Italian. His mother (not shared with Frank) came to the US from Argentina. He has unfairly good genes. They're not the kind of genes just anyone can get. I've accepted that. "And whipped cream."

"Perfect." He's a great guy, but he's not for me.

"So." Abby sets up the industrial-size, cast iron waffle maker, gracefully glancing over the fact that my kitchen is below-her-standards messy. If it were just the two of us, she'd tell me. "What have you been up to lately?"

I quit my job.

Not going into that in front of Frank and David. I also don't want to tip Abby into an impromptu lesson on responsibility.

Frank looks up from his phone, and he looks lost for a second before he pats his pockets. "We forgot orange juice."

"Oh, no!" Abby checks my fridge. "You don't have any either, Ellie." She knew I wouldn't. I never do. Stuff with a ton of sugar doesn't quench my thirst. "Would you mind running down to 7-Eleven with David? We blocked in your car. I'm sorry."

It's easier to go than to argue.

As we step out the door, she calls after us. "Drive safe!"

We're driving by the gas station two blocks away by the time I push past the hangover. *Wait a minute.* "That was a total setup, right? Plotted and rehearsed."

"Not Broadway, not even off-Broadway but small-town community theater? Definitely."

"It's embarrassing." I drop forward to rest my pounding forehead on the dashboard of David's electric SUV. Unfortunately, the seat belt catches me. I hang there like a fish in a net, my hair tumbled forward, long enough to notice a proliferation of split ends. I straighten myself.

David's eyes glint not with mockery but mischief. "You want to put on a show of our own?"

"I don't want to pretend that we're dating just so my sister and your brother will leave us alone. But, thank you. I appreciate the offer. I really do."

I don't remember much of what Joshua Jennings and I talked about last night, but I remember telling him that sometimes the truth has to be spoken. The truth also has to be lived.

I'm not going to fake my life. I'm not going to hide my grief. I am me, Ellie. And I still love Chris.

"How is Lilly?" I ask David.

His eyes are misty gray lakes of despair and heartbreak. Lilly is David's landlady like Mrs. Martinez is mine. She's eleven years older than he is. She's an artist.

"I try to help her as much as I can."

"Does she know?" *That you love her.*

"How do you know?"

"I've seen you look at her."

"I can't tell her. I can't put that on her right now. I don't want to make things awkward."

I can see how finding the right time and words would be difficult. *Hey. Um. So, I know you're taking care of a husband in the late stages of MS, but I've been in love with you since we met.*

"Have you thought about moving?"

"I've had enough saved up to buy my own house for years. She needs the money from the rent. Someone else could rent the apartment, but the new tenant might not offer to help."

"So you wait until Gabe dies?"

"It's not like that. Gabe is a great guy."

"But you love her?"

"I can love her by helping her. I can love her without us being in bed together. I see her in the morning, and I see her when I get home from work. We have long talks."

"Sounds like torture."

"Compared to what she and Gabe are going through, I don't get to whine."

We pass the dry cleaner, then the paint store. "I'm not sure if I've known a purer love, but I don't envy Lilly."

David meets my eyes for a second. "You've been where she is."

I have. I stop resenting Abby and company. I can handle guests for an hour or two. Truth is, I like David.

We pick up the orange juice, the sham that it is.

David catches me frowning at the carton on my lap, on our way back. "Wrong brand?"

"Wrong branding. They changed the packaging."

"You're right. The orange grove was better."

I run my thumb down the diagonal orange lines on the white background, straight lines that bear no resemblance to the gentle, natural curves of the fruit. "Brands are trending toward minimalism these days. Minimal color choices, minimal shapes, sparse design."

"Easy?"

"Boring. But that's all we get in the creative briefs from clients these days." Except for the Valadon request, a gorgeous piece of art from the past that radiates beauty and emotion. I wanted to work on that project, dammit.

"I've never noticed before, but you're right." David nods toward the signs above the businesses that line the road. "The old ones are detailed and artistic. The new ones are color blocks."

I point out a few particularly good ones, and he adds the ones he likes, and the shoptalk about design restores me. I'm in an okay mood by the time we turn down my street. "Let's just have a good time. Let's just chill and hang with Abby and Frank."

Somewhere, fate laughs so hard, she pees her pants.

I know this the second we get out of the car, because Joshua Jennings is standing in the open door of my apartment with an armload of travertine tiles. Usual handyman uniform: tan work boots, flannel shirt, faded jeans. Hair short enough to be spiky, if he used product, except I can't see him using product other than maybe chainsaw oil.

Abby is in the doorway, ready to break out in dance. "Come on in." Her face is so animated, she could be acting in a sitcom in front of a live audience. She grabs the flipper by the elbow to make sure he won't escape. Then she notices me over his shoulder. "Ellie, your *friend* is here."

And that's how Joshua and I and my family end up having breakfast together.

Naturally, we're seated next to each other.

"How are you this morning?" he asks.

"Fine." I do my best to appreciate his presence, if

for no other reason than because it might prevent Frank's hemorrhoids coming up as a topic.

Abby serves him an extra-tall stack of waffles. "How do you like the house?"

"Thank you. It has great bones."

"Big yard. Have any kids?"

"Not yet. Lonely and single."

He's messing with her. He knows where her line of questioning is going.

David and I exchange a look, and I almost let myself see the humor in the situation, but then Frank offers me the orange juice.

"No, thank you."

"Juice is healthier than coffee." He keeps holding out the carton.

I take it and set it on the table by my plate. "Coffee works for me."

"You should have real breakfast, every day."

What I eat for breakfast is none of his business. But he's not wrong either. I make a joke of it. "Wish someone came up with a game of chance where people could win a personal chef by lottery."

"Just drink a glass of orange juice," he insists. "It's great."

Really? I give him a smile. "You're right. I get confused at times. If only there were a man around to tell me what I like."

Then I pour a couple of inches of the damned orange juice into my empty coffee mug.

Abby shoots me a dark look. David's nostrils are trembling with mirth. Frank goes back to his waffles, and the tension eases in the kitchen, but then the flipper speaks again, in a misguided attempt to restart conversation.

"It's nice of you to all come over and support Ellie like this. When bad stuff happens, it's good to have family." He turns to me. "Take your time and think things through. Losing a job is not the end of the world. I'm sure you'll land on your feet."

Dead silence spreads in my kitchen like fog-machine mist in a bad horror movie.

"Sorry." Joshua catches on. "My bad."

What have I ever done to this man?

He's lucky I can't reach the waffle iron. And that hitting people is illegal. Also, there are witnesses—

"You got fired?" Abby is the first to demand answers, her voice thin with shock and hurt. "Why didn't you tell me?"

Thank you, Joshua Jennings.

"Just happened."

"Drinking is not the answer." Frank looks up from his phone and snaps back into father mode: somber, solicitous, sensible. "What can we do to help? The offer of your old bedroom stands. You know that, right? It's yours. You can always come back."

David piles whip cream on his plate until the can sputters empty. "Oops." He rises with a winning smile. "That's it. Ellie and I will shoot back to the store and grab another."

I *could* learn to love him.

"I didn't realize—" Joshua stutters at the same time, a thousand apologies squirming in his eyes.

I'm not going to tell him it's okay. I shouldn't have expected better from my enemy.

I want to go to the store. I want to be anywhere but here, but… "I think we've had plenty of whip cream already." Running away is not the answer. "Thank you, David."

"What are you going to do?" Abby is still frozen in motion. "What's your plan?"

As if I spent last night in a strategy session with a bottle of wine and a spreadsheet and have my three-year and five-year plans ready. *Would it kill her to give me the tiniest bit of space?*

"I'm going to act as if it were impossible to fail," I say without looking at Judas next to me.

My sister isn't appeased. "What does that mean?"

I need a project, a mission to pull me from the lava lake of grief. I need something to hold on to, so I don't disintegrate.

"I'm going to open a museum." The words spring from a still-tipsy corner of my brain.

"A what?" Frank ignores his pinging phone. He's been fidgeting all through breakfast. Maybe it's time to take his next hemorrhoid pill.

So not what I want to think about over waffles. "The Museum of Unseen Art."

"A Museum of Invisible Art?" His tone turns pitying.

I sit taller. I won't be pitied at my own kitchen table.

"Did you know that most museums only have two to four percent of their collections on display? I'm thinking about a museum that wouldn't have its own collection, just space, and it would borrow art that's not on display at other museums." My brand manager brain kicks in. "The tagline would be *From the basement to the gallery.*"

"You want to open a museum?" Abby is on time delay.

"The Museum of Unseen Art."

Four people look at me as if I'm crazy.

CHAPTER FOUR

Suzanne

1877 / Age 12

MADAME MABBIT GIVES ME BREAD FOR LUNCH. SHE DOESN'T MIND THAT I'M A BASTARD. All children are God's children, she tells me.

I'm that glad I didn't run away back all those months ago. I did, in truth, for a day. Too damn cold to run away in the winter is what I learned. I slunk back home. I could always run away again in the spring, I figured.

"Hold the hat block steady, Marie-Clémentine."

Colors surround us: pinks and purples and yellows and blues and greens. And so many textures, from tweed to real silk. When I'm here, I can barely remember the drab tenement at the bottom of the hill.

Madame Mabbit wraps wet buckram around the smooth wood with a grunt and a huff. She has hundreds of blocks in all sizes, shaped like human heads. They watch us.

"Whatcha makin' today?"

"We are *making*," she corrects my language, "full hats with brims all week." She trims the stiff cotton. "Next week, we'll make fascinators. They take less material, but they won't go any faster. We'll lose time on the decorations."

Once every hat block she's set out on the table has buckram on it, we pause to take a drink. Madame Mabbit presses a hand against her stomach. She does that a lot. Also, her eyes twitch.

She tips her cup toward the bread crust left on the sideboard. "Go ahead. My innards are off."

I don't have to be told twice.

"What do you say?"

She is determined to improve my manners. I don't see what they matter. Manners don't fill your stomach. Still, no skin off my nose to humor her. At least she doesn't beat me. "Thank you, Madame Mabbit."

She finishes her water, sip by slow sip, then blinks at me, as if she's forgotten what we were doing.

I pick a crumb off my apron and lick it off my finger. "Makin' felt?"

She went on and on about felt this morning.

"Right, then. We are *making* felt." She corrects my lowborn language, then shuffles off to the back. "Let's do a bit of carroting."

Some children have grandmothers. I imagine if I had one, she'd be like Madame Mabbit. She's not nearly as glamorous as Mademoiselle La La of the circus, but she has her own shop and lives above the shop in *two* rooms. She has carpet on her floor. I saw it last week when she sent me upstairs to fetch her spare scissors.

In the workshop in the back, we go straight to a vat of animal hair already scraped from the skin, sitting in a smelly liquid.

"Be glad it's not the old days." Madame Mabbit catches me holding my breath. "Hatters used to soak the hair in their own urine."

I make a face.

"Best urine came from the men with the Neapolitan disease," Madame Mabbit tells me. "*Mal de cour,* the disease of the court, they called it in the time of the kings."

I heard those words before. I know the modern name too: syphilis. I spent half the siege with drunks and whores in the street. I learned aplenty.

"Why would a sick man's piss… I mean, urine"— I can use the fancy words she likes, if they make her that happy—"be better?"

"The doctors treat the disease with mercury pills."

"Diseased piss, this is?" My hands hover over the liquid instead of plunging in. "I mean, urine."

Madame Mabbit cackles. "These are modern times, child. We use mercury salt now. The salt makes the hairs more readily worked, easier to press and bind into felt." She immerses both her hands up to the elbow. "You'll see."

I'd much rather see something else. All the things I'd rather see, in fact, would make a long list. Yet this is the work I have.

We strain the hair. Mercury water runs down my arms, soaks my clothes and bare legs. Then we press the wet hair into forms and crank the press. Next, we heat the felt to bind the hairs even more tightly together. I can barely see Madame Mabbit in the steam of mercury vapor.

She coughs. Her face twitches, and she laughs again as if I said something funny, even though I've been silent, wondering if Maman got paid today, if we'll have anything for dinner.

I catch myself, and instead of worrying, I give thanks for what I have, like Madame Mabbit taught me. Right now, I'm barely hungry. I have bread crust in my belly. The steam is nice and warm. I miss Clelia, but I don't miss school. I'm happy.

"You prove yourself on this work, and I'll let you help me with the nicer bits," Madame Mabbit promises. "I'll let you draw the leaves and the flowers on the felt. Then we'll cut them out for decorating."

I'd stand around in wet clothes in the smelly shed all year if it only led to drawing. "Thank you, Madame Mabbit."

She fills her lungs with the steam and encourages me to do the same. "Go on, Marie-Clémentine. We're breathing in medicine."

. . .

1878 / Age 13

THE MEDICINE DOESN'T HELP MADAME MABBIT. As the year ends and a new one begins, she coughs and coughs. Even the warmer months don't ease her poor lungs none.

"Guess what I saw today?" I burst into the shop, leaving the glorious Montmartre summer outside behind me, the overfilled space inside suddenly too small and cramped compared to where I've been.

"The gendarme's stick?"

"Ha! They can't catch me." I fetch my apron. "And if they did, it would have been worth it."

"Did you sneak into the Exposition Universelle again?"

"I saw a telephone." I tie the apron strings behind my back.

"What's that?" She coughs into the crook of her elbow, her hands full of felt.

I fetch her a glass of water from the pitcher in the corner. "Two people in separate rooms, talking to each other."

"Shouting?"

"A little. Into a black horn. There are two of those. One goes to your mouth, one to your ear."

"Why don't they just go into the same room?"

She has me there. "I saw the Statue of Liberty that Bartholdi is making for the Americans."

"Now that I'd like to behold."

"It is only the giant head so far, sitting on the ground. She has a crown of spikes."

"Like Christ's crown of thorns?" Madame Mabbit frowns with disapproval.

"I saw Braille." I try again. "Little dots on paper that the blind can read with their fingers."

"Now you're having me on." But that, at last, makes Madame Mabbit laugh. "Get to work, child, and forget all that nonsense." She picks up her scissor and sets it to the green felt, but her eyes twitch so hard, she sets the scissor back down again. "Come over here and help."

It's like that all summer. By the time the Exposition Universelle closes in November, the twitching spreads from the milliner's eyes to her arms and feet. And sometimes she yells for no reason. And she forgets things. One night, she sets fire to the millinery.

I can't believe the charred door and the last of the smoke coming out the window when I arrive for work in the morning.

"Poor Madame Mabbit." The women of the neighborhood surround her as she sits collapsed on her doorstep, while the men walk away with their buckets, all soot covered, hacking and spitting.

"It's lucky the lamplighter that went by at dawn saw the flames through the window and raised an alarm," a charwoman tells me.

I push through the crowd and help Madame

Mabbit up, shouldering her weight. "I'll clean everything."

"Lucky I didn't burn up with my wooden hat blocks." She coughs and she coughs. And then she cries. "I am finished."

"Don't you worry." I lead her to the public water pump on the corner to wash her face. "Before you know it, we'll be back in business."

1879 / Age 14

"FASTER!" MONSIEUR BERNARD SMACKS MY BACK WITH HIS STICK, AND MY SKIN STINGS, AND STINGS, AND STINGS. I curse the damned crow—as Clelia and I call him. He's dressed all in black, befitting our new place of employment, a funeral wreath company.

My fingers fly over the willow branches, and I bend and twist them to the metal frame. I prick my thumb again on the wire and I bleed, but I keep up. When my toes go numb from the cold stone floor, I dance in place. I miss the milliner shop's warm mercury steam that made last winter easy. I miss the extra bread crusts. I miss Madame Mabbit.

She survived the fire, but she didn't survive her cough. The smoke made it worse. She died the week after she lost her shop.

At the factory, all of us girls stand in a row at a long table, Clelia next to me. Her mother had another sickly babe, so she can't take on as much embroidery as before. Clelia had to leave school to help with money.

At least she got to write on paper. She did run to the fountain afterward, but she couldn't wash off the ink for me. Still, she tried, and she did give me the sheet. I drew horses in the margins.

She does a little dance too, and breathes onto her frozen fingers, before she glances toward the window. "Why ain't it warmer yet? 'T's spring."

"Eyes on your work." Monsieur Bernard smacks her on the head for talking. "You'll never be like Véronique."

Véronique, fifteen, a year older than us—sits at a table in the corner all by herself. She weaves wreathes of sheer marvel for rich merchants, from zinc leaves and porcelain roses, and lilies she paints white with lead.

"Be almost worth dyin' for such a wreath." Clelia pines for them the way I pine for sweets. She whispers, but Monsieur Bernard hears her anyway and smacks her again.

I can't tell her what a villain he is, can't commiserate at all, or he'd smack me too, and he beat me plenty today already.

I just let my elbow touch against Clelia's. To Monsieur Bernard, it looks like nothing, but my friend knows what it means. *I'm here. We're in this together.*

Our legs ache from standing all day, our fingers scraped bloody, but at least the room is dimming.

"We'll be let out soon, and hastening home," I

whisper. Monsieur Bernard has slithered away, so he doesn't hear me. He's moving down the line, busy smacking other girls.

"Speakin' like one of them fancy mademoiselles. Ooh la la," Clelia mocks me under her breath.

I don't want the girls to think that I feel myself above them. I speak as Madame Mabbit taught me, because I miss the milliner. The milliner's shop was a sanctuary for me. Monsieur Bernard's factory line is, if not the main, then at least a minor, hell.

"I will not spare the rod." He turns in a circle to look at each and every one of us. "For I mean to correct you as if you were my own daughters."

More than half the girls at the factory are bastards.

He stops at Véronique's table and puts his walking stick behind his back.

"Why doesn't *she* ever get fatherly correction?" I'm becoming so apt at talking without moving my lips, the circus might hire me as a ventriloquist yet.

"He doesn't smack her," Clelia whispers back, "but he keeps her late. I wouldn't want that."

Maybe Véronique doesn't want it either, because she shies away from Monsieur Bernard. She bends down in her chair until she's almost as small as I am.

We all know she shrinks from more than his pickled-herring breath. We all come from the bottom of the hill. None of us are *that* innocent. The worst of it is, since my breasts have been growing, Monsieur Bernard has started watching them more than he watches my hands.

"Eyes on your work!" He catches me dawdling.

I braid the willow so fast that when he reaches me, he spares me.

By the time I finish my wreath, I can barely see the thin wire, so I don't start another. The factory doesn't waste money on lamps. We are finished for the day.

"Go on, then." Monsieur Bernard throws open the door.

Of course, it being Saturday, we don't rush out into the evening. A group of mothers and older sisters hurry in. The women follow Monsieur Bernard to his office to collect our wages. Some workers are as young as ten, but even the older girls cannot walk the streets in the dark with coin.

"I found you more work," Maman says as we amble down the boulevard, the storefronts painted yellow by the gaslights. "Before you come to the factory in the mornin', you be sellin' vegetables at the market."

"Les Halles?"

"Aye."

The factory doesn't pay near what Madame Mabbit did, and there hasn't been anything else for me over the long winter.

I want to ask which farmer, whose stall, but a drunk staggers toward us. As spring brings more work, it also brings more drunks to the streets. They start sleeping in the gutters again, right after the last freeze.

The drunk leers. "How 'bout a two fer one, eh?"

Maman speeds her steps. "She's me young daughter, you poxed pirate!"

The drunk laughs in delight. "I don't mind."

"Joseph, you blind oaf." I kick at him. He used to teach me card tricks when I skipped school. "It's me. Marie-Clémentine."

"Valadon the wildcat." He whoops. "Wondered where you went."

He staggers off, but another bean brain pops up to see what the noise was. This one has the bearing of a weasel and mean, calculating eyes. "Help a man out with a coin, mademoiselles."

He steps close enough that I know that on the long list of things he steals, soap does not make an appearance. His rotten teeth flash. He'll be on us as fast as an alley cat on a careless pigeon, given half the chance.

"Father!" I raise my hands and wave at a bulky man on the corner, in a black overcoat. Then I grab Maman by the sleeve and tug her forward. "Look. Father is here."

"Whaccha goin' on about?" She shrugs me off. "Are you daft?"

I grab her again and drag her a few more feet. The man on the corner turns to us. The weasel lurches away.

We cross the street and pass people standing in line for Mademoiselle La La's performance. The music filters outside and reaches my heart. The coins I secretly earn at the stables buy me a ticket now and then. Tickets and pencils, but mostly—when hunger breaks me down—I buy bread.

"Wish I could work at the circus." The moment the words are out, I know I shouldn't have said them.

"And starve?" Maman smacks my head. "Stupid child. I know you remember the siege."

I remember that the dogs were eaten first. Dogs come when called; they were the easiest to catch. After the dogs, people hunted cats. Then the rats. You'd think rats would be the fastest, but by then, they weren't. They didn't have anything to eat either. You could tempt them out of hiding with a crumb. They were so weak, they were staggering in the street.

One thing I can say for the nuns at St. Vincent's is that they grow their own crops and raise their own chickens. They fed us until, at last, they barricaded themselves. School was out then.

"Wouldn't have been here in the siege if not for you." Maman never skips a chance to remind me. "If only I didn't have to leave them Guimbauds in Limoges, a fine house too, when I fell pregnant. Good for nothin' your father was. Just as well that the millstone crushed him. God punishes the wicked."

"Wasn't he an engineer who fell from the bridge and drowned in the river?" That's the tale I remember.

"What's it matter?" Her eyes narrow, and her arm moves as if she's about to smack me again, but then she drops her laundry-roughened hand. "He was a bad man who met a bad end."

"Remember the horsemeat?" I ask to get her to think about something else. We ate some horse too, but not that much. Horsemeat went to those who could pay for it.

Maman snickers as she shuffles along next to me. "Not a carriage could be found in Paris. And the rich, amblin' around, couldn't believe they had to walk on their own two feet."

We stop by the wineshop and go home with three bottles. Maman drinks one, and then she sleeps. On Saturdays, I don't have to go to bed listening to her yelling at me. My favorite day of the week is the day I get paid.

I draw on the wall, just one horse and one acrobat. I only have a crumb of charcoal left.

At least I won't have to go back to the funeral wreath company in the morning, on account that it'll be Sunday, the Lord's Day. Maman will spend it drinking. I'll be at the stables. The horses need taking care of, and the Lord is understanding of their needs. The stable master says I won't go to hell for shoveling shit. But sometimes, when I'm standing ankle-deep in the stinking muck with a pitchfork and a gnawing belly, knowing nothing awaits me the next day but Mr. Bernard's stick, knowing someday soon he'll be holding me back after work instead of Véronique, I feel as if I'm in hell already.

"Someday, I'll escape, and I'll be you," I tell the dim outline of the acrobat on the wall. "Someday, I'll be free. You'll see."

· · ·

1880 / Age 15

"You can't be leavin' work every time a man grabs your arse, or you'll be out of work all your life."

"I prefer waitressing to twisting funeral wreaths." I fill the iron with glowing embers from the stove, then run it over the wrinkled shirt on the table. "I like the people I meet."

Monsieur Bernard dismissed me for delinquency. And also because when he called me into the back office and grabbed my breast, I stuck him with the old hatpin Madame Mabbit gave me.

In any case, all my fault—can't argue about that with Maman. Even before the pin incident, I took to running away whenever the crow aimed his stick at me. Most of the time, Monsieur Bernard found me in the street and dragged me back to the working bench, beating me all the way. Until the day he decided, like the nuns, that I wasn't worth the effort. I don't care, I prefer adult work anyway, now that I'm fifteen. I'm no stupid factory girl.

"You fancy them artists." Maman scoffs, mired in her mending.

I admire the artists. I love the way they lay dabs of paint here and there, and their dancers swirl like they could step right off the easel and dance around me.

"They take a bit of canvas and turn it into flowers, or houses, or people. It's as good a magic as the one people pay to see at the circus." I move the hot iron over the linen slowly enough that it erases the wrinkles, but not so slowly that it will burn the fabric. "Do you believe in magic?"

"There ain't no magic in this world, Marie-Clémentine. There ain't no rhyme or reason either. There's just work and them idiots you have to put up with to keep workin'. That's all there is. You keep on working so you don't starve." She rubs her knee. "If only we didn't fall on hard times."

"The hard times are over. Everyone says Paris has recovered."

"The bad times ain't never over for the poor. Don't let no one tell you different."

She still lives in the days of the siege and the days that came after, which should have been better, but were worse instead. The government that fled from the Prussians wanted to come back into the city, but the people resisted. The Communards said a government who ran like cowards and abandoned us was no legitimate government. Fighting broke out in the city. That was when the nuns barricaded themselves into the convent.

"We live in modern times now, Maman."

"Tell that to them twenty thousand dead."

"The dead are buried." I saw the bodies on the street. And I looked through their pockets like everyone else. Maman was off most of the day searching for food. I was told to stay home. What six-year-old would? I roamed the cobblestones with the street kids barefoot.

"You stay away from them artists." Maman

straightens her back and groans before bending over her work again. "They'll fill your head with right nonsense. What do they know? I see them in the squares, drunk. Some of them have to lean on their easels."

She is leaning like a tree in a windstorm, two empty bottles at her feet. I think of the word *irony*, one of the many words Madame Mabbit taught me.

"You find you a strong husband like your sister," Maman orders. "If only you were a boy. No matter. You find you a man. That's the ticket. You don't wanna end up a grisette."

Half the girls in Montmartre are grisettes, working-class girls who make ends meet by sleeping with men for money here and there.

"No, Maman." *I'm going to be a circus acrobat.*

The next morning, I practice—as I've been doing since I've left school—while walking the horses for the stables.

I don't sit on their backs. I stand. And I bend and I twist, until spectators gather and clap. At first, when I was an eleven-year-old who could pass for eight, they tossed me coins too, especially if I broke out in a patriotic song. No Frenchman can resist a child singing La Marseillaise. That is a fact.

These days, money is rare, but I get lucky today.

"Well done!" A gentleman, graying at the temples, tosses me a coin.

I snatch it right out of the air without so much as a wobble. "Merci, Monsieur."

"I'm a generous man." His attention drops to my legs.

Now that I'm fifteen, the look in the men's eyes is different. When they offer me money, they expect more than a demonstration of my excellent balance.

He draws his gaze up my torso to my breasts. "I could be even more generous."

I laugh him off and move on. I'm no grisette.

Back at the stables, I pocket my secret wages, then go to the L'Auberge du Clou, a literary cabaret, on the avenue de Trudaine, to wait tables.

Maman is right, I do fancy the clientele. Most of them are gentlemen: artists, writers, and musicians. I watch them, and I copy their speech and manners. I don't want everyone to know, as soon as they look at me, that I'm from the tenements. This better class of men drink as much as the chimney sweeps and butchers, but they don't grab after me as often.

"Move your feet." Jacques, the manager, shoves me. And when I stumble and a glass slips from my tray to shatter on the floor, he snaps, "That'll come out of your wages." He shoves me again.

I serve Édouard Manet's table. The painter is so boisterous that his friends refer to him as the *enfant terrible*. He is drinking wine and eating fish with Claude Monet, Pierre-Auguste Renoir, and Edgar Degas. I know all their names. Of course, they have no idea who I am.

"No, no, no." Degas slams the table. He has a short-trimmed beard and a not-unpleasant face, but he looks as if when God made him, he let a drunk angel finish the eyes. His eyelids are droopy, the eyes themselves asymmetrical. "There is no need for pedantic accuracy in art now that we have the camera. Art is no longer to record things exactly as they are. We've been set free."

I exchange their empty bottle for a full one and move on, wishing I didn't have to work, wishing I could sit down among them and listen.

The next table is a couple. The man, older, won't take his eyes off the girl, who blushes and lowers her lashes. I know her from Madame Mabbit's. After the madame's death, the girl went to work at a different millinery. The couple seem to be in love. She's not here to sell herself, I can tell now, at a glance.

They've long finished their soup, but I move past and don't yet ask them to pay. I leave them to their romance.

In the corner, the composers Debussy and Satie want another drink. I bring them a fresh bottle from the bar, then hurry to the two other gentlemen who wave me over. I don't remember their names, but they're both painters—symbolists.

"More bread."

"Oui, Messieurs." I run back to the kitchen, stepping around the boy cleaning up the broken glass.

When I return, the men are deep in conversation.

"The jugglers don't work," says the scrawny one.

"It's not that they don't work," responds the other, who has the look of a well-fed aristocrat. "It's that nobody at the circus is a professional."

"That is their charm. Regardless, the circus needs fresh faces."

My heart tumbles.

I set the bread on the table and clear my throat. This is my moment. The door to my future has opened to a crack, at last. "Are Messieurs talking about the Cirque Fernando?"

"Have you been?" They look at me with interest.

"Just once or twice." *Every chance I get.* "Do you know Fernando? I'm in need of an introduction." I pull myself tall, all the way to five feet. In my mind, I'm already on the trapeze. I soar, and the audience gasps. "I'd like to be an acrobat."

CHAPTER FIVE

Ellie

Monday, March 6th

IF I WERE TO PEEP THROUGH THE WINDOWS OF MY OLD HOUSE, THE BEST TIME WOULD BE WHEN JOSHUA WASN'T THERE. Like now. Now would be perfect.

I glance at the empty driveway, the garbage can from under my sink at my feet, patiently waiting for me to finish clipping the split ends of my hair into it.

Obviously, I'm not going over.

But I could. It would only take five minutes.

I put away the scissors and sit back at the table. The grace period of the weekend is over. It's Monday morning. Time to get to work, which, at the moment, means updating my portfolio. I bid on a few projects on a couple of freelance sites. I have enough skills to pay my bills, but I'd like a company job with benefits again, eventually.

Scratch, scratch, scratch.

"I can't start a museum," I tell House Mouse, who, frankly, is as likely to be the founder of an art museum as I am. "There are dreams. There are pie-in-the-sky dreams. And then there are champagne-funfetti-ice cream-cake-on-Mars dreams. I have no qualifications or money. The only thing I know about art museums is that I like art. Okay?"

I scroll through the images of past projects on my phone to see what I could add to my portfolio. Then the pictures of *Toilette des enfants* pop up, and I stop to admire the lines that caress the figures with tenderness.

I've been reading more about Suzanne Valadon. The more I learn about her, the more I like her. She had purpose. She went after what she wanted.

Scratch, scratch, scratch.

"Why would Gibbler's wife want this small black-and-white sketch? I wonder what her connection is to Suzanne."

My phone rings.

"You've been let go?" My friend Grace is satisfyingly outraged on my behalf. "Why didn't you tell me? I kept waiting for you to show up."

"What did Tim say?"

"That you'll be pursuing other opportunities."

"I meant to call. Then I kept putting it off. I'm sorry. I was licking my wounds. I wanted to be in a better headspace so I don't just whine and complain."

"That's what friends are for."

"I'm fine. Honest."

"I have laxatives in my purse. Should I put a couple in Tim's coffee? Want me to tip off his wife about Frederica? Hide a bag of dog poop in his office?"

"You don't have a dog." But I'm in a better mood already.

"Plenty of idiots don't pick up after their pooch outside my building. I'm willing to gather up a wheelbarrowful if you want it."

"The best revenge is to be happy."

"Maybe. But it can't be nearly as satisfying as gluing your boss's ass to his seat."

Grace is twenty-four. She's like a younger sister to me. She brings a youthful energy to our friendship that I sincerely appreciate.

We may or may not plot various ways to annoy Tim for another twenty minutes before we hang up. Then I turn back to the laptop, but I'm officially distracted.

Scratch. Scratch. Scratch.

"I should go for a walk."

I grab my coat and step outside into a surprise of sunlight. The balmy weather feels more like May than March. I drum down the steps, my coat unbuttoned. I'm not wearing a hat, but I should probably wear gloves, at least. The skin on my hands is all cracked in winter. I shove them into my pockets.

Now that I don't have a job, I'll finally have time for self-care. I promise myself a paraffin hand treatment.

Mrs. Martinez's fieldstone cottage sits on the other side of the driveway, with its mossy cedar shingles. Her windows are filled with warm light. Smoke puffs from her chimney. Her home is straight out of a storybook, an enchanted cottage in the enchanted woods.

It was the first building on the property when her ancestors began farming the land, before they built the big farmhouse. After her parents died, the farmhouse burned down, and Mrs. Martinez's then husband sold the land to a developer. Mrs. Martinez insisted on keeping the cottage, even though they were living in the city at the time. Then, after the divorce, she moved back.

The cottage used to be my dream home. I talked Chris into buying our house in the development because it was across the street. If I couldn't have the magic cottage, at least I could have the view of it.

"Hi, Ellie." One of the neighbors is walking her jumble of fluffy Pomeranians.

"Hi, Dakota." I cross to the other side so I don't get tangled in her leashes. "They're too cute."

"Thanks. How is Bubbles?"

"Happy." According to Abby. I'll have to talk to her about Chris's lizard again. I haven't yet because I didn't want to start another argument.

Dakota and I move on, in opposite directions.

My house has a brand-new driveway, brand-new roof—both of which I've seen go in. *Huh.* The flipper has pressure washed the white siding at one point while I wasn't looking. Maybe he was blasting my house on Friday while I was blasting my career.

"Joshua Jennings is a busy freaking beaver," I tell a jogger who has earplugs in and can't possibly hear me.

The flipper is still missing in action when I finish my loop around the neighborhood. Fate? What could go wrong in a minute? Checking out what he's done to my kitchen would only take a quick peek.

I sneak up the driveway and around the back. I come to a screeching halt on the deck, staring through the sliding glass door into a barren wasteland.

No cabinets, no counters, no backsplash. My kitchen is as empty as my chest. I can't stand the sight of desolation. I collapse onto the wicker patio daybed I had to leave behind due to lack of room in my one-bedroom apartment.

The horror goes on. A shed, I'm stunned to notice, sits on the spot where I had my vegetable garden. I suppose the flipper has to keep his flipper tools somewhere, but... *My poor asparagus!* The indignities never end.

I knew some traces of my happiness with Chris would be gone, but I didn't expect *everything* to be erased.

I curl up on the round patio bed. I pull the shade dome over my head, until I'm enclosed in a cocoon, because my old jeans have been washed thin, and there's a chill in the air. And because I need another minute. And because I don't want to look at the stupid shed.

Chris and I used the outdoor bed all the time. Once we even made love under the stars. Our patio faces the woods in the back, no other houses, so the backyard is private. I turn on my side and pretend he's with me, big spoon to my little spoon.

I should go, but I can't bear to leave the feeling of being loved and safe behind. I need it for another minute. I close my eyes, and I don't notice when I slip into another world. All I know is that I'm walking through a house—room after empty, dilapidated room waits for me, a lifeless space with tremendous potential that's also tremendous work. Antique furniture stands abandoned in every corner, dust covered. I love the place. I can't believe it's mine. As I turn in a circle in the middle of a space large enough to be a ballroom, I say out loud, *This is going to take a lot of effort.*

"Ellie?"

Chris? I rush to the window.

"Ellie. Can I help you with anything?" Joshua is looking down at me with a worried expression.

Haven't we done this already?

I spring up and away, blinking fast to clear the cotton candy of sleep from my brain. "I'm sorry. I shouldn't be here. I don't know what I was thinking."

Let *this* be a dream. Please, please, please.

"You're always welcome to come over."

"I'm…" He would never understand.

"Homesick?"

What would a home stealer know about it? Anyway, according to Agatha Christie, whose biography was last month's book club read, *to rush into explanations is always a sign of weakness*, so I refuse to explain.

I just stand there, all awkward, which is also not great.

"So," he says. "Breakfast was wild on Saturday. I didn't realize founding a museum is your dream."

My brain wakes up a little more, but not yet all the way.

"I have other ones," I tell him. "Sometimes, I daydream that you have a nail gun accident, and there's a law that since you have no heirs, the house reverts to the previous owner."

His laugh is uncomfortable. "I can't tell if you're serious."

I walk off the patio and leave him wondering.

At home, I grab a bag of honey-mustard pretzels, Chris's favorite. He was a pretzel nut: salted pretzels, sourdough, peanut butter filled. He was a baker too. His dream was to someday come up with his own pretzel flavor. Dill pickle, bacon, and chili-lime were on the top of his list. He was seriously researching production when he was diagnosed.

I can't bake.

But I can do other things.

Toward the end, Chris's one regret was that he never did his *one* thing, the dream bigger than him.

He wasn't going to leave a legacy. I can't invent a revolutionary pretzel but….

"We're opening a museum," I tell House Mouse. "It's going to have a Christopher Waldon wing."

I launch off the sofa and drive over to the bank where Frank works.

People establish museums, right? It can be done. While I wait in line, I look that up.

Rome's Borghese Gallery is housed in Cardinal Scipione Borghese's former palace, started with art he collected. They have a bunch of Caravaggios and Berninis. All right, not exactly my speed.

King Philip II built the Louvre. Our situations are only slightly similar—in that we're both human.

The Guggenheim? The founder also isn't my twin. He was a wealthy industrialist.

I step up to the window, and the woman behind the counter smiles at me with complete insincerity. I don't blame her. She's entitled to her feelings after dealing with the public all day.

"I'd like to talk to Frank Rossi."

"Do you have an appointment?"

"He knows me."

"We still usually do appointments. He might be in a meeting."

I get it. In my faded jeans and pilled black sweater, I don't look like someone who is here to do major business.

"Could you just please let Frank know that Ellie Waldon is here to talk to him?" I want to speak to him in private. If I drove over to the house tonight, Abby would be there, putting her two cents in.

The woman slips off her stool. "Let me see."

It's fifty-fifty whether she's going for Frank or security.

A minute later, she pops out a side door. "Come this way."

I follow her down a beige hallway decorated with posters—various mountains with the tritest motivational quotes like *There's no I in TEAM*.

There's an I in IDIOT. I regret the uncharitable thought immediately, and silently apologize to corporate culture. I shouldn't let unemployment make me grumpy.

"Ellie." Frank is half-hidden behind his stacks of paper, in his own little cave of bureaucracy. He's wearing the same sweater vest that he wore to my house on Saturday for breakfast, except in green. Maybe he has to dress like that for work. Banker dress code.

Who am I to judge him for it? "Hi."

"Everything all right?"

"I'd like to open a museum."

"You mentioned that the other day." His smile grows strained.

"I was hoping you could tell me how people get started. Is applying for a loan the first step?"

"Have you ever worked in the museum business?"

"You know I haven't." I sit. "Could you please take me seriously? This is important to me."

He picks up a pen, pulls his notebook closer, and writes my name on the top of the blank page. "You no longer work at The Philadelphia Design Studio. Am I right?"

"I'm looking for another job."

"That's good news. Am I correct that you don't have a degree in museum studies?"

"I don't."

"Do you own a building that you're thinking about donating toward this new museum?"

"No."

He puts down his pen. "Do you own a collection you're hoping to show in the museum?"

"No. Listen, I know museums are founded by rich old men, and I'm not one of those. I don't have the pedigree, or the art collection, or the money, but I can make this work. I can rise to the challenge. I promise."

A lengthy silence follows my impassioned plea.

Then Frank picks up his pen again. "What kind of collateral can you offer?"

What do I have left? "The last shreds of my sanity?"

He doesn't think I'm funny.

FRANK DOESN'T GIVE ME A LOAN.

I go home and sit at my disproportionately large kitchen table with my laptop. Chris and I bought the table with a big family in mind. Now, out of the six chairs, five are always empty. I feel like they mock me.

"The kitchen table of broken dreams."

Scratch. Scratch. Scratch.

I picture House Mouse in the wall, playing the world's tiniest violin.

"It's not fair. My life wasn't supposed to turn out like this."

The mouse doesn't offer an opinion. Probably picking through its collection of sad sheet music.

I file for unemployment, and I'm closing the portal when a new email alert pings onto my screen. It's from one of those DNA sites. When Chris was first diagnosed, he went through a phase of wanting to know where his cancer came from, researching it almost obsessively. Was it what he ate, chemicals, his genes? I got him the DNA test as a gift, so my email is associated with the account. They keep reminding me to also connect his results to their ancestry database.

I start to look for the *unsubscribe* link, but a knock on the door interrupts, and I just close the page.

Mrs. Martinez pops her head in. "I thought I'd bring you a little spring." She offers me a handful of yellow tulips. "I bought too much at the store. I couldn't resist."

"They're beautiful. Thank you." I open the cabinet under the sink, then close it. "I've given away my vases. I didn't expect to receive flowers again."

"Oh, honey."

"It's all right." I grab a glass and fill it with water. "I didn't mean it as a complaint. I feel as if, lately, I'm always complaining. Sorry."

"You are entitled to your grief." She glances at my laptop. "Working from home today?"

All right. I'll have to tell her sooner or later. "I lost my job."

She doesn't ask how I'm going to pay the rent, which is so generous, it nearly makes me cry. Especially, when she says, "Oh, Ellie. What can I do to help?"

"I'll figure something. But thank you for reacting that way. I'm looking for a new job, and working on a wild idea." I arrange the tulips in the glass and fill her in on the whole museum business. "I've actually looked at a few available buildings online last night."

I wait for her to tell me that I've lost it.

"Are you looking in the city?"

"Everything doesn't have to be in Philadelphia. There's nothing wrong with bringing art to the suburbs." I turn on the electric kettle that's already filled. "Tea?"

"Found anything? Yes, please."

"Half a dozen restaurants and two bed and breakfasts. There's a small office building on Route 1 with its own parking lot, which would be perfect except for the price tag." I put our mugs on the table and drop in the teabags. We both drink Lady Grey. "It'd be easier for me to become a trapeze artist."

"Trying to picture you hanging upside down in a leotard." Mrs. Martinez squints. "That's an odd thought."

"I've been reading about Suzanne Valadon's childhood. She was a French artist. Compared to her life, mine is a breeze. How is someone so fearless at fifteen?"

"It's easy to be fearless at fifteen. The older you get, the more you realize life can deal out some deep shit. Pardon my French."

"At least Valadon asked for what she wanted." I pour hot water into our cups, and the aroma of tea fills the kitchen. "While I'm stuck here, spying on my old house. Not only am I not making progress, I'm going backward. Truth is, Valadon's courage shames me. She lived in a world with precious little opportunity for women, especially if they were poor. She barely had food, while here I sit next to my full refrigerator, a foot from a giant fruit bowl, within reach of a dozen different snacks. I have heat without having to touch wood, clean clothes without having to do laundry by hand. I have no right to be depressed."

"That's not how it works."

Her kindness might just make me cry, after all. I need to change the subject. "Anyway. I had a dream."

Mrs. Martinez rubs her hands together. "I'm good at dream interpreting."

"That's why I brought it up." I give her a quick summary.

"When you dream of a house, the house is a symbol." Her eyes brim with love and affection. "You are the house. All the rooms are your untapped potential. You are excited about the future, but scared. You know you have a lot of work ahead."

"So, my subconscious is telling me to renovate

myself? I need to be flipped?" *The freaking gall of that dream.*

"You just need to take care of yourself. We all do. And if a museum is what you want, go for it."

"I keep flipping back and forth between *I'm going to do this* and *I should pick something realistic.* Am I going nuts?"

"You're fine."

"I'm learning how to live from a fifteen-year-old girl in nineteenth-century Paris."

"Life likes to send unexpected teachers, to see if we're paying attention." Mrs. Martinez sips her tea. "What have you learned?"

I only need a second to think. "To go for it. Fight. I want to display art that nobody sees because it's stashed away in basements in musty drawers. I don't care if that's an impossible dream."

"I wouldn't want to live in a world that didn't have impossible dreams. Anyhow, *impossible* is just what women get told when they ask for something. Believe in your dream and do what it takes."

"You make it sound easy."

"It's not, but we'll definitely have to do it now, just to prove that impossible dreams come true."

She finishes her tea before I'm a quarter done with mine. She stands. "I'd better put away the rest of my groceries."

Then she's through the door.

I shout after her, "Thank you for the tulips and the support!"

Scratch. Scratch. Scratch.

"I have potential," I say out loud. "I have potential," I repeat.

Some people speak their affirmations to their reflection in the mirror. I tell mine to a mouse in the wall. I really might have gone off the rails.

And yet...

If Valadon could figure out her life, so can I. I'm a grown woman. I can do this.

Here's the thing about losing one's husband. We weren't just two halves stuck together. We became one. We were one completely stirred and mixed miracle of love. When Chris died, our entities didn't simply separate. Our fused sphere split. Half of me died with him, and half of him lives with me.

I have to make it a good life. I have to figure out how to keep going. I have to live not for just myself, but for Chris.

I go back to my laptop and read a little more about Valadon who never gave up. And then I call the bank and ask for Frank.

"Hi. It's me again. I have a new plan."

CHAPTER SIX

Suzanne

1880 / Age 15

I WILL NOT SOUND DESPERATE.

"An introduction to Molier would be even more splendid," I say the words with casual ease.

The men who were discussing the circus, at their table at L'Auberge du Clou, were talking about the Cirque Molier and not the Cirque Fernando, alas.

Patrons wave to gain my attention before the next cabaret performance begins. I bring Monet and Manet their onion soup. They're lamenting how people always confuse them with each other.

"Claude Monet and Édouard Manet." Monet slams his fist on the table. "It's not difficult to remember."

I deliver Munkácsy, the wild Hungarian, his pork cutlet. He cuts a striking figure with his bushy beard. He's having one of his melancholic days. Many of the foreign artists who are in Paris to learn turn up at the cabaret when they're sad. They need distraction. They miss their homeland.

I serve two more tables, then I make my way back to Molier's friends. "Might you be able to arrange an introduction, gentlemen?"

"Impossible."

"Ernest Molier is hounded by applicants."

In the back, Jacques, the Auberge du Clou's manager, looms at the counter with his meaty arms folded over his chest. He mouths a word, *Move*, while his mean rat eyes are glinting threats.

"I can learn anything." My tone is blithe, my stance full of confidence.

"The circus is not hiring." The taller of the two men, the one who has the look of an aristocrat, strikes a match to light his cigarette. "You'll have more stable employment here."

He is wrong about that.

Jacques stalks toward us, a vein bulging on his forehead. In about a minute, I'll have no employment. And since I have nothing to lose, I decide to dare.

I step back, then swing into motion, landing in a one-handed handstand—a move I've been practicing with the intent of performing it on horseback. My other hand is still holding the tray. Then I bend my left knee, cross the foot so I can transfer the tray to my toes before lifting it to the air. I can see nothing, because my skirts fall onto my face, but I don't hear the empty bottle crashing. I can't read the reaction of the men, but I can hear the clapping of the customers.

I choose to think they're clapping for my skill, and not because I've just revealed my pantalettes.

"Marie-Clémentine Valadon!" The weight of the tray is snatched from my foot.

I wheel upright and straighten my skirt, refusing to look at Jacques. I look only at the two startled men at the table, Molier's friends. "Messieurs—"

"Out." Jacques smacks me with the tray, and then the bottle does fall and shatter. "You're finished." He shoves me toward the door. "And don't ask me for today's pay."

He shoves me all the way out to the street, where I gape at the door slammed in my face. "Wait!"

I've worked all of the afternoon and most of the evening. Jacques owes me those wages.

Life is not fair. The strong take from the weak, Maman says. Well, there's no law against the weak fighting back.

I march back inside. "I will not leave without my money."

"You—" Jacques lunges at me.

Edgar Degas, sitting at the nearest table, leaps between us just in time.

"How old are you, girl?" Everything about the painter is severe: his voice, his stance, his eyes. Enough so to give even Jacques pause. The artists and their friends keep the gaslights on at L'Auberge du Clou, and the manager knows that.

He falls into a calculated silence.

"Ten years old, Monsieur," I respond to Degas, slicing five years right off my age. This is where being small pays. Degas looks old enough to be my grandfather. To soften his heart, I assume my most pitiful expression. "I need the money to support my family."

"A franc for each year." He counts ten francs into my hand, to the astonishment of his friends.

"Thank you, Monsieur." I shove the money to the bottom of my pocket before he can change his mind. *Why didn't I say I was twenty?*

Then I'm gone, flying down the street, past men in elegant overcoats escorting women in embroidered skirts and feathered hats. They're visiting only the most reputable establishments, taking care not to brush against me, as if they're afraid I'll pick their pockets.

Sometimes, when I can't sleep at night, I think about them. It seems like a dream that they go in carriages everywhere instead of walking in the cold rain, that they own more than one coat. What do their unused clothes do? Wait their turn on the back of a chair? And when these people are hungry, they just eat. They never open the cupboard and find it empty. And they don't launder their own sheets either, or do their own mending.

And they're still not happy.

The bankers, in particular, are as serious as dysentery.

Still, I don't want to understand the rich half as much as I want to be them.

And for an hour, I can.

I do not take the money home for Maman. I spend it on paper and red chalk, and pastels, on the rue Clauzel. I can't pass up the chance. This might be as rich as I'll ever get.

"On an errand, Mademoiselle? For which artist?" the store owner, Julien Tanguy asks. I hear artists talk about him all the time. They call him *Père Tanguy*, Father Tanguy. He helps them when he can. His shop is full of paintings. If an artist is truly poor, Monsieur Tanguy will sometimes accept artwork as payment.

"I'm older than I look," I assure him, confidence radiating through me, coming straight from the money in my pocket. "I'm eighteen, and a famous artist myself. I have a studio here in Montmartre."

"Certainly, Mademoiselle." The man's tone is skeptical, but I'm a paying customer, so he doesn't call me a liar.

I prance out the door so preoccupied with my packages that I nearly run into a couple of men outside. *Oh.* Ernest Molier's friends. My luck tonight truly has no end.

"Molier would love me if he saw me." *Too abrupt?* Best start with introductions. "I am Marie-Clémentine Valadon."

"Count Antoine de La Rochefoucauld." The tall one tips his hat.

Then his friend. "Théo Wagner. *Enchanté.*"

When they would move on, I block their way. I smile and smile and smile. "Molier would *want* to see me."

"That was quite a spectacle at the café." Wagner measures me up. "Do you also work at the stables? I think I've seen you walk horses and stand in the saddle."

Ha! People *have* noticed me. And they remember. The thought, and the box of art supplies under my arm, make me feel invincible. "I can do other tricks. I was born to be an acrobat."

"You do know that most of Molier's performers come from the circle of his friends?" Wagner inquires. "They're society people. Some are aristocrats. You think you can fit in with them?"

"I can."

I watched them enough. I want the circus, the sparkling costumes, the lights, the adoring audience. I will climb as high as I want and nobody will order me down. I will fly. I will be the darling of Paris. The crowd will throw so many francs at my feet, I'm going to need a wheelbarrow to carry all the money away.

The gentlemen before me are my only hope for an introduction, and I will not miss this chance.

"Please. Would you help me see Molier?"

MOLIER'S FASHIONABLE CIRCUS IS A GLORIFIED SHED BEHIND HIS MANSION IN THE SIXTEENTH ARRONDISSE-

MENT, ON THE RUE DE BÉNOUVILLE. It's as filled with color as my new box of pastels. Everything I've done before fades, becomes a dark dream of drudgery. I want to stay here forever.

"I need a strongman." Molier puffs on his pipe, unmindful of the ashes in his russet beard. He stands ringside, next to a bale of hay. His attention is on the horse act in the ring that's no wider than forty feet. "I don't need another girl."

"I could be a strongwoman. I'm sturdy. I've been carrying heavy trays at the café."

"You're the size of the rabbit our magician pulls out of his hat."

"Monsieur Molier—"

"Ernest, but I can't help you. My dear, I must supervise tonight's rehearsal."

Horses gallop past us.

"Not fast enough," he shouts to the boy who holds the whip in the middle. "The formation is off."

If he's unhappy with what he currently has, that means an opportunity for me. I set my boxes on the ground, and in half a dozen steps, I'm next to the horses.

I run along, then leap, then I'm in the saddle. And then, in another second, I stand. "Oh."

The ground rushes under me at an alarmingly faster rate than when I'm putting on my little act on the street. My head swims. *Look where you're going!*

The horse next to mine is a sweet mare. She doesn't shy from me. When you love horses, they can sense it, and they love you back. *This is it.* I have to show my bravest attempt.

I bend and grab her reins, then, as I straighten, I plant one foot onto her saddle.

I've only tried this once before, and I failed. I sprained my ankle.

Don't think about that.

Don't look at the ground.

Don't break your neck.

Nerves attack and paralyze me, but only for a moment. Then a deep thrill fills me. I'm riding two horses, my legs as wide as my skirt allows. My braid breaks loose. My hair whips behind me like a flag. *This is it.*

I'm flying at last.

"Stop." Molier walks up, but not so alarmed that he'd lose his pipe, and not running or shouting either. He knows better than to spook the horses. "Halt at once. You cannot do horse tricks in a skirt, you reckless child. You'll be trampled to death, and then you'll never be an equestrienne."

An equestrienne. Yes, yes, yes.

I tighten the reins. The mares slow, and in a blink, I'm back on the first one, then back to sitting in the saddle. Since it's not a sidesaddle, my dress rests high up on my thighs. I don't care. The vision of my future leaves me breathless.

"Wildcat." Molier grabs the reins when I'm in line with him again, and leads my mare to the side, while the rest of the horses gallop past us. "I suppose the gentlemen might find you entertaining." His gaze glides over my bare knees and pantalettes. "What else can you do? It's a small circus. Everyone plays more than one role. Are you scared of heights?"

Ha. "The higher, the better. I can climb."

"Might be one for the tightrope." He puffs on his pipe. "Can you start training tomorrow?"

"I can start right now."

"That eager?"

"When I tell Maman I was fired from L'Auberge du Clou and joined the circus, she will beat me. I want to do my first training without bruises."

"Practical. Can think ahead. You might yet make a decent performer."

Can he hear how rapidly my heart beats? I've heard battle drums that were quieter. I cannot appear like an overexcited child. I measure my breath. "You won't regret hiring me, Monsieur."

"That's what they all say." He turns to the boy with the horses. "Léon! Tell Augustine to give the girl Louise's old costume."

A costume in the back, for me.

I'm finally going to be the girl I've drawn a hundred times with charcoal on the wall. I nearly knock Léon off his feet, I run past so fast. *The sequins… The glitter…*

In but minutes, Augustine—a matronly clown with thick lips and red hair—fits the costume to my body with a few stitches here and there. The top is little more than a bustier, the bottom a pair of glittering pantalettes, shorter than I've worn *under* my skirt before.

"I feel naked."

"But light, yes?" Augustine tilts her head, and her face catches the light of the candles. She has a slight mustache. "Jump and bend. Easier to move?"

"Of course it's easier. I'm wearing nothing."

"You'll get used to it." She cackles. "Now get back to the ring. You'd best not make Monsieur wait."

I train with Léon under Molier's watchful eyes, that day and every day.

In a week, I'm in front of the audience on the horses. The small circus only seats a hundred, but to me it feels as if all Paris is there, the people holding their breaths for me.

My legs tremble when I stand up in the saddle.

My right foot slips.

I catch myself.

"Bravo!" a man shouts.

I let go of the reins with one hand and offer a graceful wave. I smile as if I wish to seduce every person in the audience—as Molier taught me.

"Bravo! Bravo!"

My legs stop shaking. I plant my foot in the second mare's saddle.

My next smile is true.

In a month, I'm on the tightrope. I'm above the crowd, above them all. Nothing reaches me but the applause of my audience. On the tightrope, no one knows that I'm a bastard. On the tightrope, I'm not a poor girl of fifteen. On the tightrope, I'm a queen.

I have to take a bow three times, people clap so long. When I finally run out of the ring with one last wave, I run straight to Molier's room in the back. "When can I perform on the trapeze?"

He pauses spreading ointment on his foot. The greasy substance smells like raw liver. "Not yet."

"I have practiced."

"Practice more."

"Is it so Mademoiselle Joséphine won't be jealous of me?" If I'm the queen of the high wire, she's the empress of the trapeze. I love and admire her, but my sentiments are unreturned. She says I'm always in her way.

Molier raises his eyes to the heavens. "Can you hang from a rope by your teeth and perform acts of strength?"

I kick at the hay on the floor. There shouldn't be hay back here, but it's a circus. There's hay everywhere. "No."

"Then Mademoiselle Joséphine is unlikely to be jealous of you."

"I'm almost as good as she is."

"Practice until you're better." The ring master turns from me to wrap his bad ankle.

I stamp out. I adore Molier, but he *can* be unfair.

"Mademoiselle Valadon! Marie-Clémentine." A man stumbles from behind a painted screen, around thirty, a young friend of Claude Monet. He owns and rents barges on the Seine. "You were spectacular tonight." He offers me a rose. "May I take you to dinner?"

I am tired, but I will not turn down food. "A

moment to change." I stop and hold his gaze to make sure I have his attention. "Dinner only."

Gentlemen bring me sweets and other gifts. They invite me back to their apartments. I laugh at them. I have it all—a shining future at the circus. I'm not going to lose my dream life and settle for nothing like my mother did.

I don't know yet that sometimes it's not a choice at all. Fate rolls the dice. And then your dream will be taken in a blink.

ARTISTS LOVE THE CIRCUS. I don't know if it's the colors or the movement. As I balance on the tightrope, half a dozen painters dab at their easels below.

Mademoiselle Joséphine swings by above me on the trapeze. "Monsieur Degas painted Mademoiselle La La at the Cirque Fernando last year."

As if I care. Berthe Morisot is painting *me*, right now. I hold my pose, fighting the grin that wants to conquer my face. I'm being painted by a *woman*. And she's not even the only woman I've seen painting. I know another one too, Mary Cassatt, an American.

Mademoiselle Joséphine swings back, upside down. "Monsieur Renoir painted the jugglers."

He is standing ringside. Next to him, I recognize Toulouse-Lautrec. Le Petit Gentleman, some of the performers call him, on account of his stature. He's short enough to be Renoir's son. In years too, Renoir could be his father. Toulouse-Lautrec is my age. I delivered his laundry last week—I still help Maman —but I doubt he recognizes me when I'm dressed like this.

Mademoiselle Morisot looks up. She's one of the Impressionists. Her works were selected six consecutive times by the Académie des Beaux-Arts in Paris to be shown at their annual exhibit, the Salon. And then she exhibited with the Impressionists since, every single year but one. She is important. I stop for a few seconds and hold my pose for her. Holding is more difficult than walking. Movement gives momentum, and momentum carries me forward and through. To stop is to wobble.

I hold my breath.

I will be in a painting.

I will be in a gallery, perhaps even exhibited at the Salon. Maybe someday, I'll be in a museum. A hundred years from now, people will still see me. I will not be forgotten with all the other poor girls in the tenement. I will live forever.

"Marie-Clémentine!" Molier snaps his whip below me.

I lift one foot off the tightrope sideways, swing it up, and use the momentum to turn. Then I execute a small jump. Then slowly, slowly, I slide my feet in opposite directions until I'm sitting on a rope in a full split. *Snap at that.*

"Better," says the master of the ring. "You've improved your balance."

"I am ready for the trapeze."

"No."

"Yes."

"I've trained mules less stubborn."

He exaggerates. He doesn't even have mules. He has only horses and a couple of ornery camels. They spit and they bite. I would not ride them for all the fame in the world.

I push to standing and do a backflip, land on both feet, perfectly aligned, arms to the side. I don't bother to hide the triumph in my eyes.

"All right." Molier groans. "You can start practicing on the trapeze."

"Right now?"

"Tomorrow."

Tomorrow, I fly.

I'm going to be the Queen of the Trapeze, the Darling of Paris.

Nothing can stop me.

"For the first time on the trapeze in a solo act, please welcome the incomparable Marie-Clémentine." Molier tosses back his red-lined cape and offers his hand to escort me to the pole.

I check for Maman in the audience, but she's not there. I've confessed my latest occupation at last, and when I handed her my wages, I was forgiven.

The musicians pick up the pace, led by the drum, then the soaring of the trumpet. As I climb, the clowns—Augustine and her husband—back to the edge of the ring and raise their hands to direct all attention to me, proud as if they were my parents.

The magician's upturned face shines nothing but encouragement. The performers all stand below and clap for me, including every last acrobat. And in the front row of the audience, the artists who paint the circus are there, come to support me as friends. For the first time ever, I'm part of something bigger. I have a family here.

Six months already. Six months of happiness. Six months of heaven.

At the top of the pole, I grab the bar and pause. The audience is a swirl of color below. From nowhere does the circus look more like a painting than from here. I hold the scene in my mind and memorize it. I want to draw this moment, even if charcoal could never do it justice. Maybe, someday, I will paint all this. But tonight, another kind of triumph awaits.

The familiar smell of horses and cigars and perfume embraces me. The circus smells like home, more than my mother's wine haze ever has. This is it. I know how to do this. I'm ready to soar. Everybody quiets.

I will shove off as a girl from the tenements, but I'll end this act a star, the darling of the audience, celebrated—and even more important than that, *accepted*. I will have made a career not on my back— as expected of girls like me—but on my talent.

I push away and glide through the air, swing around and catch the opposing bar with my feet. Then I'm upside down, my braid falling free. On the next swing, I right myself again.

Then back to the top of the pole. I stick the landing. My muscles wouldn't dare tremble.

This time, after I push away and let go, I pirouette in the air. I catch the opposing bar, but only with one hand. I don't need another.

It's part of my act, to show off how skilled I am, but in the audience, a woman thinks I missed, and she screams.

Nobody screamed at any of my rehearsals.

I'm only startled for a second, for a fraction of a blink of an eye. Unfortunately, you can't be late a fraction of a blink of an eye on the trapeze. The next bar flies at me, but meets only my fingertips.

And that's it.

I have time only for a single thought as I plummet.

It's over.

I land hard, on my back. New screams fill the air.

Molier is there, but the pain leaves me so breathless, I can't tell him anything. Not *thank you*, not *don't worry*, not *I'm dying*.

He scoops me up and rushes me from the ring. "The doctor! Bring the doctor! Quick!"

In this most unlikely of moments, Sister Marguerite's face floats in front of my eyes as her lesson of the frog comes back to me.

I'm the little frog who wanted to be big. I puffed and puffed myself up until my body broke. What would the sister say to me if she could see me? She would definitely *not* like my sequins. *"The queen of the trapeze."* She'd click her tongue. She never liked queens.

I don't cry. I don't hope either. My spine is on fire. I know what it means.

It's over.

I am fifteen.

I am finished.

CHAPTER SEVEN

Ellie

Wednesday, March 8th

"Wait. Is this an intervention?" I'm half out of my seat, the pale-yellow walls of my parents' kitchen closing in on me. I feel as if I'm falling, an unbalanced acrobat plummeting from the trapeze.

"We're trying to help you." Abby casts an uncertain look at Frank.

His fatherly expression grates on my last nerve. He's not the head of our family, no matter how hard he pretends that he is. I don't understand why he always makes the big decisions. Like where we go on our family vacation. I want the Poconos, but it always has to be the beach, Atlantic City. I don't get a vote. He decides, with unquestioning support from

Abby, and they take me as if I'm a kid. They're not even married, for heaven's sake.

"We're your family," he tells me.

"Not you. Not by blood and not by marriage." The words have crouched in my throat for decades, and I finally release them.

"Ellie!" Abby shoots him a look that apologizes on my behalf.

Frank puts his hand on her arm. "All we're saying, Ellie, is that you've been using your grief as an excuse and a crutch for too long."

His judgment is so unfair. I had my guard down when Abby asked me over. This is the house of my childhood. It should be my safe place.

"Why aren't you at work?" I turn the tables on Frank.

"Because your well-being is more important."

"You took a day off from work to tell me that I'm not grieving the way you'd like me to grieve?"

"I took off a couple of hours to help you with your out-of-control emotions."

I could show him out of control. I don't. "What are you talking about?"

"You won't move back here. You're staying in that apartment, paying all that rent to a stranger."

"I'm an adult. I'm responsible for my own housing."

"We would give you a much better rate."

"No, thank you."

He flattens his palm on the table. "We need to talk about your little outburst at your work."

"You haven't seen me burst out yet." But we're not far.

"You threw away a perfectly good job because you couldn't control your temper."

"That's one way to look at it. Or we could just say that I finally stood up for myself."

"You landed yourself in unemployment."

"I'll get another job. How is this any of your business? Have I asked you for money?" I wince at that last bit. "Other than for the museum, which would be a business loan from the bank."

He'd denied that again for the second time. He wasn't impressed with my plan of beginning with the museum being virtual.

"About that." Abby's eyes brim with pity. "Frank says you're serious about this unseen art thing…"

"But?"

"It's just a phase, isn't it? A coping mechanism. I don't think it's healthy. You need to find a way to cope in a normal way." She turns over the printout in front of her and slides it across the table. "I found a specialist, near where you live."

William Domotor, MD, PhD
Psychiatrist, Marriage Counseling, Grief Specialist
Address, phone number

"Doesn't he just have everything covered?" I don't touch the paper. "And aren't you two smart to know exactly what I need?"

"I wish you would let us help you," my sister pleads.

I push my chair back and stand. "You could help me by not ambushing me."

"WE MISSED YOU AT BOOK CLUB." Mrs. Martinez tells me when I get home. She's taking Karma for a walk.

"I actually picked up the book last night when I couldn't sleep." It's about Vincent van Gogh's sister-in-law, Johanna Bonger, who was widowed at age twenty-eight, like me.

"How do you like the story?"

I scratch Karma's ears. "It makes me want to know more. I keep looking things up. I've been researching a lot of art history lately. Did you know that Vincent completed close to two hundred paintings in Arles and a hundred drawings? And he was only there for a little over a year."

"I looked that up too," my landlady smiles. "When you have passion for your work, you can accomplish anything."

"The book is giving me a lot of food for thought. Especially the part that talks about using the tools we have. I don't have money, and I don't have a degree in museum studies either. I have motivation and will. I have branding experience. I know how to make a website. I'm going to make my museum virtual to start with. It'll work for now."

"Might even be better on the internet." Mrs. Martinez tilts her head. "Everyone is always looking at a screen. It'd be an easy way to reach a large audience. Some of my out-of-print books are now picking up sales in e-book format."

"I wish banks had half as much vision as you have. I can't get a loan."

"You don't need banks." Mrs. Martinez gives in to Karma and lets the beagle pull her down the driveway. "You do it on Kickstarter."

I stop with my foot on the bottom steps. "That's brilliant."

She winks at me. "When determined women put their heads together," she calls back, "nothing and nobody in the universe can stand against them."

"I didn't realize we had an appointment," is Wanda Abara's classy way of saying I should have called ahead.

I drove to the Philly Art Museum on the spur of the moment, inspired by Mrs. Martinez. "Better to ask for something in person than over the phone. When people are looking you in the eyes, they have a more difficult time saying no."

"Truth." Wanda rotates a beaded grass basket a quarter turn, in the middle of setting up an exhibit of Yoruba art.

As usual, she's a work of art herself, from her sculptural earrings to her lavender silk slacks.

Her carefully curated appearance makes me want to call Niki, my hairdresser. I haven't had a haircut since… I reached a point a while back where I couldn't tell one more person about Chris's death.

Niki doesn't know that he passed. And I don't want to tell her. I don't want to break down crying at the hair salon. I don't want anyone to fuss around me. I don't have the energy to reassure any more people that I'm fine, I'm moving forward, everything's great.

"What do you think of these?" Wanda aims the spotlight.

"I don't know if I've ever thought of baskets as art." They are a feast for the senses, the bright colors uplifting, the shapes sculptural. They can hold their own against any other piece on display in the museum. The one Wanda adjusts again has the graceful curves of a woman. The taller basket next to it reminds me of a waterfall.

"They haven't been presented by the art world as art. Do you know why?"

"I've never thought about it, but I can guess. Because mostly women make baskets?"

"And embroidery. And quilts. It's a fairly recent development that museums display quilts, acknowledging them as art. If an art museum even has quilts, chances are most of them are in storage, down in the basement. It was a neat trick through the centuries to forbid women to study art, then say that women were incapable of creating art, and judge any art women created *not art*."

"Did Suzanne Valadon study art? Or was she self-taught?"

"Self-taught."

"I have no personal connection to her that I know of." Although, I haven't given up on my Waldon-

Valadon fantasy. I just haven't had the chance to look into it. "Is it weird that I feel proud of her? Way to go, Suzanne."

"She was one indomitable woman."

We move on to a larger display, and I admire the lidded baskets Wanda displays next. The shapes are irregular, the turquoise beading exquisite, the edges decorated with shells. It's abstract art before abstract art was a concept. "I've never seen Yoruba art before."

"Few people around here have. That's what this exhibit is all about." She caresses the line of shells as if they were old friends. "Cowrie shells. They were used as money for centuries."

I didn't know that either.

We stroll past the next section that holds a treasure trove of Yoruba jewelry. Wanda blesses them with an approving nod, then moves on to an extensive display of wood carvings.

While she adjusts a few tags, I stand back. "Why am I suddenly thinking Picasso?"

"*Les Demoiselles d'Avignon,* Picasso's famous painting. Art historians consider it the beginning of cubism and modern art."

"I know the piece." I squint. "I'm trying to remember the details."

"Two of the women in the piece have faces that resemble African masks. Picasso collected African art. The wide range of styles inspired him. I like to think African artists were the first cubists." Wanda picks up a large mask and holds it up for me. "See the fragmented geometrics?" She returns it to the shelf and points to another. "See how the artist expressed his purpose with overlapping planes?"

"I kind of do." *I think.*

"Fun fact. When the Mona Lisa was stolen in 1911, Picasso was accused and interrogated. He didn't steal the painting, but he did have two Iberian statues in his apartment that were stolen from the Louvre." She notes my dropped chin. "I refuse to apologize for being an art nerd."

"You can hit me with all the art trivia you want. I was just thinking I could listen to you forever."

"Flattery will get you everywhere." She stops working. "How can I help you, Ellie?"

I explain my Museum of Unseen Art and wait.

"All right." She nods thoughtfully. "I like it."

"I sense a *but*."

"No major museum is going to lend you artwork unless you're another major museum. Not to someone unproven in the field. Have you thought about the liability insurance you'd have to carry?"

"I have not." *I should have.* "I'm a total amateur. Go ahead, laugh at me."

"No laughing." She returns to the jewelry case and switches two necklaces. "I happen to like women with big ideas, and honesty always gets points."

"As a first step, I want to create a virtual museum experience. I would just need permission to use digital images on MUA's web site... Ooh, having an acronym makes me feel like it's real."

"It's practically the MOMA."

I can't tell if she's mocking me or not. "You think I could get permission to use digital images of what you have in storage?"

"I'm sorry to say this, but unlikely." She locks the case and looks as if she wants to reach out and pat me on the shoulder. "Again, you're not a proven entity. Prestigious museums don't get involved in small projects. Should your venture turn out to be controversial or fraudulent, we wouldn't want our spotless reputation tarnished by association. Also, the works we have that are not on display can already be found on our website."

"Only if someone types the artist in the search box." I checked. "What about the artists we don't even know because they're never on display? They don't deserve to be forgotten forever."

"You're persuasive."

"My sister calls me pigheaded."

"Sisters can be a menace. I have three."

"My condolences."

She thinks for a second, and then she says, as if she can't believe she's saying this, "All right. Let's do the thing where women on a mission help other women on a mission. I'll bring your project up at our next department meeting."

JOSHUA IS STANDING ON MY FRONT LAWN.

He usually works alone, unless he hires out a bigger job, like the driveway replacement. This time, however, the people flanking him aren't a random work crew.

I don't gawk. I only slow down as I drive past them because I have to make the swing into Mrs. Martinez's driveway.

Both the older man and the younger one resemble Joshua. Father and brother? The brother has a little girl, about six years old, hanging on to his leg, wearing a little pink hard hat.

The tableau—the man with the little girl, having fun in the yard—slices straight through my heart.

Could have been is a knife.

Chris and I ran out of time for a child. We married at twenty-two, dirt poor, studio apartment, no room. Two years later, we bought the house, in as-is condition. Then two years of little-by-little renovations. We had one good year, tried, but didn't succeed. Then he was diagnosed, and radiation took further trying off the table. I wasn't going to get a little boy with Chris's eyes and my smile, or a little girl. Radiation death rays kill sperm.

I park the car without looking over, get out without glancing back, but as I hurry up the stairs, I'm literally facing them. I'm not coordinated enough to climb the steps with my eyes closed, that's for sure.

They're laughing. I don't care. Except that the men are pointing at the house's windows.

What's wrong with my windows?

"Old is not always inferior to new," I inform

House Mouse inside. "Not everything should be thrown out and forgotten. Old things have value."

I wash my hands in the sink and test myself on lip-reading. If they're going to further demolish my house, I need advance warning. I can't handle walking out one morning to the sight of the window boxes Chris made me for my birthday missing.

The men are bantering, guys having a good time, the brothers elbowing each other every once in a while—mostly with their backs to me, unfortunately. The Jennings men are meddling pests. They have no respect for anyone's hard work. All they know is, the newer the better.

"We'll leave them to their fantasies of destruction," I tell the mouse in the wall. For once, he's not scratching. I suppose even mice sleep. "I have actual, real work to do that matters."

But first, I sign in to the DNA website and opt into their ancestry database. It's as good a place to start researching the whole Waldon-Valadon connection as any.

What are the chances?

I'm immediately shown the few of Chris's relatives who are also members. I scan the Waldon family tree. Not a single Frenchman. They're English/Irish all the way. Waldon is a version of Walden, meaning a wooded valley.

Not a version of Valadon after all, no relation. I deal with the pang of disappointment. I wanted that connection more than I admitted it to myself. All the while, as I was reading about Valadon, I was fantasizing about her turning out to be a great-great aunt. I wanted there to be a connection between us.

Okay.

I move on.

I email the top twenty museums in the country, explaining my own museum plans.

Bam, bam, bam. Whrrrl, whrrrl, whrrrl.

I pop up, but only because I need a glass of water.

The men across the street are putting up those cringy fake shutters that are the blight of suburbia.

"Either something is real or don't bother."

Bam, bam, bam. Whrrrl, whrrrl, whrrrl.

I can't hear myself think. I'm never going to accomplish anything like this. I need a quiet place.

The Delaware Art Museum is within driving distance.

In five minutes, I'm in my car again. And I'm paying attention. I'm not in a huff. It's not my fault that I almost back over Joshua's brother, who walks backward out into the street at the same time, without looking at all.

I slam on the brakes, then roll my window down. "Good way to get killed."

Accidentally running over someone is one thing. But run over the brother of your mortal enemy, and the word *motive* will pop up in the courtroom, an aggravation I don't need.

"Sorry. I was checking the shutters." He gives Joshua, now on the top of a ladder, a thumbs-up.

The older man and the little girl are no longer in the yard.

"You must be Ellie," says the Joshua look-alike.

Joshua told his family about me? What would he even say? I don't want to imagine. "I'm late for an appointment."

"Jace Jennings. Nice to meet you."

He's the better-looking of the brothers. Leaner—my guess is he plays some sport—while Joshua is sturdier, borderline burly. If Joshua weren't a flipper, he could be a lumberjack. He'd fit right in, with his collection of checkered flannel shirts. Jace is clean-shaven. Joshua sometimes forgets. All the details of stealing other people's houses must clutter up his head.

I ease my foot off the brake and let the tires roll back. "You have a lovely daughter. She might need you inside. You should check on her and your wife."

I snap my mouth shut. I don't mean the words that way, but they sound like a threat from the mob. *Nice family you have there. It'd be a shame if something happened to them.*

Jace walks along with the car, the unintentional threat flying right over his head. "My wife left us," he says.

Oh, wow, I'm an idiot. "I'm so sorry."

"My daughter, Olivia, and I are all right. I'm not hung up on my ex or anything. I keep feeling like I have to explain, because when people see me with a child, they assume I have a wife. " He stops. "I'm rambling. What I meant was, I saw you watching my brother from your window. He says you're not together. I figure you like him, but you're put off by one or more of his many faults… We look alike. You could like me, and I have a much better personality."

I refuse to laugh. He's not that funny.

"I'm available is what I mean," he says. "Unless you dislike kids."

"I don't dislike kids." How did I end up being on the defensive?

"Can I have your number?"

His mischievous smile is nearly irresistible. *Nearly* being the keyword. "I'll think about it."

I will not.

I roll up the window and drive away.

The Jennings brothers should come with a warning.

CHAPTER EIGHT

Suzanne

1880 / Age 15

"I will poke my eyes out with a needle before I become a seamstress." I hiss the words at Maman. I have tasted freedom. I will never return to being a servant. Alas, I'll never return to the circus either. I can walk, but my injuries left me unable to perform. My spine could not take the pull of hanging from the trapeze or the impact of falling from a horse.

"You must earn." Maman slams her bottle on the table, and our tin cups rattle. "We need to live."

"We wouldn't need half as many francs if you didn't drink."

"Ungrateful child. If only, God would make you more obedient." She hurls one of the cups at me, and it bounces off the wall with a clang. "You think you too good for work? You embarrassed to be a seamstress? Nobody has to be embarrassed for doin' honest work. Let them lazy ones be ashamed of themselves. I left a good life for you. If only I could have stayed at that great house at Bessines. 'Twas the only easy life and happiness I ever had."

"Oh, yes. The great house." I throw up my hands. "Let us hear about it again."

"Could 'ave thrown you into the river, I could 'ave. Many women threw away their bastard children then. Could 'ave left you on the doorsteps of a convent."

She speaks the truth. I know more than one girl my age who've done that. Just a few months past, a woman in our tenement was with child, and then she wasn't. She tossed her newborn babe into the Seine. At least, that's what people whisper behind her back.

Yet, with all my dreams crushed, just now I cannot appreciate Maman. "You threw me away plenty. You sent me away every chance you had." I lived with my grandparents for years as a small child. I lived with Marie-Alix, my half-sister, right after she married Georges. I lived with others too; some faces I can no longer remember. Sooner or later, everyone sent me back.

I'm wanted nowhere.

I pick up the cup, set it on the shelf, and then I slam the door on my way out. I want the open street, and the sky above me. I want to be far away from the prison walls of our room.

I will *not* spend the rest of my life stitching other people's stockings or making petticoats for spoiled rich madams. I will not drown my dreams as if they were unwanted children. I will not turn into one of those women I grew up around in the tenement. I will not turn into Maman.

"Marie-Clémentine!"

Clelia, my old school friend, runs across the street, dodging horses and carriages to reach me. Her dark hair is no longer in tattered ribbons, but pinned up with bone combs, a few fashionable tendrils escaping at her nape. She wears the formfitting costume of young Italian women, the kind of colorful clothes artists like to paint, red and green. She carries herself with confidence and poise. I barely recognize her.

"You are beautiful."

"I'm a model now." She dips her head, the picture of grace.

"Oh."

Hurt glints in her eyes at my uncertain tone. "Of all the people, I expect judgment the least from you, Marie-Clémentine." Her upper lip stiffens. "You used to be my friend."

"I don't judge you. I truly don't." Even if models are considered barely a step above prostitutes. If I ever modeled and Maman found out... "Where are you going?"

"To the place Pigalle."

The square is just off boulevard de Rochechouart, not far from where we are. Not that I'd ever, but...

Like Maman said, we need to eat. "Does modeling pay?"

A smug smile curves up the corners of Clelia's lips. "I'm popular enough to ask for ten francs."

"A week?"

"A day."

The cobblestones spin with me.

I've never earned more than three francs for a day's work in my life. And back when Maman still did laundry, she was lucky to bring home a single coin in the evenings.

I have no paper left to draw on. My pencils are nubs. The income I make by sewing is just enough to keep us in bread and milk. I look down at my shoes that won't last another month.

Clelia reads my face and she takes my hand. "Come on."

"Maman might throw me out." But I follow the siren call of coin. "She *will* throw the bedpan at me."

"All their lives our mothers tried to prove they were good women. What did they gain?"

What, indeed.

A man left Maman with a bastard child, and everyone called her a whore—some behind her back, some to her face—ever since. They drove her to the bottle. They drove her to misery.

"I will not be like Maman." I shake off the clammy thought. "I will do what I want and not care what anyone thinks of me."

I walk beside my friend, and she tells me about

the sittings she's done so far. That's all we talk about, all the way to the place Pigalle.

The "square" is a half circle of open space at the junction of a jumble of streets. Twenty or so girls loiter around the fountain in the middle, lined up on the stone steps, most of them up from Italy like Clelia, in traditional dress. *How smart of them.* They're ready to be painted. I'm clearly at a disadvantage. Regardless, I slip among them and tug my own threadbare blue skirt straight, while double-decker taxicabs, drawn by horses, rattle past.

Artists circle us like wolves herding prey. They splatter us with commands. We obey.

"Turn."

"Lift your head."

"Take the pose of a dancer."

"L'ensemble?"

"The full?" I whisper to Clelia next to me. "What does that mean?"

"Fully unclothed, willing to model in the nude," she whispers back. Then she nods toward a newcomer, a dandy of an older man. "That's Pierre Puvis de Chavannes."

Puvis is one of the most respected artists in Paris, close to sixty, a large man still. He has the heft of a miller, but the bearing of a count. A beard covers half his long face, while his forehead reaches far back.

I'm distracted by him to the point of staring, until Clelia elbows me and hisses between her teeth. "Pose."

She stands with a hand over her heart and her

head tilted, thin lips slightly parted like a daydreaming shepherdess.

Put on the spot, I tilt forward and lift a leg behind me, balancing as if I were on the back of a horse. Acrobat poses are all I know. *What a fool I must look.* I don't belong here. I should go home.

"What is your name?"

Is he talking to me?

Clelia elbows me again.

"Maria," I blurt on impulse. I want Puvis to think I'm one of the Italian girls. Also, the later the tale of this indiscretion reaches Maman, the better.

"Age?"

Would being younger or older gain me an offer? I glance at my friend for help, but she's already busy moving from pose to practiced pose for someone else. I settle on the truth. "Fifteen."

"Your last name? Your father's name."

Would he take a bastard? "My father is François Villon."

Puvis lowers his chin to his chest as if he's peering over the rim of invisible glasses. "The poet?"

I don't so much as blink. "Oui. I am his beloved daughter."

The corner of his mouth twitches. "Very well, Maria. Follow me."

This is it? As fast as that?

I try to catch Clelia's eye, again, but she's making arrangements with her gentleman.

Puvis's apartment is a short walk from Pigalle.

Too soon, his door closes behind us, and I'm alone with the old man.

Everything happened too fast. Do I want to do this? Can I be a model?

His shelves and easels are lined up with meticulous care. His tables are laden with canvases and paint tubes and brushes, but I'm too nervous to appreciate them. No other exit but the one he's blocking. Madame Mabbit's hairpin is at home, on the little shelf above the sink.

"Take off your clothes."

This might not be the best idea I've ever had.

Ten francs.

I touch the top button of my blouse. My fingers freeze. It's not too late to run.

Ten francs. Ten francs. Ten francs.

"No need for alarm." Puvis taps the floor with his walking stick. "I must see what you look like. The structure of the bones affects the way clothes drape on a person. You understand."

His tone is mild. He does not seem to be on the verge of attack. And besides, I've seen prostitutes half-naked. I've seen plenty of people naked all the way too, when the Loyalists and the Communards were fighting in the streets, leaving corpses in their wake. A lot of those corpses were stripped of all their belongings in the night. Sometimes they stayed out there for days before they were collected and buried in mass graves.

I undo one button, then another. *Ten francs a day.* Food for our table and fuel for our fire, money to pay the rent. I shed my clothes and stand l'ensemble in front of the gentleman.

I'm steady on the outside, but inside, I tremble. Tears I refuse to shed burn my eyes. I know what some artists do with their models. *If he touches me…*

I prepare myself to fight. *I'll claw him like a stray cat.*

"I don't usually work here." Pierre Puvis de Chavannes walks around me in a slow circle. "I work in my studio in Neuilly. You will be there by eight o'clock every morning. I need to finish my current work by May, for the Salon. I expect two sittings per day. The first sitting will go until noon. You may have a lunch break. I shall provide the meal. The second sitting is from one to five. You will hold a pose for fifty minutes of every hour. You will not move. You will not scratch. You will not sneeze."

That there are rules makes me feel better. Modeling doesn't seem to be a free for all.

"Oui, Monsieur Puvis." My nerves settle.

He leans his walking stick against a table and picks up paper and charcoal. "As long as you are here, I shall make some sketches."

He does. And in the days that follow, he makes a hundred more.

Despite that first encounter, when I pose at his large studio in Neuilly, I am rarely naked. He's painting a large classical work, so I'm draped in the fashion of Greek goddesses.

While when I hung from the trapeze by my hands —I tried to go back—my spine hurt as if the flames of hell were licking my bones, the pain of posing is bearable. No sudden jerks. Posing is tiring, but not as taxing as the life of an acrobat.

"WHORE!" MY MOTHER THROWS HER TIN PLATE AT ME AS I STEP IN THE DOOR. Then she throws mine. Then she throws the cups, and then she's out of dishes. "You sell yourself to them old men in the street. The whole neighborhood is talkin'." She leans on the table, for she can barely stand. She reeks of wine. "Why must you shame me?"

"He is an artist. I am a model." I've been modeling for three weeks.

"Another name for whore." She throws a spoon. "If only I had a son instead."

I pull the day's wages out of my pocket and lay the coins on the table.

Quicker than I thought she could move, Maman snatches them up and shoves them into her pocket. "Hmpf."

We don't talk about my modeling again.

Our neighbors in the tenement shoot me disapproving looks when we meet on the stairs. They turn up their noses, as if I'm below them. I don't care. When I hear their vicious whispers, I hold my head that much higher. I won't always live among them.

. . .

In Molier's circus, I was admired. In Puvis's studio in Neuilly, I am unexpectedly respected. In that studio, I know peace.

Puvis doesn't drink to excess. He doesn't entertain prostitutes. He's serious about his work, which is a revelation to me, after having watched so many other artists sink into debauchery in the dance halls and cafés.

At times, he reminds me of Madame Mabbit. He corrects my language and demeanor. He talks to me about history and books, judging my education insufficient. He seems to care.

I hold my poses and watch him as he works.

I learn how to stretch and prime a canvas. I learn how to set up a palette. I learn how to mix colors. In the ten-minute break granted me every hour, I inspect his progress.

I learn how a composition is built, how the underdrawing is accomplished. I learn about form, the way it's born of light and shade.

From my earnings, I bring home paper and charcoal. To earn money for pastels, I pose for a photographer.

"L'ensemble," Louis Igout orders.

I slip out of my clothes. "Of course."

"In the chair."

The chair helps. With its wide, solid arms, its carvings and carpet upholstery, I might as well be sitting on a throne.

"Legs to one side."

I comply.

"One arm on your lap, the other on your chest. No. Above your breasts. Don't cover them."

I turn my head aside, in a demure pose. And yet... Manet's *Olympia* looks the viewer in the eyes as an equal. I look straight at the camera. I'm not ashamed of myself.

If I am to be a model, I am going to be a model.

The work is as demanding as at the circus, but less dangerous. I don't have to strike my poses thirty feet up in the air, nor swing from bar to bar. Holding a pose for fifty minutes at a time sets all my muscles aching, but I don't mind. I have time to think about my future life.

My current life isn't so bad, to be fair. Maman and I have food to eat every day. And when I'm at work, I'm in a different world. Puvis's studio in Neuilly is a palace compared to our sooty room at the tenement.

I shouldn't be surprised when one day, a princess appears.

She sweeps in swathed in ultramarine silk and sparkling jewels, carrying a cloud of expensive perfume with her, as if spring itself is her traveling attendant.

"My new model, Maria." The words rush from Puvis. His grandfatherly demeanor disappears, and he seems to grow an inch. I swear even his gray mustache looks dashing. "Princess Marie Cantacuzène from Romania."

He takes her hand and says to me without looking at me. "Today's sitting is finished."

Well.

Oh.

I dress in a rush, then all the way to the door, I shamelessly gawk. I've never seen a real princess in all my life. Her skin is like fresh cream, not a pockmark on her. Her hair gleams. Her hands, when she takes off her gloves, look softer than whipped butter. If I could paint, I would paint them. I envy everything about her, down to the tulle flowers on her hat.

I'm a girl, not a fool. I understand the soft light I've never before seen in Puvis's eyes. I understand why he's never required anything of me beyond being on time and holding my poses steady. I understand that I must never speak of this meeting —or any of the others that follow—for as she embraces him, I catch a glint of the princess's wedding ring.

THIS IS THE SECRET OF MY SUCCESS: I AM ABLE TO HOLD DIFFICULT POSES OTHERS CAN'T. I can hold a pose longer than anyone else. My back is strong enough to bend and stretch.

My dependability on the stand and Pierre Puvis de Chavennes's support throw open to me the doors of every studio in Paris. I pose for Forain, Henner, Steinlein, and artists from as far away as America. I pose for Princesse Mathilde, the emperor's cousin!

As the days pass, I grow into a new me. I'm no longer Marie-Clémentine the bastard. I am Maria, the sought-after model. And who knows, someday maybe I can be something else. Sometimes, when I look at myself in the paintings that hang in the best galleries, I think I could be anything.

Our neighbors believe me a glorified prostitute, but little do they know that at seventeen, I'm still a virgin.

Until I run into Renoir again, that is.

CHAPTER NINE

Ellie

Saturday, March 11th

THE FIVE STAGES OF GRIEF ARE:

1. YOU'RE SO HEARTBROKEN YOU THINK YOU'LL DIE.
2. YOU'RE SO HEARTBROKEN YOU THINK YOU'LL DIE.
3. YOU'RE SO HEARTBROKEN YOU THINK YOU'LL DIE.
4. YOU'RE SO HEARTBROKEN YOU THINK YOU'LL DIE.
5. YOU DON'T DIE.

But cemetery visits are still hard.

Our small-town cemetery used to be on the outskirts, alone in a flat field, but now the town has grown around it. At one end, there's a car mechanic, on the other a pharmacy, and then developments, of course, all around it.

Abby and I go every year, together, on the anniversary of our parents' death. I arrive early, to spend time with Chris. Except, today, my sister is early too, so I don't get nearly as much time as I wish.

"I heard scratching in your apartment when we were there the other day. I think you have mice." My sister walks up to me, teetering in high-heeled boots, which is odd. She's normally the queen of Uggs and Birkenstock.

"I know. It doesn't bother me."

She presses her lips together, then relaxes them, press and relax, press and relax. She's trying, hard, to hold something back.

"Oh, for love's sake. Don't bust a gut. Just tell me."

"You are overwhelmed."

I can't argue with that. "I've recently lost the love of my life, my house, and my job. You think I could have a minute to deal with all that?"

"I'm sorry. I'm not making light of your losses. But an expert was talking about learned helplessness on NPR this morning…"

Light travels at the speed of 186,000 miles per second. The only thing faster is the speed at which sisters get mad at each other. "I'm *not* helpless."

"Terrible events transpired that were out of your control. There was nothing you could do to change them. The absolute worst-case scenario happened. Our parents died when you were young. Then you lost your husband. Sometimes, people's brains learn that no matter what they do, it won't make a difference. Trauma can burn the message into a person's brain cells, and then when other, sometimes inconsequential, stuff happens, they don't react. So you don't get rid of the mice."

"Unless you got licensed as a psychologist since I've last seen you, could we please talk about something else?"

We walk over to our parents' grave in silence, the only ones around in the cold, two orphans adrift on a gray sea of headstones. She touches the memorial, her usual quick *hello*. I don't. She remembers them more.

"How is Bubbles?"

"Happy as a lizard in a sun lounge."

"She should come home."

"You have one single north-facing window."

My apartment used to be a garage attic. The wall in the front is the only window wall. On the sides, the ceiling is slanted for the roof. In the back, there's no room for a window, since a chimney runs up in the middle of the wall. There's an old woodstove downstairs that used to heat Mr. Martinez's workshop. But every problem has a solution.

"I ordered another heating lamp."

"How is your museum coming along?"

I've been meaning to tell her my good news. "Literally, in the whole history of the internet, I'm the first person to have thought of this idea. It either means that I'm brilliant—"

"Or crazy."

"The point is, I was able to buy the domain. TheMuseumofUnseenArt.com was still available."

"Can you believe it?"

Her sarcasm can't dent my enthusiasm. "All the Delaware Art Museum wants is to see my virtual museum up online before they agree to lend me a few pieces. They want a full project proposal. No problem. I can put together a project proposal and create a kick-ass website in my sleep. I'm going to brand the living daylights out of this. And if they decide to work with me, I can use their name when I negotiate with other museums. They'll fall like dominoes."

"Isn't it weird that they're making you jump through hoops when they're not even lending you anything? They're just letting you use digital images."

"They're a venerable cultural institute. They can't be associated with anything shady. They're protecting their reputation," I tell my sister what Wanda Abara told me.

"I worry that this project is going to distract you from your job search."

"My LinkedIn profile is up to date, and I'm looking." I tug my coat tighter against the cold breeze. The cemetery is deserted. If this were a movie, we'd be clinging together, but it's real life, and we're both grown women. My clinging days are over. "Nobody is hiring right now. I think companies are hoping they'll soon be able to replace their designers and branding people with AI."

"How about a different field?"

"Organic chemistry? Rocket science? Brain surgery?"

"Don't be glib. This is your life. The new restaurant on State Street is hiring."

"I don't want to waitress."

"Anything is better than nothing. Or you could try substitute teaching. And the stores are always looking for sales associates. Unless you think you're above honest work."

"Honest as opposed to what? It's not like my plan is to set up illegal poker games in hotel rooms. I just want to do something creative." I want to build something, a process where along the way I can also build a new me. I need something big, something all-consuming. *I need this project to save me.*

"Everything isn't always perfect."

Her words knock me back. Resentment seeps in through my many cracks. "You think my life was perfect before I left the design studio? You think anything will ever be perfect for me without Chris?"

"I didn't mean to make you upset." She taps her feet together on the frozen ground. "I worry about you. You need a job."

I'm not in the mood for big-sister hovering. I say something I know will make her back off. "If you worry about me, you can pay me my share of the house."

I moved out of my parents' home when I went to college. After college, I moved into an apartment with Chris. Then we bought a home together. Abby stayed in our old house all this time. Which isn't even something I normally think about. It's fine.

"Frank says we can't this year," she tells me. "I'm sorry. You know we're trying."

Technically, I own half the house, but it isn't as straightforward as that, because Abby and Frank pay the mortgage. Also, Abby is a middle school teacher and makes no money, so they're living on Frank's income. Also, I feel like I owe Abby for raising me. It's complicated.

"Never mind. Don't worry about it."

"Are you coming over for Sunday lunch tomorrow?"

"I was planning on taking a couple of online seminars this weekend to update my skills."

Her hands disappear in her pockets. "I hate that you make me beg for every visit."

"Maybe I'm just trying to give you and Frank some space." Because people *need* space. Everybody does. Even me.

The hint flies as high over my sister's head as a Boeing 747 heading to France.

"If you can't find employment," she says, "we'll figure something out. But please try to get a job."

"I'm doing freelance work online." I've been putting in a few hours every morning: a website update, a social media image review, rebranding a small indie band. "And I've updated my LinkedIn page." Although, to be fair, I haven't responded to any recruiter emails. All they seem to want is my résumé for their databases, without any available positions to offer me.

"You should be with people. It's not healthy for you to sit alone in that apartment."

"I don't need you to be my mother."

The temperature drops another degree. The wind picks up and chases the thin drifts of dead leaves around the cemetery.

"Good for you." Abby's voice is brittle with frost. "You can tell me off. You have someone who cares about you. Do you ever think I might want someone to mother me for a minute? To give me advice, or just to be there when everything is freaking falling apart?"

No, I don't.

I squint at her. "Do you need help?"

The question doesn't even sound right.

I was ten when our parents died, and I'm inching toward thirty now. For nearly two-thirds of my life, Abby has been my de facto mother. Maybe even more, because I barely have any memories before age six. So as far as the memory bank of my life goes, for the vast majority of it, the person standing next to me has always been Abby. She's the strong one. She's the one who never cracks, never breaks.

"I have to go." She walks away on her teetering heels.

I don't know what's up with those. Maybe she's having a midlife crisis. Her footwear is usually teacher sensible, nothing but flats.

I hurry after her. "Want to grab pizza?"

"Frank is home. I told him I'd have lunch with him. He'll be waiting."

Then we're at our cars.

"Drive safe," she tells me.

At home, I fix myself a sandwich and a cup of coffee. *Abby needs mothering.* This is a weird thought. She's thirty-nine. I've never seen her as someone in need of anything.

She's had a job for as long as I can remember. She always had everything together—and smug about it too. Responsible, hardworking, know-it-all, supporting-the-family Saint Abby.

Everyone expected me to be just like her, everyone always telling me how lucky I was to have her, how much I owed her. And I resented her all the way. I didn't want her s-mothering me. But—and I'm ashamed that this never occurred to me before—while she was tucking me in those first two years, who was tucking her in?

Nobody.

The revelation occupies my brain so much that half an hour passes before I remember something else she said at the cemetery.

Do you ever think I might want someone to mother me for a minute? To give me advice, or just to be there, when everything is freaking falling apart?

Is my sister's life falling apart?

What's happening?

I text her. *Let's talk some more. Want me to come over?*

She texts me back. *I'll call you later.*

Except, then she doesn't.

I work on my museum's website for the rest of the day. I barely spy on the home renovations across the road, just when it's unavoidable, just when I'm at the sink.

Grace calls from LA.

"How is the job search going?"

"Six-figure offer coming any minute." Might as well be positive. "Surfer boys as good as you remember?"

She snickers. "It's nice to catch up with old friends, but I miss you. What are you doing right now?"

"Figuring out how I could make this museum happen." I already filled her in on the basics earlier in the week.

"Any breakthroughs?"

"Not yet." I stare across the street. "You know the foundation garden I used to have? That small strip garden developers sketch in so they can tell you they gave you a garden?"

"Vaguely? Kind of. Yes."

"Foundation gardens make no sense. They're pushed against the front wall where the house shades them, the roof overhang stops the rain from watering them, and whatever moisture does reach them gets wicked away by the concrete foundation.

And then if you water the plants with a hose yourself, you're getting your foundation wet."

"Hello, water damage."

"Exactly. The point is, I widened mine and created a real garden. And every time Chris ran over to the store for a bucket of paint or a two-by-four or some crown molding, he brought me a potted plant. I had to widen the garden three times." Now, most of the flowers are gone, courtesy of the scaffolding needed for the new roof and the crew that trampled everything I planted. "I miss my roses." They were the last holdouts, lasting weeks longer in the fall than anything else.

"They are resplendent."

"Were. There's nothing left."

Except... I lean closer to the window. *Are those peonies that are sending up their purple shoots over there?*

The porch light glints off their fat little tips. The windows are mostly dark, one light left on in there somewhere for security. The driveway is gloriously empty. It's just my unattended house and my birthday peonies.

"Listen, I have to do something. Have fun. And don't forget suntan lotion, if you spend all your time loitering on the beach."

"SPF one thousand. Locked and loaded."

We hang up. I put down my phone, but stay at the sink.

Peonies are a symbol of good luck. Right now, for me, they're the symbol of injustice.

"Joshua Jennings is not entitled to my birthday gift," I tell House Mouse. "What do you think?"

I'm so annoyed that my sister hasn't called me back yet that I decide to do something she would thoroughly disapprove of: breaking and entering.

"No worries," I tell the mouse as I step into my boots. "I'm not really going to break anything, and I'm not going to enter either."

Scratch, scratch, scratch.

"It's a rescue mission." I tug on my thickest black sweater. "He'll kill them if I leave them."

I sneak into Mrs. Martinez's garage first, grab a bucket and a spade, then I hustle across the street.

Of course, as soon as I kick the shovel into the dirt, the metal hits a stone. *Ping!*

I freeze.

My track record for sneaking across the street is not great. Maybe Joshua pulled his pickup into the garage. Maybe he's sitting in his living room in the dark, meditating. If he heard me…

He does not appear at the door, however. Nobody stirs. Nobody comes to investigate.

I dig out the first peony—I'm going to plant them in pots outside my apartment door on the landing— then the second. I get caught on the third.

One second, I'm getting away with it all, then the floodlight flares on and a woman is standing in the open door.

Girlfriend? I haven't seen her before.

She squints at me. "You must be Ellie."

She knows me, which means Joshua told her about me.

I can almost hear it. *Crazy ex-owner. Spies on me from across the street. Can't let go. Restraining order might be safest, etc.*

I grip the shovel. "How embarrassing."

"No, no. I'm Joshua's sister. Aria. Would you like to come in?"

She's younger than me. I'm guessing twenty-two or twenty-three. She does look like Joshua, now that my eyes are used to the light and I can see.

I want to grab my peonies and scurry across the street, but understand with dawning horror that I *have to* go in. I have to explain myself, at the very least.

"I'm so sorry." I wipe my hands on my jeans. "I'm—"

"Burying a voodoo doll?" She doesn't sound judgmental.

"Saving a few of my old plants from certain death."

"A mission of mercy." She steps back and holds the door open wide. She's mini Joshua at five feet four, same brown hair shot through with the same amber highlights, cut short, with spikes. "I'm letting all the heat out. Why don't you come inside for a minute?"

I don't know what the protocol is for a situation like this.

I ease into the foyer.

My hardwood floor is refinished. The walls are

painted pale gray, with white crown molding added. The house doesn't smell like my home, which at the same time breaks my heart and sets me free.

"I didn't think anyone was here. I thought I could save the plants and Joshua wouldn't notice anything."

"He's watching basketball with my brother and my dad. Probably won't be home until midnight. The three of them together with a game on are way too noisy for me, so I came over here to study. Dad dropped me off. Joshua will take me home. I'm a grad student at Penn State. I'm the brain of the family."

"Nice to meet you, Aria." I look from her to what's behind her and drink in the sight of my home, notice and catalog every change.

"Can I offer you a cup of coffee?" The kitchen is gutted, but there's a temporary setup in the dining room that includes a coffeemaker.

"I really don't feel comfortable." I note the new rose-gold chandelier as I back toward the door. "I shouldn't be here."

"How about this?" Aria is utterly unperturbed by the neighborhood crazy lady. "I'll pop on my coat and help you outside. I need a break from studying."

"What would your brother say?"

"What he doesn't know won't hurt him. Like you said, he'd just kill those poor plants anyway."

I'm not only committing a crime, I now have recruited an accomplice. *I'm the mastermind of a criminal enterprise.*

We dig up the last peony, then Aria helps me back home with the bucket, which is pretty heavy. My stairs are steep. The help is appreciated.

"Would you like to come in?" At this stage, I have to reciprocate.

"I should get back. Front door's unlocked."

"The neighborhood is safe." I don't want her to come in. I don't know why I'm talking her into it. Maybe because I'm still embarrassed at getting caught once again. I want her to think that I'm a good neighbor. I don't want her to think that I'm a creep.

"All right. For a minute."

And then we're inside. I'm entertaining the sister of my worst enemy. In the aftermath of petty theft. What's the etiquette for that? "Anything to drink?"

"Don't suppose you have diet iced tea?" She peeks hopefully at the refrigerator behind me.

"Unsweetened cold-brew black tea from Trader Joe's?"

"You are everything a neighbor should be." She follows me to the fridge and glances out the window at the house across the street. "That must be difficult to watch every day."

I don't comment. I give her a whole unopened gallon of tea. "Take it. I have another one. You'll need the caffeine for studying."

Scratch, scratch, scratch.

Aria freezes, then rolls to the tips of her toes, ready to flee. "Did you hear that?"

"There's a mouse in the wall. Doesn't bother anyone. Good listener. Can keep a secret."

She skips toward the door. "I'm a city girl. Is this kind of thing normal in the suburbs? Does Joshua know this?"

"He's a flipper. I'm sure he's seen a mouse or two in the course of his work. But there are no mice at my old house. You don't have to worry."

My phone rings before she can say anything.

I hold it up. "My sister."

"Nice to meet you." My visitor backs outside, clearly happy to go. "Good luck with the peonies."

I pick up the call even before I close the door behind her. "Is everything okay?"

"Perfectly fine. Why wouldn't it be?"

I've heard that before and always believed it. I don't believe it now. "Can I help you with anything?"

"I went on the school's website, and they're hiring substitutes. I just wanted you to know. If you send in an application, I could walk over to the office on Monday and put in a word for you." My sister sounds distracted. The usual lecturing tone is missing.

"What's going on? I know something is off with you guys. Abby?"

"What did Frank tell you?" The question rushes across the line on a single breath.

"You're my sister. Shouldn't you tell me?" I'm rotten for playing this dirty game, but I play it anyway. I'm a hypocrite too, because I have my own secrets, secrets I plan on taking to the grave.

"He's not a bad guy."

"Never said he was." Just mildly annoying.

Silence.

Did he cheat? Because I'm already living a life of crime. If he hurt my sister, I *will* murder him.

Abby's words are slow with exhaustion. "He's trying to get better."

"Is he sick?" How bad can a case of hemorrhoids be? Isn't there a cream?

"He's working on himself."

How does one work on hemorrhoids? I try to imagine. *Nah. Nope. Not happening.* "In what way?"

"Gambling is an addiction. It's an illness. He knows he has to quit. It's been going on way too long."

"Frank is a gambling addict?"

In the blink of an eye, so many things make sense. That the annual beach vacation is always in Atlantic City. How many times have I suggested the Poconos? And then Frank always being nervous about money. He can turn ridiculously stingy at random, gifting me marketing merchandise from the bank for my birthday: bank logo pens and bags and frisbees.

He gambles away his money.

"Why didn't you tell me before? You're my sister. I'm here for you. I've got your back." I cringe at how few times I've said these words before. "Why would you think you'd have to hide this?"

"It's not a big deal. I don't want you to worry. We'll fix it. Listen, I…"

She runs out of words, and in the ensuing silence, a terrible suspicion sprouts an entire, strangling root system in my mind.

He wouldn't. He couldn't.

"He didn't put a second mortgage on the house, did he?"

"The truth is…"

"He couldn't have. I'm half owner. I didn't sign anything."

"You have to remember, it's an illness. He's…"

"Frank forged my signature?"

"I don't know what he did." Abby's voice is reedy. "I'm so sorry, Ellie."

Anger boils through me. Steam fills up my brain. I'm the mother of volcanoes, I'm so angry. But not at my sister. "You don't have to apologize for anything."

"If the bank finds out, they'll fire him."

"They won't find out."

"They might already have. His boss initiated a performance review. For the time being, he can provide customer support to his existing client list, but he can't approve any new loans."

"How badly is the house mortgaged?" *Mom and Dad's house.* Can the bank take it away? "Abby?"

The silence on the line is a dark abyss. And when my sister speaks, that abyss only deepens.

"To the hilt."

CHAPTER TEN

Suzanne

1882 / Age 17

MONEY CHANGES EVERYTHING.

Until today, I survived.

Now I *live*.

I no longer rush home after work. I help my mother, but I don't take up her mending in the evenings. I frequent the cafés that draw the artists and their friends. Instead of bringing Debussy wine on a tray, I sit at his table and listen to him talk about music. I listen as Victor Hugo tells his friends about the new production of his old play, *Les Miserables*, and how he too ate rats during the siege. But most of all, as much as I can, I listen to the men who paint.

Mary Cassatt and Berthe Morisot and Eva

Gonzalès and Marie Bracquemond might be accepted artists allowed to exhibit, but those women cannot walk alone into a café in the evening. I can. I can go anywhere. I'm a working-class girl, not a lady.

I can sit with any artist at the Café de la Nouvelle Athènes. I can even drink, although I don't like the taste. The alcohol restrictions on absinthe have been lifted. We dance in the streets.

I have nothing to lose. Street gossip already says I'm Puvis's lover, the lover of every artist I pose for, the lover of every man I dance with. The same neighbor who accused Maman of trying to steal her husband accused me of carrying on with the mailman before we moved out of the tenement. I will live life on my own terms. Let fools wag their foolish tongues. They know me not. I know who I am.

"Dance with me, Maria." Miquel Utrillo grabs my hand. He's an artist, what else.

"Yes." I'm drunk on spring.

I used to run away from St. Vincent's and the nuns to skip along the shops. All I've ever wanted was freedom, and now it's possible. The whole wild, whirling cavalcade of human existence is mine. I am the master of my life.

We swirl on the cobblestones under the stars, outside Le Chat Noir. Miquel's Catalan friends, Santiago and Ramon, clap.

Ramon's the loudest. "Rumor says you slid down the banister at the Moulin de la Galette wearing nothing but a mask."

"I don't even have a mask." I did slide down the

banister, on a dare. My skirts *have* flown up around my head. What does it matter? I have posed l'ensemble for the past two years. Anyone can see my body by walking into a gallery. "Why is it sinful for a woman to enjoy life and have a few happy moments, to own her body instead of letting her every action be dictated by men?"

"Nobody would dare dictate to you, Maria. You do as you wish."

"Why is it a mortal offense not to care about the opinions of strangers? Why do people judge me?"

"They see you free when they don't dare to be free." Miquel twirls me around. "It's envy."

I throw my head back. "Faster, Michel!"

He doesn't mind when I turn his name into French. His dark hair and brown eyes make it clear he's a Spaniard. He is only three years older than I am. Our outings remind me of playing with my school friends.

We dance down to the Boule Noir, then inside. He twirls and lets me go, then grabs a tablecloth and snaps himself into the pose of a matador. "Olé!"

Santiago and Ramon hold their index fingers to their foreheads, imitating horns, then the three act out a rousing bullfight.

"Olé! Olé!" Ramon knocks over a table. "Olé!"

I laugh so hard, I stagger as I clap.

Some of the diners clap with me, but others curse at us.

"Mademoiselle." A scowling waiter appears. "Messieurs. You must leave."

We lurch outside, still laughing.

"Where now?" Miquel, a gentleman, defers to me.

I tug the tablecloth from him and tie it around my neck. I'm a queen with a flowing cape. I prance. "The Moulin de la Galette?"

His lively eyes turn pitiably mournful. "I've been asked not to return for the time being. The last time I visited, I rode in on a donkey."

Santiago and Ramon clap him on the back to console him, and we move on, lamenting how unfair life can be to those of us who possess a free spirit.

When a group of grisettes stroll by, Santiago and Ramon slink off after them. Miquel and I sit on the lip of a fountain. While I consider whether I should sketch the mermaid in the middle, Miquel tells me about the paintings his friends are working on. He knows I have an interest. "You should try your hand at the easel."

Revelers pass us, laughing, without a care in the world, while my thoughts are swept up in a whirlwind.

"I draw." I shouldn't sound so breathless, but it's the first time I've admitted this to anyone.

Interest lights up Miquel's eyes, not a glint of the ridicule I feared. "May I see?"

"Why?"

"What's this?" He flicks water at me from the tips of his fingers, a quick smile on his roguish lips. "Maria Valadon, shy?"

"Never." I jump to my feet. "Come." We are not far from where I live. We've left the old tenement behind. My wages allow my family improved lodgings.

I have Miquel wait on the street while I sneak inside. Maman is snoring, collapsed on her bed. I move a half-empty bottle from the pillow next to her head, then grab my stack of papers and tiptoe outside. That is how the first person I ever show my art sees it, by moonlight.

And he takes his time.

I shuffle as I wait, then I almost grab it all back. I stop myself. Anyway, what does his opinion matter? Yet it desperately does. He is my friend.

"This..." Miquel's expression is serious. For once, the jokester has run out of jokes. "These are good, Maria."

"You say so because you're fond of me." Truth is, he's in love with me a little. He flatters me, that is all. I close my heart to the compliment.

"Who taught you?" He can't tear his eyes away from the paper.

"I taught myself." It's not as good as attending the Academy or having one of the greats for a mentor, and we both know it. "It's nothing."

"You must draw more." Miquel's eyes are brighter than the gaslights. "You have talent."

A window creaks open above, and an old woman in a nightcap leans out. "Be quiet, you two. Be gone from here."

We are lucky she doesn't upend her chamber pot over our heads.

I put my drawings back inside, then run down the street with my friend.

Within days, rumors fly through Montmartre that I'm Miquel Utrillo's lover.

"RENOIR IS LOOKING FOR A MODEL." Puvis paints me as I hold a Grecian urn on my shoulder, posing in a toga for his next public work on order. "He's only just returned from Algeria. I recommended you. He wants to look at you in his studio.

"I don't have the time." I've been running myself ragged, trudging from sitting to sitting, up and down Montmartre's streets. While I no longer take in laundry or seamstress work, I still help Maman when she needs me. If I have time left, it's only after dark, and I spend it with my friends. I deserve some rest.

Also, from what I've heard, Renoir is far too popular and far too exacting. He'd be a hard taskmaster. I work hard enough already.

"I asked Nini Gérard to stop by after our session and walk you over." Puvis switches to a small sable brush. Sable is softer than boar bristle, better for finishing work, because it doesn't leave brushstrokes. "At least let Renoir take a look at you."

"He'll be waiting?"

"Yes."

Models who keep artists waiting suffer a bad reputation in a hurry. "I don't need Nini." She's another one of Puvis's models. "Renoir and I already know each other."

"Do you? He said you haven't met."

"Age must be catching up with him. Fine. I'll stop by." But I will not take on more work. Posing for hours on end, day after day, month after month, year after year, is beginning to hurt my damaged back. I don't want the pain to grow worse. I've already lost the circus. If I lose modeling too, I'll have nothing left.

I pose in silence and watch Puvis apply his signature pale colors. He prefers his work to have the feel of ancient frescos. His style is soothing. Someday, when I paint, my colors will be vibrant. They will dance across the canvas, threatening to jump off.

My muscles cramp and my bones ache by the time I set the heavy urn down at the end of the session. When Nini shows up, I'm about to tell her to go away, but then I reconsider. A formal introduction, after all these years, would be more proper.

"Does he pay well?" I ask on the way over.

Nini's response is a scowl and a shrug.

"How stingy is he with breaks?"

Nothing from Nini.

"Does he seduce his models?"

She doesn't answer any questions at all, just sulks. She escorts me to a house on the rue d'Orchampt without saying a word, and then she abandons me there with undisguised resentment. A shame Puvis didn't recommend her for the project. Clearly, she wanted the assignment.

She doesn't even stay to introduce me, after all that.

I knock on the studio door. "Anyone here?" I crack the door open. "Monsieur Renoir? Hello? Monsieur?"

"Come in, come in." Renoir hurries from the back. His short beard and longish mustache are shot through with silver now. He has the same gaunt cheekbones, though, that I remember, and the same penetrating eyes. "Puvis's protégée?" He doesn't recognize me. "Maria, the model?"

"Model extraordinaire." Who is used to better surroundings these days.

Renoir's studio is crowded with paintings, his easels covered with dust. A holy mess surrounds him —no rhyme, no reason, no composition. It'd be impossible to paint. He's nothing like tidy Puvis.

He notes my dismay at the disorder. "I've been traveling."

A red and black carpet that would make a stunning backdrop for a portrait, lies tossed over an armchair. "Algeria?"

"Ah, Puvis told you. Algiers, yes. And then to Madrid to pay my respects to the work of Velázquez. Then Italy, for Titian's great work in Florence, and Raphael's in Rome, then Palermo, Sicily, to paint Richard Wagner. Do you go to the opera?"

Yes, me and my husband the count. "I prefer the circus. Monsieur Renoir—"

"Call me Auguste." He takes stock of me with his careful artist's eyes. "Where are you from?"

"Bessines." I step farther into the room, stopping in the middle, careful not to knock anything over.

"I'm from Limoges. Neighbors." The same response he gave me years ago, on the street. He walks around me, larger than life. "Healthy, young, with feminine curves," he says, as if ticking items off a list. "Mahogany hair, sapphire-blue eyes. You have flames in those eyes, Maria. Has anyone told you that?"

"In my eyes burn the flames of hell?"

His eyebrows shoot up.

I shrug. "A priest once said."

"How old are you?"

I hate that question, as if girls expire like butter.

"How old are you?" I punctuate the question with a quick laugh.

Questions asked on a laugh are often taken as jokes and are answered in the same joking manner. Asked straight, I'd be told I was impertinent.

"I'm forty-one." He doesn't flinch at the number, as a woman might. "Too old for you?"

"I've done it with older." I've been working with Puvis, and he could be my grandfather. "I'm seventeen." And then, so Renoir wouldn't look at me like a stupid child, a stupid nobody, I add, "My father was Villon, the poet."

This stops him in his tracks. "You are certain?" Then, "Have we met before?"

I quote the passage I memorized in school. *"Poor from my youth, born of humble stock, my father had no wealth, nor his grandfather, Orace. Poverty tracks us all."*

"Depressing words." Yet Renoir's eyes fill with

amusement. "Would this be François Villon, the famous poet, who died four hundred years ago?"

Damn him. I never was any good at memorizing dates. So he knew my words to be a lie, all along, even back when he had me sign his canvas.

My cheeks heat. What excuse could I possibly produce? I hang my head. Either he will send me away or won't. I stay silent.

Renoir takes my hands. "My own father was a humble tailor. I believe in one making one's own destiny."

I look up at that, not just the words, but the electricity that thickens the air, like when a storm is sweeping in from the fields. My skin tingles with an anticipation of lighting and thunder.

"One makes one's own destiny when one is a man." I won't give anyone the satisfaction of rendering me speechless.

"Become my model, and you will dance into history, beautiful Maria." There's an edge to his voice that says he feels the coming storm too.

"Women don't dance into history."

He's clearly amused. "Is that so?"

I draw away. "Women have to fight to get anywhere. And then, as soon as they die, they're promptly forgotten." The history lessons at school were nearly devoid of women.

"Such a pessimistic view for one so young."

"Do you believe Mary Cassatt, Berthe Morisot, Eva Gonzalès, or Marie Bracquemond will be remembered for having their paintings hanging next to Degas's and Monet's?"

"I would expect so."

"They will be forgotten," I assure him, then add, "Maybe not Mary Cassatt. She's rich *and* an American."

"History forgets all women unless they're rich? Is that your thesis?"

"Out of all history, the nuns only mentioned two women at school." That I remember. "Cleopatra and Marie Antoinette. Two queens. And still, neither of them was spoken of kindly."

"Is that so? No admiration for either of them at all?"

"Sister Marguerite did approve Marie Antoinette's last words as the queen walked to the guillotine."

"Remind me."

"She apologized for stepping on the executioner's foot. *Pardonnez-moi, monsieur. Je ne l'ai pas fait exprès.*"

Renoir's eyes dance with mirth. "And what did Sister Marguerite have to say about Cleopatra? Dare I hope the Egyptian queen drew more praise?"

"The sister disapproved of her, on account of Cleopatra becoming the lover of both Caesar and Mark Antony."

"To save her country from the invading Roman armies."

"She should have saved her soul instead."

"Is that what you think?"

"The sister's words, not mine. I wouldn't care if

Cleopatra lay with the whole of the Roman army. She has nothing to do with me."

Renoir laughs. "You are not what I expected. I think I'll enjoy our time together." He gestures to his sketches on the table next to him. "I am planning three large works. Dancers. What do you think?"

I do enjoy dancing. I take a peek. And then I can't tear my eyes away.

I know in that instant that I will accept the work, *any* work that he'll give me. I will find the time, even if I have to cancel another artist's sitting.

Renoir's lines are a revelation. He's a trained draftsman, a master. With a few lines, he can pull a woman out of the paper, as if he's pulling her from a well, from under the water. A line curves this way, another that way, and she's there. He draws so little, yet I can see the creases in the dancer's dress.

"Should I take my clothes off?" I offer.

"Most definitely." His lively eyes devour me. "But not yet."

RIGHT AWAY, THERE IS A PROBLEM.

"For the first painting, *Dance in the City*, I want you in a white silk dress. I usually borrow gowns." Renoir taps his charcoal stick on the easel. "I have many patronesses."

This does not surprise me. He is famous. And also, despite the bags under his eyes and his sparse beard, his angular face *is* handsome in a way. He is full of life and light. Then there's his sheer talent. I can see how that would draw women.

He clicks his tongue. "I can't think of anyone whose gown would fit you. You are rather petite."

He will not send me away.

I want the sittings with him. I want to watch him sketch and paint. I want to hear about Algiers, and Palermo, and Madrid. "I could alter a dress, then return it to its original state when we're finished."

He considers that for a breath. "No." He sketches me, his entire being absorbed in the task. "We shall have a dress made."

At our next session, there waits a seamstress and more white silk than I've ever seen. For the first time in my life, I have a fancy fitting. I keep my eyes on the mirror, and I pretend that it's all real, not just make-believe for a painting, that this is my life—the gown, the gloves, the jewels—all of it.

When the seamstress finishes, weeks later, I am an elegant lady, dancing in a ballroom. My dress is what clouds would dream of if they had dreams. My white sateen gloves stretch luxuriously above my elbows. My hair is up, carefully arranged by a lady's maid borrowed for the day. My dance partner, Paul Lhôte, Renoir's friend, can't take his eyes off me.

"Beautiful Maria," he whispers. "You look like an angel."

"Turn your face toward me, Maria," Renoir snaps. "Paul, you look the other way."

We obey, then we freeze again in our poses. Yet our nearness is no less intimate just because we are no longer looking at each other. The length of my body is pressed against Paul's. I rest a gloved hand on his shoulder. His arm is around my waist.

Renoir is not satisfied. "You must appear as if you are in motion."

We adjust again.

The master paints for a few minutes, cleaning his brush often so as not to muddy the colors. Then he frowns.

"No. This way." He peels me off his friend and snares me in his arms.

He keeps me there.

His sparkling eyes are too close. His warm breath fans my neck. He is too much. I don't know what to do with the sudden awareness. My whole body stiffens. *No, this won't do.* I force myself to relax. I smile, as if caught up in the dance.

And that is when the studio door bursts open. It bounces off the wall, the door handle leaving a dent.

"Release him, at once! You leech. You whore." Aline blows in like a country storm. She has the figure of a farmer's wife, and also the manners, never mind a face like a tomato. How she's a model, I'll never know.

She hisses at me. "Shoo. He's *my* man."

She's probably unaware that she has a wattle when she tips her chin down like that. I pity her. Her dress could not be more inferior to what I have.

Renoir backs away from me in haste and throws up his hands. "I was simply showing Paul how to hold the model for the pose. Calm yourself, Aline, dear."

Aline's eyes cut to Paul at the window, and they expand from slits to rounds. In her fury, she missed him altogether.

I dare to speak up. "I'm posing for the dancer."

Aline looks at me as if she could skewer me with a paintbrush, then back at Renoir. She transforms into the very image of a woman wronged. "Am I not good enough?"

"You're busy." Renoir's voice is soothing and solicitous. He humors her. The sooner he gets her out of the studio, the sooner we can all return to work. "We've talked about this. Maria is here to pose with Paul, nothing more."

"I started as a model at your studio."

"You are different. You know you are. She'll never be here without Paul. I'm painting them together. The pose wouldn't work without the two of them. You know how it works, ma chérie."

"Mmm." She makes a face. And then she storms off in a whirl of petticoats as abruptly as she appeared.

"Shall we continue?" Renoir strides back to his easel and touches brush to canvas again, as if nothing happened.

Paul and I assume our pose. I no longer have to force a look of amusement.

We work through the rest of the day without stopping for breaks, until Paul and I grow stiff. Only then are we allowed to leave.

"Maria." Renoir calls me back from the door.

I can't possibly stay. My spine is a column of fire. It happens when a pose is too twisted and I hold it too long. My body will not let me forget my accident on the trapeze. "Yes?"

"She's not my wife. We are not married."

He's the artist; I'm the model for hire. "No explanation needed."

"Maria, I—"

I wait, but he says no more.

There's an odd look in his eyes, the look of a man at a crossroads.

THE FIRST TIME RENOIR ASKS ME TO REMOVE MY CLOTHES, WE'RE IN HIS GARDEN SHED.

Summer has burst into flowers around us. Birds trill in the trees. He sketches me naked, although all three paintings of dancers he's working on have me clothed on the canvas.

He says these are studies for a future work. I can't wait to see what colors. I prefer his vivid pigments to the pale hues Puvis uses. I love Renoir's cobalt blue, emerald green, and vermilion.

His hand rests for a moment. His eyes do not. They roam my sun-dappled skin. "You truly *are* beautiful, Maria."

"I've been told." Yet coming from him, one of the most celebrated artists in Paris, the words touch me in a different way. Over the past few months, we've fallen into a friendship that's more than friendship. A

167

multitude of connections stretch between us, awareness that's new to me.

"That curve…" He picks up a clean brush and stalks over, drags the soft sable bristles along the dent in my waist—slowly, slowly, slowly—his intent eyes on mine. "This curve."

Tingles run across my skin. A new sensation unfurls inside me. At first, it's like a tickle, or butterflies in my stomach, and then it's—

Renoir draws the same line again, with the back of his fingers this time. His breathing grows more labored. "How perfect you are."

I feel as if I've drunk too much wine, but I don't move. I'm a model. I'm a professional. I stay still.

We work together for the rest of the year.

Sometimes, I am naked. Sometimes, he touches me. Sometimes, he then walks back to his easel. But not always.

I resist for as long as I can. Then, back in his studio again for the cold season, surprised by an unexpected storm in late March, my heart overrules my head.

I've been naked again, crouching in a washing basin. It's getting late.

"We've lost the light. I must leave." I reach for my wool stockings.

"Stay, lovely Maria." Renoir abandons his easel and comes to me. "It's not safe to be outside."

"Stay for what?" I don't understand how I am able to stand still when I feel as if every part of me is trembling.

"Stay for love." He kisses me. "I am in love with you." And then he takes my stockings, and I don't protest.

I love him too.

He takes me into his arms.

I shouldn't let him.

But I love him.

I DON'T KNOW HOW LONG I CAN HIDE BEHIND THE SCREEN IN RENOIR'S STUDIO.

"She is your whore! I know it. You don't fool me." Aline screams louder than the fishwives at the market. "Where is she?"

"Put down the broom, Aline."

We were celebrating when we heard her outside the door. After a year of hard work on *Dance in the City* and *Dance at Bougival*, we are finished. Aline forced herself into *Dance in the Country*, even though the first sketches all had my face. The pieces are Renoir's best work, according to everyone who's seen them. In *Dance in the City*, the male dancer's face is barely shown, as if Renoir couldn't bear seeing me with Paul Lhôte. In *Dance at Bougival*, the male figure can't take his eyes off me in my crimson bonnet. But the viewer will not be meeting Paul again. Renoir painted in his own face, his eyes covered by his boatman's hat. As if that could fool Aline.

The body starves for food. This I've known already. But now I know that the heart starves for love. Renoir loves me.

Except, right now, he's soothing Aline. "You know how much you mean to me."

My fists clench. Aline might be six years older than I am, and I'm shorter, true, but I would bet on myself in a fight. I'm scrappier.

"It's her, her, her," she screeches. "I'm sick of her face."

"Come on, sweet Aline. All artists have models. You'll always be my favorite."

There's a scuffle, and I almost leave my hiding place in the corner, especially when Renoir shouts, "Stop! Aline!"

"There." Then she's crying. She sobs and keens.

Then silence, a terrible silence that makes me afraid.

"Go home, my sweet." Renoir's voice is more than resigned. He sounds exhausted.

The sobbing renews.

The door opens, then closes.

I wait a moment before I whisper. "Is she gone? Where is she?"

No response.

"Auguste?"

The studio is entombed in mournful silence. I can't take the suspense any more. I step out from behind the screen expecting the worst, but the damage still catches me unprepared. I expected destruction, but I can scarcely comprehend its extent.

For several seconds, I'm speechless. It can't be. She couldn't. "What has she done?"

The large paintings lay on their easels like slaughtered bodies on their deathbed, the paint-smattered rag—the murder weapon—discarded on the parquet floor in front of them.

Aline had smeared and erased my face.

I am expunged, obliterated.

I touch my lips, my nose, my eyes—for reassurance that in real life I still have them. "Auguste?"

He's collapsed on his stool, head back, unable to look at his ruined masterpieces.

The poet Villon had gone to prison for murder. I might yet be my *father*'s daughter. "I'm going to kill her."

Renoir shoves to his feet and comes for me, for the first time showing his age, slow as if he's run a mile uphill. "I can repair the faces, my sweet."

"You allow her too much."

"She wants me to marry her." He takes my hand. "You understand."

I understood that he no longer loved her. He loves me. Over and over, he told me that.

I rip back my hands, nausea creeping up my throat. Despair darker than I've ever felt bubbles in my stomach. "You cannot marry Aline. I'm pregnant."

CHAPTER ELEVEN

Ellie

Monday, March 13th

"YOU HAVE MICE IN YOUR WALLS," Joshua tells me as
soon as I open the door.

I blink at him, returning from another world. I
was reading about Valadon. She might not be a
distant relative, but I'm hooked on her story. Sinking
into her adventures allows me to forget my own
problems. "Hi."

"Hi. I heard scratching the other day when I was
here for breakfast. I keep forgetting to bring it up."

It's Monday morning. I skipped lunch at Abby's
yesterday and took two design workshops online
instead. I don't think I could sit across the table from
Frank without wanting to strangle him. I'll eat with

him when he pays back the second mortgage he took out on my parents' house.

"You have mice?"

I blink at the flipper. Shouldn't he be sawing, or drilling, or painting? "Okay."

He waits for a stronger reaction for another beat. "You're not surprised."

"I live here. You might have noticed."

"Why aren't you more bothered?" He scrutinizes me. "My sister would jump out of her skin."

She just about did. "The mouse doesn't leave the rear wall. But thanks for the warning."

Joshua doesn't go away. He looms, his tool belt slung low on his hips. *He's ever ready to destroy something.* "I worry about you."

"I'm not your problem."

"You shouldn't live with mice. Even if it doesn't come out, it could chew on an electric wire. You could end up with a fire."

I envision my remaining possessions going up in smoke. I had to heavily downsize when I moved across the road. I only kept the essentials. I can't cope with the thought of losing *everything.*

"I'll deal with it."

"I can set a trap," Joshua offers, clearly the type that gets things done—manly man, *har har.*

I don't need him. I don't want him. I wish he would leave. "No."

"Why?"

I think rejection is new to him. "I don't want the mouse killed."

No more death.

"The store has live traps."

"I'll get one."

"If it's in the wall, you'll have to cut a hole in the drywall, place the trap, then seal the hole with tape, so you can take the trap out once it's done its job. If you want the mouse alive, you need to check behind the tape once a day."

I'm usually a capable person, but the thought of the great mouse hunt overwhelms me. Not the least because, while I don't mind the thought of House Mouse in the abstract, handling him is a whole other level. "We could just leave him where he is. He hasn't chewed any wires so far. I don't think a fire is likely."

"I don't mind helping."

"I don't need help."

He considers me. "We don't have to be enemies."

Why does he keep saying that?

"Couldn't we be friends?" He tries again, oblivious that he's standing next to a bucket of peonies I stole from his front garden. With his sister's help.

"No. Is that all?"

"Actually…" A frown cracks the smooth skin of his forehead. "I didn't come over to talk about the mouse. I remembered that as I knocked. I wanted to give you this." He pulls a small yellow tin from his pocket. "Handyman Balm. I noticed that your hands are cracked from the cold. It's made for people who work outside in winter."

I hide my ugly hands behind my back, but can't keep them there. I have to accept the gift. "Thanks?"

He noticed my hands, thought up a solution, and then got it for me. Why? I'm flabbergasted.

"Also," he rolls on. "I've been thinking about your museum. I have an empty building in Coatesville that used to be part of a factory complex. Brick, twenty-foot-tall ceilings, mostly open space. It's been abandoned for the past two decades. I bought it from the township for a song and dance. It's zoned industrial/commercial, but there was a plan to rezone residential. I thought I could fit a dozen condos in there."

"Why don't you just go ahead and do that?"

"The planning commission people changed their minds about the rezoning. I'm thinking that after some reno, the space might work for what you need. I already have the roof done, energy-saving windows in, and the polished cement floors finished. If you're looking for mostly open space, I wouldn't have to put in a bunch of framing for internal walls. Still needs to be painted. Wiring has to be replaced. Bathrooms could use an upgrade, but that's about it."

He's seriously just here to torture me. "I can't pay rent."

"For now, I'd be satisfied with the tax break I'd get for a community project."

"I can't afford any renovations either." *Obviously.* "You know I don't have a job."

"All right." He watches me with a sad look in his flipper eyes, then finally steps back. "Just thought I'd mention it. Let me know if you need help with that mouse."

"Thanks. But I'll take care of it." I close the door with a hard click.

I'm not helpless. I don't have any kind of helplessness. I can take care of my business myself. He's not my anything. I toss the tin of handyman balm on the counter. Who does he think he is to worry about me?

I grab my laptop and order a live trap. And I feel self-sufficient, right until I visualize the process—specifically, the end. What am I going to do with the mouse once it's in the trap?

Thank Google, I have the answer in seconds—the humane approach is to relocate House Mouse to a shed.

Scratch. Scratch. Scratch.

"Who do I know with a shed?"

Oh.

I like this plan more by the minute. My day is getting better and better.

I'm going to take care of my mouse problem.

Learned helplessness can kiss my ass.

Friday, March 17th

I DON'T SEE JOSHUA AGAIN UNTIL FRIDAY, WHEN HE COMES OVER WITH HIS SISTER.

"Aria wanted to meet you." He introduces us. "Our father is hosting a bridge party, so she came over to my house to study. I told her about your museum idea."

Aria taps the bucket outside my door with the toe

of her sneakers that are hand-painted with sunflowers. "Are these peonies? I love peonies. Where are you going to plant them?"

"Hi. Don't know yet. What degree are you studying for?" I didn't ask before.

"MBA. Ooh, nice bookshelf." She makes a beeline for my little home library. "I'm gonna be a boss bitch."

Joshua follows her. "Language."

Grumbly-older-brother-version Joshua is weird. I can relate to the sibling dynamics, but I don't want to relate to him. I prefer to think of him as a heartless flipper, the destroyer of homes and dreams.

A car pulls up the driveway, and I peek past him, surprised to see Abby. "I didn't realize my sister was coming over today."

"We'll go."

Aria, deep in my apartment, is paging through my big color books on design, showing no sign of intending to leave.

I wave Joshua in past me. "No, no. Come on inside." Then I wait for Abby, who apparently brought along Frank and David for her impromptu visit.

She walks up the steps with a white grocery bag. "I picked up all the local papers that still have employment sections. I wanted to bring them over. David popped in just as we were leaving."

The *we* part sets my teeth on edge. I don't want to see Frank.

David is right behind my sister. "I begged them to

bring me. I want to hear more about your museum idea. I'm a sucker for anything quixotic."

Then Frank steps in, carrying Bubbles in her terrarium, and I forget about everything else. "Bubbles!"

Chris's lizard shows no sign that she remembers me, but she's like that, always playing cool and unaffected. I hug the glass. If there are tears in my eyes as I walk to the windowsill and place her in the sunniest spot in the apartment, I blink them away by the time I turn, so nobody sees them.

Aria abandons the books. "You have a lizard?"

I leave them to introduce themselves to each other, because Mrs. Martinez is at the door.

"I saw Bubbles come home. I thought I'd step over and say hi." She walks to Aria at the window, blows kisses to Bubbles, then looks out. "What are those?"

"Kitchen cabinets came today." Aria's tone is too smooth, too innocent. It reminds me of Frank and Abby when they sent David and me for orange juice. The girl is up to something.

I walk over and check out my old driveway, and I'm instantly irritated. Any change across the street irritates me. I can't keep going on like this. I pull out my most neutral tone. "That's a lot of boxes."

"Joshua pulled his shoulder playing basketball," Aria reveals. "I offered to help him bring the boxes inside, but I have zero muscles. The two of us are not enough."

Aha.

"I thought you might give us a hand?" she asks.

And when I turn, every eye is on me.

Aria didn't mean this as a test, but it's clear that others think it is. Will I, with my own hands, contribute to changing the house where I used to live with Chris?

Am I moving on?

Am I over it?

Will I say yes?

I'd rather set the damn boxes on fire right there in the driveway.

"It's supposed to rain tonight." Aria neatly hammers in the final nail.

"I have a tarp," Joshua grumbles at his sister.

"We can heft those boxes in," David offers, the only one oblivious to the undertones. "No problem."

"Not me." Frank shuffles his feet. "I have a bad back."

Abby is at the door already. "I can help."

This had better not be part of a matchmaking plan.

We all walk across the street, even Mrs. Martinez.

"I haven't been inside since he's started renovations," she whispers.

"So, the museum?" Aria asks as David and Joshua lift the largest of the boxes.

"I'd like to bring art that's currently hidden, out and accessible to the public. For free."

"Ideally, it's preferred if an enterprise has income. Helps with budgeting." Aria grins.

"Something to think about," Abby immediately agrees.

They might have a point. "I mocked up the website. You can check it out at TheMuseumOfUn-seenArt.com. Right now, I have public domain images up."

Everybody looks it up on their phone.

"Pretty good."

"Great design."

"Easy to navigate."

"Wow. You're really doing this." From Abby.

"I don't have much so far." But I'm proud of myself, suddenly. "Still, it's oddly satisfying. It's something I created."

I spent the past couple of years reacting to the rocks life was throwing at me. Chris was sick, so I took care of him. He died, so I was sad. I lost the house, so I plotted to buy it back. I worked for a promotion, knowing that a promotion was never going to happen.

The museum is something different. *This* is moving forward.

"Next step is to raise money for paid ads. Right now, the best I can do is to share the link on social media, but I'm not an influencer. I don't have followers beyond family and friends."

Aria grabs one of the smaller boxes and walks to the open garage door. "You need publicity. Have any PR skills?"

I catch up to her and grab the other end. "I work in branding. I can do website design, exhibit design, and graphic design for posters. Anything like that."

"I'll volunteer my business skills."

"I could do exhibit setup." Joshua, coming back out, adds himself to the volunteer list. "I'm good with a hammer. Also, I offered Ellie the property I have in Coatesville."

Aria high-fives him as we pass him. "Love it."

We put the box in the garage. Apparently, we're not going inside.

"How do you feel about Coatesville?" Abby asks me with caution, once I'm back outside.

"I didn't want Philly anyway. Tons of museums there already. And there is precedence for a successful small-town museum right down the road. The Brandywine Museum of Art. You wrote a few grant applications for the school. Do you think…"

"I doubt it's the same."

"There must be grants for art. Maybe for art projects that bring art to children or underserved demographics?"

"I'll see." She looks at Frank, passing the imaginary baton.

"I don't know anything about grants." Frank fidgets.

I'm grateful that he doesn't offer to be the museum's accountant, because that would be seriously awkward.

Mrs. Martinez claps her hands. "Let's put on a show!" Then she shakes her head. "Never mind. You're all too young for that reference. Anyway, I could woman the ticket booth."

"Will there be tickets?" Aria asks. "If the museum is free?"

"We could do semifree." I relent. "Free during the week, then paid tickets on the weekends."

"Wish I could help." David scratches the back of his head. "But I think I'm too far for this, at Virginia Beach."

"No worries." I didn't expect any offers of assistance at all. My head is spinning with possibilities.

"About funds." Aria brings me back to earth. "Let's talk about how we can utilize our underutilized assets. Also, you need to start a nonprofit for this, but we'll talk about that later."

"I was a paralegal," Mrs. Martinez pipes up. "Before my first book got published."

I didn't even know that. "Perfect."

"Assets?" Aria redirects to money once again.

"I don't have assets. Underutilized or otherwise."

"You have a website now."

"Twelve visitors at last check."

"We could create merchandise with public domain art and pop it on TikTok." She scrolls on her phone. "I'll send you a few links so you can see what I'm talking about."

She's quickly becoming my favorite person. "I can design the merchandise. That falls into branding."

"I can create videos." Aria takes notes on her phone.

"How about books?" Joshua asks.

His sister gives him the side-eye. "Bookworm says what?"

I must look surprised, because he feels the need to

explain. "I worked for a roofer when I first got into construction. When the weather was bad, we didn't work. I got into books."

"What kind of books?"

"Anything and everything. Right now, I'm reading a novel about Vincent van Gogh's sister-in-law."

Are we reading the same book? I don't tell him, because it would sound like a weird kismet rom-com cliché. I do, however, repentantly withdraw my opinion of him being a complete barbarian. "I meant, what kind of books could we publish to raise funds?"

"The Book of Unseen Art. You're asking museums for permission to display their stored works, digitally and physically. Why not restricted publishing rights? And then ask them to carry the book in their museum stores. That way, they'll get their cut, and your museum idea gets seen."

I don't want to start liking the flipper at this late stage of the game.

"Would we need an agent to submit the idea to publishers?" I ask him when he comes back outside again after carrying in another big box with David.

"Self-publish," Mrs. Martinez suggests. "We can do paperback, hardcover, large print, international distribution, libraries, everything."

I look around. *An unemployed branding specialist, a middle school teacher, a disgraced banker and his computer nerd brother, a flipper, a college student, and a former romance author walk into a museum…*

A wave of optimism lifts me. "I don't care if until

now, only rich old men were allowed to fund museums. The Museum of Unseen Art is going to happen. We're going to break the mold."

"Technically…" Joshua lifts a hand as if we were in school. Maybe it's Abby's influence. God, he's nerdy. "The first museum was founded by a woman, Babylonian Princess Ennigaldi in the city of Ur, in the sixth century BC. She was a teacher and the human wife of their moon god. She cataloged and labeled artifacts from a millennia and a half of Mesopotamian history."

"I don't think I'm in her league."

"Everybody has to start somewhere."

"How do you know about her?"

"From a book."

Mrs. Martinez beams. I swear, if she could, she'd adopt him.

"All hail the reading addict," Aria mocks her brother.

All through this talk, boxes march one after the other into the garage, until the driveway is empty.

Joshua thanks us all individually, but Aria isn't ready to let us retreat across the street. "Would anyone like a drink?"

She gestures us toward the door at the other end of the garage, and people file past. I stay where I am. I don't want to go in. Or should I? If I don't, someone will read something into it. But before I can make up my mind, a car pulls up by the curb, an older model Chevy.

I call after Joshua. "You have a visitor. I think we should leave."

"Who? I'm not expecting a delivery." He returns and lopes past me. "Back in a sec. Let me take care of it."

I wait for him, picking up pieces of packing tape that fell off the boxes. I hate to even think it, but I've never seen the garage this clean. The flipper is freakishly neat.

"Ellie?" He's back in the garage in a blink. "Could you come outside for a minute?"

He has the same expression on his face that he wears every time he catches me sneaking around the house—a mixture of worry and reluctance to hurt me.

"What is it?"

I close the garbage can, then I have to go after him because he disappears back outside without responding.

I catch up to him by the curb, where he's standing next to a dark-haired woman about Mrs. Martinez's age. Where Mrs. Martinez is short and round—the quintessential earth mother—this woman is slender. She moves so gracefully that I wonder if once she might have been a dancer.

"This is Ellie," Joshua introduces us. "And this is Carol Card. She didn't realize you moved."

Is the woman looking for me? Why? I've never seen her in my life.

Her anxious gaze darts all over me, and she twists her hands while she measures me up, as if the end result means everything. "I'm told you were married to Chris."

That *were* kills me a little, as it does every time. "How can I help you?"

"My daughter is Alison Card."

The name doesn't ring a bell.

She drops her hands. "I'm Alison Card's mother?"

Several seconds pass before that finds a connection in my brain, plugs into a port, and starts up an old story. "Alison, Chris's high school girlfriend?"

Before I can begin to speculate why she's here, I'm distracted by movement in the car behind her. And even as I register the small silhouette in the back seat, the door opens and a boy of about ten steps out onto the pavement.

He has a pinched expression...and Chris's blue eyes and Chris's wavy, unruly hair.

He tugs on a loose lock, but doesn't tuck it behind his ear. He tugs again. "Grandma? I have to use the bathroom."

I look at the woman for explanation that I don't need. I know who the boy is. I know why they're here.

But I don't know everything.

Carol Card pales. Her hands tremble as she clasps them.

"My daughter passed away," she says.

CHAPTER TWELVE

Suzanne

1883 / Age 18

FATE DOES LOVE HER CRUEL JOKES.

I give birth at Christmas, the holiest time of the church that will never accept my child.

"Push!" the midwife demands.

I lie in the kitchen, on a jumble of blankets on the floor, so I won't soak our good mattresses with blood. The fire pops in the stove. I wish it wouldn't. I'm already hot, hot, hot.

"Now you learn your lesson." Maman sits in the farthest corner from me. She throws her anger and disappointment, and I'm grateful she doesn't throw anything else.

Until now, a child out of wedlock was a mere

thought, a bump on my figure, a future event. Now it's here. Tomorrow this time, I'll be a fille-mère. *Daughter-mother* is what people call girls like me. I'm a mother already, when I should still be just somebody's daughter. No father to make us a family.

"Ahhh." The pain of the next contraction tears through me, and my worries fall away. How foolish to worry about tomorrow when I'm not at all certain I will see the morning. I squeeze my eyes shut. The pain is crimson against my eyelids.

"Push!"

"Ahhh!" The contractions come on top of each other now. I'm granted no respite as I was at the beginning. No chance to so much as catch my breath. "Ahhh! Maman..."

She turns her head away.

The midwife presses on the rippling bulge of my belly, to no avail. "Push!"

The room spins around me. Dark creeps in at the edges of my vision.

"Push!" The woman sounds as if we're under water. "No, no. Do not faint. Push! You must..."

The pain ebbs. The kitchen disappears. I fall into the sweet relief of darkness and silence, a peaceful sea of black.

I'm dying. I'm the frog that grew too big. I burst open. This is my punishment. This is death.

It's over.

No more shame. No more hunger. No more backbreaking work. Just a sweet, warm ocean of nothing.

Until a baby cries somewhere.

Whose baby is that?

The moment I realize the child is mine is the moment I come back.

"There she is," the midwife says, kneeling between my legs.

"A girl?" I whisper the words past a throat that's sore from screaming. My body is a ball of pain. Falling from the trapeze and slamming into the ground hurt less.

"I meant you." The midwife dabs at my torn body, cleaning me up. "You're coming back to us."

Turning my head is a battle, but I win it.

Maman holds a swaddled babe by the fire, with the warmest smile I have ever seen on her face. "A fine boy."

Tears rush into my eyes.

The midwife dries my thighs. "Name?"

"Mathurin-Alexandre," Maman says. "Your grandfather." She looks at me at last. "Or Mathieu-Alexandre, your half brother."

She never talks about the son she had and lost before me, the one who died at age two, and I wish she wouldn't now—I don't want to think about babies dying.

"If only Mathieu survived," Maman sighs, "his father wouldn't have gone astray. We'd still be married. My life would have gone right."

She doesn't seem to realize that in this preferred version of her life, I wouldn't exist.

"Maurice," I tell the midwife. "He'll be Maurice

Valadon." I wish I could give him a different last name, but I can't.

I reach out my arms, and the midwife brings him over.

His curious little eyes meet mine for the first time.

I kiss his wrinkled little forehead. "How perfect you are."

I can't give him a father, but I silently swear to give him everything else. He might be born a bastard, but he wasn't born in a tenement, nor in a cramped, one-room let. We've moved again, from the center of Montmartre to the rue Poteau, a safer street and a larger apartment.

"You will have a good life," I whisper into his rose-petal little ear. "I will do *anything*, to make sure of that."

Maman rocks my Maurice and doesn't look up as she asks, "Has Renoir responded to your letter?"

I violently twist the water out of a diaper, then drop it back into the wooden basin on the table, my entire body begging for more sleep. The first light of the sun hits the window, but it doesn't reach where I'm standing. "He's sent no word."

No matter how many times I write to tell him that his son was born, he stays away. I don't have the luxury to break. I will not show anger. I will not feel despair. I am a mother.

"How can he refuse to acknowledge paternity?"

Maman snaps. "Does he know he's the only man you ever been with?"

"He knows."

"He's made you a fallen woman, and off he prances. A man like all the rest. You should have been more careful." Maman stands heavily. "I have to go to work."

The movement wakes the baby, and he starts crying.

"Shhh, shhh, shhh." Maman brings him over.

I wipe my hand on my apron. "Don't come back late."

Don't stop for wine, is what I mean.

Maman bundles up, then bustles off into the awakening dawn outside. No teetering basket this time. Past her fifth decade, and most of them spent in hard work, her back hurts too much to keep lifting heavy laundry. She's taken up cleaning nearby offices. Her pay is slim, but the money I saved from modeling still covers our bills.

"Why don't you smile for your mama? How you cry. What can be so bad?" I walk around the room with my son, stopping at the piece of paper I pinned to the wall that morning, my self-portrait in pastel. "Who's that? Is that your mama?"

Brown hair, the blue eyes that Renoir calls sapphire, and the gaze of a woman battered but unbroken. I created the piece when I first found out I was pregnant. I wanted a memory of who I was *before*, proof that I existed as something other than a fallen woman.

"Should we keep this one?" I've erased countless others, and reused the paper until it could no longer be worked. All I could see were the mistakes. *Not good enough.* But this time...

"Yes. This one, we'll keep."

This one says *I was here*. This one is part of the record, created when I feared I might die in labor. And then I almost did.

"Ee..." Maurice fusses. "Prrh."

"You won't go back to sleep no matter what I do, will you?" I sit with him and unfasten my blouse.

He feeds at my breast, then he does drift off, and I lay him gently in the middle of the bed. And as I watch his sweet little face, the drop of milk in the corner of his mouth, I understand why Maman didn't abandon me, born as I was without a father. I could never take Maurice to St. Vincent's and give him to the nuns to make arrangements.

I finish washing the tub of diapers, then I clean up the kitchen, wishing Michel were in Paris, but my best friend, Miquel Utrillo, is traveling in Belgium and Germany. Of course, our mutual acquaintances are convinced that he ran away because he is the man who made me pregnant.

Since Maurice is still sleeping, I pull out my red chalk. I draw my son's sleep-slackened face and his wispy hair. Drawing him settles me. Once I have him on the paper, he stays there like that, forever, safe. Drawing him lets me know him. The dip in his cheek is me. The tip of his chin is his father's. I draw the proof of his parentage. The lines prove that I am not a liar.

When he was born, the world closed a door on me, but I'm not alone in the walled-off compartment. There are thousands of girls like me in Paris. Are they resigned to their fate? Are they content? Where do they hide their dreams?

Do colors and shapes and empty canvases whisper to them? Do they have a voice wild and free in their heads that shouts, *You can!*

I'm so absorbed in my sketches that I don't look at the clock until Maurice wakes again. I change him and feed him. I'm cleaning him up when the door opens. Three hours have passed. Maman saunters in, the smell of wine on her breath.

"Where have you been?" I drag on my best clean dress. "You know I have to go out." I pin my hair back in order.

"I'm here, aren't I?" She keeps glancing at the door.

No, no, no. You will not leave again. I kiss my son's rosy cheeks before I hand him off. "Lock up behind me."

I turn back from the door and catch Maman staggering. "How much did you drink?"

"As much as I deserve after a mornin's hard work." She huffs "Go on, get. Don't you worry about me."

"I worry about Maurice." Even though worrying gains me nothing.

Maman sent me away, many times when I was

young, but she never gave me away, not forever. She could have taken me out to a farm and signed me up as a milkmaid, then left me behind forever. Or, as other desperate mothers have done, she could have sold me to a brothel. But no matter how poor she was, or how wretched, I always had a spot in her room, no matter where she bunked. And so, no matter how drunk she is or how loudly she yells, I won't get rid of her either.

The three of us are a family. I am going to hold my family together. I close the door and hurry on, toward two gossiping women on the corner who eye me with open disapproval.

"Either Puvis or Utrillo," one of them, a saggy-breasted matron with bowed legs, whispers as I pass.

I refuse to reveal the name of my son's father, so our new neighbors have connected me to a dozen different men. I might have moved, but rumors followed me. Gossip flies on the wings of eagles. Montmartre is but a big village. Everyone knows everyone here.

"Some drunk down the hill, more like," the other woman says, gap toothed and flat arsed.

I almost leave them be, but then I turn, offering my sweetest smile with a demure tilt of my head. "You know? I've had so many. I honestly can't remember."

Then I march on, while they twitter and stutter and tell each other how much better they are than I am.

I hurry to Puvis. I want to see him first. And then

I'll rush on to Henner's studio, and then to Forain's, then Heinlein's, and to De Nittis, and all the others.

Will they take me back? Because if not… I can't bear the thought of becoming my mother, scrubbing away other people's filth all my life, diluting my desperation with endless bottles of wine, wearing out my body and mind.

The artists must take me back.

Even if my body is rounder, softer, and my milk-filled breasts are…grotesque. Even if I am a fallen woman.

Fear fills my bones that feel hollow all of a sudden.

Will anyone want to paint me again?

1884 / Age 19

"Keep your face to the light," Zando tells me. Federico Zandomeneghi, Degas's good friend. "Stay perfectly still."

We were introduced by a countryman of his for whom I've modeled before, Giuseppe de Nittis. Zando is twenty-four years older than I am, but he's such a child at heart that neither of us feels the difference.

"Do I ever move?" I don't even move my lips as I speak.

"You are a marvel, which is why we all love you."

My modeling career, and my world with it, did

not end after all with Maurice's birth. Most of the artists have kept me on. That I am a fallen woman bothers them none. They don't expect their models to have morals.

"You never show exhaustion." Zando keeps up his compliments. Then he hesitates with a stick of azure pastel in hand. "Afterward, if you wish, you could stay and rest on the divan."

Now that I've been proven to be vulnerable to seduction, men do try their luck.

"I'd better hurry home to Maurice and Maman."

He resumes painting, and I watch the long, languid strokes he makes. I pose, but that's not all I do. I learn composition and color mixing and proportion and perspective. The men I pose for don't know it, but they're teaching me.

"The face, the curves, the stamina." Zando brings the fingertips of his free hand together and kisses them. "This is why we all love you, Maria."

He is a hopeless flirt—he might be older than me, but he's still in his early forties—yet I can never be angry at him. It's in his blood. He's Italian.

He often uses pastels, which allows me to learn more about this medium. I watch him as closely as he watches me. It's a fair trade-off.

He began the current piece at La Nouvelle Athènes, the brasserie that replaced the Guerbois in the Impressionists' affections of late, becoming their new favorite café. He has me dressed in a patterned pink-blue dress—he uses the typical colors of Venetians—with a large white bow around my neck and a black hat with flowers that matches the dress. He's building up the image here in his studio. Fewer interruptions. Also, the lighting is considerably better.

"Did I tell you that the Académie des Beaux-Arts rejected Seurat's *Bathers at Asnières* for this year's Salon?" Zando smudges the pastel into the paper with a few brief movements. He doesn't overblend, just enough to give his works a sense of delicacy and melancholy. "Seurat has sworn revenge."

"Will he challenge the jury to a duel?" This, I would stand in line to see.

"Better. He's gone off and founded his own group. The Groupe des Artistes Indépendants. No prizes. No jury." He sounds positively scandalized. "Just art."

"We'll see how far he gets with that."

"Sticking up for the old guard?" A dark eyebrow rises. "Surprisingly conventional of you, Maria."

"I will be at the Salon," I remind him. "Puvis's *The Sacred Grove, Beloved of the Arts and Muses* was selected by the jury." I'd like to think the acceptance has something to do with my excellent posing. I'm just about every figure in the imaginary landscape. "I am Thalia and Clio and Calliope and all the other muses."

"He does know how to squeeze every last line out of his models."

"We were just talking about Seurat the other day." Their studios are near each other. "Puvis told me Seurat is working on another colossal piece, *A Sunday*

Afternoon on the Island of La Grande Jatte. Maybe he'll have more luck with his new creation."

"La Grande Jatte? Good fortune to him with that. He's more likely to court controversy. The island had another police raid yesterday."

"I'm not surprised." Of late, the place turned into a haven for prostitutes trolling for clients, and for people having affairs.

"I've heard gossip..." Zando stands back to examine his composition. "That you returned to Renoir to pose for a significant new work."

"He begged me to return." Renoir still refuses to see Maurice, but he *is* the best painter I know. I am Paris's best model. We should be together. "I am posing for his *Bathers*."

"Hmmm." The sound carries a world of meaning. "Toulouse-Lautrec is looking for a model. Have you ever posed for him?"

"I only know him by sight." He was a frequent visitor at the Cirque Molier. "He knows some people I know." We've sat at the same tables at the cafés before. He's great friends with Cézanne, Gauguin, and Seurat. "He's an odd little man."

"Aren't all aristocrats?" Zando dashes off a few more lines. "He told me he studied under Léon Bonnat."

"His father could afford it."

"His father could have cast him aside. The comte is a fearless horseman and a gourmand of food and women. It couldn't have been easy for a nobleman to accept a son like Henri. Plenty of aristocratic families still hide away their cripples."

"Is it true that he broke both legs while still in school, and he stopped growing?" The moment I plummeted from the trapeze and hit the ground flashes back. The memory fills me with cold, and also with sympathy for Lautrec.

Zando blends again. "Would you sit for him?"

"I could. I'm almost finished with Puvis."

"I'll take you to meet Henri, but only if you promise you won't put him before me."

I hold my pose. "Wouldn't dream of it."

"I'll need a guarantee, just the same." Zando's eyes glint. "I'd like to keep you close. How do you feel about moving into this building?"

He lives on one of Montmartre's most expensive streets. "I don't have the physique for highway robbery."

"Your physique is perfect, dear Maria." He switches on the Italian charm. "A three-room apartment on the bottom floor is empty."

My heart yearns. "Does Toulouse-Lautrec pay in gold?"

Zando picks at the upper right corner of his canvas. "I've talked to the landlord."

Has he? "What the man would want for the rooms, I wouldn't want to give."

"I negotiated the rent down to a third." He sounds indescribably pleased.

"And I still don't have that much money."

"I'll help you with what you're missing."

I nearly move my head to stare at him. "Why?"

"Because we are friends. And I can. And, as I said, I'd like to keep you nearby. I am planning a number of significant works. I can't leave all the large canvases to Renoir and Puvis."

Three rooms. Two could be bedrooms. One for me and Maurice, and one for Maman. I could paint in the third. All I'd need are an easel and a desk... Unexpected possibilities spin in my head like exuberant circus acrobats.

Then there's the dark side. "Everyone would claim we're lovers."

"Nobody would have to know about our arrangement."

"They'll know I can't afford an apartment in this building. They'll know somebody is keeping me."

"We'll stay silent and let them guess." He waits for my response with a giddy little grin. Like most of Montmartre's artists, he loves to make trouble. Easy for him. For a man to lose his reputation, at the very least, he'd have to commit murder. Not so for a woman.

A room in which to paint.

The thought won't release me. And, in truth, what reputation do I have left to protect?

I don't smile, because I'm posing and I'm a professional, but I do say, without moving my lips, "Yes."

"Let the rumor mills turn and flap their sails." Zando could not be more pleased. He salutes me with his stick of pastel.

He'll ignore the grinding gossip more easily than I, but I will stand against the new storm of accusations for Maurice. I have an overriding need, a deep desire that borders on obsession, to take my son as far from the tenements as I can. I want the tenements so far behind us that when we step out of our building, we won't be able to see them. "I will pay as much as I am able. I will take on more modeling. I will sit for Toulouse-Lautrec."

I imagine the future. Maman and Maurice and I, in a truly respectable neighborhood, on the rue Tourlaque.

Our bad days are over.

Here comes the life I've always dreamed of.

1885 / Age 19

Henri Marie Raymond de Toulouse-Lautrec-Monfa is shorter than I am, but just barely, which I can tell he likes. He likes everyone who's short. At the circus, his favorites were the dwarves.

He is about my age, a comte like his father, part of the nobility. He stands about halfway up the ladder of the hierarchy, higher than a baron and a vicomte, but not as high as a marquis. He has stubby fingers, lips too voluptuous for a man, and a flat nose. If he didn't have a beard, one might mistake him for a boy. He has no beauty in him, except for his lively brown eyes that meet mine with interest.

"I have such plans for you, my stunning Maria." He rubs his hands together.

"They'd best be professional."

I haven't been completely honest with Zando. I don't merely know Toulouse-Lautrec by sight. I also know him by reputation. He has a famed affinity for the bottle and the brothel. The prostitutes on rue d'Amboise call him the little *teapot with the big spout.* His saving grace, in my eyes, is that he's a talented artist. His father paid for him to study under Léon Bonnat. Currently, he's studying with Fernand Cormon. And from now on, without knowing, he will be teaching me. It's an arrangement that suits me, even if his studio leaves much to be desired. His dusty and cluttered workspace makes me wish for the spotless order of Puvis's place.

"You may trust me entirely." He speaks with a lisp.

"Not entirely, entirely," Zando warns, his words punctuated by a howl from the winter winds that sweep by the window.

Zando was supposed to bring me by in the fall, but other work proliferated, so we are in the new year. "What do you think of this?" Toulouse-Lautrec leads me to an unframed painting, leaning on his cane. "Do you like it?"

The work is a parody of Puvis's *The Grove*, for which I was the main model. Instead of my own figure, Toulouse-Lautrec put his friends in the grove. He is there too, with his back to the viewer, in a stance that... *Is he urinating on the ground?*

He watches me to see if I'm offended.

I laugh. "Best not to tell poor Puvis. He is a good man, but he is a vain man."

"There's a reason some call him the Peacock behind his back." Toulouse-Lautrec snorts, and then he nods, as if I passed a test. "Let me see." He examines my face and body. "Perfect."

I strike a pose.

He glows with approval. "Exactly what I need. I only wish you'd come sooner. I am working on a number of new pieces. Aristide Bruant is opening his own cabaret, Le Mirliton. He'll take the building over from Salis. Salis is moving Le Chat Noir to the rue de Laval, into larger accommodations." He rocks to the balls of his feet to make himself an inch taller. "Bruant invited me to exhibit at his cabaret once it's open."

"Bruant?" I know him from Le Chat Noir where he used to sing and perform comedy in his high boots, red shirt, and black velvet jacket—a sight fit to paint—twirling his long red scarf as he sang. "Good for him."

Toulouse-Lautrec doesn't respond. He's grabbed a sketchbook, and he already has his pencil in hand.

"Then there's just the matter of the sitting fee, Monsieur." I bring money up sweetly.

Zando snickers behind me.

Toulouse-Lautrec barely looks up. "A hundred francs per sitting. Call me Henri."

I breathe in the number and it fills me up, feels like bread filling my stomach. "Thank you, Henri."

I make room for him in my schedule, and we fall into a routine. Henri sketches me and completes a number of studies. When we graduate to oil on canvas, he gifts me with a purple dress and a fancy hat. This too I accept. I work hard. I deserve everything I get.

He's thoughtful and kind. We work through the rest of winter and then through the early spring. When the weather turns warmer, he suggests that we work outside.

For a moment, I think of the shed in Renoir's garden, then I lock away the past. I haven't seen him in a while. He's been painting Aline again. "Where?"

"In the garden of Monsieur Forest." Henri looks at me as if he's already seeing a nymph. "On the corner of boulevard de Clichy and rue Caulaincourt."

"At the archery grounds? Why there?"

"It's green, and it's close by."

"They say Degas despises painting *en plein air*."

"The old goat has too many eccentricities to count. The fresh air invigorates me."

Henri speaks the truth. We spend week after week outside, and he paints and he paints.

"I feel as Adam must have felt when he had to leave the Garden of Eden," he tells me during our last open-air session. Then he laughs, switching from melancholy to joy in the blink of an eye.

I'm drawn to his hunger for life, to his free spirit. I am mesmerized by his talent, but I will not repeat the mistake I made with Renoir.

"I want to extend our arrangement," he suddenly says. "You must agree."

"I will be sitting for Puvis next week. And Henner too wants to see me."

"How the old men love to have your young body on display. You should call yourself Suzanne."

I wait for explanation.

"I thought the nuns taught you," he taunts. He loves showing off his education. "Susanna and the Elders, the story from the Bible. Didn't you learn about her in school?"

"I don't remember Susanna. All I cared about was Villon. Although, I didn't mind La Fontaine."

A salacious smile takes over Henri's face. "Susanna, a virtuous wife, takes a bath in her garden, and two old men spy on her."

"I assure you, the nuns didn't mention a single Bible story that involved naked women."

He laughs. "Artemisia Gentileschi painted the scene a few hundred years ago. Very baroque."

"Artemisia? A female artist?"

"Italian. How you would have loved her. The first woman to become a member of the Accademia delle Arti del Disegno in Florence."

"She was a famous artist?"

"Started out in the style of Caravaggio, then improved past the master. It's worth a trip to Italy just to see her paintings."

My heart beats faster. "Do you think women can be great artists?"

"Why couldn't they?"

"Degas thinks women should be banned from art, as they can never produce anything of value." He is a misogynist to the point of being a sworn celibate and dislikes female artists in particular.

"Artemisia Gentileschi certainly was brilliant." Henri dismisses the great Degas. "And you've met Berthe Morisot and Mary Cassatt. Morisot painted you, if I'm not mistaken."

"Do you think a woman could ever be accepted to the Société Nationale des Beaux-Arts?"

"No. I can't even imagine a woman ever having the temerity of applying—" Then his eyes liven. "Unless it's you, of course, my fearless Suzanne."

"Mmm."

He picks up his brush again, but doesn't touch the canvas. "Suzanne? Are you hiding something from me? Are you, by chance, an artist in secret?"

"And if I were?"

"I would wish to see your work." The response is immediate, said without a hint of mockery.

"You have too sharp a tongue. I am not certain that I could stand ridicule." I care not about the opinion of others, but if Henri called me a talentless hack, the words would eviscerate.

And yet…

I *must* dare.

"All right. I will bring you a few pieces."

Life gives you nothing. Whatever you want, you have to be prepared to take it. I *will* put my heart on the chopping block and allow Henri to dissect it.

• • •

I WILL NOT BEG.

I will not ask how Henri liked the drawings I left with him the last time. I hold my pose in the studio that's filled with the scent of turpentine and paint. Outside, rain-filled clouds threaten to ruin the light.

Henri paints in silence, a rarity. Swish, swish, swish, the brush glides across the canvas, creating a vibrant image conjured up by his restless brain. An eternity passes before he looks up. "Victor Hugo died. Have you heard? The world has lost one of its greats."

Ah, that explains his solemnity. For the first time ever, I lose my pose. My nakedness feels awkward suddenly, as if we are at the funeral already. "May we have a break?"

"A moment." Two more strokes of the brush, and he's finished.

I hide in my robe, a voluptuous red-sateen wonder that Henri procured for me. "I loved *Les Misérables*."

"I prefer *The Hunchback of Notre-Dame*, a beauty falling in love with the disfigured monster." He strides over with that uneven gait of his. And then he waits until he has my full attention. "Could you love a monster, Suzanne?"

He will not give up on his nickname for me. But while the name is a joke, the longing in his voice is so sincere that it draws tears to my eyes.

His stature, his lisp, his looks cease to matter. In art, he is a giant. He also has a giant heart. Of course, I could love him.

We embrace, and we cling to each other for a minute, in shared grief.

A brisk nod, a deep breath, then Henri recovers and steps away. "Have you read the books I gave you?"

"A chapter a night, after Maman and Maurice are asleep."

He's decided that my exposure to literature and philosophy must go beyond La Fontaine's fables and Villon's poetry. He's given me his volumes of Nietzsche and Baudelaire. And while at school I loathed learning, these days my mind is hungry. I like what Henri feeds me.

Who else would look at a fatherless girl from the countryside, a nobody from the tenements, and think I was ready for Nietzsche and Baudelaire? Only Henri.

"What do you think of the books?" he asks.

"I like Baudelaire." Enough to learn a few lines, even. *"Swan-white of heart, a sphinx no mortal knows, My throne is in the heaven's azure deep; I hate all movements that disturb my pose, I smile not ever, neither do I weep."*

"And Nietzsche?"

"I was about to say...but I like Nietzsche more."

"I thought you might."

"He says we must craft our own identity. He thinks hardship forms character. What doesn't kill us makes us stronger."

"You are the strongest woman I know, my brave Suzanne."

I've been lusted after, I've been flattered, but I don't think I've ever been sincerely admired. Henri sees more in me than all the others. He sees more in me than even I see. I want to be the Suzanne that Henri Toulouse-Lautrec believes I am capable of being.

The thought is deep enough to send me into nervous laughter. "I would have settled for a little less character and a slightly easier life."

"Montmartre's artists are begging for your favor. I predict your life will be easier going forward. Your beauty slays us all. You are the most beautiful woman I know. Certainly, the most beautiful who's ever given me the time of day." His laugh is self-deprecating. "We truly are the Beauty and the Beast."

"You do have a splendid library."

Henri steps back to me and caresses my arms. "I think I'm falling in love with you, Suzanne."

The words catch my heart in a net. Maybe it's a foolish frivolity—I have a safe place to live, food, clothes—but I also want to be loved, and Henri offers exactly that. The offer is irresistible.

"I showed your pieces to Gauzi," he tells me.

The air leaves my lungs and refuses to return. François *Gauzi* is his friend, a respected artist, also from Toulouse. "And?"

Henri's eyes glint with mischief. "I didn't tell him whose work they were."

I wait.

"Gauzi called your lines delicate and your vision sensitive."

The burst of joy is like the first strong sunshine that breaks the ice on the Seine in the spring. I'm more than a washerwoman's daughter. Maybe the colors and shapes I crave could be mine. Maybe, just maybe, I have talent. "And you? What do you think?"

"In your red chalk drawing of Maurice, the sweetness of the boy comes through so clearly. The mother's love radiates from every line. There's life in your work." Henri spares no praise. He's as dramatic as a circus ringmaster when he pronounces, "Suzanne Valadon, you are an artist. You are an artist, and you will be acknowledged as one," he promises. "You will be accepted and respected. And I will love you and support you. Do you believe me, my Suzanne?"

Lost in a dream, I kiss his cheek. "I do."

I can see my future, and it's nothing but happiness.

CHAPTER THIRTEEN

Ellie

Friday, March 17th

CHRIS HAS A CHILD, A SON.

A TEN-YEAR-OLD BOY WHO HAS CHRIS'S FACE IS WALKING TOWARD ME.

Mrs. Card looks to Joshua, then back to me, then past my shoulder.

"I forgot to take my pills before I came over." Mrs. Martinez walks out of the garage behind us. "I have to pop back home. Ellie? Is everything all right?"

All right? Nothing is even real. I'm in an alternate universe.

"I can't hold it." The boy tugs his hair again. "I have to go to the bathroom."

His grandmother pats him on the shoulder. Her

smile wobbles. "You were supposed to stay in the car, Sam."

I'm immobile. Abby and Frank and David are inside the house behind us. My brain shorts out at the thought of the boy and his grandmother going in there.

Mrs. Martinez saves me. "Come along, young man. We'll go across the street. This house is under renovation."

I stand there, numb. When Joshua touches my arm, I barely even feel it.

"I'll go and keep everyone inside." He backs away. "I'll give them the grand tour. Take your time."

And then it's just me and Chris's son's grandmother, Carol Card.

"Why now?" The question is not the most important one, but it's the one that elbows all others out of the way to fly out of my mouth first.

"Alison didn't tell us. She went off to college in California and came home for fall break pregnant. A one-night stand is what she said. She returned to school and had the baby there, early. She told us he was premature." Mrs. Card is talking fast, as if she hadn't told her grandson why they were here, and she wants to get most of the story out before he comes back.

"How did you discover the truth?" I ask the next question that pops into my head. I can't organize my thoughts.

"Alison died of complications from Covid. She was a nurse. She caught the worst strain, right at the beginning." The memories etch the woman's face with pain. "Sam's grandfather and I had him until now, but... My husband suffers from Alzheimer's." She rushes over the words as if she's running over hot coals barefoot. "An Alzheimer's care facility is out of our reach financially. I'm going to go into regular assisted care with him, and I'll take care of him. I'll watch to make sure he doesn't wander off, and I'll keep reminding him of things. It's the best plan I can come up with."

"Chris passed away too," I say on autopilot. "Last year. Cancer."

"Joshua said." She wrings her hands. "I'm so sorry for your loss."

"How did you find out that Chris was the father?"

"On a lark, I had Sam do one of those ancestor-finder DNA online things and the results just came in. Chris's name came up as a 50% match. I should have known. As soon as I saw it, I could see Chris in Sam. Is it strange that before that, all I could see was my daughter?"

"All my childhood, my father's family always insisted that my sister and I looked like my father. My mother's family always insisted that we looked like my mother." I hear how inane I sound, and I stop prattling. The boy's results must have been entered into the online database just after I checked Chris's family tree.

"If we found his father sooner..." A soft smile makes a cautious appearance on Mrs. Card's face.

"You would have been his stepmother. I worried about that. What kind of woman Chris might have married, if he married."

What am I supposed to say to that? This is a situation for which I am wholly unprepared.

"It's all right." Mrs. Card steps toward the street. "Sam can go live with my sister. I'd better go and find him."

I follow her. I want to see Chris again in the boy's face. I need to see him to reassure myself that this is all real.

Chris's son is sitting at Mrs. Martinez's kitchen table with a chocolate chip cookie and a glass of milk. I believe his story, then I'm skeptical, then I believe it again.

The scent of herbs fills the air, dry bunches hanging everywhere. Fresh herbs sit in colorful Mexican pots on the windowsills: rosemary, basil, thyme, chives, and a small pepper plant with resplendent red peppers. In another window, one long window box holds a single tomato plant—my landlady's pride and joy—that's been flowering and producing all winter. She calls it Lupe. At least she doesn't name the individual tomatoes. I'm not sure I could eat them.

Above the stove hangs an antique crucifix. There are two more just in her kitchen, but she's an equal opportunity spiritualist. She has an Earth Mother woodcarving on the back porch, and a Buddha in her garden.

The familiar surroundings settle me down, as

much as possible.

"Aren't the cookies great?" I ask Sam.

"I hope you don't mind." Mrs. Martinez smiles at the woman next to me. "I asked, and Sam told me he isn't allergic to anything. Would you like some?" She offers us the tray.

Friday, March 17th

I'M STILL UP AT MIDNIGHT. I CAN'T FALL ASLEEP. AND I WON'T AS LONG AS I KEEP THINKING ABOUT CHRIS'S SON. I looked up the DNA database. Sam is now, indeed, linked to Chris—a fifty-percent match. Exactly half of his DNA comes from Chris.

I need a distraction. I open my laptop and read some more about Suzanne Valadon. I found her because of work, then I got interested in her because I thought she might be connected to Chris. And now I just like her, for the woman she was, for her spirit. I read until my laptop runs out of battery.

Sadly, I'm still not sleepy.

I get up. Lights on. Might as well check on the mousetrap I put in the wall earlier.

Dishwashing gloves on, I peel off the duct tape, inch by careful inch. I'm not going to worry about the hole right now. In the spirit of becoming a self-sufficient woman, I watched half a dozen YouTube videos on drywall repair before I went to bed.

I reach in, and I pull out the trap.

"Oh wow."

There are two: one round, one skinny. Mister and Missus, I think. I don't know which is which. Obviously, I'm not checking.

I'm not keeping them until morning either. They're running around in the see-through acrylic tube, frantic, their little eyes begging me to set them free.

"Okay, okay, okay."

Boots. Coat. I grab a small chunk of blue cheese that has gone a little too blue, and slip it into my pocket, secured in plastic wrap. Then I pick up Mr. and Mrs. House Mouse again, and I sneak them over to Joshua's shed.

I no longer consider him my enemy, but the asparagus cries out for revenge. After this, we're even.

As a strategy to distract myself from obsessively thinking about Chris's son, the adventure fails. I can't not think about him.

What would have happened if Alison told Chris about the baby?

Would they have gotten married?

Would Chris have gotten a job instead of going to college?

If anything, I'm distracted by the million unanswered questions from what I'm doing.

Mouse relocation is so not a business I should be in.

My shivers have goose bumps. Or my goose

bumps have shivers? Either way, I'm ready to jump out of my skin.

The shed is decent, about twelve feet by twenty-four feet, Amish made, filled with reno equipment for the most part. The orderliness is commendable. The fresh scent of lumber is nice, but none of that makes me relax.

Do it and get out.

"Lots more room in the shed than in my back wall," I say to entice the mice, releasing them from the tube with shaking hands. And then I toss the chunk of cheese after them, because I want them to be running *away* from me. "A housewarming gift."

They ignore my offering and disappear under a stack of two-by-fours before I can blink.

For once, I don't get caught.

Must be a day for miracles.

I should buy a lottery ticket.

Sunday, March 19th

"What do you mean Chris has a son? It's a scam. Chris would never cheat. That man worshipped the ground you walked on."

Grace and I FaceTime Sunday morning. I sent her a quick text, in shock. She immediately called me from LA.

I explain the full story: the grandmother, and how I knew about Alison before all this, how she died.

"Oh," Grace says on the other end. "Sorry. Wow. I did not see this coming. How do you feel?"

"Disoriented. When Sam makes the exact expression Chris used to make…"

"I wish I were there."

"Me too."

"One more week."

We only talk another minute. I have to hang up, because Abby is calling.

"I need more information for the grant applications. And we should talk anyway. How about just the two of us? Could we meet and grab something to eat?"

Olive branch extended and accepted.

"How about Philly? I'm going to the Barnes." I need more artwork. "I finally got a face-to-face appointment with a curator." I suggest a French restaurant, to keep with my Valadon theme.

"I've always wanted to see that place. All right. I'll meet you there." Abby signs off with "Drive safe."

Le Papillon is a step above a café, surprisingly affordable for a place right next to City Hall. The interior is quintessential 19th century Paris. My sister and I stroll through the glass doors just as the lunch crowd is clearing out, and we're immediately shown to a table. The air is redolent with the scent of vanilla and powdered sugar—they have a formidable pastry case.

We're basically sitting inside one of the many paintings of cafés painted by the Impressionists. As far as brand consistency goes, they get an A. After all I've read about Valadon, I half expect her to stroll in on Toulouse-Lautrec's arm. I'm tempted to ask the waiter if they serve absinthe. Except, the waiter isn't coming just yet, and Abby is looking at me as if she's expecting me to speak.

So, Chris had a son.

I picture what Abby's face would look like in response to those words.

Not yet.

I want to deal with Carol Card's news first on my own. I don't need to invite guests to my freak-out party. Also, I say nothing, because if I told my sister that Chris had a son, I would also have to tell her that I am not the woman I thought I was. That's another realization in need of processing.

I feel sorry for the boy, but I also feel a tremendous amount of jealousy. Alison Card got a priceless gift that should have gone to me.

Chris's son has Chris's eyes and Alison's smile. Chris's son should have Chris's eyes, and his smile should be mine. Cancer stole Chris from me, and it stole our children. I've been dealing with that. But that fate would give Chris's son to someone else...

I shove Friday's startling revelation as deep as I can so I don't howl with outrage at the unfairness.

Abby adjusts her tidy ponytail. "You were weird toward Frank on Friday."

I was weird toward everyone. After Sam and his grandmother left and I'd gone upstairs with Abby and Frank and David, who'd all finished their grand tour of Joshua's reno job by that point, my thoughts wouldn't click back into the game. "I was distracted."

"I'm sorry Chris died." My sister's voice softens. "You are alone, and I have Frank. I'm not saying you're jealous, but could you just, please, lay off him? He's tried to be a father to you. I know he's not perfect. I know he's never going to be Dad, but—"

"I never asked him to step in for Dad." *Chris was a father and he never even knew it.* "I think it's bizarre that he pretends."

"You needed a father."

"I needed *my* father."

"Then why have you always refused to talk about him? And Mom. I know you were there when they died and I wasn't, but it's not your own private tragedy. I lost them too. They were also my parents."

"I don't want to talk about it."

"You never do. You never have. It's not healthy."

And she keeps pushing.

So then I push back.

Too much has happened lately. Whatever energy I've been using all this time to hold up the walls I've built around my parents' accident has been used up elsewhere. The walls come down. "I don't think Dad was perfect."

"He was a great father. He adored us. He taught you how to ride a bike. He carried you around on his shoulders."

"Dad was having an affair."

No, no, no. I immediately want to tell Abby it's not

220

true. I want to take it back. But the only sound I manage is a horrified gasp that echoes my sister's.

She presses her back against her chair, moving as far from me as she can. "Why would you make up something like that?"

"I heard them talk about it." The ice cracks wide open on the frozen river of my two decades of silence to reveal the dark depths. "They thought I was asleep in the back seat. Their fighting woke me up." In a blink, I'm right back there again, the streetlights zooming by in the night, the rain, the whoosh-whoosh of the wiper blades. "I used to hate when they fought. I pretended that I was still asleep so I wouldn't have to deal with it."

"You misunderstood something."

"Mom said, *If you don't stop screwing around with Jill, I'm leaving you, Eric.*"

"Who the hell is Jill?"

"I got the impression she was somebody at church."

"Mrs. Summer? Jillian Summer?"

"Maybe not. I don't know. Could have been somebody at work."

"I don't believe you."

All for the better?

Abby pushes her chair back, then she decides against leaving, and she pulls up to the table again. "And how did Dad respond in this little imaginary story of yours?"

"He didn't get the chance. Mom smacked him with her purse, and he swerved into oncoming traffic. I remember horns blowing. Then I woke up in the hospital."

I've carried this secret for close to two decades, each word a rock, filling my chest cavity. Yet when they're all out, I don't feel any lighter. I haven't removed a burden. I cloned it and dumped the clone on my sister.

"I'm sorry."

Abby holds up her hand, palm out. "Don't..." Her eyes throw hot sparks of resentment. A muscle ticks in her face as she clenches her teeth. She shoves her chair back again, and this time, she stands. "I know this is some kind of cry for help, Ellie, but it's too much. I'm not going to forgive you for this. I know you lost Chris, but it's been a year. Deal with your grief already. It's making you crazy."

We've fought a lot over the years, sisters do, but as I watch Abby hurry away, I'm not sure this time she's going to forgive me.

I shouldn't have told her. Dammit. I shouldn't have said it.

I drive home, mentally kicking myself the whole way. Now that it all blew up, I can think of a dozen better ways I could have had this conversation with my sister.

I'll fix this. I just need a break. My brain is tired. My heart is exhausted. I need to spend the rest of Sunday on the couch with Bubbles, watching the latest, endless series on Netflix. I want to get lost in drama that has nothing to do with me.

I settle in, but Carol Card calls before I can pick something.

"Sam has a lot of questions about his father. I only saw Chris when he used to come by to pick up Alison for dates. We barely talked. He was at that awkward teenage-boy stage. I don't know that much about him. Do you think we could come by again? Could you answer some questions for Sam?"

CHAPTER FOURTEEN

Suzanne

1887 / Age 22

"HOW HAVE YOU BEEN?" RENOIR INQUIRES, BUT HE
DOES NOT ASK ABOUT HIS SON.

Ask if he's a good little boy.

"Left elbow higher."

I adjust. *Ask if he's healthy.*

"Fingers elongated," Renoir instructs.

Ask if he's happy.

Renoir is the artist at his easel, I am the model on
the garden bench. We are our professional selves. We
play our roles. If he feels guilty, if he has regrets, he
doesn't show it. I don't show that he's breaking my
heart all over again.

Renoir was my sun, the famous artist, man of the

world, older, wiser, infinitely more skilled. He was everything to me. To him, I was an object to paint, no more than flowers in a vase.

He lays down his brush and strides over, tugs down the shoulders of my white chemise to reveal more of my breasts that fed our child.

"Just so…" For a heartbeat, he hesitates. His eyes hold mine. For a blink, I imagine us teetering on a high ledge, on the verge of tumbling headfirst into the past.

Sanity prevails.

He returns to his canvas.

I hold my pose, my hands up, frozen in the process of braiding my hair. My nose itches. I ignore it. At his instruction, I am caked in makeup. I don't know if it's to make me look younger or to make me look like someone else.

"I've missed you." His brush flies across the canvas without pause.

Best to stay on the professional path. "You should call the piece *Suzanne Braiding Her Hair*."

"*Girl Braiding Her Hair*." He leaves the truth unsaid, that Aline would fly into a rage, if Renoir named me in the title.

"*Girl, Braiding Her Hair*," I agree, because it'd be senseless to insist.

We have this much: the memory of our affair, the friendship that remains, and the love of art that sustains us both.

He watches me as he paints.

I watch him, and in his face, I see my son's face.

I could rage at him. I could rage at fate. I could wish for a different life, but what difference would it make?

I survived the siege, I survived starvation, I survived countless beatings. I will survive this man.

I can't change the past, but... The present moment is mine to mold. And the future grows from the present.

I'M LATE TO HENRI'S PARTY, AT WHICH I AM THE HOSTESS.

We've become lovers. In truth, I am his wife already, in everything but name. For the past year, he's been renting a fourth-floor studio in my building on the rue Tourlaque. He moved to be closer to me and Maurice. My son adores him.

I'm late, and yet I stay in the armchair in the corner of our room and draw as Maurice sleeps in our bed. He is three years old. He'll never be this sweet again, this innocent. His hair is disheveled. A fain sheen of sweat glistens on his forehead, a single drop of drool in the corner of his lips. From time to time, he smiles. He is having a good dream.

This is what I want to capture, to save for posterity. That my son is not dreaming of a cold room, or an empty cupboard. He is not searching for bread. He is not having a nightmare.

I love his face, but behind his face, on the paper, I see the ghost image of a mother who didn't give up.

And it matters not that nobody else will know this but me.

My charcoal flies over the paper. One more line. One more fix.

Perfect.

I stash the drawing on the high shelf, then run.

"I might not be back until morning," I tell Maman, in her bed already with her door ajar.

"Tell him to marry you, and then you could move in together." She harrumphs.

Out the front door and up the stairs I run, my feet carried by the joy of creation, my pleasure and satisfaction with the drawing. I knock on Henri's door with what must be an embarrassingly wide smile on my face, but if anyone can understand what I'm feeling, it's another artist.

"You've been seen at Renoir's studio." A dark cloud hangs over Henri as he lets me in. "You've been sitting for him again." Petulance turns down the corners of his mouth one second, anger snaps his lips straight the next.

"I am a model, *mon chéri*."

"Have you climbed back into his bed?"

"Play the fool twice? No, thank you."

Henri grunts and believes not a word. I can tell by the way he angles his body away from me.

"I've been to his studio," he says. "I saw *The Braid*."

Not *Suzanne Braiding Her Hair* then, and not even *Girl Braiding Her Hair*. I'm not surprised at being thoroughly removed. "I haven't seen it finished. Is it any good?"

"You are..." He uses his hands to indicate a voluptuous torso. "Falling out of your clothes. And he painted you younger. The way you were when he met you. Henri's left eyebrow slants up. "When he fell in love with you."

Oh, never call it love. Renoir loved me so much, he cast me aside, along with our child. A woman could live without love like *that*.

"The painting has nothing to do with me. He is always trying to capture the eternal woman. I pose for him, because he pays well. I can't afford to turn down work, not with what it costs to rent here. Not all of us receive allowances from our noble fathers."

"You have been going to Renoir all along." Henri ignores my small dig. "I had a chance to look more closely at *The Large Bathers*."

"Didn't Renoir tell you the model was his mistress, Aline?" That's what he tells everyone, *especially* Aline.

"I've painted you enough to know your lines. You are in all three figures. It should be called The Three Marias. And then there were *Woman with a Fan*, and *Young Woman with a Swan*."

"I don't want to quarrel." I hold my arms out to Henri. "We're lucky to have each other." He and I are the same age, have the same obsession with art, move in the same circles. We are good for each other. "Am I not always here when you need me?"

"I never know where to find you. You are exasperating."

I drop my arms. "I have to work as much as I can to keep my family clothed and fed."

He bustles. "I'll forgive you if you take off that hideous dress." He leads me to the small side room where white silk waits folded over the back of a chair, and his bad mood vanishes. When he says, "Tonight, you'll be my Cleopatra," his eyes sparkle.

"Tonight's gathering is a costume party? Where is Gauzi?" Now that he moved to a nearby studio on the rue Tourlaque, he's almost always here.

"He's run out for more absinthe. Everybody is coming. The Van Gogh brothers will be here, both Theo and Vincent. You must talk to Vincent van Gogh. You have to see his new work."

"Has he been painting a lot?" I present my back. "Unbutton me, please."

"How you tease, Suzanne." He stumbles on the buttons, but does manage after another second of struggle. When the dress parts, he caresses my skin. "My Cleopatra, my queen."

I step away, noting the time on the clock on the wall. "The guests are coming up the stairs."

"I wager they would prefer to see you naked." He hands me the white dress with its turquoise beaded collar, revealing another white costume under it. "And, yes, Vincent has been working like a fiend. He's produced a hundred pieces of art since he came to Paris last year."

Admiration and jealousy pair up to dance the bourrée inside me.

"So many?" Of course, he's a bachelor, supported by his brother. He has no family to take care of. Most of my time must go to Maman and Maurice and modeling.

"He thinks the pace will help him improve. Now, assist me." Henri sheds his trousers. "The toga is mine." He sits.

I pull his shirt over his head, then I grace the warm skin of his shoulder with a kiss. I like it that we belong to each other. With him, I don't have to act as if we're merely friends, in public.

In two minutes, he's Caesar, a golden laurel wreath he must have borrowed from a theater crowning his dark hair. I don't ask why not Mark Anthony. The short army uniform of the ancient Romans would reveal his deformed legs. The long lines of the toga make him appear taller, and the laurel wreath adds another inch.

He glances at the table next to me, at the open folder of drawings I brought by a few days ago for his opinion. "You've begun to sign your work. *Suzanne.*"

"Marie-Clémentine from the tenement is long gone, dead." Poor, hungry, little bastard. "And Maria is a model."

"Yes." He shuffles through the pages with care. "A woman reborn. A phoenix risen." He pauses on my latest self-portrait. "*Suzanne Valadon.* Perfect for the title of my portrait of you."

While I've been drawing myself at home, he's been painting me here, an ephemeral study that makes me appear more noble and beautiful than I am. And mysterious. And somber. And grand.

This is what made me fall in love with Henri, in the end: not that he is an educated man, an aristocrat, not even that he's a brilliant artist, but that he sees me. He sees inside me. He always had.

The first piece he painted of me, the year after Maurice's birth, he could have called *Fat Nude*. Instead, he called it *Fat Maria*. He named me even then. He meant to be jokingly mocking with the adjective, but I didn't mind. Nobody who lived through the siege could ever be troubled by gaining weight.

He sets the folder down. "History will remember your name."

Doubtful. Yet my vanity awakens. "Am I as good as Vincent?"

"You are as good as any of us, Suzanne." He kisses me. "Thank you for being my hostess once again." He steps back. "Did the boy go to sleep without trouble?"

"He was asleep by the time I got in. He worships you, by the way." Maurice understands that Henri isn't his father, but I think he pretends in secret.

"He is a splendid little fellow. A credit to his mother." Henri comes back for another kiss.

The doorbell breaks us apart.

I pat down my hair. "Let us greet our guests. Come along, my Ceasar."

The main room is set up for the party, the paint tubes and brushes pushed aside, food and drink taking their place on the tables. The easels are jammed against the walls, their canvases in various stages of completion. *Fat Maria*, *Suzanne Valadon*, *Hangover*, and *Rice Powder* stand next to an oil portrait of Henri's mother and a pastel portrait of Vincent van Gogh.

Vincent is the first guest to walk in, his younger brother, Theo, pushing him through the door. Theo brings his usual good cheer, Vincent his melancholy and a stack of his works, mostly drawings and a few small pieces on canvas. Theo has dressed as a tulip farmer for the party, wooden clogs and all. Vincent comes as himself. They're both red haired and blue eyed and make a handsome pair of brothers.

"Welcome friends." Henri shows them in. "You can put the artwork in that corner." He points. "We'll look at it later." Then he throws me a quick question over his shoulder. "Where's the musician? We need our bal musette."

"He'll be here. I hired an accordion player."

"Not Italian?"

"Same as last time," I set his mind at ease before greeting the Van Gogh brothers with kisses on both cheeks. "Glad you came."

Émile Bernard follows the two, another one of Cormon's students, barely past eighteen. Then Louis Anquetin whom Henri first met while studying under Léon Bonnat. Then Père Tanguy, the art dealer.

And Zando, of course. And then Gauzi returns with an armful of bottles.

He has the same close-cropped dark hair as Henri. They're both from Toulouse. Gauzi is only three years older than I am, but he's convinced he's vastly more mature. After using him as a model for forever, last year, Henri finally painted his portrait, which only adds to Gauzi's self-importance.

"You are here." He passes me with the barest greeting. He dislikes when Henri asks me to be their hostess.

"You are back." I don't have time to worry about him. More artists and critics and singers and their "companions" keep pushing through the door, until there is no place to sit. Perfume and cigar smoke fill the air. Glasses clink in one toast after the other. The accordion player in the corner knows when to play a quiet melody so discussion can proceed, and when to strike a lively tune that suits the dancers on the parquet.

I make my rounds, ending up by Vincent several times during the night. He sticks out in the merry company, more somber than the rest of us. Theo once told me that Vincent was a preacher for a while before he came to Paris from Holland.

"Henri says you have built up an impressive body of work." I glance toward the corner by the door, but a handful of arguing men block the pieces Vincent has brought. I can look at them later. "Any sales?"

The light my first sentence lit in his eyes is extinguished by the last. "No, alas."

"Soon." I pat his hand. "This much effort cannot fail to gain its reward."

"I want to mount an exhibit," he confesses into a lull in the music, in a voice that's suddenly too loud, and a group of artists gathers around. "I organized one already for Japanese art at the Café du Tambourin. But this time, I want to have an exhibit for our work." He gestures around, including the others. "I've brought a few canvases." He glances toward his art, but he can't get up. We are surrounded.

"We plan to use the Restaurant du Chalet on the boulevard de Clichy." His brother, Theo, leans in.

"I have already promised a spot to my friend Paul Gaugin," Vincent adds. "I thought we could call ourselves the Petit Boulevard Group."

I laugh at this with delight. I like that he's clever. The Impressionists call themselves the Group of the Grand Boulevard.

The interest is immediate. Suggestions fly for timing and participants.

Only when the party is over, the last guest gone, do I realize that none of us found the time to look at Vincent's art.

1888 / Age 23

. . .

"I MISS VINCENT." I STEP CAREFULLY IN THE SNOW, SO I WON'T SLIP. HENRI AND I ARE NEARLY AT OUR BUILDING.

The art supplies we carry brought Vincent to mind, how he was always worried about running out of canvas and paint. His lack of funds stressed him terribly.

He didn't sell a single work at his exhibit in November. He painted all through the winter, his pipe and drink never too far, until he made himself ill. He moved south, to Arles, in February.

"I wanted so much for him to succeed." Maybe even more than I wish for success for myself. "He's the saddest man I've ever met." No, that's not quite right. "Sad one minute, then blazing with brilliance the next. He's dazzling, but mercurial. There's a duality to him that's fascinating, but worrying too. I fear the sadness might one day gain the upper hand."

Henri, who's been laughing at the antics of two little boys and their dog, loses his mirth and leans more heavily on his cane. "I thought the sun would be good for his health and his spirit. I hoped he would shed his melancholy."

I don't like the dark tone. "But?"

"I had a letter from Theo this morning. I've been waiting to tell you." He looks at the boys again, then back. "A few days ago, Vincent had an episode."

I slow. "Bad?"

"He cut off his ear. He's in the hospital."

I am at a loss for words. We reach our doorstep, and I stop. "I could cry for him. I wish he never left

Paris. I wish he stayed here with his brother and his friends. We could have helped him."

"I'm not sure if he can be helped." Since Henri's hands are full—his packages in one hand, his cane in the other, he holds the door open for me with his elbow. His stature might be diminutive, but he's every inch a gentleman.

"When he comes back to the city, we'll do more for him. We'll make sure to raise his spirits. I feel so sorry for him."

Like Vincent, I have not yet sold a piece, but I am not alone. I have Henri. I am part of a colorful company of artists in Paris. I have more offers for modeling than I can accept. I am able to take care of Maman and Maurice. For so long, I've fought only to survive, I'm surprised when I realize that I'm happy.

I smile at Henri.

He smiles at me, and he's about to say something.

Then Maman steps from our apartment with Maurice and sees us. "About time."

"Mama!" My bright boy runs to me, his lively eyes on the packages. "Are they for me?"

I would pick him up if my arms weren't full already. As it is, I hand him a small box I meant for Christmas. I can't resist. "I brought you pencils."

"And sweets?"

"We were in a different store."

He launches himself at Henri next and hugs his legs, until Henri ruffles his silky soft hair. "No candy here either, I'm afraid."

The warm scene fills my heart. To a stranger, we

would appear a family. The way Maurice looks up at Henri…

I turn away so my eyes wouldn't mist over, and catch Maman's gaze. She's thinking what I'm thinking. Soon, there'll be a wedding.

"Come on, Maurice." She shuffles up and claims her grandson's hand. "We must catch the market before it closes."

The smell of wine wafts from her.

It's eleven in the morning.

I don't want to bring it up in front of Henri. I keep a smile on my face. "Be good for your grandmother, Maurice."

My son refuses to budge. "I want to stay."

"I've promised to model for Henri, my love. Here." I press a few centimes into his hand, and his chubby fingers close over them greedily. "You buy yourself some sweets."

Henri hands him a full franc from his pocket. "And get yourself something from me."

With all those riches, Maurice runs along with Maman quite contentedly.

Only when the door closes behind them do I look back to find Gauzi on the stairs in his silly top hat.

"Back at last? I've been waiting for you, Henri. I didn't realize you were out with *her*."

"What is it?" Henri labors up the steps. "Whatever it is, it'll have to wait. We have a session arranged."

"Don't you always?"

Sometimes, I think Gauzi resents the time we

spend together. Of course, what he resents the most is that I draw better than he does.

He was on his way out, but he turns around and comes back upstairs with us.

It is inside their shared studio, while we are unloading our supplies, that he shoots his first barb. "You have a sweet boy, Suzanne." He looks from Henri to me. "Searching for a father for him? Plotting to catch Henri?"

"It's not easy to grow up without a father." I'm too busy sorting my new colors to pay much attention to the words I see as idle chitchat. I barely notice that the mood in the studio shifts. I think little of it.

When I pose for Henri, he watches me thoughtfully. I think little of that too, just assume he's come up against a problem and he's concentrating.

On Saturday, though, he does not ask me to be the hostess of his weekly dinner party.

1889 / Age 24

"MARIA!" A FAMILIAR VOICE CUTS THROUGH THE BUZZ OF THE CROWD IN FRONT OF THE BASILIQUE DU SACRÉ CŒUR THAT'S STILL COVERED IN SCAFFOLDING, UNFINISHED, DESPITE OVER A DECADE OF EFFORT.

I jump when I recognize my old friend. "Michel!"

We run to each other like long-lost lovers.

He picks me up and swings me around. "How are you?"

The unbridled joy on his face brings back my youth. "What are you doing here? I thought you were still abroad, traveling."

"I've been tasked by *La Vanguardia* to cover the World's Fair." Miquel Utrillo embraces me over and over in the middle of the crowd, in the middle of the street.

With the Exposition Universelle in Paris this year, the city is abuzz with people from around the world, celebrating the French Revolution's one hundredth anniversary.

"This is Erik Satie." Miquel gestures at the man who steps up next to him, a companion I haven't even noticed. "We're working on a theater piece together. Erik is writing the music."

I've seen Satie the composer before at the various cafés and cabarets, but we haven't been formally introduced. He looks scholarly with his small round glasses pinched on his nose, and a little debonair in his brand-new top hat, which he immediately lifts, revealing swept-back dark hair.

"*Enchanté*, Madame." He kisses my hand.

Miquel checks behind me. "Your son?"

He's never met Maurice, but, of course, I've written to him about the addition to my family. "At home, with Maman."

"Are you still with Renoir?"

"With Toulouse-Lautrec." Since Miquel has been constantly on the move, visiting city after city, it's been difficult to keep him up to date. "We are in love. I think he'll marry me."

His expression clouds, then clears again, so fast, I can't be certain the cloud was there at all. "Come." He draws me toward the nearest café. "Let us catch up."

We used to be close friends. Yet when I needed him the most, he was gone. He could have returned before now, his support would have been most welcome. I could be cross with him, yet I find I'm unable to hold a grudge.

We go everywhere together for the next few weeks. The World's Fair is a marvel and a tremendous success. All Paris is celebrating. Everyone is happy, even Henri.

The venerated Degas, the artist most difficult to impress and please, has seen one of Henri's drawings of me at a mutual friend's house, and he praised it. Henri is walking on air. His bad mood and suspicions of me evaporate.

We are happy again. I allow myself to believe that a bright future awaits.

"HOLD THE POSE." I SKETCH MY NIECE DRYING HERSELF AFTER HER BATH. She's staying with us for a few days. I want to catch a precise angle, the unguarded, ungainly moment of it, the way women move only when there are no men in the room, when there's no need to look pretty. There's something powerful in not caring.

"My arm hurts."

"Another minute."

This is the trouble with being unable to afford hired models for sittings. The amateurs are unaccustomed to the long hours and the effort required.

Maman and Maurice are hanging laundry out back. The room is silent. The light is perfect.

"I'm close." For the majority of the work, I'm always unsure if the image will come together at the end. Then there's a moment when I know that it will.

I'm there, and the thrill is indescribable. I made something. I succeeded. I created a thing of beauty out of thin air. I can do this. I'm not nobody. I'm not nothing. I'm not a tenement rat. I have worth, is what I feel when I look at art I created.

I darken the last shadow, then I step back.

That undefinable quality I sought is there.

"All right. Go on." I release my reluctant sitter. Then I slip my newest work into my folder. "I'm going upstairs."

Gauzi is away. I want to show my latest work to Henri.

I rush up to their apartment. Knock on the door. "It's me."

"Finished?" Henri can tell from my face that I have something. "Let's see."

I hand over the folder as I cross the threshold, too impatient to wait until I'm inside.

He looks through the pieces as he walks back to the room he uses as his studio.

I follow behind. "What do you think?"

"Degas must see this."

I relax enough to notice that he was working on

Moulin de la Galette when I interrupted, finishing the moody interior scene that's shot through with green.

My heart leaps at his words, then immediately drops. "Degas is a harsh critic. If he sees me too early, he might form a negative opinion that could be difficult to overcome later, even if I improve."

"He will see your worth."

"He is convinced women can't be artists." I keep an eye on the piece on the easel, drawn to the shocking red hair of the woman in the middle, the focal point. Then the three main characters, the faces detailed. The revelers in the background are a blur, yet they're there, all movement. I ponder how I could do that. I never pass a painting without trying to learn. I want my own art to be a true reflection of reality. I want my sitters to appear alive on the canvas. I want people to hear a whisper when they look at my art. *We were here, we were here, we were here.*

The world is changing so fast. I want to create something that will remain—of my world, of me, of the way I thought, of the way we lived.

"He's never met you. You will change his mind. You are Suzanne Valadon."

I drink down Henri's faith in me like a fortifying glass of wine and let it warm my belly. "When would you have me meet him? After the World's Fair is over?"

"Only fools make fate wait. The sculptor Bartholomé is one of Degas's closest friends, and he owes me a favor." Henri snatches up my portfolio, which is heavy enough so that he has to use both hands. "We'll take this to him. Once Bartholomé sees your talent, he is sure to give you an introduction." He pauses. "Only, don't ask him about his family."

"What happened to them?" I touch up my hair in the mirror. Should I change? Do I look like an artist? It's vitally important that Bartholomé thinks well of me. "Has there been a morsel of Montmartre gossip I've missed?"

"He married the daughter of a marquis, but it wasn't a marriage for position, you see. He was very much in love with her. And then she died, shortly after. It's been two years, but... He was a painter before. He became a sculptor to create a memorial for her grave that's a wonder to see. She in her deathbed and he lovingly bending over her, trying to hold on to her. It makes hardened men weep."

True love.

In the mirror, I watch Henri behind me. Is the love he feels for me true? I hope so, because my love is true for him. We've been together for the past four years. Soon, he will marry me. He would have asked already if he weren't always distracted by his latest masterpiece. He will ask when the *Moulin de la Galette* is finished.

He pats his pocket. "We should stop in to see Maurice. I have a small gift for him."

He always does.

Maurice loves him like a father.

"Should we become a family officially?" The question escapes me. I wish it hadn't. Men dislike it when women are too forward.

But Henri is through the door already. He didn't hear me.

I can't tell if what I'm feeling is relief or disappointment. I hurry out behind him.

We stop downstairs only to find Maman and Maurice are still outside. We move along, leaving Maurice's gift—a red toy horse—for him to find when he comes in.

At Albert Bartholomé's studio, a cavernous space with ceilings that must be twenty feet tall, blocks of white marble tower over us in half-carved human form like petrified angels. The widower pages through my papers in silence. He has a receding hairline already at forty, and a beard that reaches his chest, an air of despondency and deep sadness around him. His sketches on the table by my elbow all seem to be about subjects related to death. He cuts such a tragic figure, I want to draw him.

While I become more and more subdued by the atmosphere, Henri rocks on the balls of his feet. "She's an undiscovered talent."

"Degas doesn't believe in undiscovered talent." Bartholomé inspects me. "Who mentored her? Who was her teacher?"

Here, a big name would help, but I have none to give. "I taught myself by observing."

Bartholomé scowls. "Degas doesn't believe one can teach oneself. Without correction and demonstration of better methods, the artist merely repeats and reinforces his own bad habits, oblivious to his shortcomings." He hesitates over a drawing of my mother and my son. Maman is giving Maurice a bath. "You drew this?"

Henri beats me to a response. "She certainly did."

I press my lips together so I don't explain the pose I chose for Maman, one that radiates the pain in her back out of the image. It's palpable. And Maurice's *Are we done yet?* tilt of the head. Nothing varnished. Nothing beautified. No loving glances between the two. Maman wants to be done, and Maurice wants to go to bed. Sometimes, taking care of children is a joy. But sometimes, a lot of times, for working women, taking care of children is a chore. And I dare show that.

Bartholomé scrutinizes the work, then the next and the next, and his face lightens degree by degree. "I cannot deny your talent, Madame. You are right, Henri. If Degas approves of her, everyone else will accept her as an artist."

And then Bartholomé sits at his desk and writes a letter of introduction to Degas on the spot, before wishing me good luck.

"I'll see Degas next week," I tell Henri as we leave. I need to gain my bearings first. "I want to plan out what I'm going to say."

"Nonsense." He steers me toward the rue Victor-Massé, a petit dictator. "You will see him today."

"I can't possibly. Henri, I can't. I need to catch my breath."

"You need this. It's time." Then, with the most perfunctory of kisses, Henri leaves me on Edgar Degas's front step.

CHAPTER FIFTEEN

Ellie

Monday, March 20th

I lurch into Monday overloaded with misgivings. Mrs. Card is bringing Sam around again in the evening. It's the only time she could find someone to stay with her husband, Bill.

For the ten years that Chris and I were together, the one certainty in my life was that I was the most important person to him in the world, and he was the most important person to me.

Would it have been that way if he knew about his son?

These thoughts and worse attack me, relentless hornets that deliver one painful sting after the other. I dislike the situation I'm in. And I don't like myself all that much either. I know what it's like to grow up without parents. I shouldn't feel anything but sympathy toward Sam. And I do. I do. I swear.

I want to talk to Abby about Sam, but she's on radio silence at the moment. I should never have told her about Mom and Dad. No. That's not right. I should have told her sooner. In my defense, I was only ten years old when I decided to keep the unbearable truth of that night to myself.

I text her before I even get out of bed on Monday morning.

I'm going to the French bakery later. Should I pick up anything for you?

No response.

She didn't respond to yesterday's texts either.

I prep for the day. While I wait for the life-support juice to drip from the coffee machine, I look out the window. I immediately wish I hadn't. I should ask Mrs. Martinez to have that window bricked in.

I stare at the red sign in my front yard.

FOR SALE.

Each letter is a strike of the blade, cue the sound-track from *Psycho*. Except, instead of bleeding out in the shower as in the movie, I bleed out right by the sink.

I'm across the road before I make the conscious decision to move my feet. I want to yank that sign out of the ground and beat it against the nearest tree. If Joshua Jennings knows what's good for him...

He clearly doesn't, because he walks out of the

front door smiling. "Hey. Want to see the kitchen? I installed the cabinets over the weekend."

"You're selling the house."

"I was about to come over to talk to you. The agent wasn't supposed to put out the sign until Friday, but she was in the neighborhood to appraise a new listing."

"A warning would have been nice."

He steps between me and the sign. "I feel bad about how all this happened. I wish I'd picked a different project, but this is where I ended up. This is how my business works. I need the cash to buy the next property I have my eye on."

"Money is not the most important thing in life."

"Definitely not, but I also have short-term loans on the Coatesville property from private investors that have to be paid off."

"You knew I wanted to buy the house back."

He doesn't brush me off. He considers me for several seconds. "How soon do you think you could do it?"

His serious tone shames me. He gives me more credit than I deserve. I'm living in a fantasy world.

"A year or two?" Even as I say the words, I know the estimate is wildly optimistic.

"I'm sorry, I can't wait that long." He rubs the bottom of his chin with the back of his hand. "Also, I don't think it'd be good for you to move back."

"Do you think maybe I could decide what's best for me?"

"I didn't mean—"

I turn on my heel and walk away. Maybe, if I play my cards right, I won't have to see him again before he sells and leaves.

As I stomp up Mrs. Martinez's driveway, she opens her door, leading her beagle, Karma, on a leash. "I saw you through the window. Are you all right?"

"He's selling the house."

"I'm so sorry, Ellie. I know how much your home means to you."

Don't cry. "Are you going for a walk?"

"A short one. My arthritis is acting up."

Hold it together. "Can I help you with anything?"

"Got groceries yesterday. Don't need to go out for a few days. By then the pills should kick in."

"If you change your mind, just give me a ring. I could walk Karma for you."

"Thank you, but I need to move a little, at least, or I stiffen up. We're just going around the block."

I skip breakfast, not in the mood to eat. I clean to clear my head, and what I learn from that is that homemaking gurus who say cleaning clears their heads are lying for likes on social media. I leave the sink for last.

I look at nothing but the dishes and my hands.

And then I glance up.

FOR SALE.

"I have to get out of the apartment, before I go back over there and do something I'll regret," I tell House Mouse before I remember that he's relocated. "I have to get out of the apartment," I tell Bubbles.

I've put off going into the office for my grand-mother's shamrock hairpins. Today would be a good day. It's noon. Tim usually takes his mistress to lunch on Mondays.

When I pull out of the driveway, I refuse to look across the street. I focus on the traffic, which is light until I reach the city. Then it's crazy, Philly being Philly.

I drive by Abby's school. I hate that we fought. She's the only family I have left. I need to talk to her again. I could stop by the house tonight, but I don't want to talk to Frank. It'd be better to invite Abby to my place.

I'm only a few blocks from her favorite restaurant. I could pick up a few slices of her favorite chocolate-raspberry-swirl cheesecake. A culinary olive branch.

I turn right at the next light, and in a minute, I'm at the right place. And I'm so focused on finding a parking spot, I almost don't even notice Abby.

She's exiting the restaurant.

"Hey!"

She doesn't hear me, so I start rolling the window down, but before I can call to her again, a man exits behind her. They're clearly together.

Huh. I didn't know they had teachers that good-looking. All my teachers in middle school were old. Anyway, why aren't these two in school? Why are they out instead of eating cafeteria food?

And why is Abby wearing her good black coat, the one that cinches at the middle and gives her an actual waist? She usually dresses in primary colors and shapeless tops and long skirts at work. The middle school prefers bright and cheerful, the sexless-clown look. As a teacher, you're not allowed to have sex appeal, a policy that's understandable. It's a school day. Why is Abby dressed for a date?

All my questions are answered the next second, when the guy leans in and kisses my sister. And I mean kisses Abby good. Kisses her as if this isn't the first time he's kissed her. And Abby kisses him back as if she's very much enjoying the kiss. I'm not watching a this-is-new-to-us-and-we're-awkward kiss while I'm holding up traffic. I'm watching a relationship kiss.

The driver behind me beeps his horn.

I hold up my hand. "Not now."

Why do I have to find out about everybody's cheating in a damn car?

The idiot beeps again, and I roll up my window then roll on, gobsmacked. Also, I feel sorry for Frank, which I resent. Abby was right. I don't like Frank, never did. Apparently, neither does she. *Why doesn't she leave him?*

I'm so distracted, I almost drive by the office.

I park on the next block and walk back. I don't have an employee ID anymore, so I have to sign in at security. This is all very inconvenient when I'm still reeling. I don't want to talk to anybody.

"Hi." The woman signing in next to me has the figure of a *Vogue* model and the careless elegance of a true Parisian, in comfortable heels and silk slacks, a white spring coat tied at the waist with a wide black belt.

"Hi." I wish I wore a dress from my work closet, something a little more polished, something a little bolder than a beige top with black pants. People are their own personal brand. You can tell as much about someone as you can about a product just by appearance.

The woman gives security her name as Francoise Gibbler.

We end up waiting for the elevator side by side. I'm still not altogether together, which is why several seconds pass before her name finally rings a bell.

"I'm Ellie Waldon. I used to work upstairs with Tim. I'm sorry we couldn't make Suzanne Valadon's sketch work for your packaging."

"No worries. I made it work." Even her mischief-infused smile is elegant. "There's no difficulty involving a museum that a donation can't fix."

"I've been going down the Suzanne Valadon rabbit hole since I've seen the drawings. She was an amazing woman. I've been wondering why you picked her. If there might be a personal connection."

She smiles so wide, I'm worried she's going to get lipstick on her earlobes. Not that she would. She's the epitome of classy. I bet she never even gets lipstick on her perfect teeth.

"The little girl in the drawing was my great-great-grandmother," she informs me modestly.

"Wow. I bet she could tell stories. Sometimes, I wish I could go back in time." *Most of the time* I wish I could go back in time. "There are so many amazing women completely forgotten by history. I'm reading a book about Vincent van Gogh's sister-in-law. She's the one who promoted his paintings."

"Suzanne knew Vincent," Francoise says as if she's talking about personal friends.

"I know." I clear my throat to cover up a fangirl squeal. "She knew everyone. I wish more people could find out about her. I have this crazy idea for a Museum of Unseen Art. For art that museums keep off display. If I ever manage it, I want her to have an exhibit."

"The secret basement hoards." Francoise immediately gets me. "I hope you succeed."

The elevator door opens.

I float out on good vibes, then crash the second I see Tim.

Why isn't he out, lunching with his mistress?

He acknowledges me with a look that just about frosts me, then he dismisses me in the next blink.

"Madame Gibbler. This way." All smiles, he escorts her to his office. "Coffee?"

"If it's not too much trouble."

On his way to the kitchenette, Tim pauses by me and asks through his teeth, "What are you doing here?"

"I left something personal in my desk."

"You don't work here anymore."

"It's mine, and I'm going to take it."

"I'll be watching you through the glass. Make sure you don't take anything else."

Then off he goes, an idiot to the end. It's so unnecessary—I'll only be here for a minute. Some people just can't help themselves.

I grab my hairpins, then I say goodbye to the handful of coworkers who gather around me. I didn't get to do that before. I left in a hurry.

"Keep in touch."

"You have my number."

"We'll go for coffee."

"I'll let you know if I hear about an opening at another studio."

"Let's grab a drink next week."

"You'll land on your feet, Ellie. You're good."

"We won't lose touch. I promise. Anything you need…"

"You take care, guys."

This time, when I walk out, I feel good about it. The friends I've gained, I'll keep. I leave no loose ends with the company itself. The closure is complete.

MY SISTER IS HAVING AN AFFAIR. So, obviously, I don't drive home. I drive to Abby's school, circle the parking lot until I find her small Honda Fit, then I park and go stand next to it. She finishes early on Mondays. She only has one afternoon class. She should be coming out any minute.

And there she is. All innocent looking, as if she's not conducting a clandestine relationship.

"I don't want to talk to you," is the first thing she

says when she reaches me. "Until you take back that story about Dad."

"I don't suppose you want to talk to Frank either." Having the upper hand in a conversation with her is a heady feeling. She's always had that, by virtue of being ten years older.

"Frank is going to pay you back the money he borrowed from the house. He's doing the best he can."

"Are you?"

"I'm not the one maligning our dead parents' memory." She slaps the roof of the car, which is unlike her. She doesn't have a violent bone in her body.

"No. You're the one having an affair." It feels so, so good to throw that into her face, it almost makes up for the years she's spent criticizing me.

Her head swivels to see who heard my revelation. She clicks her key fob, and the car beeps. "Get in."

"Oh, now you're speaking to me." I slip inside. "Who is he?"

She slams the door behind her. "I don't know what you're talking about."

"I saw you kissing a man."

One minute my sister is as stiff and jagged with tension as a saw blade, then her shoulders collapse. Her eyes do something they've never done before: beg me for understanding. "I love him."

"What about Frank?"

"I haven't felt this way about Frank for a long time…"

If ever hangs unsaid in the air above the cupholder between us.

"Are you going to leave him?"

"Probably?" Misery infuses each syllable. "And if he doesn't pay back your money, somehow I'll find the funds."

"We'll talk about that later. This is about you having an affair. I'm going to need another minute to wrap my brain around this. For how long?"

"Two years."

I can't be hearing her right. "Why haven't you left Frank already?"

"He helped us so much. After Mom and Dad died, you had nightmares for two solid years. You were depressed. And then I met Frank, and he moved in, and you started to do better. I was the mother figure in the family, and he was the father figure."

"I always hated that he acted like he was my father. He's not my father. He showed up two years after the accident. I was probably going to start improving anyway."

"This is what I know... When he moved in, you stopped acting out. Your grades improved. He helped around the house. We could split giving you rides to afterschool activities. I was twenty-two. I needed help raising a kid, okay? And I did love him, in many ways, for many reasons, for a long time. I wasn't using him. We *were* a family. We just grew apart."

"You've been having an affair for the past two years."

She looks away.

"Why didn't you break up with Frank before you started seeing the other guy?" I can't stop myself, even if I know it's none of my business.

"I was going to ask him to move out, but..."

The wheels in my mind whirl and whizz, a timeline is drawn, and then realization hits me as if the airbag just deployed in my face. I'm not a math genius, but I can count to two. "Chris got sick."

"The wrong time for major upheaval. I was barely home anyway."

True. She was at my house, helping me, which, I sometimes resented. Those were my last months and weeks with Chris. I didn't want Abby underfoot. Yet the humbling truth is, I wouldn't have made it through those dark times without my sister. She cleaned when I needed it, and cooked when I needed it. She spelled me for breaks. She ran to the pharmacy.

"Then Chris died..." She shakes her head, a helpless, sad, sad gesture. "You come to the house for lunch every Sunday. It's our thing. It's our place, where we grew up. My goal has always been to keep the house, but without Frank pitching in with the mortgage, I couldn't afford it. And you ended up having to let go of your house. I know it's been super hard on you. I don't want us to have to sell Mom and Dad's place too. People need roots."

I don't want to cry. I especially don't want to

break down sobbing in a stupid Honda in the middle school parking lot. It's the pits. With my eyes full of tears, I can't even see if any little kids are staring at me.

"You don't have to arrange your life around my problems." I manage to form the words.

"I know I don't. But I can if I want to. You're my family."

I sob snort. "You're just doing this now to make me cry harder. You saw my superb mascara job today, and you envied it."

We hug.

The gearshift pokes between my ribs.

I hold on to Abby anyway.

"I'm so going to get fired for this," she mumbles as we pull apart.

"For having an affair? You're not married to Frank. And I'm not telling anyone."

"Not that. Some prejudiced parent is going to report me for embracing another woman in my car in the parking lot. They're going to accuse me of being a lesbian in public and corrupting morals."

And then we're crying from laughing.

"I'm glad you're in love." I clean my face in the little mirror on the back of the sun visor. "I think you should go for it."

"You can give me relationship advice right after you have your life straightened out." Abby pats her cheeks dry too. "What about Joshua across the street?"

The name snaps me into focus. "The flipper?"

"He likes you."

"You're wrong."

"I'm a teacher. In school, the teacher is always right."

"We're in the parking lot. At best, your authority is marginal." I blow my nose. "He's selling the house."

"I'm sorry. But two things can be true at the same time. He can be selling the house *and* be interested in you. Are you interested in him? Putting everything else aside."

"I can't." My feelings are all tied up in the floors and the walls and kitchen backsplash. "I'm so mad at him."

"Want me to run him over?"

"In this car? What would that do, dislocate his pinky?"

"I want you to know, I killed a moth the size of my palm the other night. Splat on the windshield."

"You're a hardened assassin."

The banter brings a flashback to the time before everything got complicated. Because of the age difference, Abby has always been my big sister with a capital B, but still, she was just my sibling. We used to have fun together. Then we were forced into different roles, roles we both resented.

Is it possible to undo almost twenty years' worth of habit?

. . .

Joshua is prepping my house for the sale. He's planting tulips around the mailbox. They sell them at the grocery store in full bloom, half a dozen to a pot. He's popping them out of the plastic and dropping them into the ground. Big gardener he is.

I used to have a mailbox garden. It died while I was taking care of Chris. The garden died, and then Chris died. What right does the garden have to come back to life?

Joshua wipes his hands on his jeans and walks across the street.

I get out of my car.

His green eyes are troubled. "I should have told you I was putting the house up for sale. I'm sorry."

"I'm sorry too. I shouldn't have flown off the handle." I have to admit the house looks better with the damn shutters. "I wish I could have kept it."

"I know."

"I wish you never bought it in the first place."

"If I didn't, I wouldn't have met you. I'm glad that we met, but I wish you weren't hurting."

"You don't have to worry about me."

"Right. We're enemies."

"There was never a chance that we'd be friends."

"That's sad."

Is it? Yes, of course it is. And rude. "I'm sorry. I've been bad mannered. It's not how I am usually. I used to be different, but I can't find my way back to that person."

"I've only ever met this Ellie. She's not that bad." Humor glints in his eyes, and…

Attraction?

When? How? What is he even... Why would he like me?

Freaking Abby.

Teachers are right even in the parking lot, apparently. The flipper is interested in more than flipping.

No.

"Why isn't there a Mrs. Flipper?"

The question catches him off guard. He opens his mouth to respond, then closes it again. Then he says, "I messed up."

"As simple as that? How?" Cheating? He doesn't look like an abuser, but you can never tell.

"I was the typical guy in his twenties, clueless. I failed to realize what she really wanted. I thought we wanted the same thing. I learned from it, if that counts for anything."

A man humble enough to admit he's been wrong. It's not what I expected. "What did you learn?"

"We assume that people want what we want. We try to make them happy by giving them what would make us happy. I kept building my business, working double time, so later we could have everything. She could stay home with our eventual kids, if she wanted. The more I worked, the sooner we'd get there, so I worked a lot. But all she wanted was for me to spend more time with her. She didn't want a real estate empire. She wanted to travel. I was doing the whole delayed-gratification thing, and she was all *carpe diem*. And I completely missed that."

The excuse-free admission is disarming.

"I've matured," Joshua tells me, and I believe him.

He's had a haircut. His hair is shorter on the side, but still long enough for spikes on top, which he would have if he cared about current trends, but he doesn't. For the first time, I let myself notice that he has the physique of a man who hangs drywall for a living. He's the man all those *har-har, look at me, I'm a manly man* men want to be, but there's nothing *har-har, look at me* about him. He is just who he is.

"I hope you'll reconsider the friend thing," he says.

"Why? I'm a mess. I've been mean to you since you moved in. I've been practically a stalker. I've trespassed."

"You can't trespass where you're welcome. You can visit whenever you want."

"I'd make a terrible friend. I've fallen apart. I try, I honestly do, but I can't gather myself."

"You're stronger than you think. You have big dreams, and you're going to make them a reality."

I don't know what to do with the encouraging way he's looking at me. "I have to go. I have to do my laundry and pick up the apartment. Sam and his grandmother are coming at six."

Joshua's eyes say he knows an escape excuse when he sees it. "He seems like a good kid."

"He is. I feel so bad for him." Then I don't know what else to say, so I say, "See you later."

I don't run away. I make a dignified retreat.

I have three hours. I order pizza for myself, toss in

the laundry, then I clean up before I dive into job searching.

I don't find a thing.

When my guests show up, Bubbles is, of course, the first thing Sam notices. "You have a pet lizard?"

"Her name is Bubbles." I can't look away from the boy's face. He's like Chris, and not like Chris. Even when Sam is excited, there's a faint aura of sadness about him. Chris was pure laughter and mischief. He didn't have a sad bone in his body, until it was time for him to leave me.

"Can I pet her?" Sam tugs his hair.

"Slowly and gently. She was your father's." I stumble on the last word.

Sam doesn't notice. He's enchanted.

I only have the one couch, and I'd feel weird with all three of us lined up in a row, so, once the petting is over, I seat my visitors at the kitchen table. "Would you like anything to drink?"

Mrs. Card is satisfied with water.

Sam asks, "Do you have chocolate milk?"

Yuck. "No."

"I'm hungry."

Kids just have no filters, do they?

"We'll hit the drive-through on the way home," Mrs. Card promises.

Sam eyes my pizza box on the counter. It's like he can sense my leftovers. His nostrils are trembling. Thing is, his wiggling nose is Chris's nose, right in the middle of his Chris-looking face.

"How about this?" I place the pizza box with two

intact slices in front of him.

"Thank you." His contentment lasts about three seconds, then he casts a longing glance toward the fridge. "If you stir cocoa and sugar into milk, it turns into chocolate milk. That's how my mom used to make it." His voice breaks on *mom*.

I dig cocoa and sugar out of the cupboard.

"You don't have to do that." Mrs. Card nudges Sam. "Don't be a pest, Sammy."

I bristle. I don't know why. Then I do. Sam looks so much like Chris that he brings out my protective instincts. I don't like anyone calling him a pest. "It'll only take a second."

Sam watches my efforts with an equal amount of hope and doubt. "You have to turn on the stove. You have to heat the milk so the cocoa and the sugar melt."

"Right. I knew that. So, what would you like to know about Chris?" I make myself say it. "Your father."

Carol already told the boy that I was Chris's wife and that he died of cancer last year. I hope Sam won't ask too much about that, but if he does, I'm prepared to tell him as much as he wants. He has a right to know everything.

"Was he, like, a good man?"

"He was amazing."

Sam tugs his hair. "Why didn't he find me?"

The hurt in his voice adds a few new cracks to my heart, which already has the surface of Route 202, a network of damage caused by heavy loads, including potholes deep enough to go straight through to the foundation. "He didn't know you were born."

The boy solemnly chomps on the pizza and weighs my words. "That's what Grandma said."

I pour the hot cocoa into a mug, set it in front of him, and sit.

"Did my dad like pizza?"

"He did."

"How about peanut butter?"

"His favorite."

"Pokémon?"

"As much as the average adult."

"Manga?"

"He collected comic books."

The questions keep coming. We go through a long list. Sam has clearly given a lot of thought to this.

After he eats the last bite of pizza, he finishes his hot cocoa, then walks his cup to the sink, and he rinses it. He really is a good kid. He pets Bubbles again and looks across the street.

"Did my dad play basketball?"

Chris's hoop is still up on the garage. I have the balls in an oversized garbage bag downstairs. "He did."

"I can't sign up for sports." The boy tugs his hair as he turns. "Grandma can't drive me. We can't leave Grandpa alone in the house for long. He might walk off."

Worry unfurls inside me for the man I've never met. "Where is he now?"

"He has a friend over, visiting," Mrs. Card

assures me.

Sam dries his hands on the dishcloth.

"What sport would you like to play?" I ask. It's beyond strange to have this boy in my home, yet it's not wrong. Maybe it has to do with him looking like Chris, but I feel as if I've always known him.

He glances back across the road. "Basketball, I think."

He's about four feet four. *The boy with the impossible dream.* I hope he'll get that teenage growth spurt when boys grow a foot or two over summer break.

"Want to go over and shoot some hoops?"

The prospect electrifies him. "Can we?"

"If Sammy is going to stay longer..." His grandmother hesitates. "Would it be okay if I went home and came back a little later? I don't want Bill's friend to be stuck at our house. If he's ready to leave, I can just bring Bill back with me. I just want to make sure that he ate his afternoon snack and took his pills."

"Take all the time you need."

"I shouldn't be long." She kisses Sam's head. "Behave yourself, Sammy. Call me if you need me."

As she walks through the door, I have a moment of anxiety. What if she gets into a car accident and doesn't come back? I catch myself. *Wow.* It's been a long time since I've worried about *that.* I've almost forgotten how panicked I used to be anytime Abby went anywhere.

"All right." I slap my knees to snap myself out of it. "Let's put on some sweatshirts and see if we can score a game across the street."

Sam tugs on the unisex white Philly Flyers sweat-shirt I give him. He's not worried about his grand-mother. Car accidents are my hang-up, not his.

All the way down the stairs, all I can think is that I'm going to owe Joshua Jennings a favor. As if things aren't awkward enough between us already. I'm at a loss how to act around him, now that I know that he likes me.

"I don't really know how to play basketball," I confess to Sam as we cross the street. "Any tips?"

"It's you and the hoop. You get in the zone. And no matter what, you can't think you're too short."

We stop as a dinged-up pickup pulls into the driveway next to us, a twin to Joshua's, except this one is blue instead of green. A sledgehammer starts up in my chest, and I forget all about the game. Can't be buyers already, can they?

No. A little girl I recognize opens the door, wide blue eyes, a riot of blond curls, the cutest little red boots anyone has ever seen.

She runs right up to us. "I'm Olivia. Who are you?"

Joshua's brother, Jace, and niece are visiting.

They're not the type who have to be talked into a basketball game. In a minute flat, we're all out in the driveway, Joshua and Sam against Jace and me.

Mrs. Martinez comes out to investigate the commotion and ends up teaching Olivia how best to bounce a ball on the sideline. "It's easier to do it two-handed."

I think she's getting her grandchild fix. "Arthritis

pills kicked in?"

"I'm as good as new." She wiggles around. "Between the pills and the yoga, I don't feel a day over forty."

The ball bounces off my knees.

"Hey!" Jace shouts from ten feet away. "Eyes on the game."

"I don't know if you've noticed, but I have no game."

And Sam, despite his game, has no height. Basically, it's a contest between Joshua and Jace, but they gracefully include us, pretending that we're contributing, periodically passing us the ball.

None of it is weird or awkward. Joshua just runs around like a big kid. He even picks Sam up so the boy can dunk.

Jace looks at me.

I step away from him. "Don't even think about it."

Joshua grabs the ball again. He dribbles and whips around.

"So choppy. Like a giraffe doing gymnastics," Jace ribs him.

I make my move for the ball while everyone is laughing, but I come nowhere near it. I don't care. I'm having fun. I can't remember the last time I played.

Joshua and Sam win. We're all gasping for air—all right, mostly me, bent at the waist.

Sam comes over, but not to check on me. "Do you have cookies?"

Olivia snaps to attention. "Chocolate chip?"

As a matter of fact... I have a batch of frozen cookie dough in the freezer that I bought for Sam's visit.

Every eye hangs on me, I swear, even Mrs. Martinez's, who can outbake me on her worst day.

I can be a gracious loser. "Why don't you all come over?"

The game is verbally replayed around my kitchen table, with endless exaggeration and teasing. The way the Jennings brothers tell it, sneakers deals are around the corner for them. They even impress Bubbles. The lizard comes out of her terrarium and generously allows Sam to spoil her with a treat of freeze-dried crickets.

"Do you have any outfits for her?" Olivia is wide-eyed impressed with Sam's deft handling of bugs. On second thought, she picks one up and feeds it to Bubbles. She cringes the whole time, but she won't be outdone.

"I'm afraid not."

"Does she do tricks?"

"She eats spiders."

"Gross," says Olivia, while Sam says, "Sweet."

"Sweet," Olivia corrects on the next breath.

In fifteen minutes, the cookies are out of the oven. I already have another batch of chocolate milk whipped up for everyone present. Then I finally sit, my own steaming mug in hand.

Five happy faces surround me.

A lump grows in my throat when I realize that every single seat around my table is taken.

CHAPTER SIXTEEN

Suzanne

1889 / Age 24

THE EXPRESSION ON EDGAR DEGAS' LINED FACE MAKES
IT CLEAR THAT HE WISHES I WERE ANYWHERE BUT IN HIS
ORDERLY SITTING ROOM, where the afternoon sunshine
filters through the leaves of the verdant houseplants
lined up on the wide sill. The air is filled with the
scent of lemons and black tea.

The master drops Bartholomé's letter onto his
lacquered Biedermeier desk, unimpressed. I'm
surprised he doesn't crumple the page.

He sniffs.

"Close the window, please," he orders his house-
keeper, who hovers by the door. "I am catching a

draft." Then he turns back to me and states, "You are a model."

"Yes. But also an artist."

"Impossible. You can only be one or the other, Madame. You either stand in front of the easel or behind it. One does not seek to destroy the natural order."

"Why?"

He stares at me as if he cannot believe my temerity.

I was less nervous my first time on the trapeze. I grip my portfolio, lacking the courage to offer it until he asks.

"Let me see it, then." *The sooner we're done, the sooner you'll leave,* his tone says.

He lays the folder in front of him and opens it. The drawing with Maman and Maurice sits on top.

I suddenly see every mistake I made, now that it's too late. "It's—"

His hand shoots up. "Silence."

His face is inscrutable as he squints his droopy eyes. He makes no sound. He doesn't so much as clear his throat as he picks through the entire selection.

At the end, he pulls out a drawing, then closes the folder and returns it to me. "I want this one."

I blink at the red chalk drawing in his hand, a piece I titled *The Model Getting Out of the Bath Near an Armchair.* "For what?"

I half expect him to respond with *to be thrown into the fire,* but that's not what he says at all.

"I want to purchase the piece for my collection, Madame Valadon." And then he adds. "You are one of us."

NOT ONLY DOES EDGAR DEGAS THINK HIGHLY ENOUGH OF MY ART to purchase multiple pieces and display them in his dining room, but as the weeks pass by, he introduces me to other collectors. I float around in a dream world. I made it. Overnight, I am thought of as an artist. I am a member of the club whose membership I most craved.

Henri and I celebrate.

All is well until Maman falls ill.

When I go up to pose for Henri, I take Maurice with me.

I'm not posing for a nude, thank heavens. Henri is still working on *The Hangover*. I sit fully dressed at a table and stare morosely ahead.

Gauzi observes instead of working at his own easel. Then, when Maurice knocks over a tower of woodblocks in the corner, he shoots my boy a dark look. "Bringing children to sittings now?"

Henri responds with "Allowances can be made for friends."

"A quaint family picture." Gauzi's tone is droll. "I might paint that. I wouldn't be surprised if the boy started to call you father. Wouldn't that be a triumph? And quite a journey too. To the son of a comte, straight from the gutter. Everything is possible with a clever mother."

Henri lets it go without a comeback, focusing on nothing but the canvas, but he cuts the sitting short. The session doesn't go well.

And then he delays finishing *The Hangover*. And when he does finish, it's a less than flattering portrait of me, my mouth turned down in the look of a bitter drunk. I look years older than my age.

We work on *Rice Powder* again after that. I'm a woman at her toilette, a table between us, an impregnable barrier. The woman sits with a mercenary look in her eyes, her face covered up with the rice powder in a jar in front of her, her true self hidden behind a mask.

This one too Henri finishes in a hurry. And when he's finally done one day, I am not invited to go out as usual with him and Gauzi for their meal.

"Back early," Maman remarks, looking up from where she's been staring at the fire in the stove, which is filling the room with smoke. She's holding a heel of bread in her hand.

Maurice is napping in our bed. I can see him through the half-open door of our room. I quickly close that door, then close the stove, then spin back to the apartment door to hold it open, and use my skirts to fan out the smoke.

"He was a right pest," Maman tells me. "Wantin' to go upstairs and badgerin' me about it all damn day."

"I'll take him to the park when he wakes." Nannies do that with the children of the bourgeoisie. I'm no longer dirt poor, but one way or the other, I am still always at work. I barely know what to do with a child, in any case. At his age, I was left home alone and spent my days sneaking out and wandering the streets. I had no scheduled bedtime, no separate bed even, no regular meals.

Maman chews on the heel of bread with her two teeth. "Why ain't you with Henri? You best hold on to him. You're twenty-four, an old maid, and him a man with a title and money. He's your last chance. By hook or by crook, you best trick him into marriage." She harrumphs. "If only you promised Miquel Utrillo the child was his, like I told you in the first place, we wouldn't even be here. You're a damned fool if you let Henri escape."

I would never trick a friend, but I don't argue with Maman. It's a conversation we've had and had and had. I turn to close the door instead, the smoke having cleared to a bearable level.

The sight behind me, in the foyer, stills my breath. "Henri."

Henri and Gauzi are on their way out. Gauzi's eyes glint with triumph, while Henri's burn with betrayal. They must have heard every word Maman said.

"Henri?" I'm immobilized by dismay and regret, and by the time I move toward him, Gauzi is pulling him outside.

"Should I follow and explain?" I ask Maman, who only shrugs. "Surely, I don't have to run after them on the street."

I stay behind. It's such a stupid misunderstanding, I don't think an explanation is necessary.

Henri knows me. He knows Maman. He won't believe her rant. Henri and I are better friends than that. More than friends. When he gets back, he'll call on me to talk. We'll go for a walk. We'll roll our eyes at Maman's old-fashioned ways and laugh.

Except, none of that happens.

"You wish to trap me," Henri says when I climb the stairs the next morning for my sitting.

"Foolishness. I would never."

"All of it. Us." He gestures wildly with his hands, his temper on full display. "Was pretense."

How can a handful of words hurt so much? "You know me better than that."

"How did you trap Zando? What did you tell him so that he'd rent you the apartment?"

"Zando *helped* me with the apartment. I pay most of the rent."

"You tried to trap Renoir by getting pregnant."

The injustice of the accusation rankles. "I was seventeen when he took me to his bed. He was more than twice my age. I was hardly in charge of the affair. I was an innocent."

Henri huffs at that. "No woman is ever innocent."

Gauzi's words, I'm sure. "We'll talk about this another time. Let us do the work, dear."

"I already got what I wanted." Henri's face freezes into a mask. "I can finish the rest without a sitter. I will not be needing your services in the future." He closes the door in my face with "Au revoir, Suzanne."

His betrayal is a hard, merciless slap, his change of personality too sudden. Only then do I realize how long Gauzi must have been filling Henri's head with nonsense. All those small digs, the wry comments I let fly past. I never argued because I didn't want to fight with Henri's best friend. I didn't want to bring conflict into Henri's life, only kindness and love and all things pleasant.

"Henri!"

The door does not open.

I sink to the stairs, and I sit there, waiting for him to come outside, to apologize and tell me he was mistaken. We are in love. He was going to ask me to marry him. I've been planning my dress for the wedding. I've been planning how Maurice might participate.

Henri will come to his senses. He must.

Half an hour passes before I accept that he won't.

Then another half an hour before I gather myself.

I go back down the stairs, then stop, lost again. I can't possibly explain to Maman what just happened. I don't have the wherewithal to handle her questions and her reprimands for losing the man who was Maurice's best chance for a father.

Henri and I are done.

I need to breathe. I need air. I stumble outside, into the cavalcade that's Montmartre.

Henri and I are over.

The fragile tendril of hope growing inside me against all odds, all experience, is uprooted once more. It's chopped up, stamped on, set on fire, dead. What a fool I've been to dare hope again.

I walk blindly, the world a blur through my tears, and my path takes me by St. Vincent's. The school-yard is empty, the children are inside. *Maurice will be in school soon.* And like me, he'll be beaten for being a bastard. My poor little Maurice, how I did not want him to carry the heavy burden of having no father for the rest of his life.

Memories carry my feet through the gates. Not a nun outside, nobody calls my name. By the outbuildings, the overturned old pickle barrel awaits under the east window. I step on a rusty bucket first, then onto the barrel, then the windowsill, then climb up and up, eleven years old again, wanting nothing but the sky above me.

I understand at last what the word *bastard* means —never good enough. I'll never be good enough for anyone, for as long as I live.

Rejected by my own father, rejected by the father of my son, rejected by Henri. I climb all the way to the roof, my old escape. My skirt whips in the wind.

Far below, the gray courtyard is as empty as my heart.

All life is a trapeze act. You make a blind leap, over and over. I leaped to Henri, but Henri wasn't there to catch me.

What is left but to fall?

The wind tosses my hair into my face.

I look down through the jumble of strands.

What is left but the abyss?

CHAPTER SEVENTEEN

Ellie

Saturday, March 25th

"I'M NOT GOING TO LOOK OUT THE WINDOW, EVEN IF BRAND MANAGER JOB OFFERS FALL FROM THE SKY WRAPPED IN SIGN-ON BONUSES."

I don't care about the Saturday-afternoon open house across the road, the buyers that overeager agents are nudging around. I don't want to see any of the vultures who've come to pick my bones clean.

I sit at the kitchen table with my laptop, facing my apartment's entry door.

"You don't have to watch them either," I tell Bubbles on the windowsill. "Sam's coming over later." I promised the boy the last time he was here that I would go through Chris's things and find a few items he could have. "Just close your eyes and take a nap."

Bubbles is in her terrarium, watching cars come and go outside. People speak, their voices muffled as if heard through the thick, black-lacquered wood of a coffin. My house and my old life are slipping away from me, carried away on the rip current of time and fate.

I open my email, delete the spam, read a note from the book club about our new selection, and I buy the novel from our local indie store online before I can forget.

This month's newsletter from my doctor's office is about prostate cancer. I delete it *so* fast.

Next is an email from my landlady about our rental agreement, which is up for renewal. The new lease agreement is attached, no changes. I print it and sign it, then I fold it into my pocket.

I feed Bubbles some rehydrated crickets. "I'm going over to see Mrs. Martinez."

Since she's just across the driveway, I don't slip into my coat, which I immediately regret. The wind is biting. It's supposed to be officially spring, but someone forgot to tell the weather. Patches of ice dot the driveway. I'll have to run out for salt, since I didn't grab a new bag the last time I was at the store. I thought winter was finished.

"Brr." I step through the cottage's door and regret more than my underdressed state; I regret the whole visit.

Joshua is enjoying a cup of tea in the kitchen. I

haven't seen him all week. I thought I was on a winning streak.

"The real estate agent told me to clear out for the afternoon." His tone is apologetic.

Mrs. Martinez moves to mitigate. "Tea and cookies?"

I can't be so churlish as to back out. "Tea and cookies would be great."

For a second, I feel weird around Joshua, but he's so laid-back, it's impossible to stay awkward around him. I let the cozy kitchen with its colorful pottery and bunches of herbs and overabundance of crucifixes comfort me.

In two seconds, Mrs. Martinez has the tea ready. "Poleo."

"I got hierba buena." Joshua lifts his cup.

"It's good for you," Mrs. Martinez promises the both of us.

That's her tea philosophy. In her kitchen, you don't pick your tea. She looks into your soul and gives you what you need.

"Nice haircut." Joshua notices that I've been to the salon.

"Thanks." It was time. I didn't break down when I told Niki that Chris had lost his fight. She figured, since I haven't been in this past year. We hugged. I have another appointment scheduled for next month.

"I was hoping I'd run into you." Joshua scrolls on his phone with his free hand. "I have new information on my building. If you want it for your museum, we're going to need an environmental study. Also, that whole block was designated a historical preservation zone a couple of years ago. All renovation plans will have to go through approval for that. We need to submit a parking plan that meets accessibility requirements and is in compliance with the Americans with Disabilities Act. We need to have a land use permit, considering the current zoning." He looks up, his expression apologetic.

The bureaucracy is not his fault. "Keep the good news coming."

"We'll have to go through either a public review process or a planning commission review," he finishes.

I sip my poleo. Hot tea is comfort any day of the week. "So, basically, it's impossible?"

Joshua sets down his phone. "Not the easiest project I've ever tackled, but we shouldn't be dejected. Nothing's impossible."

"You can do it, Ellie," Mrs. Martinez cheers me on. "Did you come over to tell me something?"

The signed rental agreement stays hidden in my back pocket. My museum plans are stuck. And I'm stuck too. Abby is right. I can't deny that I'm still living across the street from my old house a year after Chris's death.

"I think I'm going to move." Courage commandeers my mouth and keeps tossing out one crazy idea after the other. "I need to give corporate branding a rest. I'm going to look up all Philly museums and apply for any position they might have open, even if it's for a cleaning lady. Suzanne

Valadon was a horse walker, a seamstress, and a funeral-wreath maker." Among other things. "I want to be inside a museum, so I can learn how museums work. And if I get a job in the city, I should move closer to the city. The commute to work was getting on my last nerve. It's like everyone has forgotten how to drive during Covid."

"Oh, honey." Mrs. Martinez's eyes fill with concern. "Are you sure?"

"I'll visit all the time, but I can't stay here forever. I can't wrap myself in grief and never come out. I have to move forward."

"Of course you do. Sorrow and heartache have their time and place, but we shouldn't give them everything."

"I like my grief." The horrible truth escapes me and takes me by surprise. I've never spoken or even thought those words before, but as soon as they're out, I know they're true. "Grief replaced Chris in my life. For the past year, it filled the empty space. Grief is my connection to Chris."

"It's not your only connection." Joshua speaks with care. "You have all your happy memories. And you have the years you had together. You have his love. You will have it always. Nobody can take that away."

When did the flipper get so smart? And why is what he's saying making me swallow back tears? *Get your act together, Ellie.*

"Grief replaced Chris, but grief is not my partner." The revelation hits me where it hurts. "Grief is not here to help me. Grief wants to consume me."

"We're not going to let that happen." Mrs. Martinez gets up and envelops me in a hug.

"You're not mad at me for leaving?"

"All I want is for you to be happy."

Joshua asks, "What can I do to help?"

"I haven't nailed down any details yet."

Silence settles on the kitchen, in which I'm unwilling to admit that the move has been a spur-of-the-moment decision, and I haven't actually made specific plans.

Mrs. Martinez thumps back into her chair. "Did Joshua tell you he's got a cat?"

That does distract me. "Can flippers have pets? Aren't you about to move out?"

"It's not ideal, but he showed up at the house three days ago and won't leave. Apparently, I have a mouse infestation in my shed."

One skinny mouse, one round. Oh. I suppose it's possible that the round mouse was pregnant. *Oops.*

Poor Mr. and Mrs. House Mouse. I can't believe I put them in harm's way. "Did the cat eat them?"

"I used live traps and relocated them to Olivia's school. One of her teachers took them as classroom pets. They have a whole tricked-out habitat. Anyway, while I had the trap out, I was feeding the stray cat so he'd stay away from the mice. Now he thinks we belong together. If you want the trap—"

"I'd better go." I gulp my tea and stand. "I have

to put cookies in the oven. Sam and his grandmother are coming over."

On the way back to my apartment, I glance across the street. Six strange cars are invading my old driveway. The next car turning at the corner, however, brings visitors for me. They're a few minutes early. It doesn't matter. The cookies can wait.

"Let's start down here." I open the garage door, as Sam and his grandmother get out. "This is it. Behold the piles upon piles."

Sam's eyes snap wide. "Wow."

"Not all mine." I lead him forward. "Only these are."

Books fill the first box: Patterson, Child, Koontz, Connelly, King.

"Chris loved thrillers."

"Sam is reading Harry Potter," his grandmother tells me.

Right. Of course, he is. I open the next box. Comic books. "Maybe these?"

He shuffles through them, so excited that he goes too fast and has to backtrack. His fingers flit from one volume to the next and the next. "Can I pick two?"

He's never looked more like Chris. Even his nostrils tremble the same way.

His childish excitement hits me in the heart "You can have the whole box. Take it all away."

Mrs. Card is less enthusiastic. "That'll need a lot of space."

"Please, Grandma?" Sam tugs his hair. "Please?"

We exchange a glance over the boy's head.

Who's going to say no to those eyes?

His grandmother relents.

I keep size in mind going forward. I dig out a shoebox from the bottom of my pile. "It's Chris's old Matchbox collection. Do you like cars?"

Sam's permanently anxious expression, those pinched lines between his eyebrows that children shouldn't have, disappear little by little. An irrepressible smile brightens his face.

I also give him Chris's tricked-out backpack, even though it holds a lot of good memories of the two of us camping in college.

"Were those Dad's?" The boy spots a pair of spiderweb-covered fishing rods next.

"Mr. Martinez's. He used to fish in the Brandywine. Have you ever gone fishing?"

Sam wrinkles his nose. "I feel sorry for the worms."

"I feel the same way. How about this?" I hold out a signed baseball that came from Chris's father. "Unfortunately, the signature is illegible, but maybe you could research it on the internet."

He holds the battered ball up like gold treasure. "Thank you."

"Chris's father passed away a few years ago." I suddenly remember that Sam had/has other grandparents. I glance at Mrs. Card to make sure this is an acceptable topic, and she nods. "His mom sold the house and bought a cruise ship pass. Her plan is to live on a cruise ship and travel the world through retirement." They lived on the West Coast and spent all their time traveling even before my father-in-law's death. I wasn't that close to them. We only saw each other a few times a year. "Would it be all right if I emailed her? I think she's in the Mediterranean."

Sam looks at his grandmother with hope, and she hugs him before she tells me, "Of course, it would be all right, dear."

Then we go back to the boxes.

When Sam has seen everything, he hauls the box of comic books to the trunk of their car.

I carry the rest of his loot behind him. "I was about to put some cookies in the oven. Would you like to come upstairs?"

I don't know why I even ask. He's on the stairs before I finish the sentence.

"Did my dad like cookies?"

"He was a sugar fiend."

"Grandma says sugar is bad for my teeth."

"You listen to your grandmother." I look back at Mrs. Card coming up behind us. "I'm baking oatmeal-raisin cookies today."

The thought that ten-year-old boys might not be into oatmeal only hits me as I say the words.

Sam is unbothered. He goes straight for Bubbles. "Hey, buddy!"

I pop the cookies into the oven. "Chocolate milk?"

"I already had chocolate milk today." He glances at his grandmother, then back at me. "Regular milk, please?"

Mrs. Card and I have tea.

While we have our snack, Sam chatters on about

school and his grandfather, randomly dropping in questions about Chris. The apartment echoes with the sound of his voice. One kid can fill a lot of space.

I've been having problems talking about Chris when people bring him up—every memory is tinted with pain—but talking with Sam about his father fills him with so much joy that I can't help but feel it with him. We keep talking until we're interrupted.

"Knock, knock. It's Joshua."

"Come in."

He opens the door, reaches behind him, and drags in Chris's hoop. "I switched it out for a new one last night. I was going to repaint it, then give it to you to give to Sam, but since they're here…"

Sam is already on his feet. "Really?" He touches the beat-up hoop as he skips around it. Then he stops, and his shoulders sag. "I won't have any place to put it."

Aw, dammit. Joshua doesn't know that Mr. and Mrs. Card are about to move into assisted care.

"I'm sorry." Mrs. Card's voice is reedy. "Let me think about it, all right, Sammy?"

Joshua stands in the entryway, confused, then catches himself and at last closes the door behind him, stopping the cold air from coming in.

Before I can find the right combination of words for the delicate situation, Sam speaks up, and his childish simplicity cuts through the clutter. "I was supposed to come and live with my dad."

"I'm sorry, I—"

"It's okay." Sam puts on a brave face. "I can go and live with Grandma's sister instead."

His grandmother looks away. I can't imagine how difficult this must be for her. My heart breaks for both of them.

"I have an idea." I take the hoop from Joshua. "How about I keep this until Sam is ready to take it?" I'd like to keep my boxes in Mrs. Martinez's garage even if I do rent another apartment. I'd be happy to pay for storage. I could leave the hoop with the rest of my belongings until the boy's situation is sorted out.

My offer doesn't fix everything, but the general mood improves enough so we can all sit down and enjoy the rest of the cookies.

Sam keeps looking at us, from his grandmother to me then to Joshua. His nose is wrinkled, he's thinking so hard.

"What is it?"

"If a stranger peeked through the window, he'd think we're a family," he says quietly, dropping his gaze to his plate.

That just about kills me. The longing in his voice is twin to the one that lives inside me. I've never wished more that Chris was with us still.

"Who's your favorite player from the 76ers?" I ask him.

His eyes light up as he names three. I'm ashamed to say, I don't know any of them. When Chris was watching games, I was usually reading.

Joshua steps in. "Who do you think improved the most last year?"

Then the two are off to the races, talking statistics, while Mrs. Card and I exchange a glance over the table. *Boys.*

Joshua leaves first, then Sam and his grandmother slip into their coats. We're in the driveway—I'm carrying the basketball hoop to the garage—when Mrs. Martinez steps outside.

"I wanted to say hi." She lifts the bag in her hand, her eyes filled with warmth and grandmotherly care. "I have a little gift for Sam." And then she walks toward us, but just as I see the patch of ice, she's already going down. It happens in a blink. It's indescribably sudden.

"Watch out!" Horror steals my breath.

Sam reaches her first. "Are you okay?"

I'm one step behind him. "How bad is it?"

Mrs. Martinez holds up the hand she used to brace herself. Her palm is skinned; her expression is confused, as if she's unsure how this happened.

"Hold on." I put a hand under her elbow for support while Sam shores her up on the other side.

"All right. I can do this." She has to psyche herself up for it. She huffs. "One, two, three." She moves to rise, but immediately drops back down. "Or maybe not. I think I broke my hip."

And that's not the only terrible thing that happens.

After the ambulance takes Mrs. Martinez away and Joshua goes home once again—he heard the commotion and ran to help—Mrs. Card climbs back upstairs to use my bathroom, and I'm left alone in the driveway with Sam.

"Does your grandmother's sister live nearby?" I ask to distract him from worrying about Mrs. Martinez. "Are you excited about living with her? Will you have to change schools?"

I've never considered school districts before. I hope Sam's transition will be easy. The move will be upheaval enough. I can't imagine having to add a new school on top of all that.

He shuffles his feet.

He looks up at the staircase behind me.

I finally pin down his peculiar, pinched expression. He's a worried little man who doesn't want to show that he has problems.

He tugs his hair. "Grandma doesn't have a sister. We made her up, in case I couldn't stay with Dad, in case he couldn't take care of me. We didn't want him to feel bad."

CHAPTER EIGHTEEN

Suzanne

1890 / Age 25

"HAVE YOU HEARD THE LATEST ABOUT TOULOUSE-LAUTREC?" Miquel Utrillo blows through the door and snaps off his hat. "You won't believe this."

Spring sings outside. Our baskets on the shelf are filled with fresh vegetables. Even the air is cleaner. We've switched the old woodstove for a coal one—a lot more efficient.

I've spent little time with Henri since I climbed the roof at St. Vincent's.

For a dark moment, all I could think of was that another hope, maybe my only chance of a better future for me and Maurice had been taken away. Then I looked down at the street, at an automobile passing an omnibus drawn by horses. Life is nothing but change. Things I don't know to expect and can scarcely imagine are on their way.

"The last time Henri and I talked, he told me Theo van Gogh bought *Rice Powder* for the Galerie Goupil for a hundred and fifty francs."

"Good for him."

"Mmm." He didn't ask about Maurice, while Maurice cried for months, missing him. Henri wasn't right for us after all. I refuse to pine for the man.

Henri is not my life. My life is my son. I learned that standing on St. Vincent's roof last year. I stood above the rooftops and let the wind blow all my feelings for Henri away. Then I climbed down and returned to Maurice.

"What has Henri done now?" I hand my son a carrot stick. I've been trying to cook, but he's been tearing through the kitchen with his new wooden horse—a carved horse head on a stick—acting like a ruffian.

"He challenged De Groux to a duel." When Maurice runs to him, Miquel swings him around, then sets him down and hands over a sweet treat from his pocket.

Of course, Maurice immediately trades the carrot stick for that.

"Over what provocation?" Henri is oversensitive to comments about his stature, and he's not the greatest sportsman, a bad combination. I freeze midturn. "Is he dead?"

"At the banquet of the exhibition of Les XX, a

group of twenty Belgian artists, in Brussels, De Groux said he wouldn't let his paintings be hung next to Van Gogh's. Toulouse-Lautrec challenged him on the spot. And then, try to imagine"—Miquel swings his arm—"Paul Signac stood up and said he would continue the duel should Toulouse-Lautrec fall."

"I wish I'd been there." I catch myself. "Forgive me. I sound callous." I wipe my hands on my apron. "Was anyone hurt?"

"De Groux backed down."

"I hope someone wrote to Vincent. How it will entertain him." I imagine a wide smile on his melancholic face, and it makes me happy. I pull out a chair and clean off that corner of the table. "Come. Sit. I'll make you tea."

"I thought we might take Maurice to the park. Or a boat ride."

"Boat! Boat! Boat!" Maurice waves his horse as he jumps in place.

"Almost forgot. I have more news." Miquel ruffles his hair. "They're opening the Eiffel Tower to the public at the end of March."

"Are they?" I nearly start jumping with my son. The tower was supposed to be a temporary structure for the World's Fair. I've been dreading its dismantling. "I want to climb to the top. Can you imagine seeing Paris from there?" So much higher than the rooftops.

"I bet Maurice would like that too." Miquel hands out another treat, then steps to my easel that holds a canvas instead of my usual drawing pad, tucked away in the corner. "What's this?"

"I want to paint."

"But?"

"I admire Mary Cassat and Berthe Morisot. I love that they broke new ground. They made it clear that the women's domain, bathing your children, sleeping little boys and girls, and the domestic scenes are every bit as worthy subjects as heroes on horses, or mythological figures on Mount Parnassus."

"But?"

"I want more." I wipe the knife I've been using.

"Meaning?"

"The female artists we know get a pass from the establishment because they paint like women. They paint the women's domain, in soft pastel colors, romanticized. They don't encroach on the subjects men prefer. They don't threaten the men."

"And you?"

"I want to paint everything and everyone, exactly the way I see them, without the distraction of ribbons and ruffles. I don't want to paint women sitting in proper poses. I want to paint them yawning. I want to capture the way a young girl, limbs caught between the proportions of a child and that of a woman, climbs awkwardly into the bath. Neither sweet, nor seductive, but something in between. So that the viewer would want to say, *Don't worry, you shall grow out of this.* Every shape is valid, even if it elicits neither lust nor sentimentality. It has the right to exist on canvas simply because it exists."

I snap my mouth shut. Such a passionate outburst. I don't want Michel to think that I've taken leave of my senses. Yet I can't make myself feel embarrassment. I lift my chin.

"If that's what you want to paint, then that's what you should paint."

This is why we are friends. He judges me not. "I am interested in the human form."

Several seconds pass before he catches my meaning. "L'ensemble? Female nudes?"

"In a natural style. Not to tantalize."

"I don't know how you've missed this, but the raison d'être of female nudes is to tantalize."

"That is precisely what I mean to rebel against. It is accepted that women's bodies are there to be used by men, as willing or unwilling objects of desire and satisfaction. As visual and physical entertainment. As a source of titillation or, at best, a source of comfort. Or as the provider of heirs."

"Yes?"

"But if a woman uses her body to survive, she's a whore. If she willingly shows her body, she is shameless." How many names have I been called by our neighbors for being a model? "Dare she appear eager for marriage, she is a gold digger."

"Models might not want to pose nude for a female artist."

"You might be surprised. And if they don't, I'll paint myself in the mirror. I will record myself growing old."

"You will paint wrinkles?"

"Why not, if that is the truth? I want to paint myself nude when I am a grandmother. The first time I posed nude, I was fifteen and an innocent. Nobody complained about that. Nobody proclaimed it anything but *art*."

"You also draw youth. You drew your niece and son in the bath."

"As real children, doing what children do, their grandmother drying them. A slice of their life that is theirs, not posed for anyone's benefit."

"You are convincing. I will give you that."

"In any case, I want to paint nudes, female *and* male. Are they not both human? Have they both not been made by the same God?"

"Female artists don't paint naked men. It's not done." His eyes spark with mirth. "None have even tried. You'd be a scandal."

"Let them be scandalized, then."

"They'll burn you at the stake."

I think of Jeanne d'Arc as I toss the onion skins into the bucket at my feet. When it comes to women who defy convention, being burned—one way or the other—is never an idle threat. "I know you are right. I've barely just gotten my drawings accepted. They are starting to sell. I have the moon and the stars. I shouldn't reach for the sun."

"True," my friend says in all seriousness. "You must remain the Valadon we all know. The picture of shyness and modesty, and that endearing timidity. You can't be reaching for things others think you shouldn't have. That would be too far out of character."

"Stop mocking me." I throw the end of a carrot at him, then hang my apron on its peg. "In any case, I can't go to the park with you. Degas is expecting me. I was going to wait for Maman to come home, but I can't. She went out for milk hours ago. She should have been long back. No doubt she's in a tavern somewhere."

"I'll walk with you," Michel volunteers.

"Boat," Maurice begs. "Can we go on the river?"

"Not today, my love, I have to go out. But I'll hurry back. Tell your grandmother when she gets home to put the meat pie in the oven." I kiss his sweaty forehead, then fasten my bonnet. "Be a good boy. Don't touch the stove." I don't really have to tell him that. He's seven. Maman says I'm a fusspot of a mother.

"I have other news too," Michel says once we're outside, his eyes measuring and wary. "Renoir is marrying Aline."

I stumble on the edge of a cobblestone. Stupid old street.

He offers me his arm. "He doesn't deserve you. He never has."

I've long relinquished hope that he would acknowledge Maurice, but now, faced with the absolute certainty, this final abandonment of us still pains me.

"I have two choices, forgiveness or bitterness." I step forward. "I refuse to be bitter. Aline bore him a son." Two years after Maurice was born. "He's doing right by her."

"I despise him for what he's done to you."

"Don't."

"Don't you?"

"I can't." And that's the maddening truth." He's too good an artist."

"Art above all?"

"As he says, pain passes, but beauty remains. His work will live forever."

"So will yours. Someday, you'll be more famous than he is."

Michel is ever my supporter. "I wish I had half as much talent as you have optimism. I fear someday you'll see the real me and stop being my champion."

"Never." He steps in front of me, forcing me to face him. His always merry eyes grow serious. When he speaks, he speaks with gravity. "Marry me, Suzanne."

The street, the carriages, the people fade into the background. *Could I? I should. I can't.*

"Michel, you are my best friend." I love him, but I'm not in love with him. I'd ruin both of us with a marriage of convenience. "I can't."

"I want to give Maurice my name. I'm willing to acknowledge him as mine."

The offer breaks my heart. How many times has Maman demanded that I trick Michel, that I tell him Maurice is his son? She wouldn't believe that I haven't lain with Michel, that he could never fall for such a ruse. And here he is, willingly offering himself.

He is a dear, dear friend.

If I could ever make myself fall in love with someone, he would be the man.

But I can't.

1891 / Age 26

THE MOST UNLIKELY OF ALL UNLIKELY THINGS HAPPENS. EDGAR DEGAS, WHOSE OPINIONS MAKE MEN TREMBLE, BECOMES MY FRIEND. Of course, people accuse me of being his lover. Never mind that he's a known celibate and, on the whole, doesn't even like women.

Months go by as I visit him nearly every day. Together, we mourn Vincent—that sweet, troubled, brilliant soul—who, in July of 1890, killed himself.

"He respected and admired you much," I tell Degas during one of my afternoon visits. Now that Vincent is gone, I don't feel as if I am breaking his confidence. "He studied your work, did you know?"

Degas's eyes mist over. "And I admired his undiluted passion. I am going to buy some of his work for my collection." He looks away so I don't see the mist well into tears. "I should have done it sooner."

"And now Theo is gone too, at the height of his happiness. Married at last, with a son." Vincent's brother survived Vincent by only six months.

"Theo brought me into the Galerie Goupil. Before

he began working there, they wouldn't accept any of the Impressionists, which is how they labeled me, never mind that I am a Realist." Degas's voice breaks. "How is Theo's wife, Johanna? Have you heard?"

"She's gone back to Holland."

"I fear for the woman. I don't want her to become lost."

"Not her." I met her once. She couldn't have been more different from me—a puritanical Dutch Protestant, a proper wife, her only thought how she could support her husband. But in one way, we are similar: she also has steel for her spine. I grew mine on the streets. I don't know how she came by hers, but she has it. "In whatever she chooses to do, Johanna will succeed."

Degas turns to the window and stares out. What does he see? He confessed last time that his eyesight is worsening. When he returns to me, after several seconds, he scrutinizes my face. "Now tell me why you've been fidgeting since you came in."

Failing eyes or no, he still sees aplenty. "It's Maurice."

"He's not sick?"

"Lively as ever." And growing *too* lively for poor Maman. "Last year, Miquel offered to claim paternity. He's willing to grant Maurice his name. At the time, I did not take him up on it."

"Good man, Utrillo. And you're not a fool." Degas's tone warns I'd better not be. "You are rethinking your decision. You will not say no."

"Maurice is becoming a handful. He is teased at

school. Having a father would settle it all down. I've wished this for my son for so long." *No longer a bastard.* "I am almost too scared to believe it."

"You are Terrible Maria." His nickname for me. "You're not scared of anything."

He is wrong about that. My fearlessness ended when my son was born.

I don't promise Degas anything, but I do commit to talking to Michel. And I'm presented with the opportunity sooner rather than later. I run into my friend on the way home. He is with another man.

He introduces us to each other. "Paul Mousis, meet Suzanne Valadon."

Paul is a year or two older than me, his frock coat and top hat of good quality. He's of sturdy build and steady gaze, sporting the most magnificent mustache. I immediately want to draw him.

"A sculptor?"

He laughs off my guess as he kisses my hand. "A businessman."

"Have you ever sat for an artist?"

"If anyone could tempt me to model," his brown eyes flirt, "it'd be you, Madame."

He could not be more different from my usual bohemian artist friends. He has a calm and sure way about him—a man secure in his place in the world, and secure in his abilities. He is well-built. He probably rides a lot or belongs to a fencing club somewhere.

"If you—"

"We're expected," Michel draws him away. "But I

wish to see you. Soon. Don't forget that you promised to sit for me, my Suzanne."

An acquaintance calls to Mousis, and he moves on, while Michel stays another moment. "Will you accompany me to dinner tonight?"

"I will. I want to talk to you." Blood rushes to my heart. And then suddenly, I can't wait, not even a few short hours. "I would like you to be Maurice's father. If the offer still stands."

His smile is instant. "I'd be honored."

He doesn't offer marriage again. He knows it's not what I want. His offer has always been unconditional.

I trust him, but over the next few days, every time I think of him, I think *Will he? Will it really happen?*

When he shows up at our apartment with a fresh paternity certificate, the relief I feel is indescribable.

My hand trembles as I hold the paper. "It means the world, Michel."

Maurice runs around us, drumming with two sticks in the air. He doesn't understand the significance.

Maman sits by the stove, her toothless grin a sight. She probably thinks I finally fooled Michel into thinking that Maurice is his son. I won't waste my time to convince her otherwise.

I hug Michel again and again. "It means the world."

Then I lay the precious certificate on the table, and I swing my boy around. And we whoop. It's the happiest day of my life.

Maurice Valadon is now Maurice Utrillo.
My son is no longer a bastard.

1892 / Age 27

EVERY NEW PAINTING IS LIKE THROWING MYSELF INTO THE WATER WITHOUT KNOWING HOW TO SWIM, Édouard Manet once told me. He's been gone for nearly a decade, lost the year Maurice was born, dying in agony, his left foot amputated from gangrene, a complication of his syphilis. I will never forget him, nor the lessons he taught me.

I have been drawing since I can remember. At age twenty-seven, I start painting at last. How many times have I heard Maman say, *if only*. *If only* will not be my life. My gravestone will not say *if only*. My gravestone will say *she dared*.

I still can't afford models, so I keep working with what I have: Maman and Maurice, and my niece, Marie-Lucienne who's living with us for the moment. I have no studio, no elaborate backdrops, so I paint them in our apartment.

Edgar Degas, and Miquel Utrillo whom I also paint, encourage me. I paint because I've always wanted to, and because plenty of people think I can't, and I won't back down from a challenge.

The sentiment that life is short is no less true for being a cliché.

I want to do something with my life while I can. I

want to paint for myself, and for the artist friends we've lost: Manet, Vincent, and Seurat. Our residence on earth is not guaranteed. No one knows when the landlord will put you from the room and ask for the key back.

In July, on the side of Mont Blanc, a hidden lake burst from behind a glacier and flooded the valley below. The water killed two hundred people in the village of Saint-Gervais-les-Bains.

Take no moment for granted, the warning seems to blow on the wind. And I don't. I work as hard as I can, which leads to my first triumph. Some of my studies are exhibited by Le Barc de Boutteville in his shop on the rue Pelletier.

For most of my life, I had little. Now the canvas is mine, and so are the colors, the shapes I paint, the images I conjure from nothing. I touch up highlights on the tiny petals of the lilacs I'm painting. And after that, my first female nude is next. I already have sketches laid out on the table.

"Mama!" Maurice runs into my studio, his face red. "I will not go back to school. I hate it!"

"You have to go to school. You're eight years old. I am almost finished. Go eat."

"I don't want beans."

"You'll be nice to your grandmother and thank her for cooking."

"She's stupid."

"Maurice!"

I've always thought if my son had a father, it

would solve all our problems, but his unhappy face says otherwise.

"I want to stay with you." He stamps his foot.

"You know I have to work." More than ever. He outgrows a set of clothes every time I turn around. He needs paper and ink for school. And Maman could drink away a banker's wages.

Maurice chucks a paintbrush across the room. "You're always in here."

Maybe he's acting out because he senses that emotions are boiling all over France. A few months back, in Fourmies, government troops fired on people demonstrating for an eight-hour workday, and tensions haven't yet settled. The bullets killed nine and wounded thirty. Peace is fragile once again.

"One more minute. I have my colors mixed. I know where everything goes. If I don't finish now, it'll take me hours to place my brain in the same spot and mood tomorrow. I'll finish this, then I'll wash my brushes, and then I'm all yours for a little while. All right?"

He marches off.

"Don't jump on the canapé with your shoes on," Maman shouts the next second.

"I don't have time for this," I call through the door Maurice left open a crack. "In half an hour, I'll have to leave for a sitting."

I deepen the shadow under the vase, then I switch brushes and add reflected light to the bottom of the round terra-cotta vessel.

"Do your homework," Maman orders Maurice.

"You can't make me!" Maurice shouts. "I want to go with Mama!"

I add highlights to the peonies in the vase too.

"Stop that." Maman shouts. "Stop it at once. Marie-Clémentine!"

"One more minute." I adjust the curve of the vase. I want to get it right. I'm self-taught, I'm a woman, I come from nothing—I'm always aware of the increased scrutiny I face. And now I am showing at Le Barc, my pieces next to Camille Pissarro's and Toulouse-Lautrec's. Makes one nervous to think about it.

"I hate school. I hate it. I hate it. I hate it!"

"Put down the knife, Maurice."

I'm so focused on my work, several seconds pass before Maman's words reach my brain. And then I run out, loaded brush in hand, my entreaty for another moment of peace cut off by the tableau that confronts me. Maman stands on one side of the table, heavily leaning against it. The bottle she bought this morning is empty. Maurice's homework is in the middle, ripped into pieces. Maurice faces his grandmother with a knife, his face distorted with hatred.

Our golden armchair, and the sofa too, lie stabbed to death behind him.

"Stop!"

"I will not go back to school." He whirls to me, and a sudden onslaught of tears washes down his face. He dashes them away. He throws the knife at the disemboweled armchair, then runs into his room and slams the door shut hard enough to shake the frame.

Maman reaches into her pocket and pulls out a crumpled piece of paper. She holds it out for me without letting go of the table. "Teacher sent it around."

She grew up speaking Limousin, a dialect of Occitan that people speak in the southwest of France. She had her learning before the Third Republic decided to modernize us all and forbid any other language than French at school. She wouldn't admit to any deficiency, though, just blames her worsening eyes when she leaves the reading to me and Maurice.

"Maurice was in a fight in school," I tell her as I scan the note, not the first. "He doesn't pay attention in class. He doesn't do his homework. He talks back to the teachers. He curses at the other students. Sometimes, he runs off halfway through the day…"

A headache slices through my brain. I close my eyes. *Am I a bad mother?* I almost ask Maman, but how would she know? I remember little mothering on her part. She was always off somewhere, while I ran wild.

And now, I'm always painting or off modeling, leaving my son behind.

The realization has me staring at the closed bedroom door in horror.

Am I no better than Maman?

Every fiber of my being denies the charge.

I might not always be around, but I don't curse or hit Maurice. I pay for a good school for him. I'm not the perfect mother, but I am correcting the mistakes of the past. I can't be expected to leap from terrible to perfect in a lifetime, can I? We learn what we learn, and if it's not the best, we try to do better. If Maurice will be even better than I am to his children, they'll have the perfect life. A single generation cannot fix all the mistakes of the past.

Or maybe I'm just desperate to give myself a pass.

I walk to the bedroom door, but stop with my hand on the wood, while my son is howling with fury and misery inside. Painting at last might be my dream come true, but dark clouds push in at the edges of my heaven. I'm at a loss for what to do with him. I fear for his future and what it might bring.

"He ain't right." Maman wheezes and coughs, collapsing into her chair. "You teach that boy what's what."

My anger rises. "Should I shout at him because he's upset? Should I beat him?"

"I beat you aplenty when you needed it, and it didn't hurt you none. Look where you are now. A famous model, and yourself a painter. La-di-da."

"I succeeded despite your methods not because of them, I can assure you of that. No child will become calmer or smarter for having been beaten." I open the door and step through. I sit on the mattress. "Your mama loves you, my sweet."

He shoves me away and hides under the blanket.

"You must not treat your grandmother that way. That was wrong. Please, talk to me, Maurice."

He hides in silence.

"You must go to school. You know you must. I want you to be a learned man, a gentleman. I want your future to be full of opportunity. Don't you want that?"

He says nothing.

The next day, I take him to a doctor. I will find a cure for this terrible anger my son holds inside him, I don't care if it costs our last coin.

"Mental problems…special institution…best send him away…" I don't hear half the doctor's fine speech. It all adds up to one thing: he's telling me to give up on my son, to have him locked away. "You can leave him now." He adjusts his round wire spectacles on his pale face. "I will make sure he is transported to where he needs to be. It'd be the best for him."

Would it?

I think of all the times Maman took me somewhere and left me there. I take Maurice home. We never return to the doctor.

"I'm keeping you home from school," I tell my troubled son when he wakes in the morning. And while he eats his breakfast, I set my drawing pad on the table next to him. I had a thought while I lay awake in the night. "How do you feel about drawing?"

I pray that what saved me will also save him.

CHAPTER NINETEEN

Ellie

Sunday, March 26th

I can't put Sam's quiet admission out of my head.

Half my brain just sits in an empty room some-where with the words *my grandmother doesn't have a sister* hanging in the air. The rest of me keeps going because when the world throws earthshaking revela-tions at us, it refuses to stop while we adjust.

"I'm visiting Mrs. Martinez at the hospital tomor-row." I set Abby's signature mini cupcakes on my kitchen table, when she comes over on Sunday. I'm still not ready to resume our weekly lunches with Frank, so I invited her over for midafternoon coffee. "I'll take her a piece."

"How is she?"

The mood in the room is civil, if strained.

"Sounds good on the phone. If all goes well, they're going to release her on Thursday."

"Four days doesn't seem long enough to recuperate from a broken hip."

"If that's all health insurance pays for, then that's all people get. Almond milk?"

"Yes, please."

I step to the fridge. Once again, there are cars in my old driveway—a real estate agent with a family. Two little girls are running around the front yard. "Can we have a swing?" They squeal loudly enough to be heard from across the street. "Can we have a puppy?"

One of the kids is about three, the other maybe ten. They remind me of Abby and myself. The parents walk around the house, holding hands. I can only see them from the back. The husband has short dark hair, the wife a blonde ponytail. The kids run around the garage to the back.

This should have been us—Chris and me and our kids.

The thought hurts, but doesn't level me.

I bring Abby her coffee. "After Mrs. Martinez recovers and I get a new job, I'm moving."

She stops with her glass halfway to her mouth. "What brought this about?"

"I keep reading about Suzanne Valadon. She's quickly becoming my favorite artist. I think she and I both have daddy issues."

"How so?"

"Her father didn't acknowledge her. Her son's

father didn't acknowledge her son. I don't think she ever could truly trust a man."

"You don't trust men?"

I want this conversation to go well, so I don't bring up Frank. But there's another topic that needs to be addressed. "I didn't lie about Dad."

We can't tiptoe around the subject forever.

"I know you have no reason to lie." Abby twists away from me on her chair, as if looking for something on the counter, but she doesn't get up. Then she turns back. "I accept that it must be true." The skin tightens around her eyes. "Why didn't you tell me about it before?"

I've thought and thought and thought about this.

"Part of it was that I didn't want to say anything bad about them. I loved them and I missed them. I didn't want to believe that it could be true. If I didn't speak about it, maybe it would go away. Nobody knew but me." I wrap my fingers around my tea. "It sounds stupid."

"You were ten years old."

The next breath I take comes easier.

"It's just that Mom said it, and then they died. So I didn't want to say the words. And then, I told Chris. Our wedding anniversary was coming up, and we were talking about our parents. And he kept going on about how solid marriages used to be, and how now so many people get divorced. And I just blurted it out." His stunned look is etched on my mind. "And he went for his annual physical on

Monday, and the doctor found a lump and sent him for a test."

"I'm sorry."

"I'm sorry too. I should have told you everything right when it happened. I definitely shouldn't have waited twenty years to throw it at you at a restaurant like a weapon. I don't know what's wrong with me. Since Chris died, I can't find my way back to myself."

"You're on your way."

"I hope so. Because I want to do better."

We fall silent for a few moments. It's not an awkward silence. It's a sisterly silence, where two sisters are just there for each other.

Then I speak again. "It's not that I don't trust men. I think I don't trust people to stay. Mom and Dad died. And then Chris died. Everybody leaves. I know I've been pushing you away. I think, deep down, I thought you'd leave me too, sooner or later."

"I would never leave you. We're sisters."

"What if you get married and your husband decides to move away?"

Abby straightens the junk mail on the table. "Not a huge concern right now, considering that I'm single. I broke up with Frank yesterday. We're no longer together. He stole money from me. And maybe I could have forgiven that, all things considered, but he stole money from you. Nobody messes with my little sister."

I drop into my chair. "I don't know what to say."

"You've got big dreams that we need to make reality. There's no room for people on the team who're pulling us backward. We're only going forward, dammit."

"What about the other guy?"

Abby looks up at the ceiling, then back at me with a sigh. "He was just the symptom of a bigger problem. I ended things right after you caught us."

"I'm sorry."

"I needed that wakeup call. I'm going to get my life together."

I watch her, reeling. "I've never seen you with your life disheveled."

"I'm good at keeping up appearances. Do you know why people never look behind masks? Masquerades are pretty. Who wants to see ugliness?"

"Sooner or later, all the pretty masks crack."

"You're wise beyond your years."

"I've been hanging with Mrs. Martinez. Anyway, if we don't live in truth, what do we have?"

"We'll always have each other."

"That's the truth. I'm sorry I've been weird lately. I think I was doing that thing when we give other people what we'd like to get. I wanted space, so I was giving you space, thinking that must be what you want too. And you were trying to give me stability and family. I think you want those."

My sister blinks a few times. "There you go, being deep again."

"Can't take credit. It's something Joshua said to me."

"He's not a bad guy."

"I know. I'm just not ready."

"And your hands are full with the museum." She drops the matchmaking just like that. Maybe she's growing. Maybe we both are. "I know you can do it without me," she says, "but it's an awesome project. I want to be part of something big. You know? This will matter. I mean, long term. Maybe even after we're dead. I want to help."

For the first time in a year, I don't feel alone. "Thanks."

"The other day, at the house." She gestures across the street. "People were offering help. Let's put a team together." She watches my face. "What?"

"I have another secret? Not really a secret," I rush on. "It's a recent thing."

Abby shoots back an incredulous "What is it?"

I should have told her sooner.

"Chris has a son. I sent an email to Helen. She needs to know she has a grandson. She hasn't responded yet. She might be in the middle of the Atlantic for all I know, without access to Wi-Fi. Or could have lost her phone in the water."

"Slow down. What do you mean Chris has a son? "My sister's chin drops. "From where? How? Since when?"

I share her bewilderment. I still have to convince myself every morning that Sam is real.

I explain how Mrs. Card found me, ending with "Technically, kind of, you have a nephew. I'm sorry I didn't say anything right away. I needed a minute."

And then for a few seconds, we just stare at each other.

Yeah. Welcome to my world.

"Wow," Abby says, shell-shocked. "How do you feel about it?"

"Do I have to pick just one feeling? Because I have a jumble of them."

If I want the museum to become reality, I do have to build a team. I start after Abby leaves by calling Francoise Gibbler. She tells me she's at the Brandywine Museum of Art, ten minutes from me, having a look around before a sponsor's cocktail reception. She invites me over.

"How is your Museum of Unseen Art coming along? I keep thinking about it. It's a brilliant concept." She's wearing a cashmere caftan with leather riding boots, and it shouldn't work, but it does. She looks like the head of a small European principality. Princess casual.

The rotunda where we chat is a piece of modern art in the style of Frank Lloyd Wright. The simple, confident lines focus my mind.

Time for brutal honesty.

"No significant forward movement. Yet. I've dreamt a big dream, and I eventually found the courage to go after my big dream, but I've still been playing it safe. I haven't gone after my dream with all I have, not with all my heart. I've been taking steps, but I haven't gone to ridiculous lengths. Maybe, deep down, I don't want to look ridiculous if I fail."

"I felt exactly the same way when I started my skincare line. But then I was inspired by my grandmother, who was in the French Resistance during World War II."

"Oh, wow." I try to imagine what that must have been like. And here I am, thinking I have problems. "She must have told you some amazing stories."

"She was involved in saving the artifacts of the Louvre. She was a department store sales girl at the Grands Magasins du Louvre. The museum director closed the Louvre for three days for repairs. The store employees wrapped and crated the art, and then it was shipped out to save it from the Nazis, who were closing in on Paris."

Wow again. "It's astounding how many exceptional women did amazing things and we never hear about it."

She nods. "They somehow found the courage and went ahead, and never received the credit. Later, during the occupation, she put her life at risk day after day in the resistance, delivering messages. If she'd been caught, she would have been killed. After hearing her talk about the past, I realized that if I fail, the worst that could happen is that I lose my business. How could I be a coward with such low stakes?"

We circle around, admiring the paintings on the walls, while I marvel at all she's just revealed.

"I can see how your grandmother inspired you to do great things. Would it be weird if I said I'm inspired by Suzanne Valadon?" I pause and look another hard truth in the face. "Except, I'm starting to think that while I've been learning a lot *about* her, I've failed to learn *from* her. Valadon *lived* her life, in all capital letters. She lived every single day to the fullest. She took it all, whether it was on offer or not. She grabbed her chances, and to hell with the consequences."

"My grandmother was the same. She used to tell me that there was no *safe* in life. The adventure of life is just that—an adventure."

"I think Valadon would have agreed. She didn't put off her dreams until a better time. She drew on the wall with charcoal while her drunk mother raged into the night. She drew while she worked at the funeral wreath factory. She drew while she worked at the circus. She drew while she recovered from her fall from the trapeze. She drew while she modeled for other artists. I want to put together an exhibit of her unseen art for my first show. I'm assembling an unofficial team. Would you consider—"

"Count me in."

I'm so excited, I'm giddy. "What we have so far is an old factory building on offer, but it needs finishing, not to mention a million permits. You're on the board at a nonprofit that supports emerging artists. Since my idea has to do with the arts, do you think it might be eligible for a grant?"

"Let me bring the idea up to the other board members. And until your building is ready…" Her eyes light up. "Come with me."

She leads me down a hallway, then another, through a Staff Only entrance.

"Where are we going?"

"The old archives." She opens a set of double oak doors, and then we're in a cavernous space. "The museum has just transferred all their archives to electronic format. They had boxes and boxes of hundred-year-old receipts in here, deteriorating. They moved everything to humidity-controlled off-site storage. Which leaves the museum with all this empty space."

Hope swirls through the air, diamond dust. It sparkles. "You think—"

"That," Francoise points at the far wall, "is the back wall of the main gallery. All they need is a door, and this can be brand-new exhibition space. I don't mean as a replacement for your museum idea. But I'm sure we could talk with the people in charge and arrange a Valadon exhibit."

"That would solve my *reputable venue* problem. No institute would hesitate to lend work to the Brandywine Museum of Art. Perfect."

I stand there for another minute, imagining the possibilities. I can see it, all the colors, those wonderful paintings around me.

On my way home, I call Wanda Abara. She knows me already, and she does have three Valadon sketches.

"If the Brandywine Museum of Art makes the request, I bet we could arrange a loan. How are your own museum plans going?"

"I need to learn more about museums. I

submitted an application for a paid internship position at the Philadelphia Museum of Art. I don't suppose you could put in a good word for me?"

"I'd be willing to put in a hundred."

"Do you think they'll consider my application? I'm not studying toward a degree in museum studies."

"Not strictly required. What do you have?"

"A degree in design with a minor in marketing. BFA." Bachelor of Fine Arts, the umbrella that design falls under.

"Graduated in the past five years?"

"Barely."

"Close counts not only with horseshoes and hand grenades, but internships too. I'll write a letter of recommendation."

"I can't even tell you how much I appreciate that. I don't suppose there's a housing stipend? The listing didn't mention."

"Let me check into it."

When I get home, I dance around the kitchen table with Bubbles.

"It's happening."

I'm on a roll. I'm motivated. I'm ready to fight for my dreams. But I still put off talking to Joshua until the next morning. I keep thinking about how he reacted to my decision to move, how he said all the right things. I've resented him for so long, I have trouble adjusting to this new reality where I appreciate him.

I wait until 9:00 a.m. to ring his doorbell with two

cups of Starbucks's best in hand. I could have brought over coffee in my own two mugs, but I want him to know that I went to the trouble.

He opens the door in work clothes, his smile instant and welcoming. "Surprise guests are the best guests."

"You are so weird. I hate surprises."

He laughs.

He's always quick to laugh. Chris was quick to laugh too—I stop myself there. I'm *not* going to compare them.

"You had a lot of bad surprises, to be fair." Joshua takes the cup I hand him. "What's in this?"

"Plain black."

"I look like a tough guy with a tool belt on, don't I?" He ushers me in. "Not when it comes to coffee."

I haven't been inside the house for a while, not since it's been completely finished, not since it's been staged for showings. It's pristine, all white. I love all white. I don't like having to hunt for dirt. It's spacious and sparkling, and modern. It's—

Joshua watches me for reaction. "Hate it?"

"I want to." So little of Chris and me is left behind. I don't feel as if I've come home. I feel as if I'm visiting. I note with surprise that the thought doesn't hurt. "It's different."

"Different good, or different bad?" He walks over to the counter.

Oh, for heaven's sake, Ellie. Give some damn credit where credit is due. "It's great."

"Thank you. Coming from you, that means something." He fixes up his cup, then goes for the taste test and smacks his lips. "A good sugar rush can carry me right through the first hour or two of hard labor. Now, what can I help you with?"

"I might have found a temporary space. I want to put together a team of volunteers to figure everything out. I don't suppose you'd be interested? I'm going to do this thing."

"I never doubted you would. And I would love to be part of it."

"Thank you."

Then there's a moment of awkward silence, when I'm not sure what to say next. I know what I *should* say. He's going to help me with MUA. I have to ask about his project, no matter how much it kills me. It's common courtesy.

"Any bites on the house?"

"I got an offer." His eyes are wary.

"Oh." That's all I have. I need another second. "Nice family?"

"You've met them. My brother, Jace, and Olivia. He's been here helping a lot. He's fallen in love with the place. They're in a small townhome right now, and he wants a backyard with a swing set. Well, Olivia wants it. The kid can be pretty persuasive."

And just like that, all my misgivings disappear. The smile I give Joshua is genuine. "I'm glad. I hope they'll be happy here. Get ready for Mrs. Martinez spoiling Olivia. She's been pining for a grandkid."

"Children need all the love they can get. She can spoil away. How is she? Have you talked to her? I was thinking about going to see her tomorrow. Does she know yet when she can come home?"

"Possibly Thursday. I'm going to see her later this afternoon." I almost ask Joshua if he wants to go together, but I don't.

"I'm picking up lumber for a wheelchair ramp for her front door. I figure she'll be in a chair for a while."

"That's really nice of you. I'd like to contribute. I should have noticed sooner that we were out of salt. I should have taken care of that ice."

"The ice isn't your fault. You aren't in charge of winter. And no worries about the lumber. I'm only buying a few pieces. I have a ton of scraps."

Now that we're talking about mobility, a whole new set of problems surfaces. "It's an old house."

"A beautiful old cottage."

"The doorways are narrow. I don't know if a wheelchair will fit through. I don't know if she'll even be able to go to the bathroom. There's no way she'll be able to go upstairs."

"She definitely shouldn't be sleeping on that lumpy couch with a broken hip. She should be comfortable. How long does it take to fully recover from hip surgery?"

I tap my phone. Google has the answer. "Up to a year."

We stare at each other.

"So." He points me to a barstool. "Emergency meeting."

"Best-case scenario," I say as we sit, coffee in

hand, "she'll need a place for a few months that's fully handicap accessible."

"Worst-case scenario, if she doesn't fully recover, she might never be able to go upstairs."

"How about one of those chairlifts?"

"Like you said, old house. Her staircase is too narrow."

"I'd love to take care of her. I can put off moving. But obviously, my apartment is even worse."

Joshua sits up straighter. His eyes light up. I can tell he's thinking home improvement thoughts. "Is it?"

"More stairs, no room for an extra bed?"

"No extra bed needed if you two switch places. She could live upstairs, while you live in the cottage. She might not come outside for a few days or even weeks. Jace and I could carry her up. Your apartment has no internal doorways other than the bathroom. Do you have a shower or a bathtub?"

"Shower. And I'd be happy to switch places with her, but she'll want to come outside at some point."

"By then, I could turn the garage into a handicap-accessible apartment. All one level."

I don't know how people live like that—thinking that everything is easy, that everything is possible. I don't know if I envy them or pity them. They seem unaware that when you least expect it, reality has a way of rearing its ugly head.

"I doubt you have that many scraps, and how would she pay for all that?"

"I have to move out in a few weeks when Jace

and Olivia move in. I could build out the garage in the meantime. When that's done and Mrs. Martinez moves down into her new apartment, I could move over into the upstairs apartment until I find something else. Would save me having to pay for a short-term rental."

His plan twists my brain into a pretzel. "You're a good problem solver."

"That's the definition of being a flipper."

"I've defined it in a few other ways in the past."

He snorts, shaking his head. "I bet. I like your dark sense of humor, you know that?"

I'm glad he sees it as a dark sense of humor and not just plain bitchiness. I scrutinize his plan for cracks, but I can't find any. "*If* Mrs. Martinez agrees."

"It's not a bad solution. You and I would be here to help her out. And then Olivia and Jace too. Olivia doesn't have any grandmothers."

"What happened to your mom?"

"Elbow cancer."

I don't know if he's serious. I don't dare laugh. "Are you messing with me?"

"I swear. Synovial sarcoma. By the time they diagnosed it, it metastasized. It's a rare cancer. She would joke about it, even toward the end, how she was always extra. The worst was that she never got to meet Olivia. She died when Jace's wife was pregnant."

"I'm sorry. That must have been terrible."

"They would have loved each other." Joshua falls silent. Then he speaks again. "Since we're talking about kids, is Sam coming back again? Jace and I are thinking about going into Philly to see the Sixers. We thought we could take the boy. If it's all right with Mrs. Card."

"Oh, I want that for him so bad. Would you really take him? Please? If his grandmother says it's okay, of course. The Sixers would make Sam so happy. I'll pay for his ticket."

"Not necessary. We'll have fun. He's a good kid."

Don't say anything else that's nice.

Joshua Jennings has to stop. Because if he doesn't, I'll have to admit that I'm starting to like him, and what if that kills me?

I'm saved when his phone pings with a text.

"Go ahead." I sip my coffee.

He reads the small screen and scrolls and scowls.

"Bad news?"

He sets the phone on the counter. "I was hoping this wouldn't happen." He picks up the phone as if to double-check he's just read what he read, but only glances at it for a second before he puts it down again. "The township rejected my parking plan at the Coatesville building. I figured no matter what I do with that building, it'll need parking, so I submitted the paperwork last week."

In my mind, the image of my beautiful museum that I built from hopes and dreams crumbles brick by brick.

He winces, as if he too can see it. "I'm sorry, Ellie."

I can only nod. I was so excited about this, I was

so ready to leap, that I'm in shock at the sudden end to the dream.

"I was going to apply for the land use permit today," Joshua goes on, "but I suppose there's no point."

"Thank you." I get up. "Thank you anyway."

On the way home, I pull out my phone to call Madame Gibbler, but she beats me to it. My phone rings while I'm still scrolling for her name in my contact list.

"I talked to a couple of people on the board about your idea," she says, and I can tell from her regretful tone that this conversation is going to be as bad as the one from which I'm walking away.

"They said no?"

"It's not so much that they're not supportive, but the room can't be designated as exhibition space. It's their closest room to the Brandywine Creek. The creek floods every spring. Those stone walls are old. The chances of a breach are too high. That's why they moved the archives out of there in the first place."

"That makes sense. Thank you for trying."

Up in my kitchen, I sit down by my laptop, look at my Philly apartment search, and close it.

I thought I was on a roll. It's difficult to accept that I'm back at the starting point.

I don't mind staying at the cottage. I'd happily help Mrs. Martinez with anything. But the museum I do mind. It's more than a legacy I want to create for Chris. It's more than not letting history forget an exceptional woman like Suzanne. More than bringing hidden artworks up from the basement.

This project was a test for myself. In a way, I was trying to bring myself back, I realize as I stare at Bubbles sleeping. I wanted to be the type of person who was strong enough to do something like this. Someone who, like Suzanne, could dream impossible dreams. And then she could make them come true.

It hurts that I failed.

CHAPTER TWENTY

Suzanne

1893 / Age 28

"WHO IS THAT?" PAUL MOUSIS WATCHES THE MAN AT THE PIANO AT AUBERGE DU CLOU. He's taken me out to celebrate the new year at one of Montmartre's favorite literary cabarets. We've become friends since Miquel introduced us. Paul is nothing like the others of my circle. For one, he's not an artist. He's reassuringly conventional and normal. He works for a bank. "The man knows music."

"His name is Erik Satie." I trace the shape of the empty chair next to me with my eyes, the back support imitating the petals of a lotus. I should like to draw it. The place is packed, the crowd merry. The yellow haze of the gaslights and the smoke haze makes the scene look like an Impressionist painting.

"You know everyone." Paul doesn't hide his admiration. In fact, he's been openly admiring me all evening. His attention is flattering.

"We've been barely introduced. He's another friend of Miquel."

"Miquel is too busy with his paintbrush to spend time with me these days." Paul refills my wine. His attention never strays from me for too long. "And what are *you* working on, Suzanne?"

"I've been painting in oil, but drawing still comes more naturally. When I have an idea, I find myself reaching for charcoal instead of a brush. I'm trying my hand at nudes, the female form through the eyes of a woman. I thought it might be interesting." I wait for him to express discomfort or outright disapproval. Nudes are not considered an appropriate topic for a female artist.

"Do the models find it strange to pose nude for a woman?" His smile is awkward, but his tone is free of condemnation.

"I'm working on my own form for now. Self-portraits with the help of a large mirror."

Paul, the prim and proper banker, blushes and downs his wine in three gulps. He's looking at everything but me. "I see."

I find him not only attractive, but endearing.

Before I could tease him for his puritan sensibilities, Erik Satie finishes his piece.

He leaves his piano and strides straight to our

table, straightening his glasses. "I thought it was you, Suzanne."

I make the introduction, and the men shake hands, but Satie doesn't return to performing. He looks at me. "I'm finished for the evening."

Oh, does he want to talk to Paul? He must have known who Paul was. Maybe he wants advice on something related to finance.

"Why don't you sit with us?" I nudge the chair I've just admired away from the table.

Satie is part of the young and talented set of Montmartre. If I can, I want to help him.

"Suzanne tells me you're a composer." Paul is the picture of good manners. If he resents a stranger interrupting his dinner, he doesn't show it. This too I like about him. "Are you working on anything?"

Satie's shoulders droop. He opens his mouth, but only a dejected sigh escapes him. He makes a half-hearted gesture with his hand, out of sorts.

The lost look on his face reminds me of Vincent van Gogh when he was in low spirits. Oh, how I miss him still. "What is it?"

"I heard Debussy play *Clair du Lune* at his apartment a week ago." Satie's voice is raw with naked misery. "The master isn't finished with the piece but…it's perfect. I find his genius paralyzing."

Paul waits for an explanation, his bewilderment obvious, if not verbally expressed.

When Satie simply makes another helpless gesture, I venture my own thoughts, based on my own experience. "As an artist, sometimes when you meet with superior work, it either inspires you to work harder to reach the next level, or it depresses you and makes you want to give up."

Erik's eyes fill with gratitude for my under-standing. "If I'll never be that good, what's the point of trying? I will never be able to compose anything nearing his level. Why even struggle? Wouldn't it be smarter to quit? Let the master be the master."

"I've been envying Suzanne." Paul smiles at me. "But maybe I'm lucky to have no creative streak. Numbers tend not to inspire this kind of despair. You learn how to work the mechanical calculator and there you are. The rest is easy."

He orders more drink and food for the table, then he asks Satie about Debussy, whom Paul also admires.

Both men are animated. Paul is clean-cut, with a magnificent mustache, well-to-do, confident, with a reassuring stability to him. Satie is nervous, a couple of years younger than Paul, long hair, little round glasses, a true Bohemian.

"Would you sit for a portrait for me?" I'm suddenly inspired. I've already drawn Paul and his dog.

Satie freezes as if he's in front of the easel already. His eyes fill with wonder, his misery temporarily forgotten, just as I've planned. "I'd be honored, Madame Valadon."

"She claims her victims where she can," Paul says under his breath good-naturedly, and we all laugh.

"Beauty is the undoing of all men," he adds. "How could any of us resist such a splendid woman?"

I strike a pose in my chair, and the gentlemen applaud, and then I've had enough of attention for the moment. I almost bring up the anarchists whose bomb killed six people at the police station at the avenue de L'Opera. But instead, I ask about the Panama Canal scandal. "Do you think Clemenceau will be charged?"

"Very likely. Looks like the company's bankruptcy involves eight hundred thousand investors," Paul tells us. "Over one and a half *billion* gold francs lost on the venture, by latest estimates, but I think it will be more once all's said and told."

I can't comprehend so large a number, and I'm impressed that he can.

Satie's shoulders dip again. "I still can't believe Baron Reinach committed suicide. Herz fled to England."

"Comte de Lesseps will be charged, for certain," Paul says with assurance. "Who would have thought that the builder of the Suez Canal would disgrace himself so? And Gustave Eiffel too. And then the ministers who are being accused of taking bribes." He pauses, as if hesitant to say more. In the end, he does go on, but lowers his voice. "A new French company is interested in buying the permits and assets of the failed venture. And so is the United States. I'd put money on the canal eventually ending up with the Americans."

He knows everything, and the width and breadth

of his knowledge appeals to me immensely. I love his brain. Paul says he likes me because I know how to live.

We barely notice the time pass as we flit from topic to topic, the discussion of wide-ranging subjects exhilarating.

When Satie brings up Nietzsche, I comment, and Paul gifts me with an approving look. And I silently give thanks to Toulouse-Lautrec, regardless of our parting.

There's only one awkward moment, at the end of the night, when both men offer to escort me home. It doesn't occur to me until then that both are interested in me. Most of my friends are artists, and most artists are men. I am always surrounded by them. Sometimes, I forget I am not one of them.

"We could discuss when I might sit for the portrait." To my surprise, Satie comes up with the winning argument.

"Until next time, then." Paul bows out with grace. "Au revoir, Suzanne."

And so Erik Satie and I walk the cobblestones side by side in the low light. He looks at me more than he looks at where he's going. He nearly walks into a lamp pole. He pretends nothing happened. "I very much admire your strength."

"You mustn't let anyone intimidate you or put you off your work," I advise him. "From before I even seriously began pursuing my art, I've been surrounded by the greats. Puvis, Renoir, Toulouse-Lautrec, Degas. If I thought I shouldn't create anything until I grew as good as they are, I would never have picked up a charcoal or a pencil."

"You are so full of light and energy and all that is positive," he tells me and grows more breathless as he goes on. "You are the muse herself, Madame."

Flattering, but nonsense. "Tell me more about the piece you're working on."

He speaks, and I ask questions, and he speaks, and I nod. And he flies, and I realize only then how badly he's needed encouragement.

When we stop in front of my building, Satie takes my hands. With his top hat and frock coat, and then that long hair sticking out every which way, the wild excitement burning in his eyes, he looks possessed. "I have never felt about another woman as I feel about you. May I call you Suzanne? I cannot lose your company."

"You may. And you won't. We can be friends."

"Must we be only that? Could not we be more? Marry me, Suzanne. I wish you by my side forever. You are a muse. You will be my muse. I recognized you as such the moment we met."

I nearly start laughing, but the tumult of emotions in his eyes makes me realize he means the words.

"Before today, we've barely been introduced. We've only just had a single conversation tonight. Do be reasonable, Erik. Don't you think this is a little too fast?"

"I needed only this night to fall in love with you, Suzanne. I know my mind."

"I'm at a loss for words." I don't recognize myself.

Money, I've lacked before, and food, and opportunity too, but words I usually have in abundance. I don't have a bashful temperament.

"You don't believe me." His shoulders collapse, but only for a moment before he fills with enthusiasm again. "I will prove myself to you. May I come by and visit tomorrow?"

Oh, I can't wait to see Maman's face. I'm more amused than anything else. Satie is happy, and he's begun the night so sad. I haven't the heart to hurt him. "You may. The afternoon would be best."

"ARE YOU AND ERIK LOVERS? THE TRUTH," Miquel Utrillo demands, the skin around his eyes tight. "He said he proposed."

We are standing outside Le Chat Noir, on the rue Victor-Massé, where we first met. He is my closest, dearest friend. He saved Maurice from having to live the rest of his life as a bastard. He's helped me teach Maurice to draw and encourages him at every step. I hate to hurt him. But I won't lie to him either.

"I didn't say yes, but we've been together for the past few weeks." After his first visit, more followed, and Erik surprised me by sweeping me off my feet. I find his open adoration and unbridled enthusiasm difficult to refuse. He composes music for me. He does make me feel like a muse.

"Do you love him?"

"I think I could. I've been painting his portrait and getting to know him. The same flame that burns inside me to translate life to the canvas, burns inside him to translate life to music. Two small but stubborn flames. Maybe together, we'd be more difficult to extinguish."

Michel's expression hardens, becomes a mask. "I am leaving Paris."

I reach for his arm. "Maurice will miss you too much."

He steps back, pretending he must because the door opens, but he moves farther than needed, out of my reach. He stands there and looks away. He can't bear looking at me.

Pain cracks my chest. "Michel?"

So this is the bargain. I gain a lover, but I lose my oldest friend, the man who gave my son his name, the one gesture that meant—and still means—everything to me.

I won't rail against the unfairness of fate. If I wept every time life knocked me down, I would do nothing but cry. The only way to fight back is living fully and loudly, every minute of every day.

I step after him and reach for his hand. "I wanted to paint you again."

"You can paint me from memory." He allows me to touch him for a moment and no more. "By now, you must know the lines of my face."

I do indeed. I know, by heart, all the shapes that make him. I've drawn him a dozen times. "When are you leaving?"

"As soon as I can book passage. I've received an offer to participate in the new World's Fair. They're calling it The World's Columbian Exposition, to commemorate the four hundredth anniversary of Christopher Columbus's journey. I am told there will be no expenses spared. Chicago wants to prove to the world that the city is fully recovered from the great fire." He looks through the cabaret's windows at the colorful world we've been part of together, and he lingers on the tableau as if wanting to take it with him. When his eyes return to me, they're filled with profound sadness. "No matter how great a devastation, recovery is always possible."

"I wish you only the best." Would he stay if I asked? I don't, because I can't give him my heart the way he wants it. And he deserves nothing less than that.

He walks me home, always a gentleman. And I watch him leave, wishing life could be different.

Maman is mending an old apron in the kitchen when I walk in. She barely looks up. She hums a country song, deep into her cups. Age has bent her back. The years deepened her crosshatch of wrinkles. Wine has stolen the spark from her eyes. What scares me is that when I paint my self-portrait, I see parts of her in the mirror sometimes.

I take off my hat. "Maurice?"

"Sleeping."

He must have been outside, playing all afternoon. I've done that at least, gifted him a childhood. He doesn't have to work at a factory or the stables or the market. My son has as much freedom as I could give him.

I turn toward my studio, then turn away. I had a four-hour sitting in the morning and another four-hour sitting in the afternoon, both difficult poses, their ache lingering in my body. "I'll go to bed too. I need the sleep."

I walk into the bedroom on light feet, but Maurice, in the bed next to mine, isn't lost in the world of dreams. He's sitting on the mattress, staring at his hands.

"Have you drawn anything today?" I still teach him when I can. He's becoming quite adept.

He mumbles. Then he gets up, and he staggers.

"Are you sick?" I rush to hold him up, then turn my nose from the smell of wine on his breath. "Have you been drinking?"

His grin is feeble. "Just with Grandmother."

I'll deal with Maman later. My son comes first. I sit him back on the bed. "You're too young to drink."

"Wine doesn't bother me." He giggles. "Beer makes me fart."

"When have you drunk beer?"

"We drink what we got."

"When?"

"I don't know."

"All right. Before today, when was the last time?"

"Yesterday."

Anger hardens my insides. "When was the first time?"

"I don't remember. We always drank."

"When you were still going to school?"

"Before I started going to school." He hiccups. "If

339

Grandmother doesn't give me any, I steal it from her." Maurice flashes a proud smile. "Or I steal it where I can."

I sink onto the mattress next to him. I have to work to comprehend what he's telling me, then work even harder to accept the reality of the words. All the times Maman watched him and I came home from work and found him sweetly sleeping... *What a good boy*, I would think, tired from playing.

But he hadn't been.

My son is nine years old, and he's a drunk. I'm shaking with a storm of emotions I can't even name. I lay him back down, then I whirl out of the room.

"How could you?" I charge at Maman. "He reeks of wine. His feet won't hold him up. This is what you do all day?"

"He's a handful." She barely looks at me. "You're always working. He gets a cup, it makes him calm."

"You made him as you are."

I could cry. How I hated, all my life, how Maman is, how she drinks. And now my son. My only child.

For the first time, I want to strike Maman as she struck me so many times. I want to drag her from her chair and shove her out the front door. I want her gone. I want her far away from my sweet son.

And I almost grab her, but Maurice staggers from the room and steps between us. "Don't yell at Grandmama."

His eyes are unfocused.

"Oh, for heaven's sake, sit."

So many things suddenly make sense. His rages,

his problems at school--none of them were his fault. They were mine. To put food on the table, I left him behind.

I thought to be a good mother meant that his belly was full, that he had warm clothes, that he had toys. I gave him everything I wanted when I was a child. But I should have given more. What he needed was my time.

The fine apartment, the paintings, the recognition matters not. All my aspirations fall away. I fold over from pain, from the realization of how many different ways I've failed. And failure has a price.

I am losing my son.

I can hear Sister Marguerite's voice in my head, La Fontaine's tale of the stupid, stupid frog that wanted to be too big. *To reach too high is a sin. You must know your place.*

Have I sinned?

Am I being punished?

I cannot, I cannot lose Maurice.

CHAPTER TWENTY-ONE

Ellie

Monday, March 27th

"Joshua is such a lovely young man." Mrs. Martinez props herself higher on her pillows to bathe in the spring sunshine pouring through the window. Her hospital room is on the sixteenth floor. She has a view of Philadelphia you can't get outside a million-dollar penthouse apartment, looking over the Delaware River and the Benjamin Franklin Bridge. "He's as hardworking as any man I've ever seen. A self-starter too. The way he is with that little Olivia, and your Sam too, that tells a lot about someone."

The *your Sam* part is heavy enough to set aside for another time. The Joshua issue, however, has to be addressed immediately, before Mrs. Martinez runs away with it. "No matchmaking. I mean it."

I could distract her by telling her of my museum plans falling apart, but I don't want to dump anything depressing on her.

"I've held myself back for a whole year," she says.

"What's another year, then?"

"I'm a romance writer. I see romance everywhere."

"Really? The occupational-hazard defense?"

"I'm on drugs."

"And here I am, goofing around. I'm sorry. Are you in pain? I'm so sorry I didn't take care of that ice the second I saw it."

"I'm the landlady. I'm responsible for keeping the driveway clean. It is what it is. I'll just be sitting around for a bit. I won't wear out my fancy new sneakers so fast." She waves off my concern. "Honestly, right at this minute, I don't even remember what pain feels like. How is Karma doing?"

"I thought about sneaking her in."

"You should have."

"She wouldn't get in the bag," I tell her. "Sorry."

"Karma does what Karma wants. Beagles are that way."

"I've been feeding her and walking her. I brought her upstairs last night so she wouldn't have to sleep alone."

"What did Bubbles think about that?"

"I think they're growing on each other." I secured

the lid on Bubble's terrarium to make sure there were no mishaps.

Mrs. Martinez laughs. "I bet." She tilts her head to the right, then to the left. Her muscles must be sore from the hospital bed. "That's a beautiful green jacket. I always thought it brought out your eyes."

"I've been looking at Suzanne Valadon's art so much, I realized I've missed color. And I'm tired of winter. I wanted something that says spring."

"Perfect with the navy-blue shirt. I'm glad to see you wearing more color again. I never said anything, but I was worried about all your blacks and grays. Anyway, back to Joshua."

"You're shameless."

"I just had surgery. That should grant me some allowances, but romance isn't even what I'm talking about," she says in the most unconvincing tone ever. "I like Joshua's idea of transforming the garage into another apartment. I've been worrying about the stairs at the cottage, as I grow older."

"That's a long way off."

"Still, something to think about. And with this accident…"

"You'll heal."

"I do plan on dancing again, but in the meantime, I still have to live somewhere." She takes a sip of herbal tea. She told me which jars to bring from her pantry. "Anyway, here's a thought. The property consists of two lots. When we sold the farm to the developer, we asked to keep the cottage and the small lot next to it. A good thing too, because he sure lowballed us on the price. He told us he'd be subdividing into two-acre lots—just a few houses, keeping the country character and all that. The way he told it, he was barely going to make money on the deal. Then he subdivided into third-of-an acre lots, put up thirty houses, and made out like a bandit." She holds up her index finger. "Don't get started on flippers."

"Who? Me? I'd never."

She rolls her eyes, and maybe it's the drugs, but for a second they cross. "If the garage had a downstairs apartment and I moved there," she unscrambles her eyes, "I could sell the cottage is what I meant to say."

"Should I tell Joshua to go ahead?"

"Yes. God bless that man."

The way she talks him up at every chance, I wouldn't be surprised if she had a petition for sainthood ready for him under her pillow. "What are we going to do with everything that's in the garage?"

"You said Jace bought your old house. I don't suppose he'd let me rent your old garage for a while?"

"They're moving from a small townhome to a large house. I doubt he has a ton of stuff. I'll ask."

"When I'm back on my feet, I'll go through it all. I haven't used anything from there in years. I need to donate the lot. And if you move over to the cottage temporarily, there'll be room there for your boxes. This will be a good change. You'll see."

"How are you always so positive?"

"I think of life as a book. It's full of twists and

turns. Some of it is comedy, some is tragedy. I'm not going to pause on the darkest chapter and reread it over and over. I don't want to miss all the excitement that happens next. I want to keep turning the pages. I know there'll be redemption and blessing and joy still. I trust that God is a good writer."

"I swear, sometimes, when you talk, I feel as if I should be taking notes."

Mrs. Martinez reaches for my hand. "Thank you for being here for me." She squeezes my fingers. "The greatest disappointment of my life was that I wasn't able to have children. It always made me worry about old age. When you and Chris moved in across the street, I felt as if I gained a daughter and a son."

"We've always considered you family."

"I know, honey."

Talking about family... Should I share Sam's revelation? Mrs. Martinez also cares for the boy. But she has enough problems of her own. On the other hand, haven't I just recently learned a lesson about keeping secrets?

In the end, I blurt it out. "Mrs. Card doesn't have a sister."

"What's that?" Mrs. Martinez squints.

I keep forgetting that she's on drugs. I shouldn't bring up any heavy topics. But I have, so now I have to explain. "You know how Mrs. Card said she hoped Sam could come and live with Chris, but there was a backup plan all along? If Chris couldn't take Sam, the boy was to live with the grandmother's sister."

"But you just said Carol doesn't have a sister."

"And that is exactly the problem."

"I'm confused. Maybe my brain is fuzzy."

"No, it is confusing. Mrs. Card made up the sister so Chris wouldn't feel pressured to take Sam. She didn't want Chris to take Sam out of obligation, only if Chris really wanted the boy."

"I see."

"Did I tell you I emailed Helen about him? She just got back to me. She's so excited about having a grandson. I think she and Sam are going to start talking online. I put her in touch with Mrs. Card."

"Can Helen take the boy?"

"She didn't say anything about it. She sold her house to buy some kind of an unlimited cruise ticket. She likes the cruise because she couldn't clean her place anymore, and it was difficult for her to cook every day. There's a cruise doctor. The ship is completely handicap accessible. She put a lot of thought into it before she committed. I don't think she could just back out of the deal at this stage. I hope Mrs. Card and Sam aren't counting on that. I really like Sam. His situation is killing me."

"What are you going to do about it?"

This time, I blink at her. Because, that's the question, isn't it? The *only* question, through all life's endless battles. *What are you going to do about it?* No other question exists. It should be stapled on telephone poles down on every street.

Not *How will I get over this?*

Not *Why me?*

Not *Why is life unfair?*

Just *What am I going to do about it?*

The question flickers in my brain like a neon sign on the fritz. Then the answer appears, clear and steady.

"I am going to ask Sam's grandmother if Sam could live with me."

Tuesday, March 28th

"WHY HAVE I NEVER HEARD OF SUZANNE VALADON?" Mrs. Card pages through my printouts of Valadon's art on the table.

The Book of Unseen Art I'm putting together heavily features Suzanne. I've found a number of her works in the public domain. She'll be in good company with two dozen also forgotten but brilliant artists. My museum project might be dead in the water, but I can still do the book. Baby steps. And I'm not letting go of my museum dreams either.

What am I going to do about it? is the question.

I made an appointment with the town planner. I'm going to convince the man. I'm going to make the museum happen.

And I'm not giving up on Sam, which is why I invited them over. It's Tuesday pizza night. I figured young boys and pizza were a good bet.

"The colors are absolutely stunning." I hold up *The Blue Room.* "And the women are so real, aren't they?"

"She's as good as any big-name painter."

"That's what I'm trying to tell everyone. She created two hundred seventy-six paintings, two hundred seventy-three drawings, and thirty-one prints. But when she died, the paper *Le Figaro* never even mentioned that she was an artist. Not a word of all that she created."

Bam. Bam. Bam.

Across the road, a basketball game is in progress, the ball slamming against the driveway again and again. Joshua and Sam against Olivia and Jace.

"How is Bill?" I ask.

"At the doctor's office. They're running a couple of hours' worth of tests. He got accepted into a clinical trial."

"I hope it works."

"That's my prayer. I don't think they'll be able to turn back time, but if they could stop his decline, we'd be happy with that."

"And Sam?"

"Worried." Mrs. Card buries her face in her hands before she drops them. "We're all stressed. He loves talking to Helen, though. It's good that he has another support person in his life. It's another connection to his father. She's making travel arrangements to meet him. Of course, she can't take him back to the ship with her, but I think just meeting her will be good for him. We'll be fine. We'll just put off the retirement home a little longer. I don't mean to sound as if he's a problem. He's a gift. It's just that a boy his age shouldn't be stuck in the house with people our age, day after day. I don't have the time or the energy to give him rides, not after I drive Bill and myself to all our appointments. Neither of us can play basketball with him in the driveway, that's for sure."

"I'm not that coordinated myself. Chris had the sports gene in the family."

"I tried to call him, you know. A few times."

"When?"

"I started as soon as the DNA results came in. I found a number for him on the internet. My calls always went to voice mail. I thought maybe he didn't want to call back. But then, my policy is always to assume the best about people instead of the worst. What if he simply changed his number? So I thought we'd drive out to see him. Drive by, really. The internet record had the address too. I shouldn't have brought Sam, but he likes getting out of the house. And I didn't expect to make contact on the first run. Then I saw strangers in the garage. I stopped the car to see if Chris might come out, to confirm that I at least had the address right. And then Joshua walked down the driveway."

"I'm glad you talked to us."

"I was hoping to find Chris settled down with a wife and kids. I wanted Sammy to be surrounded by parents and siblings."

"You don't know how much I wish that it could have happened that way."

She rubs her arms with a sad smile. "Life isn't a fairy tale, is it?" As she shakes her head, the bucket in my foyer catches her eyes. "I meant to ask you when I came in, but I got distracted. Why do you keep dirt in your apartment?"

"Peony tubers. Weather forecast was threatening with a serious freeze overnight."

I'm not going to let those flowers die now, not after I saved them. I'm glad I noticed their little tips popping up across the street. I thought they were destroyed along with all the other plants, but they weren't. I didn't lose them over the winter, and I didn't lose myself either. The peonies were buried in dirt, while I was buried in grief. But we aren't dead.

I draw the deepest breath I've ever drawn, a breath of starting over. "How would you feel about me becoming Sam's guardian?"

Hope, doubt, and indecision flicker across her face. "You don't have room here."

"I'm moving into the cottage."

I planned on moving away after Mrs. Martinez recovered, but…

There's more than one way to move on. If Mrs. Martinez likes her garage apartment, maybe I'll stay. Sam needs people. He could be happy here, I have no doubt about it.

Mrs. Card presses her hand against her chest. "My grandson does like you. He likes your Joshua as well."

"He's not *my* Joshua."

"And that Jace too, of course. And little Olivia. He's always wanted to be a big brother."

"It's funny how much Olivia looks up to him."

"We'd visit as much as we can. We won't be locked up at the retirement home. And you'd visit us?"

"Every week. You'll always be his grandparents. I know he barely knows me. So we can just start by him spending more time here. We can go fishing. Or to the zoo. I could take him to games at his school. Or if he needs a ride anywhere, and you don't have time. We'll hang out, and when he figures out what he wants, if it's living with me, I'd love that. We'll wait until he's sure. But I'm sure. I'm sure now."

"Let me ask him."

Only when the possibility of Sam saying *no* appears, do I realize how much I want this.

CHAPTER TWENTY-TWO

Suzanne

1893 / Age 28

"GENERALLY SPEAKING, WE PAINT FROM BACK TO FRONT, LARGE TO SMALL, DARK TO LIGHT," I tell Maurice at the table as a carriage clatters by outside. It's the first of September, a warm autumn day. The window is open. "Background first, the largest shapes, find the darkest dark and compare the rest to that." I point to the darkest spot on the postcard in front of us, then hand him a piece of charcoal. "Try."

He examines the image of the elegant buildings that line the Seine. Then he touches the charcoal to paper. He draws his lines with confidence. I don't think I'm biased when I say he has talent.

My own half-finished painting of a new self-portrait awaits on its easel, with the first appearance of faint lines around my eyes. I don't want to paint women who are eternally beautiful. I want to paint women who are unapologetically tough. And I will, but right now, Maurice is more important. Giving him paper and pencil isn't enough. I have to be with him. I have to teach my son.

"See the shadow of the bridge?" I point. "The shadow is always darker than the object itself."

Maurice corrects. "Like this?"

"Like that, my love. Well done."

He beams. Then he refocuses on his task. "I don't know how to draw the bridge's reflection on the water. The lines are not straight there."

I show him. Then, when he does it exactly right, I praise him again.

Maman snores in her room, and my son and I exchange a glance. I forgave her. I can't throw her out. She wouldn't survive without us.

I will make it work. I will keep my family together. Because I'm the only one who can. Because we are all we've got.

I model when I can, and I paint when I can, and I keep working with Maurice.

By the time Miquel Utrillo returns to Paris after the Chicago World's Fair closes its doors at the end of October, I am exhausted, and I'm more than ready to have my friend back.

"Erik Satie is despondent," he tells me as he walks into my studio.

"We only lasted six months." I put down my charcoal and dismiss my two models, who quickly dress. "He wanted me to be his, but I only know how to be mine. I couldn't take care of Erik. I had to take care of Maurice and Maman."

"How are they?" He hangs his black hat on a peg. He shaved off his beard, but kept his mustache. Other than that, he barely changed at all.

"Better. They're at the market. Maurice might become an artist. He surprises me with his progress."

"Like mother, like son." Michel takes his time inspecting my latest sketches. "What's this?"

"*Femmes au bain.*" Women after bath.

"Study for a painting?"

"For a soft-ground etching."

"You etch now?"

"Degas taught me."

"How are his eyes?"

"Failing more by the day."

"A shame."

"He's making more sculptures. He says he needs only his hands for that."

"I missed Paris," Michel admits.

"I missed you too." And then, because hope glints in his brown eyes, I add, "Paul Mousis, the banker, proposed."

Michel's expression doesn't change, yet he seems to withdraw inside himself. "Will you marry him?"

I choose my words with care. "I'm spending time in his company."

For years—for a decade—all I wanted was a last name for Maurice. And now that my son is respectably an Utrillo, thanks to Michel, suddenly proposals keep popping up on my doorstep. Fate does love irony.

Michel stares at me and stares at me, and then he laughs, and the laugh has a bitter tone, but his eyes are not shot with pain as before. "Life is a comedy, my Suzanne."

Isn't it just? A full cabaret act. And how we scramble on the stage. "How was Chicago?"

"It wasn't Paris, but the Fair was a success. I'll tell you all about it if you come for a stroll with me."

"I'm always happy to stretch my legs."

We are on the street when Michel picks back up his tale of the fair. "Nearly fifty nations, each with its own pavilion this time. Enough innovation to make me believe in a brighter future. The fire in the cold storage building that killed seventeen people was a shock, of course. And then the dark shadow of the mayor's assassination at the end, as well. The closing ceremonies had to be canceled."

"How terrible. I read about it in the papers. Weren't thirteen of the victims of the fire firemen?" I can see the scene—swirls of gray smoke and orange flames--but I wouldn't want to put the subject on canvas.

"Gave their lives to save others." Miquel bows his head in a moment of silence. Then he looks up. "Tragedies aside, I wish you could have seen all the marvels."

"Le Figaro published a drawing of a giant wheel people rode sitting in carts."

He dances ahead on the cobblestones like a child. "Eighty meters high."

"How I wish I were there. I miss the heights. I keep meaning to climb the Eiffel Tower, but I never find the time."

"I had a chance to talk with the inventor, George Ferris. He's hoping to make more and install them in other cities."

"I hope one comes to Paris." I want to see the rooftops again. "What else?"

"A moving sidewalk."

"Impossible."

"Mechanics, Madame. It's called a Travelator. I don't see much use for Ferris's Wheel, but mark my words, the Travelator will catch on. Anyone will be able to go anywhere without having to walk."

I'm giddy with the possibility of a world changing so rapidly for the better. "What else?"

"Life-size replicas of Christopher Columbus's three ships, the *Niña*, the *Pinta*, and the *Santa Maria*, built in collaboration between the United States and Spain," he says proudly, a Spaniard to the bone.

"What else?"

"Buffalo Bill's Wild West Show. I truly do wish you'd come with me. If for nothing else than to meet the White Rabbits."

"We have rabbits in France. In every color possible."

He laughs. "The buildings almost weren't finished in time for the opening. Taft, the sculptor in charge, asked if he might bring his female students from the Chicago Art Institute. The chief architect told him, *Bring anyone, even white rabbits, if they do the work.* The women completed the task in record time and with stunning artistry. The White Rabbits name stuck. And now they're celebrated."

A shame they were not offered the opportunity from the beginning. "I would have loved to meet them."

"There were parts you wouldn't have liked. At times, as I walked around, I could hear you complaining in my ear."

"About what?"

"The White City, for one. A creation of the perfect city in the main park, a monument to the power and ideal of white men. Women were relegated to the Women's Building. Anyone not white was barred altogether from participating and were pushed to the Midway exhibit."

"In 1893?" The thought is shocking. "France first abolished slavery a century ago." Although, Napoleon reinstated it in the colonies. But the Second Republic put an end to that.

"Only a quarter of a century over there. But I have hope things will be improving. Frederick Douglass was present because Haiti elected him to be their representative at the Fair. He wrote a protesting pamphlet with Ida B. Wells and other civil rights leaders."

"I'll have to tell Degas." He talks to me often about his time in New Orleans, his Creole mother, and his grandfather who was born in Haiti. "Come to dinner? Paul will want to hear all this. And Maurice."

1894 / Age 29

I NEARLY BREAK MY POSE, I'M SO JITTERY WHILE PUVIS draws an endless succession of sketches of me. I'm going to ask him today. I'm going to ask for it all. The world.

The same God who gave me my dreams would not punish me for reaching for them, I've decided. I am becoming a better mother. I am also becoming a better artist. If men deserve accolades for their hard work, so do I. If my paintings are judged inferior when displayed next to theirs, so be it. But I want them displayed, at least.

Puvis is constructing a large piece for City Hall, working out gestures and placement. The people he draws will be a group of men at the end. He only needs me for my limbs and the line of my back. His focus is so complete that he forgets my break. "Arm higher."

My muscles burn. I hold the pose. It's important that he doesn't become frustrated today. If I hurt, I hurt. I will feel better later.

Then, at long last, once the early-spring light begins to fade, he says, "That's enough for today."

My legs are so stiff, I can barely scramble off the

pedestal. I wrap myself into a robe and limp over to his stack of drawings. "A majestic vision."

"Stop buttering me up, Suzanne. What is it? You've been distracted."

I pull my belt tighter. *Now or never.* "I am thinking about submitting a handful of works to the Académie des Beaux-Arts for this year's Salon."

He blinks. "Whatever for?"

"I believe I am improving." And being accepted at the Salon is a stamp of approval, an acknowledgment that Paris sees me. The best of the best compete for a spot on the hallowed walls. It's everything. When one's work is accepted, it's as if the world says, *this person is an artist.*

"The judges will ask where you received your formal education."

"The École des Beaux-Arts doesn't allow women."

"Then have you studied at an *atelié*? Which of the greats has accepted you as his student?"

"You know that I'm self-taught."

"You see my point. Great artists who have studied at the École, meticulously executing lessons, then were mentored in the studios of the greatest artists for years, will never believe that a woman could learn just as much, be as good as they are, by teaching herself."

"Degas said the same when we first met."

"Then he and I agree on something. Go back to him and have him explain it to you again."

"He now believes that I am ready."

"People do say he's going mad." Puvis stalks to the pedestal I've only just vacated, and he sits.

"In truth, I don't understand why he supports me."

"Even grumpy old fools can't resist lining up behind true talent. Like calls to like. The living art inside you calls to the living art inside him. For argument's sake… What subjects are you considering?"

"A nude." I'm proudest of those, drawing women as they really are, not copying the idealized forms of the ancient Greeks.

"A nude?" He grips the edges of the pedestal as if he is at risk of falling. "Do be reasonable." He shakes his head so hard, his glasses nearly fly off. "A nude by a woman? Do you wish to cause a scandal?"

"Degas asked the same." I dislike this growing consensus, but I'm willing to take advice. "He recommends drawings of children."

"Quite so."

"Will you support my submission?" He is the president of the Société Nationale des Beaux-Arts.

"I must first see the work you are proposing."

The door of opportunity opens a crack, but a crack is all I need. I leap through. Or rather, I leap to the chair that holds my clothes and, under them, my portfolio.

On top are the drawings of children Degas helped me select, and two pieces of Maurice and Maman.

Puvis pinches the bridge of his nose, but he does look. And then he looks some more. "Oh." He

361

glances at me with suspicion. "Are these traced? I don't see eraser marks."

"I don't use an eraser. I want my lines to be bold, not tentative. I want people to see that I know what I am doing."

"You drew a profile in a single go?"

"And the body."

"But that would take an impossible amount of time to perfect." He scrutinizes my drawings again. And when he hands the portfolio back, he says, "I will be proud to support your submission, Suzanne."

"Thank you." I'm light-headed. I open my mouth to say more, but he holds up a charcoal-stained hand to hold off further gratitude.

"My support alone will not be nearly enough. We must recruit others to your corner."

DEGAS IS OF THE OPINION THAT I SHOULD TALK TO ALBERT BARTHOLOMÉ, THE SCULPTOR, ANOTHER MEMBER OF THE SOCIÉTÉ. He's believed in my art from the beginning—he was the one who introduced me to Degas in the first place—so he's on board immediately, but...

"You'd best prepare yourself for battle," he tells me.

"Why, if the works are good? It can't be merely because I am a woman. Other women have exhibited in previous Salons."

"Mary Cassatt studied at the Pennsylvania Academy before coming to Paris. And then here, she studied under Gérôme. Berthe Morisot trained under Corot and Millet and more. They followed the rules set by the establishment."

"There had to be more women beyond those two."

"Daughters of the bourgeois."

"And I am a bastard from the tenements. How long will my past follow me? The classes must be separated, is that it? The world works to keep us where we are. A poor man isn't allowed near any opportunity that would help him out of his poverty. While a rich man could commit murder and walk free."

"And probably handed a position in the government," Bartholomé agrees. His old melancholy still clings to him. I don't think he will ever lose it. The sadness has become part of him, a second skin.

"I expected more from the Société Nationale des Beaux-Arts. I thought they were a gathering of free-minded artists, and—"

"Paul Helleu!" Bartholomé shouts the name. "He is one of the most respected members. If we can gain him to our side, you are in. Helleu is one of the most popular portraitists in Paris." Bartholomé grabs pen and paper from the desk next to him. "I will write him a letter and we'll send it along with your portfolio."

And so we do.

And then we wait.

. . .

THE SALON DE NATIONALE OPENS ON THE TWENTY-FIFTH OF APRIL, ORGANIZED BY THE SOCIÉTÉ NATIONALE DES BEAUX-ARTS AT THE CHAMP-DE-MARS.

As I walk into the Palais des Beaux-Arts with the crowd, I know my drawings will be on the wall—I delivered them myself—but I can't fully believe it. Someone might have snatched them off at the last second, although I signed up for the catalog simply as Valadon S., without a Mademoiselle or Madame. I don't want people to look at my work and think *Not bad for a woman*. My drawings are as good as anyone's. I am a competent artist, and I want to be accepted as one.

Zando, who also threw his support behind me, walks on my right with Michel. Paul Mousis walks on my left.

"When this is over," Paul whispers into my ear, "I wish to show you something, Suzanne."

Then we step inside the Salon bleu—the blue walls nearly covered in art—so many spectators inside already that we can barely see the Salon rouge straight ahead. We are handed a catalogue. I don't draw an easy breath until I find my name, in the section *Dessins*, drawings, behind *Peinture*.

Valadon S.

1670 La toilette du petit-fils.

1671 Grand'mère et petit fils.

1672 Étude d'enfant.

1673 Étude d'enfant.

1674 Étude d'enfant.

Drawings of Maurice and Maman.

"You are the first self-taught woman to exhibit." Zando squeezes my arm.

The space is divided into fifteen areas, several for paintings, then drawings, aquarelles, pastels, sculpture, architecture, and decorative arts. We pass by and admire superb if endless renderings of women, portraits of Madame this and that, and landscapes, and fields with working peasants—all so expertly executed that for a moment, my self-confidence wavers. "Do I truly belong here?"

"You do." Paul draws me forward.

Then we are there. I lose my breath. Five of my drawings hang on the wall.

For a second I lose them, then I blink the tears from my eyes, and I see them again.

"It's difficult enough to have one work accepted." Even Zando is impressed.

My pieces are hanging on the same wall as the artists I've been posing for all these years. It's unheard of.

"The model among the masters." Bartholomé stops by. "Congratulations, Suzanne." He points to one of the studies of Maurice. "I wish to purchase this one. Do not sell it to anyone else. And Degas said to make sure to tell you he wants the drawing of Maurice with his grandmother."

For a moment, I can't speak, so I merely smile my gratitude at the men who surround me. Some men, a great many of them, have worked through history to keep women like me out of their "sacred" places. But others, my friends, helped me get here. Such change is coming. Such a tide. It fills me with hope for our future. In my lifetime, equality will happen. It can't be long now before in the eyes of society, women will be equal to men in all aspects.

After Bartholomé leaves, other artists stop by to wish me well. They praise my line work and the freshness of my approach. One even calls my work virile. Each of my five pieces is inspected and accepted.

I look up and blink to clear the moisture from the eyes, and only then does the ornate ceiling register. I look around, noticing for the first time the ornate room behind the paintings.

I am in a *palace*.

My art, my family is in a palace. Not garbage from the tenements. Not gutter rats. We are seen at last. It's not just that my skill is acknowledged, this is so much more than that. It's an acknowledgment of our existence.

Better yet, not only is my work exhibited, but it *sells*. By the time we are ready to leave, I am walking on air. And then I don't have to walk at all, because Paul hires a taxicab.

"Where are we going?"

"A surprise," he tells me before he calls to the driver, "18, avenue de Saint-Denis, Pierrefitte."

Pierrefitte-sur-Seine is a suburb of north Paris. Not a terrible distance, especially since the whole way out, as thought after dazed thought swirls through my mind, Paul holds my hand.

We alight from the cab in front of a magnificent

country house, the scent of fresh-baked bread greeting us from the bakery next door. Two young German shepherds run out to greet us as Paul opens the gate. He pets them, and they jump all around him in wild abandon before they run to me.

They're just like the sweet puppies I used to draw back in school, on my slate. I'm so happy to see them, I drop to my knees and rub behind their ears, and then, when they flop over, their bellies. "Who lives here?"

I envy him the house, but I envy him the pups a thousand times more. And then there's the garden, a giant stretch of green, which immediately makes me think of Maurice. Such fun he could have playing here, in all this space.

"I bought the house." Paul offers his hand and draws me to my feet. "In the hope that you would live here with me."

I am so stunned, my first answer is an awkward laugh. "Are you proposing again?"

"I am. One should never give up one's heart desire." He flashes me a pointed look. "I learned that from the best."

I grip his hand, clutching a dream I don't want to slip away. "I don't know if I'm ready. I don't know if I'll ever…"

"Come live here with me on whatever terms you will. I shall take you any way I can."

"And your family?" Catholics. Bourgeois. "They would never approve. They are conservative."

"Your approval of me is all that matters, Suzanne."

The dogs jump on my skirt and yip, begging along with Paul, as if trained.

"I couldn't without Maurice."

"Of course Maurice has a room. I picked one for him already, but he can have whichever room he wishes."

"I cannot leave behind Maman."

"I would never suggest that."

"She can't take care of a house this size. And I wish to paint. I will never be the kind of woman who spends all day in the kitchen."

"You are an artist. I've known that since I've met you, Suzanne. And your Maman deserves her rest. I think two maids would be sufficient."

"And if I miss Montmartre? I couldn't live without the company of artists."

"The house comes with a mule and a mule cart." He holds up his hand when I would interrupt. "You must have an art studio, of course. If none of the rooms suits you, I know of a studio for rent at 12, rue Cortot."

I know the house on rue Cortot and the half dozen artists who rent there. Renoir painted there at some point. "Paul, I—" For once, I'm not sure what to say. Here is a man who wants me for more than my body, someone who sees in me a true partner, someone who thinks beyond how I could benefit him. "I don't know if I can leave behind my wild ways."

"I love your wild ways. And you haven't said no yet," Paul observes. "Allow me to show you the house." He escorts me inside with a spring in his step. "The space is plentiful, including a room for a live-in maid. The second maid will only come for the day. The garden rivals Monet's."

Room and peace for Maurice. Rest for Maman. The dogs. A man who considers my wishes. Time and space to paint. Everything I ever wanted. "I won't be a kept woman."

"You sold multiple pieces today. And they're not the first ones. The more you paint, the more you'll sell. I might yet have to work harder to keep up with you, Suzanne."

"You're a man difficult to say no to." I wish I didn't love him. Love has never gotten me anywhere with men.

"Impossible to say no to," he corrects, with the confidence of a banker.

Which makes me smile.

A man who makes me smile.

I unlock the iron bands from around my heart. "You would take me with all the missteps of my past and all the rumors?"

"Happily."

"I am not a saint."

"I love that about you."

"I am not the devil either."

He laughs. "I won't say I want you to be mine, Suzanne. But I would like very much if we belonged together."

To live is to risk. To hide from life is to fade away. We must swing on the trapeze, or we'll never fly. And without flying, what is life worth? I want to fly, even if I might crash to the ground now and then.

I have never forgotten the freedom of flight, and I will never forget.

So I say, "Yes."

And I still scarcely understand why now, why this man. I don't need him. My son has a name, and, as Paul says, I have increasing income. I can support myself and my son and Maman. I don't need anyone.

The women I know who marry do so for security.

The women who have financial security already, like Mary Cassatt, don't usually marry.

When I look at the deep joy in Paul's eyes, joy at just having me near him, I can almost envision a third option, where one marries for love.

Lucky for me, right now, he is content with what I am willing to give.

"All right." I push away on the trapeze.

THE DAY MAMAN, MAURICE, AND I MOVE INTO THE HOUSE IN PIERREFITTE IS THE DAY PUVIS VISITS. The house is an unpardonable mess. Everything we own is in crates and boxes.

"I looked for you at your old apartment, but you weren't there. They said I could find you here." Puvis is startled, if not alarmed, by the mess.

"You could have sent a note." What could possibly be this important?

GIRL BRAIDING HER HAIR

"Not about this news." Three canvases leaning against the wall distract him. "Yours? Are you trying a new style?"

"Maurice's." He's found himself in the work.

Puvis hums. "Not bad. The boy will have to be watched. Anyway, back to the purpose of my visit."

The first artist who's ever invited me into his studio turns solemn, draws a letter from his pocket, and unfolds it.

"The Société Nationale des Beaux-Arts respectfully extends an invitation to Suzanne Valadon to join its members," he reads.

I've dreamed about this for so long, I don't trust my ears. What if I merely heard what I wanted to hear? But Puvis is smiling. And then Paul picks me up and whirls me around.

When he puts me down, he kisses my cheek. "Bravo, Suzanne."

"But they don't accept women," I look from one man to the other. "They never have."

I live in a fine house, I've sold many works, I've been exhibited, but deep inside, I'm still that little girl from the tenements, hungry and covered in dirt. The one that always gets sent away. The one that nobody wants. I might have fought for this, but part of me never believed I deserved it. I'm choked up with emotion as I smile at Puvis at last.

"We were not looking for a woman, but neither will we overlook true talent. Suzanne Valadon," he says dramatically, "are you ready to walk into history?"

Then Maurice runs in from the garden, the pups at his heels, followed by Maman, who takes one look at my face and asks, "What happened?"

Puvis has to explain it all over again.

Pandemonium in the foyer.

"Will you do us the honor of joining us, Suzanne?" Puvis hands me the letter.

I don't get past the letterhead. My eyes fill with tears. I never cry, I don't understand what is happening to me lately. Since I can't see, I have to trust Puvis that the writing says what he said it says.

I am going to be the first woman to join the Société Nationale des Beaux-Arts.

"Yes." And then, to make sure history hears me, I say it again, louder this time. "Yes!"

"You will be in the public eye. People will have opinions."

"I'm not scared." It had been my mantra as a child, to convince myself and everyone else. I used to pretend not to be scared of hunger, or the cold, or war, or the rats we had to eat, or anyone's sticks and slaps. But this time, it's not pretense. I trust my skills, and myself. "I am not scared."

CHAPTER TWENTY-THREE

Ellie

Saturday, April 8th

"IF THE BUILDING IS TO BE A MUSEUM, IT SHOULD BE A MUSEUM OF THE TOWN'S INDUSTRIAL PAST, TO OUR STEEL," THE TOWN PLANNER TELLS US. He's a short man in his forties, rotund, with thinning hair. He could be Danny DeVito's humor-deficient brother.

Madame Gibbler, Joshua, and Abby are with me at the meeting. Somehow, I ended up with a team.

"One does not preclude the other," I say, reasonably. "The more tourist attractions, the more tourist traffic, the more income for the township."

"We have no grants for the arts left in the budget."

Abby brought her own paperwork, and she hands

it in. "I've applied for a grant from the state. We meet all the requirements. There's no reason why we wouldn't get it."

"And we have future funds," I add, "from a book we are publishing."

Then Madame Gibbler speaks up. "I'm one of the private donors who will also be contributing."

The town planner smiles at her, helpless, unable to look away from her for several seconds. He finally clears his throat and gathers himself. "What about an environmental study?"

Joshua steps forward and hands him a folder. "Completed." A friend of his cut us a generous break on it.

"And these are…" I present the next folder, "the preliminary sketches of the exterior. As I understand, only the façade and roofline have to be completed to historical specifications. The sides, back, and the interior can be altered." I'm going to drown him in competence. I've done my homework.

"There's still the matter of parking."

"We're appealing the parking plan," Joshua says.

And I add, "We're adding green space and a culvert for stormwater runoff."

Another question is posed.

I am ready with the response.

The pattern is repeated, over and over, until at last the man leans back in his seat.

"All right." He shores the folders up in a neat stack in front of him. "I'll send my decision in the mail."

. . .

CHRIS AND I HAVE NEVER GONE FISHING, BUT IF WE HAD, IT WOULD HAVE BEEN LIKE THIS.

Spring has kicked off her blankets, splashed water on her face, drunk her double-mocha latte, and finally showed up for work. No, not for work—for play. She cups your face with her hands and covers you in warm-breeze kisses, that's the kind of spring day it is. Monet himself couldn't paint a scene prettier than the emerald banks of the Brandywine Creek.

"Has the town planner made a decision yet?" Grace asks, eyes closed, boneless on a blanket.

"Still waiting to hear back. For now, I'm still pushing preorders for the book, and the virtual museum online, perfecting the branding. At least, the idea is out there. If an influencer discovers us, we'll be set."

"What does smallmouth bass look like?" Sam holds his fishing rod like people do on their first-ever fishing trip—as if he's hanging on for dear life.

I sit to his left; his grandfather, Bill, sits on his right. Bill is having a good day, jaunty in his overalls and Teamsters baseball hat. We invited him along so his wife could have a break.

Grace, back from LA even more beautiful with the golden glow that only California sunshine can bestow, sits up on my other side. She runs a quick search on her phone and shows the resulting picture to Sam.

He shrugs. "Looks like any other fish."

Chris's shrug. Grace catches it too, and we exchange a glance.

"It's also called bronze bass," she says, referring to the screen. "Bronzeback, brown bass, brownie, and bareback bass."

"We used to call them smallie," Bill adds. "My father used to take me fishing for them before he went off to Vietnam." His tone roughens. "He didn't come back from the war."

Sam must have heard the story before, because he just gives a sage nod. Then he adds, "I'm glad we don't have to deal with worms."

"Smallies go for artificial bait best. Topwater buzz bait is where it's at. Floating minnows." Bill might not remember where he lives, but he remembers fishing just fine, and he enjoys the activity.

Sam is fiercely concentrating on the water.

We've been FaceTiming a lot in the evenings. I've been telling him stories about Chris. I thought dredging up the past would make me sad, but it's just the opposite. In our talks, Chris is alive again. I'm reminded how much time we did have together, the entire mountain of happiness.

"How's school?" I immediately regret the question. What kid wants to talk about school over the weekend? I have a lot to learn here. "How's basketball?"

Sam shrugs again. "Tommy says I'm the runt of the litter."

"What does Tommy know?"

"He's the tallest boy in my whole grade."

Well.

"Was Dad tall?" The question is asked with breathless hope, while he keeps his eyes on the creek, not wanting me to know how important my response is to him.

"Five eleven."

"Way tall," Grace adds.

I've never seen a kid turn so happy so fast. He yanks his rod back hard enough to smack himself in the forehead. He doesn't care. "I'm gonna be five eleven!"

Grace and I are smart enough not to argue with the pronouncement.

"If you don't end up being a basketball player, what would you like to be?"

"In the real world or any world?"

I like that his future plans are nuanced. "Any world."

"A wizard."

Then we talk about Harry Potter for a while. I also recommend Percy Jackson, which he hasn't read. I promise to lend him my set.

"But I'm definitely going to be a basketball player." Sam circles back to his favorite topic. "Joshua and Jace are taking me to a Sixers game." Then he falls quiet for a few seconds. "Do you think Grandma Helen will like me when she meets me?"

"She will love you. She loves you already." She's been FaceTiming with Sam too, from the cruise ship. Helen will be on a plane to come to see us, the second her ship docks in Miami next week.

377

"All right." Bill pulls his line from the water, and we both look, but the hook is empty. He lays his pole on the ground. "Gotta see a man about a horse."

"Me too." Sam scrambles off after him into the woods.

I turn to Grace. "What horse?"

"They're going to the bathroom."

"Sam went ten minutes ago. Do boys get UTIs? Should I say something to his grandmother?" As soon as the last word is out, I realize what's going on. *Oh.* "He's going to make sure Bill doesn't get turned around. He wants to make sure that his grandfather doesn't get lost."

"He's a good kid."

"Yes, he is."

By the time my misty eyes clear, they're returning, and we settle back into fishing.

"Grandpa, look!" Sam surges off the turned-over bucket that's his seat.

Bill has a bite. When his arm trembles, Sam switches his own rod into his left hand and grabs on to Bill's with his right.

He's so good at taking care of his grandfather. He deserves someone to take care of him too.

"Watch your own line!" His minnow has dipped under. I help out Bill so Sam can focus on his own catch.

Bill brings in his fish. Sam's escapes, but he couldn't be happier.

"Did you see how big it was?" He hops around.

"It might come back."

He throws the fake minnow back in, since it's intact.

"Try a little walk-the-dog action." Bill demonstrates, his bass already in his bucket. "Twitch, reel, twitch, reel, twitch, reel."

By the time Sam gets it right, Bill falls asleep in the warm breeze. Out of the four of us, he ended up with the only folding chair. He's not too uncomfortably slumped back.

"Did you love my Dad?" Sam asks, looking at the water.

My throat tightens. "Yes."

"Do you think he would have loved me?"

"Absolutely, yes."

"Definitely," Grace concurs.

"Do I really look like him?"

"You've seen the photos. You're his Mini-Me."

Sam frowns, too young to get the Austin Powers reference.

"You look so much like him, it's ridiculous," Grace promises.

He is the picture of contentment. Minutes pass with him glowing next to me, before a cloud floats over his happiness. "I wish he didn't die."

"Me too, Sam."

"I was excited about living with him. I thought we'd go to games together."

"He would have loved that."

I catch Grace hiding a few rapid blinks. She clears her throat as she stands. "I'll get us some water from the car."

Then she leaves, and Sam glances at Bill. "I worry about Grandpa. I don't think he's going to get better."

What could I possibly say to that? "He has good people to take care of him. His friends visit. And there is your grandmother. And I bet you're a lot of help."

He nods.

"How would you feel about living with someone else?" *Please, God, Fate, Universe. Please.* "If your father didn't pass away, you would have ended up living with him and me. How about if you live with just me, at the cottage?"

Mrs. Martinez is living above the garage. Joshua is working hard on turning the garage into a handicap-accessible living space. He should be finished next week.

"Grandma said you asked her. I would have to switch schools," Sam says.

This could be a stickler. "Yes."

He brightens up. "I'm the shortest boy on the team right now. Maybe I won't be shortest at the new school."

"It's possible."

"Did you always want a kid?"

"Yes."

He thinks on that long and hard. "Harry Potter was an orphan."

"The closet under the stairs at the cottage is full of coats. You're going to have to have your own room upstairs."

"Could I put up posters?"

"Everything can be negotiated."

"I would still see Grandma and Grandpa, right?"

"You bet."

Bill snorts himself awake and checks on his bass in the bucket.

Sam looks too. "Are you taking it back to Grandma?"

Bill yawns. "Do I dare?"

"Grandma said no slimy fish scales in her sink." Sam casts me a quick glance. "Can we fry it at your house?"

I don't want slimy fish scales in my kitchen either. "Sure."

How much trouble can a single medium-size fish be?

Not a question to ever ask. Because then Sam pulls another one. And then I do too. And then Bill again. And again and again.

The cottage's kitchen ends up resembling a murder scene at a pop-up restaurant. Mrs. Martinez's small square table is nowhere near enough, since we invite Joshua and Jace and Olivia over. Joshua and Jace carry Mrs. Martinez down from the garage apartment, in her wheelchair. Karma shoots inside, right behind them, and runs straight to the terrarium to greet Bubbles.

Mrs. Martinez is, as always, undaunted. "You know how a reporter asked Stephen Hawking once if he felt bothered that his body didn't work? And he said he was lucky all he needed for his work was his brain. If he could sit in a wheelchair all his life and become the most respected physicist of our time, I can sit around for a few weeks. Now that I'm not running around all the time, I started writing again."

"How do you come up with your ideas?" Grace brings my cast iron skillet from the stove with her famous cornbread.

I slide one of my old travertine tiles under it. They cleaned up fine and make the perfect trivets.

"People pop up in my head, and they start talking." Mrs. Martinez laughs. "I don't usually tell people that. I don't want them to think I've gone off my rocker."

"You're the sanest person I know," I tell her. "I hope the book will be a runaway bestseller and make you famous."

"I'll settle for runaway bestseller. I never wanted the limelight. I want to work hard, put out quality, and keep my life nice and boring."

The door rattles. I skip over to open it for Joshua and his brother again, so they can carry in my large table from my old apartment. My kitchen is bursting at the seams with people, no space to spare.

One year later

"Tonight, us." Joshua raises his glass of French champagne gifted to us by Francoise Gibbler. "Tomorrow, the crowds."

The town planner came through.

The night before the MUA's opening, we're having a moment in the main gallery after we tidy up everything. It's called the Christopher Waldon Gallery, Chris's legacy. We have no restaurant, but we have a coffee bar that stocks nine different flavors of soft pretzels. I found a local artisan baker to make them.

The second to last thing Chris told me before he died, right before *I love you*, was a quote from Joseph Campbell, his favorite writer.

"Life is like arriving late for a movie, having to figure out what was going on without bothering everybody with a lot of questions, and then being unexpectedly called away before you find out how it ends."

The gallery is not the end of the movie, but it's the end of a chapter in the book from which the movie of our lives was written. The end of one chapter, and the beginning of the next.

Chris is gone and, at the same time, with me, always here.

I think he would approve of the direction my life has taken.

Suzanne Valadon's vibrant colors adorn the walls. I have a magnificent new dress at home that'll match. I've put away my grays and blacks.

Suzanne's first show, at the Brandywine Museum of Art that lent us their main gallery for a month at Madame Gibbler's encouragement, was a success.

Since I managed that first show without mishaps, almost all the lending museums let me borrow

Valadon's art again for the grand opening of the Museum of Unseen Art.

The air is filled with possibilities. Tomorrow, after the opening, we'll have the full team here for a celebratory dinner catered by Le Papillon, but right now, it's just the three of us.

"Did she make it at the end?" Sam asks. "Suzanne."

"She did. When she was almost sixty, she and her son received a ridiculous amount of money from an art dealer as a retainer for work they would create that year."

"How much?"

"I don't know. A million francs? They bought a nice house on the rue Junot. And, just for fun, they bought an old castle that had a drawbridge and a moat. They also bought a car, back when practically nobody had cars."

"Sweet. Can I have champagne to celebrate?" Sam jumps on the opportunity.

"No, you may not."

I wait for him to tug his hair. He doesn't. He only does that now when he's tired, and rarely even then. He doesn't grumble either, but moves right on. "Can I go out to the car so I can play my game? Phone battery's dead. I only have a USB charger."

"Go ahead." I hand him my keys. "We're almost done for tonight. We'll be out in a few minutes."

"When will Grandma Helen be here in the morning?"

"We pick her up at the airport at eleven." It's her third visit. The first two could not have gone better.

Helen is coming to the opening, and so are Sam's other grandparents. He might not have a traditional family, but he has a family. He's a pretty happy kid. He's doing well.

He flashes us a content smile before he lopes out, and then it's just the two of us, Joshua and me.

Suzanne Valadon's luminous work graces the walls, dozens of drawings, pastels, soft-point sketches, and paintings. Her self-portrait, portraits of her son, her mother, Utrillo, and all her other friends tell the story of her life, her losses and her triumphs, the obstacles in her path and how she overcame them.

"I'd say I feel like I'm dreaming." I sip the champagne. "But I'd hate to use a cliché in a room with so much original talent."

Joshua toasts me. "You had a dream, and you made it reality. I am impressed."

"You create homes for people."

"You no longer hate flippers?"

"I can't speak for the whole field, but I don't hate *this* flipper." I tip my glass toward him.

"Progress."

We walk around and read every single info board I wrote. I'm still checking for typos. "David is coming tomorrow for the opening. He's bringing Lilly. Gabe is in the hospital, and she's stressed. She needs to get out of the house. I don't think Gabe has a lot of time left."

"How does David feel about that?"

"He's sad for Lilly. And he'll be there for her, come what may."

"He could be a hero in one of Mrs. Martinez's romance novels."

"That's what Mrs. Martinez said. She's almost finished with her new book."

"Is she coming?"

"A pack of wolves couldn't keep her away. She's completed her physical therapy."

"My father asked about her. He'll be here too."

My mind jumps straight to matchmaking, but I stop myself. I always resented when people did that to me. Mrs. Martinez will choose when she's ready for another relationship.

Joshua stops in front of Valadon's last self-portrait. "Do you think she was happy?"

"From time to time. But I don't think happiness was her goal. Her life wasn't always easy, but by God, she *lived*."

"I like the way she looks at us in the mirror. She didn't pretty herself up. Didn't erase that she's tired, or her age. As if she's saying, *Yeah. This is me. What about it?*"

"She lived life on her own terms."

"Did she end up marrying Paul Mousis?"

I talk so much about her, Joshua is familiar with her story.

"She did, but they ended up divorcing. Then she married another artist. Her first solo exhibit was an unmitigated success. Serious collectors bought her work. A few critics maligned her for having a *masculine quality* and *unfeminine bravado*, but I doubt she cared."

Joshua steps to the next piece. "I see she did paint l'ensemble."

"Her realistic, unvarnished female nudes revolutionized the subject." I move on to the next piece. "Her male nudes gave the critics fits."

"I bet she enjoyed that."

We walk the circumference of the room, stopping by every drawing, etching, and painting, as if they are friends. Then we come to the end.

"Better go see Sam."

Lights out. Security set.

Outside, the parking lot is empty, save for our two cars. I stop by mine. Sam is asleep on the back seat, hair mussed, phone dropped on his lap.

I love this kid, I think. Then the movie stops rolling, the screen freezes.

I love this child, and not just because he's Chris's son, and not because he looks like Chris. I love Sam's sense of humor. I love his mischief. I love his occasional worries.

We started out as a team, coming together in the service of a common goal: finding him a place to live. And now we are a family. My heart squeezes.

Joshua steps toward me. "What is it?"

"Life catches you by surprise. But sometimes, it catches you by surprise in a good way. I almost feel like Suzanne brought Sam to me, in return for me bringing her out of the past. I don't usually believe in the mystical, but… I only made Chris's profile public in the ancestry database because I thought he might have been related to Valadon. Waldon—Valadon. Anyway, that's how Mrs. Card found me."

"I'm glad she did."

I open the driver-side door, but I don't get in. "I meant to tell you… I kind of did a thing."

"Yeah. A whole museum." Joshua's tone is dry. Suppressed humor glints in his eyes.

"Another thing."

"Bought an orchestra?"

"I bought Mrs. Martinez's cottage. I finally received Chris's life insurance, and the grant that makes the MUA possible has funds for salaries. I qualified for a mortgage."

"Congratulations. Both on the museum and the cottage."

"Any chance you'd give me an opinion on repairs and a few upgrades? I'll pay a consulting fee."

"You know what the best time is to ask for a home evaluation? Before you buy a home." Joshua puffs out his cheeks. "I built a cabin from popsicle sticks in elementary school that was structurally safer than that back porch."

"The appraiser said it could be fixed."

"Yeah, but for how much? You should have asked a flipper." He makes disapproving noises, then softens. "Don't worry about it. I have some scrap wood."

"I don't want to owe you more than I owe you already. You donated the building to the museum."

"It got me a huge tax break from the city on

another development deal I'm putting together. You don't owe me anything."

I lean against my car and take in the pressure-cleaned brick façade, the darkly glinting windows, the lights over the entrance, the sign that's new and crisp and delightfully original, flowing hand lettering, no mass-produced font, nothing bare-bones and minimalist about it.

"It's popular with the public," Joshua says. "People have been posting pictures in community FB groups. They like it."

"Do they?" The thought gives me a thrill.

"It's you. You know that, right?"

I look at him and find him looking at me.

"You're the soul and spirit of the thing. You want to make the unseen, seen," he explains. "The hidden come to light. The suppressed potential to come out into the open and be fully utilized. When Chris died, you hid yourself in the basement. Nobody got to see you. You shut yourself off from your full potential. You wasted yourself at your city job that you didn't like."

"And now?"

"You came through and out into the light."

He sees me as a better, bigger person than I see myself. But maybe he's not wrong. "This is just the beginning." A sudden confidence buoys me. "Soon, we'll be adding another wing."

"I wouldn't doubt anything you say." Joshua takes my hands.

At least my skin is no longer cracked. I don't have

to be embarrassed about that. His Handyman Balm worked.

"You know what you need?" he asks, and I know he's going to kiss me. "A guy who knows how to upgrade properties."

Then his lips touch mine.

The five stages of grief are:

1. You're so heartbroken you think you'll die.
2. You're so heartbroken you think you'll die.
3. You're so heartbroken you think you'll die.
4. You're so heartbroken you think you'll die.
5. You don't die.

I am alive.

AUTHOR'S NOTE

This book only exists because of you.

When I published THE SECRET LIFE OF SUNFLOWERS, I didn't know how it would be received. I'd never written anything historical before. Without your amazing response—the emails, Facebook posts, online reviews—I would probably not have written anything historical again. Words cannot adequately express how grateful I am to you.

Suzanne Valadon was a celebrated artist of her time, the equal of any Post-Impressionist artist, but after her death, history only remembered the men. She was forgotten for the most part, and quickly. In her obituary, the newspaper *Le Figaro* calls her the wife of an artist (her second husband, Utter) and mother of an artist, but says nothing about her being an artist herself, despite the fact that she created hundreds of works of art, had four retrospective exhibits during her lifetime, and suffered her fatal stroke (at age 72) literally while painting at her easel.

Her son, Maurice Utrillo, became a famous artist, to the point that in a few sources I consulted, Suzanne was only mentioned as Utrillo's mother.

So how much of this book is true? The historical half is based on real people and events; the present-day story is entirely fictional. But even the historical parts are not a hundred-percent fact. I could only work from what material I could find in books and online. Extended research trips to Paris are not in my budget. I stayed as close to the truth as I could, and when I didn't know what the truth was, I made a choice, for the story's sake.

A couple of things made my task more difficult. One, some of these events were described by Suzanne's contemporaries, colored by their own prejudices and all the gossip around her. Two, Suzanne liked to tell a good story and often bent the truth herself. She, in fact, misstated her year of birth all her life, making herself younger. On this, I went with the official birth record. As far as I can tell, nobody knows who the father of her son was. Nearly every source I consulted said something different. I personally think Renoir is the most likely choice, but obviously I can't guarantee paternity.

Suzanne Valadon was a larger-than-life figure, and so the rumors and stories that swirled around her, before and after her death, were many.

When I first outlined this story and started writing this book, she'd not yet had an exhibit in the United States. However, in September of 2021, the fabulous Barnes Foundation in Philadelphia debuted her first US show. Like an idiot, I missed it, because I was in a fit of unsubscribing from newsletters, because my email was becoming unmanageable. (Yes, I'm still crying about that.)

To take a break from feeling sorry for myself, I will give you an update on Ellie...

The Museum of Unseen Art is a major tourist attraction. The Suzanne Valadon exhibit was a huge success. Other museums took note and are bringing this artist to the attention of audiences everywhere. Suzanne Valadon is a respected and beloved artist once again.

Frank fell off the wagon and ran off to Atlantic City for three days. He came back with the jackpot ($1.2 million) and paid off the equity loan on the house. Then he ran off to Vegas.

In spite of numerous late-night calls, Abby will not take him back.

Ellie and Joshua are still together, living happily with Sam. They are expecting kittens.

P.S.: If you like my books even a little, would you pretty please sign up for my newsletter? https:// martamolnar.com/newsletter/signup It's my only way of reaching you to let you know when my next book is out. I don't send any spam or what I had for breakfast, I promise. I don't have the time for that.

And if you have another minute, would you please leave a quick review on the website where you bought the book? Reviews make a huge difference for authors. They can make or break a book. I really want to write the next novel. Your kind help would be appreciated beyond words.

Thank you!!! —Marta

BOOK CLUB DISCUSSION

Thank you so much for picking my book for your book club! I would love to know what you all think about the story. If you don't mind telling me, please stop by my FB page. It would make my day.

Sometimes, reader groups ask me for discussion points, so here are a few in case you can use them.

Did you know about Suzanne Valadon before reading this book? Did you look up her art while reading? What do you think of her work?

Why do you think the female Impressionists (Berthe Morisot, Mary Cassatt, Eva Gonzalès, Marie Bracquemond, Cecilia Beaux, and Lilla Cabot Perry) were never as famous as the men?

. . .

In what ways do you think Valadon's childhood affected her later life? Do you think she was able to overcome generational trauma and become a good mother?

Do you think growing up without a father in a century when that wasn't socially acceptable impacted her relationships with men?

What did you think about Ellie's present-day storyline? Could she have dealt better with her grief? In what ways?

Family relationships are difficult. Did you think there was too much unnecessary drama between Ellie and Abby, or did their interactions ring true to you?

What did you think of Ellie's idea of a museum for unseen art? What types of art are still underrepresented? What would you like to see on the walls, if you could visit the MUA? (I'll give you my answer to this one. If I had a museum, I'd do a huge exhibit of artists who died before their art could be recognized. I'd let anyone bring their wife's, husband's, mother's, father's art and put it up, so people could see it all.)

. . .

Do you have a pie-in-the-sky dream? What is it? If you were to reach for this dream, what could be your first step?